Vow of the Undead

Vow of the Undead

The Bloodrune Saga

Book One

Elsa Frey

CONTENTS

For those who have no spoons left to run, but still want to be pursued by the villain who would burn the world down to keep you warm.

CONTENT WARNING

This work contains explicit sexual content and scenes with dubious consent. As well as death, violence, blood, stalking, mental health references - especially anxiety and panic attacks, and mentions of physical and mental abuse.

CHAPTER ONE

I ce webbed through my eyelashes as wind needled every inch of exposed skin. I swung the scythe at another golden stalk and added the wheat to a bundle I'd collected on the ground. My shoulder throbbed, the muscle tightening from hours of cutting, gathering, and binding.

It didn't help that the stupid scythe was kept dull.

Since Ragna's oldest son used one against an executioner, the king's council deemed scythes potential weapons, and like all other blades, swords and axes, they were either outlawed or required to maintain status as a tool. Which meant dull and nearly useless even when it came to harvesting.

I rolled my shoulders back and sucked in a breath of painfully cold air before swinging the scythe twice as fast. As twilight beckoned darkness, the chill would only hurt worse. That gave me ten minutes to cut this row down before night cut *me* down.

This late in the spring, Skaldir should only have slush on the ground in the mountains, but winter became longer and more brutal with each passing year. Only five years ago, when I was eighteen and just out from under my father's thumb enough to help harvest the fields, the fjords had melted by the time the summer sun had stretched across the sky.

Now, snow lasted for most of the year, so I spent every waking second on Ragna's farm, or foraging in the forest with the other gatherers to stock up on food before snow hit again.

Thanks to the witches of Skaldir who were skilled with the magic of flora, we had an occasional stroke of luck with crops that would normally never survive, much less thrive, in the cold. But it hadn't been enough for everyone to make it through last winter.

The faces of the seventeen we lost to starvation hovered in my mind as I cut fast, faster, faster until I caught a figure waving at me from the corner of my eye.

Ragna stood at the edge of the field and waved her muscular arms over her head to catch my attention. I could see her lips moving but the wind swept her voice away. Beyond her, a small stone house was one of many in Skaldir, the northernmost village on the continent of Vylheim.

Ragna dropped her arms and shook her head. I couldn't hear her, but I had no doubt she was scolding me for staying out so late. She'd sworn my father, the Vyl and leader in Skaldir, would have her head if I froze to death.

Of course it wasn't true, my father had no authority to take anyone's heads. Any kind of violence was only allowed by the hands of the executioners, and only to kill those who'd dare to break Vylheim's most important law; *don't shed a drop of blood.*

The bloodshed law kept those of us who obeyed safe from another outbreak of war, and alive.

Unless we starved.

I hacked at the wheat again as Ragna shouted my name. I pointed at the row of golden stalks, but Ragna was not having it. She stormed toward me, marching into the field, and I knew she'd insist I give it up for the night.

"Silver!" Ragna barked as she came closer, picking

through chopped stalks. Years of working in the wind as a farmer left her pale skin cut with wrinkles that only deepened with the crease of her brow. "You foolish, amazing, stupid, beautiful woman. It's as cold as Rolf's balls when he fell in the fjord and you're still out here cutting away at the wheat like Odin himself will come down and kiss you on the damn lips."

I stopped cutting to smirk at her. Only Ragna was gutsy enough to mention a God's name aloud and out in the open.

"And what if he does?" I said. "Will you be jealous that I'm his chosen witch?"

A shiver cut down my spine as I dared call myself a witch out loud. I'd spent too much time around Ragna's bold behavior. Letting something like that slip from my lips proved I was as foolish as she said. I didn't have the wiry muscle or the resilient strength of the witch standing in front of me so, I rarely dared to admit what I was.

Ragna threw her head back and laughed. "Not even the Allfather himself will pry me from my precious Rolf's arms. Now will you stop risking your life to get another bundle or two?"

"No," I said as I gripped the scythe harder and readied to swing again despite my muscles protesting every movement. "I need another vision as much as we need food, and working myself weary will get me there. Just give me another hour."

I continued hacking away while she placed her fists on her hips and shook her head.

Working like this was the perfect combination to solve both the lack of food and my lack of visions, so I wasn't going to stop, even with Ragna glaring at me. The line between harvesting and preparing for next winter was as thin as straw, and the harder I worked, the closer I came to pushing my body to the edge of collapse where I'd be granted a vision.

Ignoring Ragna's angry rant, I swung the scythe back and forth over the stalks in a painful rhythm of strained muscles. I hoped for that collapse to come soon, before bitter night blanketed the fields. My black out would only last a few moments, but I didn't want to wake to dark skies.

Between consciousness and collapse was the only place the Gods could reach me. Once I fainted from exhaustion, a vision would take over my senses. Being a seerborn witch often meant being inundated with confusing visions, but mine had been narrowed in on one single focus since my mother was exiled.

Ragna sighed. "I know you want to see your mother, Silver, but beating yourself into the ground every chance you get isn't healthy for you."

I wiped at the ice in my eyelashes and met her gaze. "It's not just her. I had a vision of the sagas last week." Only occasionally would my visions wander from focusing on my mother. When they did, I received glimpses of sagas that recounted both our recent history and ancient events, back when witches were revered instead of in hiding.

As much as I wanted to see my mother and know that she was safe, sight of the sagas was worth more than gold.

"You're not the savior of all witches, Sil, you're my half frozen friend. Now—" she jerked her head to the side. "Let's get you out of this chill. You can come back out here tomorrow when the sun is high and try for a vision then."

I only shook my head.

If I could piece my visions of the sagas together, and then track down the original runestone on which the history was recorded, I could prove witches weren't a threat to King Drakkar.

I would prove my mother wasn't a threat, before the wasteland stripped away her life.

Ragna must have sensed the turmoil thrashing around inside of me because she finally stopped scolding me and grabbed the scythe from my hand.

She winked. "This is mine now," she quipped. "Unless you want to fight for it."

Coming from her, this was as much a challenge to get it back as it was a distraction from the frayed nerves that so often plagued me. She knew a playful fight would rein in my nervous mind.

A smirk twitched at my lips. "Only if you're ready to lose."

I'd fought her plenty of times in the forbidden hall, or rather, the dugout beneath Ragna's home. There, those of us brave and stupid enough to practice self-defense trained against one another, because even if violence and fighting weren't allowed, even if bloodshed was strictly forbidden for the safety of our society, some of us still believed in the monsters of old, the undead and the giants who slipped into our world from the other realms.

Of course, those beliefs were forbidden too.

But I didn't need to merely believe in monsters, I saw their red eyes in the forests dozens of times. I had felt them watching me since I was a young girl.

Ragna waved the scythe back and forth to catch my attention. A glint of mischief flashed in her eyes and I knew she'd won this argument. I'd follow her to the dugout buried below the little stone house at the edge of the field.

I'd clash tools with her, wooden swords and branches, because even in secret, we didn't risk hiding weapons. Sparring could grant me the collapse and vision I sought just as easily as toiling away in the fields, if Ragna didn't go soft on me for being the Vyl's daughter.

I trailed her, and within five minutes, I found myself in a huge hole in the ground beneath the floor of Ragna's home. Earthen walls smelled pungent of damp soil, teeming with wriggling larvae and other creatures whose species survived the ice of Vylheim's worsening winters. I blew out a breath and picked up the broken piece of a fence post, my weapon of choice. I steeled my muscles, knowing Ragna was about to beat what little stamina I had left out of me.

Though exhaustion pulled at my bones, fighting her had the opposite effect that I'd wanted.

It energized me.

A swell of excitement and sense of safety pushed me to keep wrestling Ragna as a second wave of energy rippled through me. I slammed the cut of wood against her branch over and over until another sound overpowered our sparring.

Thundering hooves shook the ground above us, and a bolt of nerves flayed open within my veins. We froze mid-clash and locked eyes.

We had plenty of horses in Skaldir, but somehow, we both knew this was not a group of villagers riding back into town. Or maybe we were just scared enough not to risk being caught fighting.

If executioners found us training like this, they'd have our heads. Even without a drop of blood, practicing at battle proved that the king and his council were right; the people of Vylheim were bent toward violence and must be controlled through the fear of execution in order to maintain civilized society.

I never could decide if they were right. I relished the feeling of power this training gave me, but maybe that was exactly the tendency toward violence that they were trying to suppress.

We were a danger to ourselves.

"Ragna!" Rolf's voice echoed from the house above. "More Grimward are here. Get out here before they think you're hiding." He called the executioners by their collective name out of nervous respect, and the shrill edge of his voice hinted at his growing worry.

Ragna's brow wrinkled, a sure sign that she didn't hear Rolf's warning clearly. Having suffered several infections in her ears, her senses weren't as sharp as mine.

"We have to be out there, in plain sight," I said, pointing to the ladder that led to our exit.

She nodded. As a witch like me, any little suspicion could blow her cover. Because even though violence was the executioner's crime of focus, being a witch was just as illegal.

Arrivals like this—of more executioners than the ones who constantly patrolled our borders—were unpredictable so that they might catch more villagers in the act of shedding another's blood. Somehow, the Grimward always appeared when two young men got into a scuffle, or when a lover's quarrel turned violent, as if they could smell the blood of battle before it hit the ground.

We tossed the makeshift weapons aside, and I paused, grabbing the discarded scythe instead. Angling the scythe's blade to catch the glow of candlelight, I checked on the enchantment that concealed my eyes.

The shimmering metal reflected my face back at me.

No black eyes.

I breathed easier. My enchantment had held up. Even if it only concealed the black with a watery film of magic blessed to me by the Gods so that I may slink through the world unknown as a witch.

Not that other witches even had this curse.

I was the only one, and when the black first spread, my mother spent every waking moment creating an enchantment to hide it. She'd placed it on me years ago, and now, as the enchantment slowly faded, it was proof her life was slipping away. The more the black seeped out from the center and spread across my eyes, the closer she was to death.

I threw the scythe down and climbed above ground in time to see the dozens of horses carrying masked men and women.

Extra executioners weren't the only visitors in Skaldir. Guards and the king's council were riding with them today, and they were galloping straight toward the Vyl's home—my home.

Ragna and I exchanged a knowing glance as Rolf herded

us out the door and with the other villagers who emerged from their homes, a mixture of curiosity and fear painted across their faces.

That all-consuming fatigue after a full day in the fields returned, and the walk back into town only doubled it. By the time we reached the longhouse where my father held council, the largest and sturdiest home in Skaldir, a crowd had gathered, and my bones ached.

I carefully pushed through bodies, my stomach sinking farther and farther into my bowels. I kept my eyes off of the executioners because my nerves told me that if they merely looked at me they'd identify me as a witch and I'd be dragged away to the wasteland.

I'd see my mother there, but I wouldn't be able to save her.

Never had the king's guard and members of his council rode in with the Grimward before, and I couldn't fathom why they'd come here.

Pieces of whispered conversations clung to my ears as I wriggled through the crowd. The executioners and the bloodshed law kept plenty of us cowed and scared, but plenty more dared to breathe their traitorous feelings.

"They never stop marching around us like we're a bunch of criminals. I'm fucking sick of being watched," an elderly man grumbled.

"They're waiting for someone to slip up so they can stop fights," another chimed in.

"Stop fights? They're here to keep our necks under their boots," his wife said.

"It's all about control…"

I didn't disagree with the sentiment, but control was necessary. Our villages had gone to war before and stained the earth with our blood. Too much blood had soured the soil like a curse and left half of Vylheim a wasteland that starved thousands of survivors of war.

Many believed the law was disingenuous, since the punishment for breaking it also spilled blood, but this was the only threat that kept people in line. Otherwise we'd be at each other's throats.

Our history was proof of this. The nature to fight was in our blood. The same blood our ancestors had spilled in ancient wars and passed down to us.

After I squeezed my way inside, I saw my father at his chair on the left of the large room. My tired muscles tensed at the sight of the grimace twisting his mouth. His frown wasn't directed at me, but habit said he'd still find a reason to scold me.

I swept my gaze away from him before I caught his eye.

Every inch of open space was filled with bodies except what seemed to be invisible boundaries around more executioners. I kept my eyes off their masks and the axes at their sides to keep my nerves from fraying even more.

A skeletal woman with a small, upturned nose and a hefty, pale man stood at the front, blocking my father's chair. He was going to chew on the anger from it for days.

The woman addressed Skaldir by staring down her nose at us, her peaked brows permanently in the shape of shock. The detailed embroidery along the hem of her dress pinned her as a courtier, and the all-black dress signaled she was a member of King Drakkar's council.

"Like Darius said, population has waned," she said, waving to the male councilmember. "We are losing our people, our heritage, and our history."

I snorted. We'd lost most of our history long ago. Villagers only shared it through oral sagas now.

The councilwoman continued on. "With the winters growing worse, we fear an all-consuming loss over the next few decades. Less food means more deaths and fewer births. We must find fertile land, and our only option is expansion beyond The Sea of Skalds."

Unrest rippled through the crowd. Going beyond the sea meant losing more lives to unforgiving waters.

She ignored the added restlessness. "For the next three years, our efforts will be focused on preparing for exploration, and as such, we've deemed the end of the Polar Nocturne in the third year, the seventh year of King Drakkar's reign, The Dawn of Exploration, when the people of Vylheim will finally set sail. By then we will have prepared enough ships and explorers to fill them with."

Darius laid his hand on her shoulder and then turned to us. "Thank you, Ylva. Able-bodied men and women of Vylheim should consider taking to the seas."

"That's sacrifice!" Ragna shouted.

All together, the Grimward snapped their heads and scanned the crowd for the source of the woman who dared speak out. She didn't shrink back.

Darius continued. "Sacrifice to the seas is better than starvation in the wasteland or total extinction. With hunger, unrest grows, and we've been forced to cut down more and more of those who shed blood."

"If you don't want us to die out, then stop killing us!" Ragna dared shout out again.

Frowning, Darius spoke through clenched teeth. "If we don't send a message that bloodshed ends in execution, then we'll descend into war again, and all of Vylheim will be as barren as the wasteland. It is the way of all humans." He flicked his hand out and two members of the Grimward, one in a boar's mask and another in a bear's mask shoved through the crowd, searching for Ragna.

But she did not take the bait. If she moved, they'd know she was trying to run. She stood her ground and their eyes passed right over her.

Ylva jumped in again and directed the speech back to this exploration. "Many of the king's guards will take to the seas with you, and every exiled person will be required to join them."

My heart stuttered and it seemed a hand clamped around my throat.

My mother would die at sea. I had no doubt. Every single one of the witches that had been hunted down and dragged to the wasteland would be sacrificed to The Sea of Skalds.

And I should be one of them, instead of her.

She never should have outed herself to protect me.

My pulse thumped erratically and my eyesight blurred. I thought I had more time to piece the visions together, to make a case for witches based on real, true history that the king couldn't deny.

We aren't a threat. Don't kill us.

Don't kill her.

But Ylva spoke again, sealing my mother's fate. "With the passage of three years and at the end of the Polar Nocturne, the age of exploration will dawn."

Three years.

I could no longer hope for visions while cutting away at the fields, I had to start running again, to beat myself down every chance I got for the glimpse of a vision from Odin or Freya. It had to come with emotional and mental pressure too, because without it, I didn't always get to the point of collapse. Fear too easily stopped me short, a self-preservation that reminded me my heart and nerves were frail.

It had to be a total collapse to quiet my body and mind so my spirit could understand the language of the Gods. The language of Asgard.

I only had three years.

CHAPTER TWO

Nine of us women lined up for the first challenge of the autumnal twilight. While children played in the streets, and villagers made bets on the race's outcome, I steadied my breathing. Nerves rippled through me, buzzing with impatience for the running to begin.

I anxiously waited for the start of each new season when we'd gather as a village to celebrate the changes with footraces, wrestling, swimming, and stone lifting. I wasn't particularly skilled at any of them, but that worked in my favor because this—running—was my opportunity to push my body to the edge of breakdown.

And that's what I craved most.

The competition, the bets, the thrill of running in front of others, all of it was enough for me to push and push and push until I finally got what I wanted; a vision from the Gods.

I shook the tingling from my arms as Ragna patted my back. She was the favored winner because of her wiry muscle and that she shaved one side of her head to keep it from blowing in her face and distracting her. Trades exchanged hands, coin and furs, with Ragna's name on their lips. It only encouraged me to run harder.

"Alva is cheering for you, Silver," Ragna said with a laugh. She pointed to her daughter who jumped up and down at the row of villagers, all eager for the challenges to kick off. Her blond braids shone bright among the fading green and ragged browns, the muted colors of autumn made darker by an overcast sky.

Alva's little hands fluttered in erratic claps and my heart matched its pace. If I wasn't careful, I'd cross the frail line from nervous excitement to unbidden panic.

I blew out a slow breath and gave Alva a little wave.

"No, she's hoping you win," I said to reassure Ragna. But she was not offended by her daughter's choice.

She shook her head and winked. "She doesn't have to hope for that."

I managed a smile until Alva suddenly stopped waving and chewed on the sleeve of her dress. Her father pulled her closer to him, silent concern tugging at his frown. Even Ragna's good nature vanished.

Their gazes panned across the village to where the race would end.

I snapped my head to the end of the foot path. Masked men and women marched down our racetrack, not an unusual occurrence except that these were extra members of the Grimward, more than we normally had patrolling our village.

Thirteen executioners had arrived, along with members of the king's guard mounted on horses behind them.

Their footsteps and the clop of hooves grew louder and heavier as they marched toward the competitors. Years had passed since they'd ripped women from their houses, testing to see if they claimed themselves as witches. The Grimward was too busy patrolling for violence, and experience told me that even now, with the king's guard in tow, they were likely only patrolling for any fools who'd gotten into a fight and drawn blood.

But my frayed nerves said otherwise.

They're hunting witches.

They're hunting you.

And you deserve it.

Blood rushed in deafening waves through my ears. My heart hammered painfully with the storm of dread building inside me.

Someone called out for us to get into position, daring to break the tense silence as we all afforded the Grimward respect laced in bitterness.

Since their visits grew more frequent, we tried to lay low, focus on the activity, and continue our celebration. How they even scented the lost blood, I didn't know. They eyed us as they scanned the crowd in search of whoever had broken the law.

I bit my tongue and kept my eyes on the ground. I had to believe they didn't know what I was so that I didn't collapse from nerves and give myself away. Collapsing was reserved for during or after the race only, when my unconsciousness would be considered nothing more than the strain of the sport, not a moment to commune with the Gods.

Each woman dropped to one knee as if bowing before royalty, our heads low.

An executioner's boot stepped into my line of sight. The Grimward were a necessary evil and we'd been visited by the king's guard, even courtiers and council members before, but something about today felt different—or rather, familiar. Familiar to a single horrific memory from my childhood.

A shiver snaked between each bone along my spine. If I thought about the first time I saw their masks, and the swing of their axes, darkness would cloud my sight until I collapsed in the crystal-wet leaves.

If only the damn race would start.

I needed to forget.

I glanced at my father in hopes he'd call for it to begin. He was eyeing the executioners, clearly annoyed that he had no control over them and that their search interrupted our celebration.

I gritted my teeth, focusing on the feel of bone grinding against bone to divert my mind from the invisible claws enclosing my throat and lungs. The race hadn't even started and I was already breathless.

I squeezed my eyes shut to try to block out the echoes of that day triggered by the sight of their masked faces, but pieces of the memory I'd buried popped up anyway.

The darkness of the hatch under my bed. The screams. The lies that left my tongue bitter ever since.

Like my mother had taught me to do, I shifted my focus from the past to the present. I tasted bitterness on my tongue. I smelled the rot of early autumn leaves. I felt the damp earth bend beneath my knee. The world narrowed, my pulse slowing just enough to keep me upright.

My heavy braid tumbled over my shoulder, the amber-brown ends mingling with the leaves covering the ground. I fought every urge to abandon this race and run from here, but if I left now, I'd only call attention to myself. I'd only draw the interest of the executioners looking for criminals.

I couldn't help that I was born one.

Two of the executioners marched behind the row of women, circling us like birds of prey zeroing in on their kill.

But it was the glare of my father's wife that caught my attention, her irritation for my very existence as a witch obvious with her twisted frown. At twenty-six, I no longer gave in to her pressure. It once molded me, like heat in a forge while my father was the fire, burning me with every slap on the cheek, a bitter occurrence that grew more frequent the longer my mother had been gone. Ten years banished to the wasteland meant her life would end soon. Nobody had ever survived longer than a decade there.

My heart tripped. I had to get a glimpse of how to free her. The Gods' help was my only hope.

This damn race needed to start now. The pressure of competition had worked every other time, but I only glimpsed pieces of the sagas, up until my most recent vision.

A vision of an ancient runestone with the image of a witch carved into it.

Was it stored with the others in the king's castle?

Another vision might tell me that, too. Thankfully the Grimward had no clue that when I fainted from physical exertion, I was also seeing magic painted on the inside of my eyelids—painted by the hands of the Gods. To them, I was just a weak competitor, a stupid girl in this for the fun of competition.

The executioners finally cut left, and I prayed for the race to begin, when another pair of boots stopped before me. This rough black leather didn't match the blood-stained brown of the Grimward and guards' boots.

I dragged my eyes up, but the man had already turned and followed in the executioners' wake. His dark hair was knotted at the back of his head, a style that I'd only heard described in stories. A heavy sword was slung across his back instead of the executioners' typical axes hanging at their sides. Nobody was allowed to carry weapons anymore, except executioners and the king's guard, and...*the king*.

It couldn't be King Drakkar.

This man looked like a warrior from the old and forbidden sagas that spoke of Odin and Freya and recounted historical battles fought in their names. Plus, the king had never traveled here before.

He strode toward the Vyl's chair where my father sat to survey the race and autumnal celebrations.

Despite this distraction, my father's voice finally—finally—rang out in the call that started the race. "For glory!"

We bolted forward.

My feet pounded the slick path coated in wet leaves. I forced one leg in front of the other, ignoring the pain thumping between my ribs just like a warrior would. Cold air filled my lungs as I sprinted out ahead of the other competitors.

My heels struck the path one after the other. Fire enveloped my lungs as my failing heart hammered too fast. I'd started in front of the other racers, only to quickly fall back. Two, then three women passed me, their eyes set on the rotted ash tree.

Ragna easily breezed past me while I heaved painful breaths.

I had to push harder, faster. If I failed to collapse, the Gods would not be able to reach me. While the barrier between Asgard and Midgard was thin and their influence accessed us through the tree of Yggdrasil, a connection was only possible for witches who put in the effort.

I forced my feet forward, but it was too late.

Ragna pumped her fists in victory as she stopped at the ash tree. The short sprint and the thrill of competition had ended before I could hurl my body past its breaking point. I hadn't pushed hard enough.

Once I finished the race, running my palm over the rough tree bark, I doubled forward, the heel of my hands on my thighs. While I heaved, the other women chatted easily. My breathless lungs wouldn't even let me congratulate Ragna.

Just then, she laid her hand on my back and I sucked in a choking breath, giving her a smile that she didn't return. Ragna's resilient beauty remained despite the worry twisting her face.

"Silver." My heart thumped when her voice came out in a whisper. "Have you found yourself in a bloody fight lately? Or have they found out about you?" She moved to stand in front of me, her muscular body blocking my sight of the village. If she'd been a witch from ancient times, her gift of strength would have been used to fight off Jotnar, the giants who pillaged human villages—creatures everyone now said never existed—though she could only summon it with the rising of the dawn sun.

My back was to the ash tree as I blinked up at her. "I—no. Why?"

Despite the heat of the exercise, my blood ran cold as her fingers gripped my shoulder.

"They're staring at you," Ragna said. "The *king* hasn't stopped looking at you since he arrived."

I dared to look past her and immediately my gaze met the man with the warrior's hair. His pale blue eyes stared at me, unblinking. He towered over my father with the muscle and widespread stance of a fighter. His thick beard accentuated the cut of his jaw.

Everything about him, down to the arrogance slightly curling at the edge of his mouth and the delicious fierceness in his icy eyes, was what I imagined a warrior before battle to look like.

My lips parted and I sucked in a sharp breath.

When he noticed my reaction, his mouth cut into a crooked grin. It did nothing to soften the intensity of his all-consuming eyes.

My heart slowed enough for me to notice the brief skips with every other beat. How is it that a man who refuted the existence of Gods and witches and our history could embody the heroes from the sagas I loved?

And his eyes were on *me*.

Heat bloomed in my chest, thawing the cold fear that had rendered me frozen only moments ago. His gaze roved over me, dropping to where I heaved in another breath, and then trailed back up to my eyes.

My father was speaking to him, but the king didn't seem to listen. He merely folded his thick arms over his chest and tipped his head ever so slightly. Though I hadn't won a message from the Gods, I'd received the king's message.

He'd come here for me.

This man I'd never met was fixated on me, and because he was nothing like I expected, I couldn't look away.

"Does he recognize you?" Ragna's voice broke through my thoughts.

Shit. Did he know what I was? My eyes darted from her to the people behind her. Two members of the Grimward marched toward me. Only their stark brown eyes were visible from beneath carved masks, one a boar with jagged tusks, the other curved with the lithe lines of a lynx.

"Which of you is Silver?" the boar asked as he made his way down the path we'd used for the short sprint. Their stares matched that of a predator stalking its prey.

And perhaps the king's stare had been the same, I was only too foolish to notice.

"I have to run," I whispered.

"Go into the forest," she breathed back, just low enough that they couldn't catch her words as they marched closer. "If they catch you, they'll exile you. And if for some reason they decide they must kill you, they'll only do it where there are witnesses."

She was right. The more alone I was, the safer I was.

They were instructed to send a message, and if nobody was around to see my head severed from my body, it was a waste—nearly as grave as a villager wasting a drop of blood when our very lives, every bit of our energy, was wrapped up in a system that supported one another. Farmers, trappers, gatherers, Vyls, weavers, even royals all played a role in keeping Vylheim from becoming the wasteland our ancient home had turned into. Each life had value to the system. Value not worth sacrificing without witnesses.

The message was more important than the execution, so that others didn't get any ideas.

My gaze shifted back to the king. He lifted his brows as if to challenge me.

Run.

I spun on my heels and ducked past the rotted ash. I ran into the heavy shade of trees where even the bright moon at the beginning of autumn could not break through the tangle of branches above.

I ran—another chance to push my body to the breaking point, to survive, and perhaps even to glimpse a vision.

CHAPTER THREE

FREYA'S TRIAL

The forest's darkness enveloped me, stark and cold but protective. Shadows gave me cover from the executioners who hunted me. After foraging food from this forest for two decades, I knew every tree, every spot to hide.

I ducked to the right, forcing my feet to keep moving, keep running.

I would not stop.

The flap of a bat's wings fluttered overhead. I could no longer hear the beat of the executioner's boots striking the earth, but I knew they were close behind and I'd yet to break down my body. I'd only lose them by winding my path, because they'd quickly outpace me.

I weaved through a maze of trees and ignored the thwack of branches hitting my body as I pushed through.

Mercy would come from the forest itself, even if it wasn't a safe place.

I usually only dared take to the shadows of trees in the daytime with the other gatherers, many of whom were women who'd just bested me in the race. Witches knew wild animals were not the only threat in these trees. Ragna had sworn she heard the footfall of a giant deep in the forest. Others had reported sightings of fanged people, but my father promptly shut down such claims. Bears and beasts existed, but not giants or the undead— called Draugr—mentioned in Thor's saga.

For once, I prayed my father was right.

I ran until black spots dotted my vision.

The king wouldn't let me live, whether that death came swiftly or achingly slow through starvation in the wasteland. Witches weren't supposed to exist because Gods weren't supposed to exist. I suspected the king didn't appreciate villagers worshipping Odin and Freya instead of him. As the Gods' chosen vessels, a witch's very presence in Vylheim proved him and the rest of his beliefs wrong. We were here, and though we were in hiding, we existed, some of us seer-borns, others with the power to heal, or manipulate the elements.

I sucked ragged breaths into my burning lungs. Cramps seized my legs, but it was my heart that hurt the most. The beats thumped off rhythm, and it threatened to give out at any moment. It would soon stutter into a brief stop before reawakening.

In the interim, perhaps I'd hear Freya's voice or glimpse through Odin's single eye and see what he saw.

I drove my feet forward, step by step, despite the ache radiating up from my heels.

Glancing above, I caught sight of the heavens between branches. Soon ribbons of purple and pink, and blue as stark as King Drakkar's eyes, would dance across the sky—a colorful reminder from the Gods that even in the depths of winter, there was hope.

They were there, waiting for witches to reach out to them for guidance and help.

Tell me what to do. Where can I go? How can I help my mother?

Myself? I begged silently. Frustration mingled with desperation as my tongue swelled, my mouth growing drier.

How would I survive now? If the king knew I was a witch, his pursuit would be relentless. I could never go back to Skaldir. I couldn't dare to commune with other witches in the hopes of digging out an answer that would free my mother from exile.

Give me a vision!

I trusted the Gods would reach me if they could. When I lacked visions it was because of my own failure, my resistant fear of the inevitable collapse. I hated that I wasn't pushing myself hard enough.

Cold sweat trickled down my forehead, slipping between my brows. Salt stung my eyes. I squeezed my eyes shut for as long as I dared. Peeling them open again, I saw only darkness and the vague shapes of tree trunks.

The bushes rustled with a wild animal startled by my presence. A thin stream of moonlight broke through patchy branches, and the dim light illuminated a black bird flying in front of me. The raven cawed and I took the sound as a cheer, as if Odin himself had sent his precious Huginn or Muninn to watch over me.

Icy air crackled in my chest. Every breath left my throat raw as my body slowly failed, my throat squeezing tighter and tighter.

Help me.

Soon I would collapse, but that didn't always guarantee a connection with the Gods. I'd need days of recovery before I could push myself again in hopes of another vision.

I didn't have days.

Survival in the forest, alone, at the dawn of autumn wasn't an option. Especially not after I ran myself ragged.

The black clouds at the edges of my vision grew. Heat flamed over my neck and into my spinning head. Collapse was imminent, and I prayed it was enough for them to reach me.

I blinked again, and when I opened my eyes I didn't see the raven, the trees, or the shadowed forest. My world shifted into an all-consuming vision. Before me stood a grand castle with stone turrets. Rose bushes twined and tangled over the walls, their thorns as sharp as the look on the king's face.

King Drakkar stood at the top of the steps in front of towering double doors. His lips shaped around words I could not hear yet somehow understood.

"Come to me. I have what you seek."

My foot caught a root or rock and my body was thrown forward. The vision vanished and night filled in around me. I expected to slam into the ground, but hands gripped my arms and wrenched me backward, forcing me upright again. The water I'd gulped before the race sloshed in my stomach with the sudden recoil.

A man and a woman's voice floated, disembodied around me. My head spun because I couldn't draw enough breath into my lungs. Through the haze of pain and confusion and desperation, a single thought struck me.

The executioners had caught up to me, and I was collapsing in their arms.

Heat and darkness encased me.

Chapter Four

When I came to only moments later, nobody was there. I was alone, suspended by the grip of something I couldn't see. I narrowed my focus, gazing into the darkness until my eyes adjusted and I could make out the shapes that melted from the shadows like black clouds forming into a human.

It wasn't a boar's mask and a lynx looking at me. In the pale light stood a man and woman dressed in fine clothing. They each held one of my arms to keep me upright. Like a doll, they propped me up with what seemed to be unusual strength.

These people dressed in royal finery were not only an oddity this far north and away from Mara, they were the last thing I expected to see in the forest.

Mara was the largest and most powerful village in Vylheim, nearly a kingdom of its own, though the king who sat on the only throne in the entire continent ruled over us all, every single villager from Skaldir, to Torsholt and Einnland, as well the other towns.

What would bring courtiers *here?*

I stared, my mouth gaping, waiting to see if this vision

would dissipate as easily as the mist crawling across the forest floor.

After a moment, I determined that not only were they real, they were a threat. They gripped my arms so tightly they could snap the bone beneath my reddened flesh with a mere flick of the wrist.

Without a word, they stepped forward and yanked me along beside them. My numb feet padded heavily as they forced me to walk with them.

Slowly, they picked through the forest, cutting a new trail to the south of where I'd run. With my throat still dry and my head spinning, I couldn't conjure words. I merely wrenched my neck to scan the woman.

Had the executioners taken off their masks? Her eyes were a pale gold, not that of the deep brown I'd seen beneath both the boar's mask and the lynx's mask. Executioners also didn't dress in finery with detailed embroidery.

My mind had been right the first time, these people truly were courtiers.

A shiver cut through me as the woman's eyes flashed with a spark of red, like blood, before it vanished just as quickly. Her gaze raked over me as she dragged me alongside her.

"What do you want with me?" I asked. Shudders rippled through my breathless words.

This wasn't the first time I'd witnessed shadows lurking alongside me, but they'd never come this close.

"You'll know soon enough." Her voice cracked like a frozen lake, the tone sending my heart into my stomach as if I were falling through the ice.

Every nerve in my body fired warnings at the sight of hunger and hatred mixing in her eyes. The sudden and sickening urge to attack her swelled in my mind. She hadn't hurt me, or even threatened me, and yet I wanted to shove her away, hard.

This was more than the need for survival. Was it from fear? Or was this the darkest part of me itching to break free?

I tried to focus on studying her.

Curiosity prickled through the dizzying fear that twined around my heart like the mist at my feet. Everyone said giants and trolls, spirits and the undead didn't exist, but neither did humans with gold eyes who could emerge from the darkness faster than a blink.

I scanned the shape of her cheekbones and the chestnut hair piled messily atop her head, noting her golden eyes again. It was a shade I'd never seen on anyone before. A shade my mother taught me was reserved for creatures damned by the Gods.

"You've followed me before haven't you?" I refused to let them drag me along in silence. The man only laughed as the woman ignored me.

I could have screamed, but I'd strayed too far from the village. Running wasn't an option, and fighting—*No!*

Even if I could hurt them, I wouldn't, not unless it was absolutely necessary. I'd spent too long locking that vile part of me away, as if I could bury memories like a key in a hatch under the bed.

"Why grab me now?" I asked.

Her fingernails dug deeper and deeper. "Because now we know what you are."

The man's hand squeezed tighter as he shoved me forward so hard I slammed into the woman. She bared glistening white teeth at me. Anger flared in me as I tried to wrench away from them both.

If I dared stab him with the tip of the silver pendant weighing heavy in my pocket, I'd lose my head to an executioner's blade. All for a mere prick from the sharp edge of a necklace, a piece of jewelry my mother said represented the tree of Yggdrasil, and was purified with the power to cut through cruel humans and monsters. Even if the undead couldn't die, she said it could hurt anyone who defied the Gods.

The tree's trunk was long and fashioned into a sharp tip while the top had only two split branches like arms reaching up to the Gods. She'd called it my Y Tree, a silver pendant designed in the exact shape of the ancient king of Vylheim's signature. On the side, a small carving of his name was left in the same cut and style as on the runestones; *Volrik the Rune King*.

While the witches believed this shape was the tree of Yggdrasil, the king and his council claimed the ancient king used this shape to represent two choices. That it had nothing to do with the Gods and witches.

I couldn't use it as a weapon. It'd be stripped away from me and I'd lose my chance to prove it matched the indent in the ancient runestones.

"And what are *you?*" I demanded, staring into the woman's strange eyes.

She only scoffed and yanked me forward.

A skip in my pulse told me these people who'd slunk out of the shadows as if their bodies had been molded from the darkness, were not human. Monsters only existed in the sagas, but that was what the kings and leaders said about the Gods too, and I'd witnessed Freya and Odin's visions in my own life.

Had it been a trick of the light or did they blend with the shadows the way undead did in the stories?

"Don't look so pitiful," she said. "We won't hurt you."

"Much," the man added, as he came up behind me while his partner prodded me from the other side. His breath brushed over the back of my neck. "Silver Norn," he said, his tone mocking. "You can't hide who you are. Did your parents think your name would spare you from us?" A raspy laugh erupted from him, sending my blood boiling.

I hated that he taunted me, that he knew to bait this urge to attack them I had building inside of me.

Despite the woman's hold on me, I spun around to face him. "You better hope *I'll* spare you," I spat.

The wicked side of me had slipped out.

"The wretched witch spat on me." He stopped walking to put space between us.

Satisfaction spread like warm mead across my chest—the mark of someone disturbed.

The woman clucked her tongue as if she were a disapproving mother and I a child. "What a foolish girl. Don't you know the executioners will have your head?" The woman's fingernails slowly dug deeper into my flesh, splitting the skin apart in crescent slices.

I tried yanking away again, but when she only squeezed harder, the flood broke loose, the hatch unlocked, and my wickedness spilling out. "I could say the same to you. You're hurting me, and when the executioners find out, you'll no longer have a tongue to speak. They'll brand your face with the death knots and then they'll exile or behead—"

"Shut up!" She cut me off. "Do you not recognize royal embroidery when you see it?" With her free hand she ran her palm down the front of her dress, the stitching intricate, obviously too detailed to be from a seamstress in Skaldir or any of the surrounding villages.

She thought she was untouchable. I'd never been to King Drakkar's castle, but I heard rumors, tales that those who lived there didn't answer to any of the same judgments held against the rest of the people of Vylheim.

Though I'd never heard of royals inciting violence, they'd skirted other crimes, like bribery, abduction, or breaking an oath. These stories were merely nightmares, unreal to someone who lived their entire life in the distant village of Skaldir, weeks' travel from Mara where Mara's Keep, the castle itself, housed the only throne in Vylheim.

Had King Drakkar sent them in case the executioners didn't carry out their mission?

"She doesn't have a lick of sense," the woman drawled with annoyance. To her partner she said, "Sten, are you so sure she's the one?"

"Are her nasty little beetle's eyes not enough proof for you, Astrid?" he said.

My stomach flipped. The enchantment had never faded before the next morning. Could he see through the magic? I eyed him as he toyed with a bronze ring that held a ruby jewel at the center of the thick band, emphasizing his wealth as a royal.

She glared at me, taking in the black apex of my eyes that'd spread like a perfect circle of spilled ink. She could see it too. "Hideous. We should scoop them out—"

"So you do intend to hurt me," I interrupted. The pendant weighed heavier and heavier in my pocket. "The king sent you after me?"

Astrid's eyes flashed and, for a moment, our roles as predator and prey swapped. I knew the strange place in between fear and anger too well.

Was she afraid of me? Angry at the king? I couldn't begin to understand it.

Perhaps they wanted to impress King Drakkar by bringing me before him, but that didn't explain why shadows like them —moving too quickly and with inhuman eyes—had lurked at my heels since I was a young girl. King Drakkar had only held the throne for seven years since he'd replaced King Roderic at only nineteen.

Both kings had been on a witch hunt my entire life, while skillfully denying we existed at all. A king who looked like the warriors in our sagas was no different. Just because he had long hair, wielded a weapon, and carried bloodlust in his eyes did not make him sympathetic to our history, to witches.

"Are you taking me to King Drakkar?" If so, everything would be easier. I could go with them without a fight and follow the vision.

My pulse fluttered. The king's gaze had left me unsteady, his presence everything I didn't expect.

Sten spoke, letting Astrid stew in silence. "Hoping we won't kill you before you see Mara's Keep?" He stepped so close his hot breath blew over my neck. I recoiled as my own breath hitched. How could he throw that threat around so easily? To his partner he said, "She only has to be alive, not conscious."

"Sten," Astrid growled. "Don't tempt me."

"She'd be easier to handle as a limp body." Goosebumps prickled across my neck and arms.

"You won't be able to control yourself," she said.

"Her blood smells like wine…"

His voice crawled over me and ignited the mix of fury and fear building in my veins.

I could no longer hold back the flood of words on my tongue. "I don't care what you think you can avoid as a royal. My father is a Vyl, a leader in Skaldir, and he will call for the fair use of executioner justice when he sees you've hurt me."

My free hand found its way into my pocket, my fingers wrapping around the cold silver Y.

As if sensing my thoughts, Astrid ripped me toward her, forcing us face-to-face so that I'd give her my full attention. My hand twitched, ready to pull the makeshift weapon from my pocket.

"Hurt you?" She gripped my chin with her other hand, her strength unmatched, my head locked in place so tightly it seemed she could merely twist her wrist if she wanted to snap my neck. "Not until we make use of you." She spoke through her teeth. The flex of her jaw revealed her anger. I'd hit a sore spot. "Then, and only then, will I taste your blood until you're nothing but a lifeless human husk."

"Astrid! Your hands!" Sten's voice became background noise along with the brush of leaves overhead. We both ignored him, but something warm trickled down my arms. I glanced at Astrid's hold where her fingernails dug in so deep they left crescent wounds in my flesh and drew hot blood to the surface.

Blood rushed through my ears, my heart pounding louder —a thumping applause to cheer for my next move. All thoughts of starvation, exile, the possible execution I'd face, washed away at the sound of the feral and sickening hunger that laced her every word.

Her fingernails had sliced into my skin, leaving the back of my arm stinging when she suddenly let go.

I seized the moment of freedom. Pulling the Y Tree from my pocket, I sunk the sharp end of the pendant into the soft spot just below her collarbone. When Astrid's gaze fell, horror filled her eyes.

Bright red blood trickled from the wound in her chest, but it was her hands that transfixed her. The tips of her fingers bubbled as if dipped into a boiling pot. I had no idea how or why, but my blood, red and hot, had become fire to her flesh, slowly melting her skin and turning the shell of her fingers to ash.

Where I'd stabbed her, her flesh congealed and melted around the Y that still impaled her.

"What is happening?" she choked out, mirroring my own thoughts.

How had the Y Tree burned her? How had *my blood* burned her?

Perhaps Freya was watching over me. My mother always said witches were given the most divine opportunities. But she also said witches helped others, they never hurt, and yet my blood was melting this woman's fingers.

My heart slammed into my gut.

It wasn't just my blood hurting her. I'd stabbed her. I'd chosen to commit the very violence that I'd been trying to forget about, to resist.

Astrid's body crumpled, and only then did I remember my other captor.

Expecting the worst, I stooped and ripped the Y Tree from her flesh before spinning around to protect myself from Sten. He stood stunned, frozen, horrified at the sight of blood—not Astrid's, but my blood—trickling down my arm where her sharp fingernails had cut into me.

For a moment, I thought he wasn't going to hurt me. That I'd be able to run. But I dared to blink, and in an instant, he lunged at me. When I turned to run, my heel caught on slick leaves and we went down together, wrestling until I thrust the end of the Y Tree into his neck.

It didn't stop him.

In a mess of limbs and dead leaves, I couldn't see what weapon he'd wielded when something sharp sliced across my face.

I cried out, the sound piercing through the forest.

When his skin bubbled around the pendant, his strength waned and he quickly grew limp. I rolled out from under him. His lifeless eyes were left peeled open, staring into the realm of the dead.

I turned to see that his partner looked the same. Astrid gazed at nothing while her spirit roamed the underworld, claimed by Hel, the God of dishonorable deaths. They were dead, which had to mean they weren't the undead or strong monsters my frayed nerves had led me to believe.

And I'd *killed* them.

Scrambling to my feet, I only stayed long enough to rip the Y Tree from his throat before I ran, praying to the Gods I wasn't supposed to believe in that nobody would ever find out what I'd done.

The Gods were my only hope. The vision they'd granted me of the king was just enough to guide my next step.

I knew where Odin wanted me to go—back to Skaldir, back to the king whose courtiers I'd just murdered.

CHAPTER FIVE

Night passed shrouded in shame. When the next day descended into all-encompassing darkness and early snow dotted the ground in crystal white, I finally dragged myself back to the edge of the village.

Nearly two days had passed before I could bring myself to show my face in Skaldir again.

I'd just shed blood, royal blood. *No, worse*, I'd murdered two people. Their limp bodies and unseeing eyes filled every corner of my mind.

Their deaths confirmed they weren't the monsters I suspected. They must have been people from Mara's royal court who sought to drag me before the king after I'd ran from his guards.

Monsters didn't drop dead so easily, and neither Astrid nor Sten looked like the beasts of rotted-flesh that the sagas described. I'd practiced in the dugout to fight and kill creatures like that, not people, but I'd let out the evil I kept beneath the surface.

My twisted darkness had once again emerged, twenty years after I'd buried it and had sworn I'd never let myself do something so unforgivable again.

They had to be people because now they were dead.

There was no escape from this memory no matter how deep in the forest I'd left them behind, or how far I walked. All I could do now was hope to follow the Gods' guidance so I could forget myself in pursuit of what they wanted.

And what they wanted was for me to surrender to the king who'd come to kill me.

I paced the edge of the forest just behind the rotted ash tree. Beyond the trees, Skaldir was quiet. No screams rang out from the executioner's punishments, and no shouts of glory nor echoes of celebration filled the air.

The autumnal revelry had been cut short by King Drakkar as much as the now falling snow.

"What can the king do for me?" I whispered as if the Gods could answer now. Even a witch had to sacrifice a piece of herself to hear them.

Perhaps if Midgard was closer to where they resided in Asgard, it'd be easier for them to reach us, but the Nine Realms spread vastly across Midgard's sky, with Jotunheim separating us. The realm of giants and trolls, battle and chaos. No wonder it was so hard to hear Freya's voice or see through Odin's eye.

Come to me. I recalled the words I'd understood from the vision.

If I went before King Drakkar, how would I survive? I had to live at least long enough to honor the Gods so Hel could not drag my soul to the depths of the underworld where I'd never feast with Odin or roam in peace with Freya.

But survival at the king's hands made no sense. Especially after I'd killed.

Steadily, snowflakes gathered on the ground, blanketing the patchy brown and gold leaves in white. Autumn had ended as quickly as it'd begun, which meant Vylheim was in for a dangerously long and dark winter. I shuddered, but not from the cold.

I'd killed. I'm corrupt. Broken. Evil.
Evil.
Evil.
Evil

My stomach twisted, and I wrenched my thoughts away from the darkness that stirred within me. If I didn't focus on one thing at a time, my thoughts would descend into a spiral of madness where this incessant dwelling would overcome me. I'd be left paralyzed, incapable of following the vision that fluttered with hope in my heart.

My muscles had already stiffened and my heart skipped painfully.

This was my chance to find my mother.

According to the Gods, *he* was my chance to free her. Was it certain death? The king stood at the helm of the system that exiled my mother for being a witch. If he knew I was both a witch and a killer, spilling my blood wouldn't be a waste at all. It'd be a glorious message for all of Vylheim to witness.

And yet, the Gods had answered.

I was to go to him. If I did not, if I ran like I had when I hid under the hatch in the floorboards…

I shook my head, disgust coiling in my gut like sour mead. I would do this. I would do this because it was the clearest vision I'd had since my mother was taken from us ten years ago, just when I'd grown from a child into a young woman.

I ran my palm down the rough trunk where the bark was stripped and peeling and black. If I touched the tree of victory long enough, perhaps I'd gather the courage to force my feet forward. I'd march out into the village and track down King Drakkar, wherever he'd taken up camp.

Memory of his warrior's stance and fixed stare sent uneasy flutters through me. He'd been fixated on me and only me, with a smile and the lift of his brows. Heat crawled up my neck at the memory. I forced a breath out and palmed my chest. I hated him. He was the man responsible for ripping my mother away from me, *not* the warrior I dreamed of no matter how he knotted his hair or carried his weapon.

I sucked in a breath of icy air so quickly it felt sharp in my throat. The shock of the cold sent away the shameful heat gathering within me every time I thought of the king's eyes on me.

Perhaps it wasn't so terrible for me to want to see him again since it was the Gods leading me to him.

In the vision, King Drakkar said he had what I sought, but that was the Gods speaking through the image of the king. Maybe they wanted me to track him because the runestone with the image of the witch could be with the records stored at Mara's Keep.

I had to prove that witches were more than the Gods' vessels. If she wasn't a threat to the king's beliefs, he'd have no reason to keep her in exile, and in a world bound by honor, he'd have to honor the truth. This truth was a piece of lost history, a saga that spoke of the first witch, a woman who served the ancient king of Vylheim until his dying breath.

The saga shifted and altered from the mouths of hundreds over the years, twisting to claim the witch had Odin smite the king.

But my mother's visions said otherwise. The witch was loyal and I had the Y Tree to prove it. My mother had sacrificed hundreds of plants, burning them for glimpses of these details.

If I found the original runestone with the saga and the indent to fit the Y Tree—the ancient king's signature—then King Drakkar would have no choice but to acknowledge that witches existed, and that we were capable of both believing the Gods *and* recognizing human authority.

We weren't a threat.

We were capable of keeping peace. All we wanted was to come out of hiding, to honor the Gods, and to share the history the people of Vylheim had forgotten.

Even the king and his council were bound by tradition.

I finally emerged from behind the tree, tapping the scab where Sten had cut a wound across my cheek. I never saw what kind of weapon he'd wielded, but it would scar my skin all the same.

Stalking through the quiet village, I noted no changes. No blood stained the ground. No royal camps were set up in the fields. Everything remained the same except for my home.

While other houses were dark, a candle flickered in the window.

I surveyed it. Had they waited up, hoping for me to return? Or would the king be asleep in my fathers' bed while he and his wife took to the furs on the floor?

The heavy door groaned as I pushed my way through. Shutting it behind me, I blocked the chill of night, and the goosebumps on my neck finally sank back into smooth skin.

Without a candle, I had to feel my way through the long hall, and when my eyes adjusted, I caught the dim light streaming out of the vast front room. The houses in Skaldir were one or two large rooms in an open space. Each area was split for privacy with beaded curtains, tapestries, and a few strung-up animal bones. The bones were extras we did not use to snap and create tools with which to hunt small animals and skin any larger ones we caught in traps.

The beads dangled on the other side of the opening to the front room, catching the flicker of the candle in the crystal blue glass.

I expected to turn the corner and step into the king's presence, but I was met with the hard slap of an open palm. The slap wrenched my head to the side and threw me off balance.

I stumbled back, cupping my stinging cheek.

The force of the hit wasn't unfamiliar. My father's hand found my face whenever I dared defy royalty, whether it was whispering Freya's name or even speaking my own, as if saying my name somehow conjured my powers as a witch.

"Foolish woman," he spat. "What have you done?"

My heart stuttered. There was no way he knew about the bodies in the forest. They were so far from Skaldir, shrouded in darkness and soon to be buried in the snow where they'd remain. They would be frozen and hidden for months. But fear still struck me harder than his hand before the feeling quickly shifted to the same disgust carried in my father's voice.

"How weak and selfish do you have to be to call attention to yourself like that? Did you think of us? Did you think of Skaldir when you ran from the king?" His dark eyes flared. "Did you ever consider what would happen to the rest of us if they found out what you claim to be?"

Claim to be.

Claim to be.

I claimed nothing, I was only what I'd been born as. A seer, and a supposed threat to the king. And now? A murderer, too.

Disgust manifested as bile in my tightened throat.

"He was going to exile me," I said between my teeth.

"No, he was going to kill you." Breath left my lungs and sudden numbness swept over my body. I could no longer feel the dull ache from the wound on my cheek when he spoke again. "But I saved your life."

Had King Drakkar taken to killing witches instead of exiling them?

My father turned and marched back to the chair at the center of the council hall. My mother had once said it resembled the throne the king sat on in Mara's Keep. She'd visited Mara when I was a young child, having returned with curious news of the strange king before King Dakkar came to power. I'd always fantasized about what the king's castle looked like after seeing the similar chair.

When my father turned and took a seat, I met his harsh gaze. I folded my arms, bracing for what he'd say next. What had he bargained for my life?

"You are to serve in the royal court of Mara for the remainder of your life."

"No," I breathed. My mother had told me stories of the servants in Mara's Keep, dazed men and women who were never heard from again. Though, of course, this servitude was safer and more palatable than living in exile or a beheading.

"I suspect it will be more than working as a cook or a maid," he muttered.

I opened my mouth to protest again, but stopped myself. This was my invitation to the king—to follow the Gods' guidance.

The castle I'd seen in my vision must have been Mara's Keep. Odin and Freya had paved the way for me, perhaps bargaining with the Norns, goddesses who determined our fates, to weave this into my life's thread.

"And what if I collapse and he deems me unworthy of this service?" I asked. I willed my heart to slow, but of course, it did not obey. Laying bare my illness in front of my father was as foolish as it was humiliating.

My heart failed me every day, and he denied the pain I suffered as my legs and feet swelled, my hands were always cold, and exhaustion bore down on me heavily even after a decent night of sleep. The erratic pulse wasn't like Dain's severed foot after it'd turned black from frostbite. I didn't wear it on my skin like the burns on Bjorn's hands and arms.

Because my father could not see this suffering, he refused its existence. I was simply a disappointment.

Of course, he didn't acknowledge what he could see either, not when my eyes first turned black from magic, and not when my fingertips became blue with lack of blood. More proof of this came when he didn't so much as glance at the scabbed wound cutting across my cheek.

To my father, I wasn't a witch, and I wasn't suffering.

To me, I wasn't really Silver. I'd never truly identified with the name my parents had thrust on me. Maybe because I just wanted to deny something he'd given me the way he denied who I truly was.

"You will manage," he said, irritation lacing his voice.

"Where is King Drakkar now?" I shifted the conversation away from my worries before I lashed out at him and earned another palm to the face.

He sighed and took a gulp from a tankard of ale. "South of us. Torsholt. We are to join them on their journey back to Mara now that you've been found."

"You weren't looking for me."

He laughed. "Winter has arrived early. I knew you'd be back before the first snow hit the ground."

That wasn't entirely true. I'd lasted almost two nights, and I'd only returned because of the vision. But if I told my father that, he'd simply deny my nature as a witch. To him, I'd come crawling back because I was weak, pathetic, and scared.

"What's in Torsholt?" A criminal to be executed? More witches to exile or force into servitude?

He laughed again. "Perhaps the king will tell you."

I gritted my teeth. If I were a mere servant, would I even have the chance to speak with King Drakkar?

Come to me. The vision hinted he'd talk to me, that he'd invite me into his castle. This promise meant I could at least ask him about the historical records stored there.

"If they're in Torsholt, we should leave tonight to catch up with them." I spoke louder, my chin lifted. I was eager to leave.

My father coughed, spluttering with ale. He slapped his chest to clear the shock away and get his choking under control. The glint in his eye was one I'd never known. Curiosity?

No, wait. I'd seen this before, whenever he sat in that damn chair in front of the people he respected in Skaldir the most. Pride.

For a single second, he was proud of me.

Maybe I'm not so weak. But I couldn't relish the thought or the look on his face because the memory of Astrid and Sten's lifeless eyes clouded my mind. I was far worse than merely weak or foolish.

Evil.

Selfish.

Murderous.

No, stay the course. I repeated words my mother had said to me before the executioners dragged her away and into exile. *Stay the course. Don't let your dwelling paralyze you. Use it.* Like she used her talent with weaving to keep the history alive, to communicate with other witches, and to protect them. I had to reach her, and I was given a direct invitation to Mara's Keep to find her, even if it cost me my life. Whether in servitude or worse.

I buried all other thoughts, locking them away like a prisoner. Memory of Astrid and Sten's limp bodies thrashed against the prison walls.

Stay the course. I could hate myself for what I'd done once my mother was free.

I lifted my chin, holding my father's gaze until he looked away. He sniffed and took a quick swig of the ale.

He kept his eyes down on his drink when I spoke again. "Since you knew I'd return, I expect you have provisions ready?"

He nodded, eyes still on his ale. "I will accompany you, and my wife will take over as Vyl here while I'm gone."

I said nothing else as I strode out of the council hall, ready to gather my things and leave. Eager to run from Skaldir and leave every disturbing memory behind. Maybe in Mara, I'd forget what I'd done.

If I could keep the thoughts locked away.

CHAPTER SIX

My father was a liar. Provisions were not ready.

After leaving him behind in the council hall last night, sleep had sucked me in. I'd collapsed in my bed and slept hard, waking only because my frayed nerves had plunged me into cyclical nightmares.

As soon as morning arrived, I forced my aching body out of bed and made my way to the stables where my father said he'd stored packed provisions.

Provisions was a strong word for the meager collection of pelts for blankets and animal hide tents. And though the horses had been fed, their hooves were not yet cleaned and inspected for sores. Their saddles and packs were left at the door of the stable where the wooden shelter opened up into the wide pen.

I knelt before the packs and inspected the rest of the supplies. The men he'd handpicked to travel with us packed flint and steel to start fires, but no pots or wooden spoons or bowls with which to eat meals.

And if we couldn't cook, we'd rely on hard meat and cheese. There wasn't enough of that to last us one day of travel, much less an entire week to Mara. Salves and bandages were forgotten too.

Dawn light stretched from the open side of the stables. The sun almost warmed my cheek but another gust of icy wind sliced over my skin. The direction of the wind angled just right to sweep through the stable from the back to where I'd left the door propped open.

I'd come straight to the stables expecting to see my father and his men preparing the horses to mount, but I'd beat him here and spent the last few minutes scanning the packs.

The sound of gravel crunching underfoot came from behind me and I didn't have to look up to feel his looming presence.

"Do you want us to die before we arrive?" I shot my father a sharp look over my shoulder.

He stood at the threshold of the stables, staring down his thin nose at me. The pale morning sun washed him out and his skin looked clammy, unlike the tanned skin of farmers and the rest of the villagers. As the Vyl, he'd spent most of his time indoors. Though I'd heard Torsholt and Stormdal's leaders worked out in the fields with their farmers. They hunted with those trapping wild game to supplement villager diets.

But my father did none of that.

He'd been a Vyl my entire life so I didn't know the side of him my mother claimed he once had. Strong, resilient, a legendary trapper. According to her stories, he'd trained falcons to hunt rabbits, ducks, and other smaller birds, but I'd never so much as seen him speak with the other falconers in Skaldir.

His slim lips twisted into a grimace before he spoke. "I'm as frustrated as you. I expected them to work faster."

His gaze trailed behind me to where Bjorn tethered a horse to a post. The lanky man ran his fire-scarred hand over the animal's back to calm it. He'd run it over my bare ass plenty of times too, but it'd been months since we found ourselves in one another's beds. While it was pleasurable for our bodies, it did nothing to keep us attached. He was just a friend, and unfortunately, he'd wanted to stop our nightly visits when he thought my father might discover us.

It wasn't that my father would care beyond the fact that as one of the Vyl's men, Bjorn was supposed to tell my father everything. He wasn't allowed to have anything hidden, no secrets, and this just wasn't something Bjorn was comfortable sharing with him.

After a moment of speaking softly, Bjorn brushed his palm down the horse's leg, and she allowed him to lift her hoof. Of course Bjorn was the one doing the work while my father watched.

"Perhaps your men expected you to help with preparations." I wanted to bite the words back, but they'd already slipped from my lips. Though I'd challenged him plenty of times before, now wasn't the time. Not when he was already on edge after I'd ran from the king.

I busied myself by standing and grabbing a brush to run over the hindquarters of the horse who stood alone in the stable. The older horse didn't even need to be tethered. She enjoyed the feel of the bristles running soothing circles over her back. Just the sight of Bjorn taking out the brush had had her trotting toward the stables, ready for her turn.

My father sighed. "Perhaps one of my men shouldn't have been so weak and pathetic as to abandon us. If we had Rolf helping, we'd be ready to leave."

"Rolf?" I said as I searched his face. Ragna's husband had been a type of right-hand man for my father while Ragna ran the household, raised their children, and tended to their farm. "What do you mean he abandoned us?"

He scoffed. "He refuses to go to the king. We have an opportunity for King Drakkar to invite us into Mara's Keep, to sit and counsel with him so that we may speak up and bring Skaldir and the northern villages to his attention." The king had just traveled here. Wasn't he already aware of us? But I didn't have time to ask what he intended by the comment as he continued. "We need trade to get us through the winter. We need defenses against bears and wolves. Which means we need representatives to stand before him, as many of us men as we can spare, to tell King Drakkar that we will starve without spears and axes for hunting."

"I've been saying we need weapons for years—"

"Yes. To defend against…" his voice trailed off as he shook his head, his frown more twisted than ever. He couldn't bring himself to say it. He never could bring himself to acknowledge the shadows that I believed were monsters from ancient days—monsters from the sagas.

My mother said most of them died out when humans scarred Midgard with the wasteland, our ancestors' battles causing so much blood to spill that it poisoned the very ground we walked on. But she knew they existed, while my father denied it.

And perhaps he was right, since Astrid and Sten, who had seemed all monster to me, ended up being nothing but mere humans.

They had to be, because the only other alternative was to accept that monsters were following me. That the red eyes I'd witnessed in the shadows my whole life were powerful creatures coming to devour me, not people who could be tried and punished for their crimes.

Of course, if Astrid and Sten were human that didn't explain why their skin had boiled at the touch of my blood and a simple pendant.

That was magic from the Gods. It had to be.

I'd been grasping for explanations lately, trying to convince myself of these things so that I could make sense of the world around me. None of it had really made sense since I lost my mother.

And even before that, when I lost control of myself.

"I'm well aware of your foolishness," his curt voice cut through my thoughts. "You and Rolf both. Witches are creatures in a saga that odd humans claim kinship to in order to explain their oddities."

Bitterness stained my tongue and I recoiled. This wasn't the first time I'd heard him deny my existence aloud. He knew I had visions but had refused to accept them as anything more than the ramblings of a foolish woman.

"So Rolf wanted to stay here with Ragna?" I asked, though I spoke it more like a statement. As loyal as Rolf was to my father, he practically worshiped his wife. If Ragna needed him to stay in Skaldir, it wouldn't be a second thought.

"Ragna is gone."

My pulse skipped. I snapped my attention from brushing. The sudden twitch of my wrist startled the old horse. His front hooves danced nervously and he almost reared back until I blew out a slow breath and calmed myself. When my energy settled, so did his, but I couldn't help the nerves still buzzing beneath my ribs.

Villagers didn't often disappear, but each time they did their absence left an unexplainable hole. Most assumed the missing person had succumbed to poor weather, buried in snow, or frozen.

I'd left Astrid and Sten the same way.

A shudder took control of my body for a second.

Other villagers usually insisted that the disappearance was the fault of wild animals catching the person and dragging them away to be devoured.

My mother said it was both of them, *and* monsters. *Everything comes back around. Nothing is truly ever over. The undead are proof of that. Draugr existed once, they'll claw their way back to Midgard again. Giants and trolls can cross over from the other realms if the Gods are distracted. Nothing is truly ever ended, Little Spider, not even you.* The memory of the nickname she'd given me pricked my heart.

"Gone?" I whispered.

He only scoffed. "Forget whatever foolishness you're think-ing. It's not that. The king took her—"

"No!" My outburst sent the horse skidding out of the stables. I stood with my arms limp, the brush still hanging in my hand.

"The executioners deemed her in violation of our law, Silver."

I shook my head, taking a step back from him. "No. She never shed anyone's blood. They took her because—"

"Dammit, Silver! Don't say it!"

She was a witch. I'd seen what they did to my mother when they claimed she'd broken the law. They made her vow that she wasn't guilty with her breath over the flame of a candle. When the candle flickered, changing from yellow to black, they bound her wrists in shackles.

This gave her away, but she wasn't guilty of anything other than existing. My father had conveniently forgotten that. He'd said I was remembering the moment wrong because I was young and emotional and it was so long ago. But I wasn't that young. I was only sixteen when the Grimward caught my mother burning a sage branch and whispering incantations.

I'd never forget that day. How my father denied knowing about her nature as a witch to the Grimward, pleading his innocence instead of defending my mother's right to exist.

"What law did she break then?" I pointed the brush at him like it was a weapon. "Tell me. What law? If she shed blood, they would have executed her in front of the entire village. So why take her and exile her?"

"There are other crimes. Theft. Denying food or shelter to executioners or royal travelers. Adultery."

"Adultery?" I laughed without joy. "You're seriously suggesting that Ragna fucked another man when her entire world is Rolf? Besides, nobody has considered adultery a crime in years. People fuck who they want."

"Keep that filthy word out of your mouth, daughter."

"I am a woman, Father, not just your daughter." He opened his mouth to cut me off again but I spoke louder, unafraid. I was marching myself to the king anyway. "And I am a witch." My stomach fluttered as I heard the words out loud. This was me, my identity, and it felt damn good to say it. So good that I didn't care about the string of curses he released, or when he screamed at me as I spun around.

"Silver!"

I ducked away from him and ran out the back of the stables. I'd face him later, when we finally left for Mara. For now, I would find Rolf and get the real story. Had King Drakkar placed Ragna before a candle's flame? Or did they test her another way?

I didn't want to think about it for too long. Executioners were brutal, ruthless. Even something as simple as a dispute between two young men where their wrestling led to cut lips and a bloody nose had damned them both for execution. They'd been beheaded only days after news of their fight had spread to the nearest executioners. I never understood how the news always spread so quickly and easily. Who was stupid enough to turn their own neighbors over to death or exile or a lifetime of service in the royal court?

Running wasn't the right word for my hurried limping toward the opposite end of Skaldir. Exhaustion still wracked my bones, and my heart was too weak to pump enough blood to keep me moving.

Cold air nipped at my ears, but I kept going.

I averted my eyes from the communal hearth, the small stone building that was built for the purpose of baking bread and large meals together.

I caught the echo of chatter from within. No doubt the women were discussing Ragna's disappearance. Because I'd run into the forest, I was likely the last to hear of it.

Their muttered conversation sent a pang through my

chest. The last time I stepped foot in the shelter of the hearth was ten years ago with my mother at my side.

Not an hour later she'd been dragged outside by the executioners. The bread we'd kneaded together hadn't even finished baking when the masked men and women claimed my mother had hidden a young girl from them. A girl who stabbed a boy in the eye with a sharp stick. They failed to mention that this boy they named was a bully, a cruel young man who delighted in leaving bruises on those smaller than him. Though I didn't doubt my mother would harbor this supposed criminal, I'd been with her constantly and had never seen the girl anywhere near her.

It was all a lie.

What they'd actually seen was her burning sage and whispering incantations for the enchantment that concealed my eyes. But they conjured a lie that skirted around the existence of witches.

I winced. Lies were the worst kind of offense, and I'd been as guilty as the executioners. I shoved the thought away, always trying to forget that I wasn't really who I said I was. Parts of me would always be kept hidden.

And I may have become a killer, but I didn't have time to let my darkness overcome me.

My mother was waiting.

And I knew she wasn't dead. I just knew I'd have a vision if she'd died. I'd *feel* it. She was still alive, but that meant she was also suffering. This long in the wasteland would have stripped everything from her—just as the king hoped.

I assumed he wanted a rough life in the scarred earth to strip the magic from the witches he banished there. Otherwise, why not just kill us?

The warm scent of baking bread filled my nose. My eyes stung with tears as I hurried past the hearth.

"Anna!" a small voice shouted.

I blinked the tears from my eyes. Through the blur, I

spotted Ragna's youngest, a girl of only six years old. At three, Alva could not pronounce Silver, and since Ragna had once told her I was the spitting image of my mother who went by Anya, Alva had called me 'Anna' ever since.

I went by many names; Silver, Little Spider, but Anna was my favorite.

Alva stood in the doorway of her family's longhouse. Only days before, I was in the dirt beneath their feet, sparring with Ragna to train our bodies for self defense, and now she was gone.

Rolf appeared behind Alva with an infant boy in his arms, the child Ragna swore would be her last.

She'd been right.

Alva hopped up and down at the threshold. It was as if she was waiting for me, though she was likely looking outside in wait for her mother's return.

Tears sprang up again. My throat tightened as Alva ran out to me, her short legs kicking up dirt. "Mama is gone, Anna! Mama is gone!"

I could not stop the tears from spilling. Even with the scabbed skin, the wound still stung from the salty tears slipping down my cheeks.

Weak. Tears are the salt of the spineless. People cry when they cannot do. My father's voice echoed in my head, but I focused on my breathing, slow and steady, until his harsh words faded.

The tears that trailed down Alva's plump cheeks looked large and heavy, not at all weak. They were tears for her mother. And in this case, my father was right. Alva could not do anything about her mother's disappearance and the pain of it needed to go somewhere, so it spilled out of her body with every tear that dropped.

She mirrored me all those years ago, but instead of running away and hiding, she was out in the open. Of course, she wasn't the cause of her mother's disappearance.

She hadn't damned an innocent person to certain death.

Don't think about it.

I finally allowed myself a full breath with the smell of bread in the air. I trailed my fingers over my braid, noting the feel of my smooth hair. I focused on the small child barreling toward me, the shine on her cheeks, the sadness and confusion swimming in her eyes.

When we reached one another, I crouched and wrapped my arms around Alva's little body. I enveloped her and let my own tears fall until a thought struck me.

Alva could not *do* anything about Ragna's exile, but I could.

I could find that damn piece of missing history and prove to King Drakkar that witches were not a threat to his authority.

"Alva," I said as I pulled back. I held her tiny shoulders in my hands and felt her body shudder with a long and desperate breath. Tears dried in tight lines across her pink cheeks. The chilled wind tossed her dark hair around her face. I brushed a thumb beneath her eye to catch another tear. "I'm going to find your mama, and I'm going to bring her home."

You can't promise that. Doubts thrashed in my mind. *You're weak, you've always been selfish. Think of what you did when you were Alva's age. Think of what happened to your mother only a few years later.*

Silver, Little Spider, Anna, Witch, Selfish, Killer.

Evil.

Evil.

Evil.

I gritted my teeth until my jaw ached and the feeling pulled me out of the dwelling spiral.

"You will?" Alva asked, eyes round and widening more and more as she stared at me.

"I have to."

She only cocked her head. My promise was enough to stop the flow of tears for now. Both of ours.

I wanted nothing more than to look away from her. To forget the person I'd become since I gave in to my darkness at the same age Alva was now. I was even more desperate to leave Skaldir and every scarred memory behind.

My heart squeezed as Alva leaned into me again. I hugged her close, protecting her from the cutting wind as Rolf marched up behind her, the baby now wrapped in several layers of fur.

As he spoke, he confirmed every fear I'd had. Ragna was tested, taken, and told she was sentenced to a lifetime in the wasteland.

"If she dares leave the wasteland," he said, wetness shining in his eyes, "they'll kill all of us."

Another message worth the shedding of an entire family's blood, because if anyone got any ideas of fighting or breaking any law, we'd descend into chaos, we'd damn Vylheim to become a wasteland again.

That blood of war would scar the earth until nothing could grow and our children starved.

"I'm going to find the lost history," I said.

Absent-mindedly, I'd pulled the Y Tree out of my dress and fingered the sharp edge that I'd washed off in the stream at the border of Skaldir, rinsing away Astrid and Sten's blood. The story went that the king of the ancients, Harald, had used this symbol, this very necklace, with its cross shape and unique tilt where the cross met, to mark the original runestones with his seal. Once his council of witches smoothed the stone with elemental enchantments, it could only be broken with this seal. Showing the king the true history would prove the existence of witches and their history of living with kings in harmony.

Without this runestone, our king and the council denied witches and all manner of magic, monsters, and Gods.

Rolf said nothing as he looked down at his infant son.

"I can use it to help," I said.

That was a lie. I only hurt people.

No! I could at least try, I could fight this darkness within me. I could forget the bodies I'd left in the forest. I could forget everything I'd done and take on a new name.

Servant. For the king.

I'd gladly live out the remainder of my days within the walls of Mara's Keep if it meant access to our history. If I lived at all. How long would it take for King Drakkar to realize two people in his royal court never returned from Skaldir?

Rolf's tired eyes and sagging mouth didn't exude belief in me, but Alva's hope was enough for now. She didn't know, yet, that I was a killer, that I'd always been wicked, wrong.

A flash of the hatch beneath my bed crossed my mind. Echoes of screaming followed until I buried the memory and conjured a smile for Alva's sake.

She smiled back and I knew I'd carry the sight of her little grin with me as I forced myself to face the king.

CHAPTER SEVEN

Just beyond Skaldir's borders, my horse was already breathing heavily as we caught up to the tail end of the royal party. Almost a hundred travelers from Torsholt and other nearby villages had joined for the same reason a dozen villagers from Skaldir trailed along behind us.

Winter had already begun.

Travel to Mara would be slow and rough enough, but survival in the north with snow starting on the second day of autumn would be brutal.

Anyone who was born in the north and opted to run to the south was not only considered weak and a traitor to their ancestors who'd established themselves here, but they were rarely welcomed back after running away.

Unlike my father and his men, those who trailed us intended to live in Mara, except the few who bravely declared they were offering themselves to the king's exploration efforts. Survival was dependent on if a southern stranger took them in and taught them how to live. Or perhaps gave them a new job.

And survival for the souls who planned to explore was

impossible. If the arduous journey didn't kill them first, they could be chosen for the Age of Exploration where the sea would claim their lives.

The parade of horses clopped alongside people on foot. Some rode in wagons pulled by the oxen they hoped to transport to the new home and farm they envisioned in the south.

Two nights passed with ease.

We always stopped at sunrise to set up camp. On the third day, we resumed the journey the same way we had for two days; at twilight, and in silence.

Why we always set up camp in the morning, I didn't know. Night was colder with more risk of wild animals hunting the stragglers at the back.

Perhaps it was to prepare for the Polar Nocturne. In only a few days, the entire world would be plunged into darkness for half the winter. I'd heard some of the villages prepared for it this way, readying their minds to accept weeks of no sun, no morning, no light.

Each evening was quiet before the children woke for the all-night travel. Miraculously, the little ones adjusted to sleeping during the daylight better than the rest of us. Or maybe they were just so exhausted by the time we stopped that they collapsed. I could relate to that.

But the sounds of night, the cold especially, kept me restless. My heart beat too fast, a contrast to my heavy limbs and eyelids, keeping my nerves on edge as I curled my frozen fingers to check if they could still move.

Once the sun set, everyone stirred, and slowly, the buzz of eager conversation kept us going through the winter weather, even on the longest nights. Nights like this one that stretched into near impenetrable darkness. Nights where your mind wandered, wondering if we'd ever reach the relief of the southern villages.

My legs and butt ached from riding, so it was a welcome

reprieve when one of the king's guards rode to the back of the traveling party and demanded we dismount.

Though I hated having to listen to him.

I frowned, mirroring the other men and women who shot the guard looks full of venom. But we obeyed, shaking out our legs and allowing our poor horses a moment of rest.

Especially mine. The old horse already looked ragged, and I resolved to walk for a while after this.

The guard frowned right back at us.

None of us were used to dealing with the king's guard, but we knew what happened when an executioner came to our villages. Somebody either vanished or lost their head. The guards embodied that same authorial and aggressive aura with axes swinging from their belts. Others carried knives tucked into their boots—all weapons banned from the commoners. It was all to protect the king.

To protect us all. The phrase all Vyls chanted echoed in my head.

Every life was valuable, both the king's and a villager's, and without the rules keeping our world from unraveling, we'd end up damning all of Vylheim.

The guard slid off his horse and stormed through the maze of men and women and children, yanking his horse along behind him with a violent jerk of the reins.

He paused in front of a woman with hair the color of autumn. Wind carried her hair away from her face, revealing her pinched expression behind thick tendrils.

His abrasive manner left her stumbling back when he brushed her aside with the back of his hand.

Buzzing nerves rippled through the crowd. A woman behind me stooped to scoop up her crying child.

One of my father's men looked to him for guidance, but my father merely gritted his teeth. His jaw slid back and forth as he kept his narrowed eyes, tracking the guard.

No doubt my father wanted to tell his people to return to their mounts and keep going. He wasn't used to dealing with authority this often.

How he planned to win over King Drakkar with that attitude was beyond me.

The guard marched past the woman in front of me, scanning her, before he stopped at me. His eyes flashed. Staring at me, he grimaced.

"You're the one he wants," he said.

My heart rate tripled. The king already wanted to see me? Was I to start my servitude on the road?

I'd thought I would answer to myself for the remainder of the trip. I'd hoped to have my freedom a little longer.

I glanced at my father who kept his gaze averted. This was what he'd bargained for; my service for my safety.

Had he saved my life, or damned it? As much as he denied the Gods, he knew I worshiped and revered Freya, the god of beauty, of prophecy, and of freedom. When Loki traded her hand in marriage to a giant, she refused to be controlled. She embodied independence, and the witches surviving in hiding, in secret, strived for that same freedom.

I was no different.

Still, this trade had kept me alive, and since I'd yet to bring honor to the Gods—at least according to my own standards— I knew I wouldn't be granted an afterlife in Valhalla or Folkvangr where warriors feasted and challenged one another in games like our seasonal celebrations. I hoped someday becoming a seerborn as skilled as my mother would honor Odin and Freya enough to call me to an afterlife with one of them.

Otherwise, Hel would claim my soul for the underworld.

The guard gripped my arm and my heart skipped. He squeezed my scabs and bruises, sending a bolt of pain skittering over my skin and sinking into my muscles. I bit down hard on my lip to redirect the focus of pain.

The ghost of Astrid's hold on me sent a shiver through me.

He prodded me the couple of steps toward his horse while others climbed back on their mounts or into their wagons, slowly resuming the long haul to Mara. When we reached his horse, he released me and shoved past me. He held up the end of a thick rope that was coiled around a hook on the saddle.

No fucking way was he going to tether me to his horse.

"You try to run, I tie you up," he said. With that, he climbed into the saddle. Flicking his hand, he indicated for me to walk alongside the horse's canter. I swallowed the scoff in my throat. "We'll move fast to catch up to King Drakkar's party. Fall behind and I'll drag you."

"Drag me?" I challenged him, as frustration with this binding servitude slowly built. Freya would never allow herself to be tied up. "Can't I ride on my horse?"

Without a word, he nodded at my mount. I twisted to look over my shoulder. The poor old mare was worn thin, her nostrils still flaring from the exertion even though we'd been at rest for several minutes.

The guard said aloud what I didn't want to admit. "That pathetic excuse for a mount won't keep up with me, and I'm not waiting around. You'll be faster on foot."

I gnawed at my lip, walking was the best choice. I'd never push my horse to go faster than the pace we'd already set. I turned and stepped up to my sweet horse's face. Petting her neck gently, I gave Bjorn a knowing nod. He returned it, glancing quickly at my father, who ignored the entire interaction.

Knowing Bjorn would keep my horse safe, I faced the guard again. Defiance stiffened my muscles. "I'll ride your horse." He only laughed, and it steeled my resolve. "You can't let me bleed. Doesn't the king want me alive?"

He glared at me with deep brown eyes. Had he been one of the masked men? Did the guards and executioners ever trade duties? Was he experienced with severing people's heads from their bodies for causing a mere scuffle?

"For his service, I mean," I said.

The guard snorted. "Your kind doesn't bleed the same way we do."

Your kind. It was the closest I'd ever heard an executioner or guard, or really anyone who wasn't a witch or close with a witch, admit that we were something other than human.

And what the hell did that mean? I bled…

But my blood also burned Astrid and Sten. That wasn't like other humans. The flesh on Astrid's fingertips had bubbled and congealed as quickly as the skin touched by the silver Y Tree. Wasn't that from the help of the Gods? Or was I really a threat?

Evil

Selfish.

Yes, I was, but not all witches.

He kicked the horse into a canter and I followed in a daze. My feet moved of their own accord. Evening stretched into night and stars slowly greeted us, each with a unique shine. Looking up too long, I lost pace with the guard's horse.

The guard snapped demands at me until I forced my legs into a weak run to catch up with him. Walking eventually descended into me dragging my feet.

After passing hundreds of travelers, exhaustion tugged at my bones.

Men from Stormdal eyed us curiously. Why was a village woman trailing the king's guard?

Women from Torsholt furrowed their brows. The jagged lightning strike embroidered into the left breast of their dresses carried the symbol of their village. A subtle but ancient reminder of Thor. It was a wonder the king didn't banish anyone who dared stitch it into their clothing.

Freya would be proud.

Odin too.

One of the women reached out and brushed my arm. I felt the magic crackling at the tips of her fingers. I glanced back at her and nodded reassurance to ease the worry twisting her face. Some witches carried potent divination within, their silent chants and prayers enough to create a pathway to the Gods where they could share their divine guidance for the people of Midgard.

"I'm okay," I whispered.

It was a lie. I could collapse at any moment, but my heart kept ticking. If I ignored the tingling in my legs as my feet and ankles swelled from the effort, I could focus on keeping my hands warm. The tips of my fingers had turned blue hours ago, but with enough squeezing my hands into fists and blowing my warm breath over them, I'd been able to keep it from spreading.

As hours lengthened into the dead of night, harsh beliefs drowned out all other thoughts, leaving me shaky and dizzy. Anxious thoughts often plagued me worse when I was tired.

My pulse fluttered and my eyesight narrowed with every memory of my corruption resurfacing. Damning my mother, killing the courtiers, my blood burning them, and the hatch. The screams. The swing of an axe.

Foolish.

Weak

Evil.

I doubled forward.

Breathless, I palmed my eyes as if I could scrub my mind from dwelling on what I couldn't change. I wanted to wipe the words away, wipe the memories, wipe my hands clean of the blood that once stained them.

"Move!" The guard barked from ahead.

I lifted my head and tried to take a step forward. Stumbling, I grabbed a man's arm. He startled and pulled his arm away from me before realizing I needed help. When he scooped his arm under my elbow and righted me, I whispered a breathless thank you.

The guard kept moving with his neck twisted so he could glare at me from several feet down the path. "Run if you have to. I can see King Drakkar from here. We're not slowing down now."

Run.

I could try it. Riding the horse and the stops we'd made to set up camp and rest each dawn had replenished my strength. Hopefully the walking hadn't stripped every bit of it away again.

I straightened.

We were within sight of the king. It wouldn't be too far.

I shoved my feet forward, starting at a tentative walk.

Focusing on each step, one after the other after another, buried the taunting thoughts. If I would succumb to dwelling, it would be to dwell on the ache in my feet.

I'd fear collapse instead of the memories.

I sucked in a deep breath and focused on the distance between me and the guard. It was only a short sprint, nearly the same distance of the race to the rotted ash tree.

My heels numbly struck the path. I dodged past the rest of the Stormdal travelers as an executioner with a wolf's mask turned at the sound of my footsteps.

Only a few more steps.

My legs burned, but if I pushed harder, maybe the Gods could show me more with a new vision. Where in Mara's Keep were the historical records kept? Perhaps there was something else in the castle that would grant my mother freedom from exile.

I kept my eyes fixed on the guard, determined not to lose my dignity. He would not tie me up, the king would not meet me in tethers, even if I was his servant.

Sweat and pain blurred my sight. I slowed when a vague shape stepped in front of me, but not soon enough. I smacked into someone's back and the wind knocked from my chest.

The woman whirled around, her eyes flaring from beneath a mask carved with the face of a wolf—the animal whose species now became her name. It was the way of all members of the Grimward. They were assigned a mask, and so became their identity.

Wolf spat out a string of loud curses and several guards turned to stare at me. Others setting up camp stopped to see what the commotion was about.

A villager had collided with an executioner. No doubt it was a sight to see. Nobody was stupid enough to get that close to the executioners.

The guard I'd caught up to laughed as Wolf hissed obscenities at me.

Breathless, I apologized and stumbled back away from her. I slammed my palms against my knees and dragged painful breaths into my throat. My eyes fixed on the dirt in front of me as I tried to contain my spastic breaths, but my head spun from the effort. Even on the edge of collapse, a vision didn't come over me.

It was just as well, because with a clear head I caught Ragna's voice.

"Drakkar!" She didn't address the king formally.

My skin prickled at the tone in her voice.

I snapped my head up. King Drakkar had already dismounted from his horse. He stood at the front of the party, a good distance from the guards and executioners as he led his horse to be tethered. His sword clung to his back, shining against the dawn light.

Through the crowd of executioners and guards climbing down from their horses, I spotted the side of Ragna's shaved head. The hair on the other side of her head was bound in three tight braids that she'd coiled into one heap at the base of her neck.

A dozen guards and executioners stood between her and King Drakkar. They gave her no attention, but the king turned at the sound of her voice. They didn't regard her as a threat, so she easily snaked past them until a guard finally grabbed her. She shoved him off and kept going.

I recognized the shine of determination in her eyes. It was the same look she got right before a race. She knew she would win.

She would not stop until she did win.

And though Ragna wasn't in a race now, she broke into a run.

Another woman twined through the crowd from the opposite end as a third shoved past me, nearly knocking me to the ground with her shoulder.

Something glinted in her fist. A pendant. Similar to the Y Tree, the tip was sharpened, long enough to stab through someone's eyes—or into their collarbone.

Three women all slipping through the distraction of everyone setting up camp was either an escape or...no, my stomach dropped.

Ragna was running *toward* the king, not away in an attempt to escape.

This was an attack. A coordinated attack that I had no doubt was headed by Ragna who would guide the other witches to fight against their captors.

And perhaps my entrance had given them the distraction they needed. While half of the guards laughed and stared down their noses at me, the king was exposed.

"No!" I whispered, my lungs not filled enough to shout out. "Ragna, no!"

This was certain death.

They would not be able to kill him and get away. These witches were sacrificing themselves. I knew many witches believed that if we could only replace the king, we'd change everything. An empty throne was safer than a witch hunter at the helm.

But I couldn't let Ragna kill herself, not with Alva's hope in me.

Ragna jumped on the king, and because her strength was God-given, she knocked him off his feet, if only for a moment. Though King Drakkar was taken by surprise, he easily threw her off of him.

No blood was shed yet.

Yet.

The other woman grabbed at the sword hanging on his back and tried to pull him back but he did not budge. It didn't matter because the guard nearest him finally reacted. One ripped the woman away from the king's back and slammed her into the ground.

The third woman charged him, dodging the reach of another guard as she raised the pendant in her fist. Behind him, Ragna struggled to her feet with a rock in her hands. If I knew her, she intended to bash it into the side of his skull, which would surely lead to plenty of blood.

This attack was a clear and obvious affront to the bloodshed law.

Afterwards, executioners would bring an axe down on Ragna's neck for all to see, to squash any other thoughts of fighting. Even if the king only lost a single drop of blood.

Despite the flaming in my chest, I broke into another run. I didn't know what I could do against Ragna's strength, but I had to try.

"Don't!" I screamed.

The chaos left a wide open path for me. The guards were too scattered by breaking to set up camp. The attack was too unexpected for them to grab their weapons in time. They must not have thought the witches would ever dare. Nobody would ever dare. Not after years of witnessing executions, beheading of loved ones who'd gotten into a fight or even while defending themself against an intruder.

They believed we were cowed.

Black spots dotted my sight with every strike of my foot against the ground. I blinked, but they only grew bigger, making everything around me dimmer and dimmer. This run would end in collapse.

Wind cut through the reddened skin around my wound. My scabbed cheek burned with an icy sting.

The king reached to unsheath his sword when I ducked past him.

My throat ripped with another shout at Ragna as I threw myself against her. She was a stone wall, and I was a child's ball bouncing against it. But the force of my impact got her to drop the rock in time, her mouth agape at the sight of me. I hadn't pushed her over, but I'd shocked her enough to stop her from hurting the king.

She blinked and ducked to grab the rock again.

Guards converged on the woman with the pendant. Before they could grab her, she'd sunk the sharp end into the middle of King Drakkar's hand where he gripped the hilt of the sword.

I didn't know what kind of magic this witch possessed, but it'd surely helped her get past the guards and close enough to the sword-wielding king to stab him. When he dropped the sword, she moved with inhuman speed, pulling the pendant from his hand and then burying it into his eye, the weakest spot for a small weapon to do maximum damage.

If it impaled his brain, he'd be dead. They'd have achieved their victory.

King Drakkar stumbled back, and when I was distracted, Ragna grabbed the rock to finish him off.

Without even bothering to scream at her, I snatched her braid and pulled with every ounce of strength I could muster.

She stopped short, the force of her hair yanking her back for one startling moment.

Every muscle in my body ached as I tensed and tried to drag her back. My arms burned as my legs shook.

The black spots spilled darkness over my sight and I was plunged into another realm.

One moment I was interrupting Ragna's attack, the next I was inside a castle. I stood at the center of a vast room where King Drakkar sat on a throne, his legs spread wide. The grin on his face was unsettling.

A woman's voice came from somewhere behind him.

"You must pass the trial.

Three are granted to you from Freya, Loki, and Odin, along with our gifts.

Pass and you will be granted a piece of the sagas once lost.

The first from me, Freya; track the king like a hunter, uncover him when he is at his most vulnerable. Follow the blood he leaves behind, it will lead you to answers.

Victory of the first comes with a visit from my companions. Bygul and Trjegul.

Victory will earn my favor and understanding that I can only give you when that comes.

Victory over these trials will spare your fellow witches for years to come."

Trials? The Gods weren't just guiding me, they were inviting me to share in their power.

I'd heard pieces of a legend where a witch was given challenges so that Odin and Freya could reach through this chosen woman and into Midgard to gift the people wisdom of the other realms. She shared in their knowledge as divine entities which helped the people of this realm survive.

Better even, Freya offered me her favor. If the God of beauty and independence gave me her approval, I could forget every wrong and wicked thing I'd ever done.

But how could she choose me?

I wasn't worthy.

The vision vanished and I found myself on my back in the dirt. I blinked as the world filled in around me. The executioner with the eagle's mask stood over me, her shadow cast long across my body. Ragna was crouched with her head in her hands beside me.

Bright red trickled down from a tear in her scalp.

"No, no, no," I whispered.

I may have stopped Ragna from hurting the king, but I'd pulled her so hard I'd made her bleed.

CHAPTER EIGHT

In the last seconds of my life, I watched the man who should have been dead pull the pendant from his eye socket.

He'd lived. The damn king had fucking lived.

I didn't know how to feel about it. The witches' plan had failed, but at least the woman who'd stabbed him wasn't as disturbed as me. I'd buried my silver pendant into Astrid and Sten's bodies far deeper. Deep enough to kill.

She'd only injured King Drakkar's eye, though I supposed she had intended to kill him.

She and I both had drawn blood.

Any moment, I expected the executioner standing over me to swing her axe down on my neck. I lay flat on my back, staring up at her eagle's mask like an animal sacrifice laid out for the slaughter, a secret ritual practiced by few witches, and one I'd only witnessed twice.

A small rock dug into my spine. My legs and arms throbbed with the effort of stopping Ragna. Miniscule stars simmered in the inky gray sky as night crawled closer to dawn. Thick black clouds were scattered above, rolling in to slowly block any sign of the realms beyond Midgard.

I'd never see the sun again.

This was my end, and yet my heart didn't slam against my chest. I had full use of my lungs, and my eyesight was clear of black spots.

In facing death, I should have screamed, fainted, or at least lost myself to a spiralling descent. But hundreds of overlapping thoughts didn't crowd my mind. Everything was entirely clear, and I was...calm. Focused even, just as I had been when I fixed my sight on Ragna and threw myself in between her and the king.

Only one thought sent my heart skipping; I'd failed my mother.

I barely breathed as I ripped my eyes away from Eagle. Time slowed as I looked from Ragna to the eagle mask, then to the king again.

Blood trickled from King Drakkar's eye. He held the pendant in his fist as the two executioners restrained the offending woman. I gritted my teeth at the sight of them dragging her by her hair, but at least it wasn't Ragna.

The woman screamed and cursed at King Drakkar, but he paid no attention to her cries. He tossed the pendant into the mud and buried it with the sole of his boot. Pain must have consumed him because he turned away from the executioners when they made their announcement.

Another voice spoke in my mind, her tone different than mine.

"There is a time when he is more vulnerable. You're not there yet, huntress."

Where had these thoughts come from?

"Come!" A man's voice bellowed, tearing me from the voice haunting my head. From beneath his bear mask, he shouted for everyone to gather for the routine announcement.

I'd heard every version of the executioner's call before.

It was our duty to watch the criminal die so that we would remember the wasteland, remember the blood that was shed, that poisoned the soil and plunged our ancestors into starvation and the extinction of all but one small group of survivors in Mara.

He paused and asked the witch her name. They purposely and loudly announced the name of the offending person to drive the knife into the heart of their loved ones.

Her only response was to spit in his face.

I would be next, except my father was too far in the back to be affected by it. If he even loved me at all.

My ribs were met with the toe of a boot. Lightning pain crackled up through my bones and I grunted to hold back a curse. Eagle stooped to snatch the fabric at my shoulder. Pulling me forward, she forced me to sit up and watch.

The announcement continued. "By the law of Vylheim since the dawning of the wasteland, you are required to witness the execution of one who has spilled blood."

Stormdal villagers slowly crowded together. They formed a crescent around the two executioners and the witch as the masked men shoved her to her knees.

"Gather and see this criminal's blood stain the earth as a small sacrifice of life, and an important reminder that we will never again suffer the poison of our land that comes with great loss. We refute war and all fighting beneath it for the survival of our posterity."

This was when we were supposed to echo the Grimward, but I couldn't find the words on my tongue.

The witches' attack was self defense, however reckless. These women were bound for the wasteland already, so I could not blame them for taking one last opportunity to make a change for their families.

Kill the king and perhaps the witch hunts would end. Perhaps executioners wouldn't prowl our villages. Perhaps we could live without the threat of a beheading and choose to refute violence just because we valued life.

But history said otherwise. The wasteland was proof of it.

Many people carried corruption within them, even if it wasn't as dark as mine.

The second executioner pushed the witch's head down, holding her there with the nodules of her spine protruding at the back of her neck. Her entire body convulsed, either with anger or fear—likely both. The first executioner in the bear's mask listed her crime one final time before unhooking the weapon at his waist.

Sickness swirled in my gut as he tested his grip on the axe.

When my gaze sliced to Ragna, I recognized the cool relief that'd been washing through me. Sickening. How could I feel good right now? Since she hadn't drawn the king's blood, it wasn't her neck beneath the blade. They wouldn't waste her life, though how could she contribute to our society when she was bound for the wasteland?

Another one of the mysteries my father had brushed off as something we simply couldn't fully understand from the remote village of Skaldir. We weren't part of the southern kingdom, and we didn't border the wasteland, which meant we didn't have the experience to speculate on it.

The offending witch cried out as sobs wracked her body, and still, I was thankful it wasn't Ragna on her knees.

You selfish wicked fool.

After Bear finished announcing her crimes, a hush fell over the crowd so heavy that the only sound was the rush of wind through the trees. The world gifted this witch with a sound like the fjords in spring for her final moments.

Everybody watched and waited except for the king.

King Drakkar stayed turned away from us as he removed his cloak and stripped off his shirt. I blinked at the dozens of tattoos covering the muscles of his back. Crouching now, he tore the fabric of the shirt into strips. Three guards each individually attempted to help him, but he sent them away.

Eagle kicked my hip and I snapped my attention forward.

I was taught from a young age not to close my eyes when

they brought the axe down, so I stared forward, unblinking like the corpses I'd left in the forest. Just like the executioners, I was a killer, but it wasn't sanctioned by law. The violence I'd caused came from within, the sickest and most wicked part of me.

With practiced ease and the entire force of his body, Bear cut into her flesh, through her spine, and split her head from her shoulders.

Bile stained my tongue in the familiar seconds that followed.

The spray of blood. The dull thud. The chilling echo of hundreds of breaths released at once.

It was over.

Until mine.

And still, my head was clear. Perhaps hours of being consumed by circling thoughts and the dizzying weakness that came with it had prepared me for the worst.

Every day I found myself shaky, scared, spinning out of control over a small reminder, a single thought like: what if the corrupt side of me emerged again and I couldn't stop it from damning another innocent person?

Now, with pain cutting through my bones and muscles, and death looming, I breathed easily.

Perhaps the Norns threaded the constant and consuming fear into my life's thread so that it would prime me for this end. Perhaps I needed to stay calm as Hel claimed me for the underworld.

Or had my fight to save Ragna been enough for the Valkyries to choose me for an afterlife in Valhalla?

No, because my effort wasn't honorable, it was selfish.

I did it because I couldn't bear to watch her give her life, not because I was a hero like the warriors from the sagas who fought giants and the monsters from other realms.

Eagle gathered my collar in her fist again and forced me to my feet. I stumbled into her when my knees gave out.

Ragna looked up at me between the trickles of blood splitting into two streams around her right eye. I'd never seen her cry, not when her sisters had to cut her son out of her stomach, not when she lost those same sisters to a bear's attack, not when three of her pregnancies ended in still, blue babies. Ragna released her pain through screaming, not tears.

So today she must not have felt pain, but regret. Or perhaps fear for the unknown she'd face in the wasteland, and now without one of the other witches to keep her company.

She swallowed and her voice came out smaller than I'd ever heard from her. "It should be me."

Hissing came from beneath the eagle's mask as the executioner shoved me forward.

My feet couldn't keep up with her pace, so she half-dragged me across the path. Eagle shouted something I didn't understand to the Grimward—the collective group of executioners. The one holding the axe dripping with the witch's blood nodded before turning back to the crowd.

Eagle threw me to the ground beside the witch's body.

I refused to look at the witch. I would not see this woman at her worst. Hopefully, she was already being taken to Valhalla by the Valkyries. Or if Freya had chosen her for a more peaceful but less honorable afterlife, she'd be in Folkvangr.

Eagle shoved my head down where I was forced to look at the blood pooling in the dirt. I closed my eyes and listened for the rush of wind, the sound like melted fjords.

"Remain to witness a second execution—"

"No." A deep voice echoed from behind.

Footsteps approached and my eyes sliced to the right to see a shadow nearing. Black boots stepped up between several browns.

King Drakkar's stride was unmistakable, each step deliberate and unhurried, but with more weight than the stomping feet of guards or the Grimward.

"My king," Bear said. "She has drawn blood and will be made an example of."

"No," King Drakkar repeated. He dropped to a crouch before me. "Sit up."

I did as he commanded.

Straightening to balance on my knees, the back of my head bumped into the executioner's hand. I glanced behind me to see the blood on the axe drip down and land on my braid. My stomach revolted but I swallowed the bitterness back down and faced the king.

He'd fashioned thin strips of his shirt and tied it across his face to cover his injured eye. Now he only wore the cloak on his shoulders with his torso bare underneath. My gaze slipped to the ink decorating his broad chest.

A tattoo of a tree spread over his left breast. A serpent was coiled at the base of it.

This image couldn't be Yggdrasil. That was the Gods' tree, the tree Odin hung from for nine days, the tree that witches believed connected us to Asgard. Without it, we would not be able to hear Freya or see through Odin's single eye.

A tree I'd hoped to see someday before I died.

That wasn't possible now.

But this tattoo of it was a mercy. Even if this tree wasn't really an image of Yggdrasil.

The king certainly didn't believe in the Gods, but even if he refuted the sagas and our true history, perhaps whatever he believed about our ancestors was inspired by the truth.

This was just a tree. Just a snake. And he had dozens of other images painted into his skin that certainly did not match with the Gods.

Perhaps my mind wasn't as clear as I'd thought, because the ink in the tattoo seemed to catch the light of the moon and brighten with a hollow hint of blue, like water between depths, shimmering near the surface with darkness beneath. Impossibly, the tree that was etched into his skin glowed.

"You don't cry out," he said. "Why?"

I blinked at him. He'd interrupted my execution to ask why I wasn't screaming? I opened my mouth but couldn't find the words to respond.

His eye narrowed, their intense blue another reminder of the crystal water in the summer fjords. "Do you think your Gods will save you?"

I said nothing. That wasn't how Odin and Freya behaved. The Norns weaved our fates, Odin and Freya and the other Gods only offered what they could to affect the lives of the people in Midgard.

His gaze raked over me again and his mouth split into the same smile he'd held when he spotted me back in Skaldir. Right before I ran from him. Like this was all a game, I was a hare hunted by the wolf. "You're too calm."

"Do you want me to be afraid?" I asked. I'd lived my entire life on the edge of fear. Only in the most intense moments did my panic subside. This was the culmination of all of them, and it was about to end.

His eye flashed and his grin broadened. He dipped closer to me, bringing with him the scent of a smoky oak tree mixed with cold steel. "Are you not even angry at the injustice of it all?"

Injustice? This was the system of which he stood at the helm. Was he trying to bait my frustration? It was wrong that we couldn't even defend ourselves, but there was a fine line between allowing weapons and the chaotic descent into war, so I didn't think it was entirely unjust.

I knew all too well the dark tendencies within a person.

And was this execution an injustice when I'd killed two of his courtiers? I didn't have to end their lives. I could have simply hurt them long enough to get away. My choices haunted me.

But he didn't know. He couldn't. If he did, I'd risk a long and painful death, torture, before my end.

I returned his sharp gaze, eyes narrowed.

Lifting his hand, he snaked it around to the back of my head and pulled me to him. His lips brushed my ears as his breath touched my neck. "I know you've fought back before."

My skin went alight with hundreds of goosebumps. I fought back only with Astrid and Sten. *There's no way he knows.*

"Where is that fire now?" he asked. "Show me."

Breath was suddenly scarce. I could not drag enough air into my lungs, and I did not fight back.

In the last moments of my life, I refused to succumb to the corruption that poisoned me. Even if the witch's death was an injustice, even if I shouldn't be beheaded for merely stopping Ragna. In fact, I *saved* the king. If she'd brought that rock down on his skull, he would be lame, if not dead.

"You will show him the fire when you burn him, Huntress." The voice's sharp tone sent a shudder through me.

King Drakkar pulled back and scanned me. His icy gaze flashed with something akin to suspicion. It vanished as quickly as it'd appeared.

He swallowed hard and his tone came out more ragged, heavier. "Show. Me."

I wasn't going to be selfish now when the gods, Hel and Freya and Odin's Valkyries were each waiting to decide where I'd spend my eternity. Surely, Hel would claim me, but my death didn't have to be entirely dishonorable.

I lifted my chin and his eye dropped to my lips.

He grabbed my jaw, his fingers pressing into the soft spot of my cheek. "Pretty witch you are. Come on, Silver. Show me you're scared. Show me your fury."

When my mouth twitched, he stared at it again.

I smelled the smoke of cut oak burning in a fire. I felt my heavy braid trailing down my back. I saw the fjords in the king's eye. I heard his unsteady breathing, as if I had somehow ignited *his* nerves.

I did not give in.

"Good girl," he finally breathed. His fingers clamped around my wrist while his other hand found my waist. He stood, guiding me to my feet with him.

I'd stayed calm. For once, I'd kept the darkness at bay and for this, the king rewarded me. Even though I'd refused his commands, he rewarded me.

He called off the Grimward and walked me toward the camp. I should have been thankful, and eager to serve him even, but I had no appreciation, no love or loyalty to the man who'd exiled my mother.

He sanctioned the witch hunts. If it weren't for him, Ragna would be at home by Alva's side.

Death would not greet me today, but a new hatred for King Drakkar flourished in my veins, because he'd tried to bait my corruption to the surface, and I'd spent years carefully burying it like a box covered in chains, only for him to recognize it and play with the lock.

And even though he did not have the key, he'd enjoyed taunting me.

CHAPTER NINE

Only hours after the witch's execution, a storm rolled in. The heavy rain washed her blood away by the next twilight when we woke to continue traveling.

Though I rode with King Drakkar like both his chosen prize and his prisoner, tethered with a sea knot around my wrists, he rarely spoke to me.

Hardly anyone spoke at all.

When I told the king he was damning every exile to their death, he only grunted like the animal he was. And then when I switched to asking what purpose the weakened exiles would serve on ships bound to explore beyond Vylheim, he demanded I stop talking about the exploration.

It was the only time I witnessed a flash of anger across his arrogant face.

All wild thoughts of convincing the king and his council to call off this exploration diminished. They wouldn't listen, and daring to defend the witches exiled to the wasteland would only put another target on my head before I had a chance to save them.

My only option was Freya's suggestion.

Find the lost history.

Show the people of Vylheim.

Expose King Drakkar.

Four days of pelting rain had me grateful for the furs over my head and shoulders. Since I sat in front of the king, sharing in his horse, I was at the front of the entire party. He'd insisted I ride with him so that whenever the storm lightened, he could test me while the guards kept their eyes on me.

At least that was how his questions felt, because I had no clue what else their purpose would be.

What would he stand to gain from asking me about how I dealt with jealousy? And, what did I consider the definition of chaos?

I answered each one through my teeth. At first I thought he'd purposely waited until the rain fell in sheets to speak to me, like the storm provided some sort of privacy. Then I thought that maybe he expected a cold and miserable witch would be easier to bait into some sort of a confession.

He never stopped interrogating me long enough for me to consider the vision from Freya and how I might track a king's blood, and maybe, after all, that was his intention. Though he'd have no way of knowing about the trial granted to me. He didn't even believe in the Gods.

King Drakkar released another string of prying questions as the rain eased. These were more personal, which made it even more impossible to identify a pattern to his seemingly random interrogation.

Did I want to give up or work harder whenever I lost a race? Why had I never taken a husband? He asked if I preferred women, and then said that if so, he wouldn't blame me.

"Women have a way of drawing everybody's attention." His hand brushed against the bend of my torso but did not linger. "Your curves are a place of rest and comfort."

"I prefer men," I said.

I felt his smile in the silence that followed. I didn't mean that I preferred him.

"Have you ever wanted revenge?" he asked. It was another question vastly different from the last to throw me off guard, and it worked.

"I have," I said. The answer slipped from me so quickly that I didn't have time to swallow it.

The revenge I wanted was against him. Send *him* to the wasteland for ten years and see if he survives.

A low rumble built in his chest and was felt through my back. His laugh was surprisingly warm, but his amusement made my blood boil.

"Good," he said.

Was this all a game to him? Toy with the servant witch who saved his damn life?

If I wasn't tied up, I might have slapped him. The exhaustion of travel and endless rain, and the nerves about the unknown life ahead left me raw and impulsive, stupid even. Or perhaps it was the darkest part of me tempting me to attack him.

"I should have known," he said. "You're not the first person to want to gut a courtier." He leaned closer and my heart skittered. "You're just the first to succeed."

My pulse hammered in my ears. This was another bait.

Two of his courtiers were missing but that was likely all he knew. How many other witches did he try to draw a confession out of? This was a calculated witch hunt. Of course he blamed us, because this was another excuse to rid Vylheim of the women who proved authority more powerful than a king existed.

And anyway, what he'd said about me being the only one to succeed wasn't true.

"Did you not dethrone the last king?" I asked. "I'd say that's close to gutting a courtier."

Another laugh rolled through him. I almost liked the feel

of it. The movement warmed me. His body flush against mine was almost a small comfort, because when the horse cantered too quickly, I didn't have effective use of my hands to hang on.

And when the horse picked up even more speed, King Drakkar gripped my waist. His fingers hooked into the bones at my hips.

"Almost like gutting a courtier," he said. "True. But a king is not a courtier, and I didn't gut him. In fact, he didn't bleed at all when I snapped his neck."

I bit my lip to keep my gasp muffled. He didn't deserve the satisfaction of my shock. Or was it curiosity? This was nothing new. I'd heard the stories of how King Drakkar overpowered the former king, ending his life without wasting a drop of blood, because somehow, King Roderic didn't have blood at all.

That was the story anyway.

Why did my mind paint a picture of what he'd said? Why did I replay the flash of King Drakkar murdering the former king over and over in my head in the seconds that followed his words? And why did I like it?

Because we're both corrupt.

Sick

And evil...

"You see, Silver," he said, as if he'd prepared a defense against my thoughts. "I never tell a lie."

Now it was my turn to laugh. It came out sudden, loud, and inappropriate, as I sat with the king's hands on my waist when I should have been executed alongside the brave witch who'd tried to change life for all of us.

Two members of the Grimward snapped their attention to us. A guard brought his horse closer until the king waved for him to back away from us.

With the rain lightened to a quiet drizzle, the guards could hear our conversation if they rode alongside us. It only took one look and the flick of King Drakkar's wrist to make sure they didn't. Apparently, he did want a little privacy with his captive witch. Goosebumps lifted across my collarbone.

"You don't believe me?" he asked. "Test it."

I chewed on my lip. Was this another bait? What could I ask him to test this claim?

If I asked him what he thought of the Gods, was that proof that I was a witch? Did it even matter? The guards, the Grimward, and the king himself had already called me a witch. They'd already captured me and tied me up.

I twisted my hands, trying to alleviate the rough cord scratching against the sensitive skin on the inside of my wrists. It only left darker red marks.

The cool rain was a relief, at least, but it left my fingers shaking and devoid of a healthy pink. I opened and closed my hands into fists to force blood into my fingers.

King Drakkar reached around and tugged at the cord. I seethed at the rope scratching my flesh raw, but as soon as he flicked his wrist, the knot released and he tossed the cord to the ground. He brushed his thumb over the red marks and I sucked in a breath.

Propping my fingers in his palm, he paused and held them there as if inspecting them. "Your skin matches the sea, and it's just as cold."

"Only my hands." I tried to pull away but he clamped his fist around my hand.

He tugged my arm across my body so he could examine my fingers closely. "They're entirely devoid of blood."

"Yes." I turned my hand over in his palm, no longer feeling the urge to recoil. Children had been the only ones brave—or foolish—enough to ask about my blue hands, my black eyes, or why I sometimes couldn't even keep up on a simple walk to the communal hearth. My father had made sure nobody spoke of these weaknesses in his daughter, but he hadn't been able to silence Alva. "I'm used to it."

"Do they hurt?"

"The cold hurts. But everyone feels the chill of winter."

He shook his head. "Not like this." My throat tightened, but I didn't know why or where the sudden rush of emotion came from. This was the enemy king and I was his captive servant, his acknowledgment of my cold hands was likely more about concern for how well I'd do my job rather than concern for my well being.

He wrapped his arms around me and buried my hands with his. "Now where were we?"

"Lying."

With a laugh he said, "Testing, actually. Go on, ask me something important."

"Why?"

"I want to know what you value, Silver."

My mother. Freeing her from the exile he'd placed her in.

"I value life." It was a regurgitated, basic, and vague response. It was perfect to keep him at a distance. He already had his fingers holding mine and his chest pressed against my spine, but I could keep this barrier between us.

"That's unoriginal, and a lie."

I twisted to glare at him. "How dare you say that!"

His wicked grin dipped to my ear again, and his lips brushed against me as he spoke. "You've killed, Silver."

"Fuck," I said, another word slipping out without my consent again. His bait had worked. He was right, and he damn well knew it. My muttered curse was the reaction of someone who'd just been bested. How did he know what I'd done? And how did he see through me so easily? All he knew was they were gone. "I defended myself." This was a half-truth. I'd *wanted* to hurt Astrid and Sten for taunting me. I didn't want to kill them—no, I never wanted to kill them—but I needed for them to know I could harm them.

That I wasn't weak.

I was just selfish instead, and corrupt enough to finish them off.

"I've only ever acted to preserve my life," I said. That wasn't entirely untrue, just not as immediate as I made it sound. Still, it was vague enough to avoid a confession. I couldn't admit I'd stabbed them.

"Good girl."

"Don't toy with me," I snapped.

"I meant it. Your life has value and you're bold enough to recognize that beyond what the law says. It's admirable."

A blush warmed my neck and ears. He knew I murdered two of his courtiers, and he admired that about me? What the fuck was wrong with King Drakkar?

What was wrong with me?

My shoulders had eased back and my spine straightened a little taller. This wasn't a compliment, even if it sounded like one. Half of me craved to bask in the feel of it though, to relish it. I'd done a terrible job keeping this darkness locked away with the memories.

Something about King Drakkar coaxed them out. He triggered me to both stay calm and react with fire at the appropriate times, almost like he already understood parts of me I couldn't even comprehend.

"We're the same," he whispered, unprovoked.

My neck prickled with goosebumps as his fingers tightened at my waist. I told myself I only liked his hands on me because he kept me from sliding off the horse. There really wasn't room for both of us.

We're not the same.

"We both see that we're meant for more," he said.

"Every life has value. Even the witch who did that to your eye." I shouldn't have said it. He could throw me off this horse and force me to be dragged behind in the mud. He could call the Grimward to bind me again and force me to my knees. He could do whatever he wanted —-but if we were the same, as he claimed, then I could too.

"You're not wrong, but order is necessary, and for that to be maintained, we must make sacrifices."

"And what have you sacrificed?" I asked, speaking through my teeth again.

He laughed. This time it came out cold and cutting and it sent a shiver through me. He drew his hands away, and I shouldn't have missed the steadiness of them. I didn't expect him to respond, but when he did, it was only a single word.

"Enough."

What could a king know of sacrifice? My mind sat with that to keep from spiraling. If I thought too long about why I enjoyed his touch, panic would grip me. I was already shaking from the bone-cold of persistent dampness, and if I passed out, I didn't know if King Drakkar would catch me. But I hoped he would.

I shook off that thought.

Only a wicked fool would be attracted to a king who just sanctioned the beheading of the witch from Stormdal.

I hate him.

But I liked his voice, his bold questions—even if they dug into the places I didn't want to explore.

It was selfish of me to let him live. Ragna could have killed him. I'd stripped our chance for hope, for a new sovereign ruler who was brave and humble enough to accept the existence of the Gods and allow witches to exist openly.

Selfish and cruel.

He left me alone long enough to spiral twice and then pull myself out of it by listing every sensation one by one, so it was a relief when his deep voice overpowered my thoughts until they vanished completely.

I drew in a full breath for the first time in hours.

"Do you ever feel there is someone else inside of you?" he asked, even though the rain began to pour again and almost drowned out his voice. Even with his mouth so close to my ear. His warm breath broke up the constant chill.

"I'm not sure what you mean."

How was I supposed to answer that? *Yes, the sinister side of me is her own person.* That simply wasn't true, I'd *wanted* to stab Astrid. I hated that she threatened me and I'd wanted to shut her up, even if I didn't plan to kill her.

Perhaps he was trying to bait the confession from me—get me to admit I was a witch who had visions of others, and heard voices from the Gods. Even if he already knew what I was.

"Do you ever have voices in your head?"

I didn't respond.

"Fine, how about this?" King Drakkar leaned in closer. "Do you want someone inside of you? Not a voice, someone real. Your preference suggests you like to be filled." His palm landed on my thigh and a small gasp escaped me.

The suggestion in his question became obvious as his fingers pressed against the soft flesh of my leg. I should have recoiled at his touch, but there was a fine line between hatred and heat, both inspired by flickering passion.

A fevered blush crawled up my neck, a welcome warmth in the persistent storm. He brushed his knuckles down the side of my throat, having pulled back my cloak's hood enough to bare my skin. Rain trickled down from my forehead to my collarbone.

I shivered, but was no longer cold.

"Answer me, Silver."

I'd lied about a lot in my life. My life itself was a lie, really. I wasn't the witch I was supposed to be. As a seerborn, I should have been able to see how to protect my fellow witches. I didn't feel like lying about this too, and I knew exactly what he implied.

It'd been far too long since I felt the ripples of pleasure that came with being filled. Bjorn was a kind man, loyal to my father, and loyal to our arrangement to delight in one another on a physical level, but that was where it ended. We were a means to an end, nothing more.

"Yes."

The king sucked in a sharp breath and I felt his body tense behind me. "Silver, have you ever lied?"

The heat of his last question quickly vanished with a sudden and painful chill that washed over me. It was as if he'd heard my thoughts. Or did he know the secret I'd kept buried since I was just a girl?

Lies had poisoned my lips ever since.

I couldn't respond. There was no right answer, so when he spoke again, I welcomed the sound of his voice. "You value life, but I'm willing to guess you value truth more. Perhaps as much as I do."

I opened my mouth, but it was a guard's voice that cut into our conversation.

"It's time to make camp," the guard said. "The winds are changing, and the chill has dropped. We need cover before frostbite sets in."

King Drakkar sighed but nodded. "Set the canopies." He directed our horse to the left where the dense trees protected us from the wind. He slid down from the mount and offered me his hand as if he wasn't a witch-hunting king, but a kind and gentle man.

After hesitating, I slipped my fingers into his hand where his fist covered my blue skin. His hands weren't especially warm, but they blocked the wind, and with the way his thumb brushed over the numb tips of my fingers, heat unfurled through me.

He led me to the base of a towering tree where he pointed for the guards to set up 'our' canopy. Each order barked from his mouth like a demand, but I didn't flinch at the sound. As rough as King Drakkar was, he'd stopped my execution. For now, I had nothing to fear.

Travelers slowly drifted off the path beaten by hooves and mirrored the guards' work setting up camp.

Once our canopy of animal fur and leather skin stretched between the trees, King Drakkar left me with a demand.

"Stay here where the wind can't reach you," he said. His gaze dropped to the hands folded in my lap. I sat at the center of the tight shelter. "They're blue again."

I followed his line of sight to my achingly numb fingers. I'd hardly noticed. "I'm used to it."

"Yes, so you've said. But I'm not. I will not have you suffer needlessly. I'll be back to..." his lips twitched. "To help keep you warm."

"Where are you going?" I asked, but it didn't matter, he'd already disappeared into the shadows. The darkest part of the night came before dawn, and the king was slinking through it for reasons unknown.

I didn't know how much I cared. Exhausted, I lay back on the furs. Despite the well-built canopy, wind still howled through the openings.

I drifted in and out of a fitful sleep, seeing Ragna's face, the witch's head fall to the ground, and then the ink on King Drakkar's chest. Was it Yggdrasil? Why would a king who hunted witches paint himself with the tree that connected us to the Gods? And what had given it the glow of the moon? It made as little sense as my congealed nightmares.

Shivering, I woke to the wind bellowing like the wolves battle-weary men shifted into from the ancient sagas. I curled within myself, tucking my aching hands between my legs when a figure appeared at the opening of my canopy.

Red caught my attention, and I thought I'd fallen into another nightmare, another dark dream about the creatures with glowing eyes the color of blood following my every step. I blinked and sat up when the king ducked into the canopy.

Without a word, he stepped over me and lay down,

molding himself to the shape of my body. My pulse pounded loud enough to wake the entire camp.

"You're shaking," he whispered. "Come closer."

It wasn't a suggestion. King Drakkar palmed my stomach and gently pulled me flush against him. He plucked my wrists from between my legs and blanketed both of my hands with his. His fingers were surprisingly hot, nearly burning.

Without thinking, I squirmed to press more firmly against him, soaking every bit of this unexpected warmth. He'd just come from outside where he should have been wind-bitten, not carrying the fiery invitation of a flaming hearth at the tips of his fingers.

I didn't know when or how I fell asleep with my heart skipping so erratically, but I woke to the king's nose buried in my braids.

As much as I wanted to pull away, he was still warm. Not fiery anymore, but enough to keep me comfortable.

I squinted at the world beyond the canopy. The embers of an evening sunset blanketed the trees in gold. We'd slept the entire daylight away. Soon, the guards would wake and rouse King Drakkar.

I closed my eyes and felt his breath on my neck, telling myself I only liked the warmth of it, nothing more.

We resumed our journey though the wind made it nearly impossible to resume our conversation. The king could no longer interrogate me with the wind carrying our voices away. The air whipped around us, violent and needling my nose and cheeks.

By mid-night my thighs were sore from riding, and all the heat I'd maintained after the night of curling into King Drakkar had been sucked from my bones. Even in summer, the wind was relentless. Winter would claim twice as many souls as last year. Of that I had no doubt.

King Drakkar leaned into me and did what he could to protect my hands from the wind, but curiously, he was no longer able to keep the heat he'd somehow gathered the previous night.

One of the king's guards stopped the travels at the front. He swung one leg and hopped off his horse, handing the reins to another guard as he fixed his eyes on us.

King Drakkar sighed as he slid his palm down the curve of my torso before he dismounted, but it wasn't enough to cause any heat of friction other than the traitorous heat building at the base of my belly. The cold grew worse when the king dismounted and left me alone on his horse.

He met the approaching guard halfway.

"Time to split parties." The guard said. "The king enters Mara first. Three days ahead. Three riders together. Three kingdoms combined." The guard spoke in a monotone voice as if having recited this a hundred times like the Grimward relaying the execution announcement.

King Drakkar released another rough breath. "Bring me a new horse, Silver will stay with this one."

The guard gave him a single curt nod before turning around. After a few minutes, he reappeared on his horse with a riderless horse cantering at his mount's side. The king climbed into the saddles and flicked his icy eyes toward me one last time before directing his horse away from me.

Without another word, he took off on his new horse, a guard at one side and an owl-masked executioner at his other.

And though I was surrounded by guards and members of the Grimward, I was alone, the cold air slicing through my animal furs and cloak.

CHAPTER TEN

Shame tormented me for three days. The sickness twisting my gut grew worse with my monthly bleeding. Whenever the stomach cramps and flow of blood cropped up, my obsessive dwelling and nervous energy became all-consuming. I didn't have the energy to keep the thoughts at bay.

This slow journey to a lifetime of servitude didn't help. What would my days look like as I worked in the castle at Mara? My skills with cooking, baking, and cleaning were basic and attuned to village life in Skaldir. I was best skilled at reciting the sagas and solving riddles buried in the history of the Gods.

My favorite duty had always been as a gatherer. My mother taught me how every plant served humans either as a salve, an oral medicine, food, to burn for scent, or to sacrifice to Odin and Freya. Of course I could identify any poisonous leaf as well. But none of that would serve me well in Mara, where much of the flora was different, if I even worked as a gatherer at all.

Dull pain clawed through my lower stomach. Each month I dreaded the bleeding because it never failed to leave my nerves more frayed than ever. The flow was as heavy as the weight of each painful reminder.

I almost missed having the king at my back, which meant I was a traitor.

I almost lost my chance to free my mother because I was short-sighted and selfish.

I almost died, and I should have.

The Stormdal witch's life was not less valuable than mine, despite whatever King Drakkar was attempting to suggest. I hated his interest in me as much as I craved more of it, and this sent me into another spiral that only a careful focus on the senses helped me crawl out of.

I felt the rhythmic canter of the horse's stride and the ache in my thighs. I smelled the remnants of rain as we left the storm in our wake. Taste was trickier, since I hadn't eaten for hours. Bleeding either stripped me of my appetite, or sent me into an insatiable hunger. This month's wave turned my stomach inside out, leaving no room for a desire for food, which was just as well since we'd nearly run out of provisions after the storm slowed our expected travel by two days.

Closing my eyes, I narrowed in on the next sense. An owl hooted from nearby. The horses' hooves struck the earth with steady purpose. I heard tentative cheering…

My eyes peeled open to the sight of a valley stretched out before us in the bright light of the full moon. We'd finally reached the top of the hill we'd been climbing for the past few hours. Below lay our first glimpse of the vast kingdom of Mara.

Tiny structures dotted the landscape, homes and stables. Snow had not yet blanketed the terrain here. Winter reached all of Vylheim, but I'd heard it was slow to arrive in the southern kingdom and quick to leave, the majority of the snow and ice would come only with the Polar Nocturne.

In the denser areas, the buildings were organized in rows like the main part of our village back home in Skaldir. Except here, there would be no council home to house the Vyl and his family. Mara's Keep, the king's home and the castle where all the courtiers lived, was the only place for council, if King Drakkar counseled with the people at all. My father seemed to believe he did, or else he wouldn't have traveled this far for a single meeting.

The people of Stormdal crowded in behind the remaining guards and Grimward members, everyone scrambling for a glimpse of their new southern home.

Hope lifted my chin. At the top of an opposite hill sat the largest structure visible in Mara, a stone castle with spires and towers lifting into the starry sky. I finally had Mara's Keep within my sights.

Within a day, we'd be inside that castle where I could *follow the blood he left behind.* I would track the king just as Freya instructed, and I'd pass this trial. This was a thought I hadn't allowed myself to consider until I knew I'd make it to Mara, because I couldn't bear more failure.

I will track him. I had to trail his blood to find the lost history, but King Drakkar reigned in a time of peace, and drawing blood was outlawed. Nobody even carried a weapon besides the Grimward, a select few of his guards, and the king. The only time fighting was sanctioned was by the king himself, and that was merely a rumor.

But King Drakkar was said to be skilled with a sword, which meant he must practice with his guards. People had claimed he clashed with members of the Grimward who tried to defect, publicly. He stayed as sharp as his sword so that nobody could overthrow him the way he stole the previous king's throne, and to hold his power over the executioners.

Did he duel in practice with the guards near wherever he kept the runestones hidden? Or perhaps he'd be attacked and in his most painful and vulnerable moment I could pry the answer from him. Where was our history stored?

What if I didn't need the history at all, and when he bled,

he sought help from a healing witch who, with my partner-
ship, could force him to acknowledge that we weren't a threat
in front of Mara? That all witches in exile did not have reason
to be kept there, nor reason to fear existence in Vylheim
because he'd no longer hunt us—if she healed him.

If only I had the gift of healing. But this vision was
enough.

There were countless possible outcomes. I'd just have to
wait and see what opportunity presented itself.

Freya would lead me to the answers to free my mother and
send Ragna back home. I'd be victorious when I saw two cats
representing her beloved companions, Bygul and Trjegul, like
my mother saw Odin's ravens when a crop she'd planted
would be successful. They were visual, breathing representa-
tions of the Gods' promises.

For this, I was grateful.

The rest of the journey passed with ease, and my monthly
bleeding subsided by the time we entered the settlements
closest to the castle.

Mara was a single village on the continent of Vylheim, but
since it stretched over so much land, the gatherings of houses
created what were almost their own separate villages. This was
why the people of Vylheim called Mara a kingdom—as if it
was separate from the rest of Vylheim.

Now that I was seeing it with my own eyes, I understood.

I also understood why the kings of old had chosen Mara
to build a Keep. Though Mara bordered the wasteland, this
land was prosperous, close to the fish at sea, away from the
unforgiving winter in the north, and simply stunning.

Stone houses dotted the countryside. Mara was beautiful,
full of lush green farms along the perimeter. Soon they'd be
covered in snow, stripping the last of our chance to grow food
for the season, but for now, the southern village was a relief
from the relentless winter weather that was slowly looming in
our wake.

Candles flickered warm orange hues from behind windows. People filled the centers of the settlements, gathering with excited energy as if for a competition or celebration. As we traveled through the heart of the settlements, I caught pieces of conversation, talk of a wedding in the kingdom of Mara rippled through the villagers.

Somehow, anticipation for this wedding spread across multiple settlements, as if those who were to be wed were royals. And perhaps they were.

As we rode up to the castle, our party had dwindled to only those planning to meet with King Drakkar. The guard who'd kept his eye on me approached from the left side of the towering stone building.

Once we were dismounted and guards guided our horses to the stable, he spoke.

"The king wants you to rest," he said, grabbing my arm. "The rest of you," he addressed my father and his men. "May wash up at the servants' bathhouse."

He pulled me away from them and I yanked back. "I want to stay with the people of Skaldir," I said.

"The king says you will rest."

"I can rest knowing they're close." It wasn't that my father's presence offered me any solace, but Bjorn was a friend, and at least their faces were familiar.

"As long as you rest, I don't give a shit what happens," he said. "King Drakkar was clear in his command that I ensure you get the opportunity to sleep and restore yourself after the journey. He said you need it." Though the guard's voice dripped with irritation, my heart lifted. Nobody had cared to allow me rest before—certainly not enough to command it.

And I definitely needed it. After washing up, I fell into an open bed, sleep enveloping me. Dreams of King Drakkar's body molding to the shape of mine welcomed me.

———

When I woke hours later, the same guard dragged me from my bed and led us back out to the front of the castle.

My throat tightened at the sight of animal masks. Executioners joined the guards as they pulled my father and I through the crowd.

People parted for the Grimward, like the clouds separating after a rainstorm. Mara's villagers spread apart just enough to let us pass. They pushed forward in our wake and I was pleasantly surprised that the king allowed for commoners to trample the halls of his castle. Of course, it was far vaster than a Vyl's home, with plenty of room for visitors, but it seemed the entire crowd had their sights set on a single destination, leaving the other halls empty.

Bodies pressed in around me as I finally crossed the castle's threshold and the people of Mara's Keep scrambled for a glimpse of the king. Inside was a maze of stone. We followed the narrow halls to the throne room.

This castle wasn't built to invite the kingdom's subjects inside all at once, but with the arrival of the northernmost village in Vylheim, the king had opened his doors for all to come. I could only hope it wasn't to come witness my beheading.

I kept my eyes to the ground with the hood of my cloak draped over my head as servants guided us into the castle along with the rest of the visitors from Skaldir seeking alliance with the king.

"Silver." A man's voice rolled my name over his tongue and my skin prickled like it had when Sten came up behind me. I glanced back at my father, knowing it wasn't him. He rarely called me Silver and opted to address me simply as 'daughter' instead. Who else here knew to call me by this name?

My gaze swept over the crowd.

A figure in a dark green cloak pushed through the throng of bodies. Two men spoke to one another on my left, one of them with flashing red eyes. Blood rushed through my ears with every erratic beat of my pulse. I blinked and, though he still raked his gaze over me, hungry captivation darkened his brown eyes, making the red fade away.

The figure's mouth, partially obscured by shadow, formed around the shape of my name again. I didn't know if I heard him say it or only understood it by the movement of his lips.

"Keep moving," my father barked, ripping my attention away from the strange man. "We need to meet with the king before he changes his damn mind."

I blinked and looked ahead of me again.

With frayed nerves, I forced one foot in front of the other. Every step I took was a step deeper into the royal court, from which I'd stolen two lives. The flash of the figure's red eyes brought my mind back to them and held my thoughts hostage.

Shadows had lurked around me as a child and that same sinister energy crawled at my back now. The feeling of my flesh turning inside out was as familiar as the ghost of Astrid's hold and Sten suggesting he wanted to taste me.

Though I was terrified that maybe monsters had tracked me my entire life, it was the courtiers who finally captured me.

Either way, the energy felt the same, and I wanted to strip it off like a dress soaked in lye.

A foot caught the hem of my cloak, and my heart stuttered. I yanked the fabric but it wouldn't budge. My father pushed me forward and the force tugged the cloak off my head and shoulders. I yelped and clutched the fabric in my fists, snapping my eyes to the culprit. The same man, shrouded in the shadow of his own hood, glared at me with golden eyes.

As every muscle in my body froze as my father growled something about my weak countenance.

The man's lips parted, and he shoved in closer, taking the second before my father pushed me forward to whisper a warning. "Don't go in there. Come with me."

My father ignored him like he had with every other shadow who'd lurked outside my window or followed my footsteps. He simply jerked past the figure, and the flow of the crowd pressed us forward, swallowing the shadow at my heels.

Finally, I yanked my dress from beneath his boot and allowed my father to nudge me forward.

Excitement buzzed through the people of Mara as alive as the unease swimming in my gut.

The golden-eyed man could have been one of my captors, had they survived my attack. Did he want to devour me like Astrid? My blood went cold as a shudder rippled through me with the memory of her words. The memory that had haunted me with every shape I caught sight of in the woods during our journey to Mara's Keep.

Don't go in there. Could this message be a warning that King Drakkar had decided to execute me after all? The second half begged to differ. This shadow wanted me to come with him, just like Astrid and Sten.

We spilled into the vast throne room where the ceiling stretched into the sky with a massive arch, and the open space allowed me to suck in a breath that was cut short when I felt someone watching me.

I flicked my gaze from the candles flickering across dozens of hanging candelabras to the throne. King Drakkar stood, keeping his sharp eye fixated directly on me. His other eye had been fastened with a leather eye patch, a blot of smooth black covering one side of his skull. Two council members flanked his throne, Ylva and Darius.

My throat tightened. Was I marching to my execution?

Didn't I deserve it? But I was so close to Freya's trial, to reaching the opportunity to follow the king's blood to the answers I craved.

When his mouth cut into a charming smile that split sideways across his face, I drew another breath, this one shallow. All I could do was move forward. I'd made my decision. In a daze, I floated to the throne with my father at my heels and dropped into a respectful curtsy, with my head tucked, my knees on the cold stone floor, and my copper skirts splayed around me.

Conversations fell silent, and the only sound echoing through the throne room was the approach of footsteps. My heartbeat doubled as a shadow stretched over me.

The king crouched in front of me and, with his thumb and forefinger, lifted my chin.

Every breath I dragged into my stiff throat became more shallow until I met his gaze once again. His icy eye, the color of melted fjords in the summer, held mine. He released my chin and brushed his thumb over my wound that had since become a scar.

It'd only been three days since I'd seen him last, but for the majority of the time we had been together, he'd been sitting at my back where I couldn't see him. Now, I took all of him in again, noticing the details my distracted mind had left out before.

His wicked grin was as dark as his sleek hair and beard, and held my thoughts captive, rendering me senseless, foolish, like a young shieldmaiden enchanted by a battle-weary warrior from old tales. The longer I looked at him, the more I wanted to look. Everything about King Drakkar was the living vision of a man from the sagas my mother had dared to share with me. A man *I'd* dared to dream of, and he'd even stopped my execution. He'd saved my life just like a warrior would do.

He'd unknowingly given me the chance to pass a God's trial and shirk off the shameful parts of me once and for all. That was the true rescue, whether he knew it or not.

Humming low in his chest, he dropped to one knee and leaned in to me. "Silver, I've missed you." His gaze raked over me, and I expected another one of his unbidden questions. "I have a proposal for you."

CHAPTER ELEVEN

King Drakkar's thick arm wrapped around my lower back while he held my other hand. My heart flipped as he guided me to my feet. The memory of him lifting me from my knees was an echo of my stopped execution.

Just like the moment he interrupted my execution, what might come next was impossible to predict.

"I plan to marry you," he said, his voice low but cutting with confidence.

Marry me? How could I become the wife of the king who exiled people like me? My stomach revolted with a pulse of bile pressing up into my throat. I swallowed it and lightly palmed my throat to feel the ripple of my swallow. The action grounded me enough to process his words.

It wasn't even a question, or the proposal he'd promised, but neither was it a punishment nor servitude. At least not in the way I expected.

He tilted his head, eyes scanning every inch of my face before he held my gaze. "Silver?"

I sucked in a tight breath, but relief didn't come. If I accepted, I might share in the secrets he held as king. As his wife, how much easier would it be to find the lost history? Or to convince him to free my mother?

"This isn't what I thought I came here for." It was all I could think to say.

"Do you deny the heat between us?"

Heat? That was just the burn of hate.

I said nothing.

If I bound myself to him, this would be my sacrifice. This would help me pass Freya's trial. Who better to see the king at his most vulnerable than his wife? Despite all this logic, I couldn't bring myself to accept. Which was another one of my selfish choices.

Now the tingle of nerves fluttered in my chest. They buzzed in my fingertips and I slipped my hand deeper into his steady hold.

A slight smirk curved at the edge of his lips.

How could he want me after I'd killed his courtiers? Standing before him, we were surrounded by people who must have been friends with the man and woman I stuck like suckling pigs and left in the forest to rot in blood-stained snow. They were dead by the very hand the king now held in his.

"Say you're mine," he said as he dropped to one knee before me. It wasn't a question. He didn't ask me to marry him as was tradition for most couples in Vylheim. He spoke it into existence as if I didn't have a choice. And, of course, I didn't, though something about the way he waited for me to respond told me he wanted me to at least give me the illusion of choice.

He gripped my hand, staring up at me like I was fowl waiting to be shot out of the sky with an arrow and then devoured alongside a plate of potatoes. "With me, you'll want for nothing. But I need you to say it. Say you're mine, Silver. Or shall I call you my wife?"

"But I'm not your wife." The words slipped out before I

could swallow them, my natural inclination for the independence that Freya spoke of in her sagas.

King Drakkar stood, still gripping my hands as he stepped toward me and lightly tugged me into him. His voice dropped to a volume only I could hear. "Perhaps you shouldn't announce that in front of inquiring ears. Your father informs me you need safety, as you have..." he paused to lift the back of his finger to the scar Sten had left across my cheek, tracing it with the slightest touch as he seemed to search for the right word. "Persistent admirers. When I say you'll want for nothing as my wife, I mean there is no admirer who'll be allowed within reach of you ever again. No human, or monster."

My heart thudded in my throat. Did he know I still spoke of the old tales, spreading the sagas of monsters and Gods?

When had my father told him this? I'd suffered nightmares my entire life, but I never breathed a word of it, nor of the gods I still prayed to and the monsters my mother taught me to fear.

My gaze slid to my father only a few steps away. He beamed, seemingly proud that they'd finally, truly made a deep connection with the wealthiest ruler in Vylheim. I flinched at the sight of his smile, so unnatural on my father's cruel face.

Turning my attention to King Drakkar, I conjured my voice. "What do you know of monsters?"

He grinned. "Everything."

Did the records show glimpses of giants and the undead? "There's rumors about lost history here—"

"Yes, but you're not part of Mara's Keep, Silver. Not until we're married." King Drakkar dipped his mouth to my ear, blocking everyone's sight of his face with me. His voice was nothing more than a whisper, a breath on my neck. "Many have come here excited for my betrothal. Let's not keep them waiting. Kiss me to show them who you belong to."

Heavy silence coated the room. Some three hundred pairs

of eyes watched, breathing scantily while the people listened for my response. A shiver trickled down my spine, but I lifted my chin and met his gaze as soon as he pulled back from my ear and faced me.

He didn't move. He didn't even blink for an unnatural amount of time. The crushing weight of his hold made me want to rip my hand away, but he'd promised me the one thing I needed. The only thing I wanted—save for a way to go back in time and change what I'd done—was access to the records. And protection too? It was all I could want, especially after a lifetime of being followed by glowing red eyes.

I hated my shadows for frightening me, my captors for pushing me to the edge, but I hated myself the most. I'd let the idea to destroy Astrid and Sten overcome me and it had made me the very thing that haunted my nightmares, a monster.

I shoved the thought away before it spread like poison in my veins. Before the incessant and nervous dwelling left me questioning my own identity.

He waited patiently as I processed this.

Then, I tipped my head back, my chin lifted, my lips meeting his as I rolled to the balls of my feet.

To my surprise, he melted into me, soft at first, then firm and hungry for far too long in front of so many people. He cupped my jaw with one hand and pressed his other palm against my spine, pressing me flush against him.

My cheeks flamed, and when he pulled back and our lips parted, I missed the bite of the sharp, spicy wine on his lips, the firmness with which he held me—a promise that he'd keep me so close nobody would sink their fingernails into me or threaten to taste my blood again.

King Drakkar turned to his people with a savage smile cutting his face. He'd gotten exactly what he wanted. Now he'd announce our betrothal. Could this have been what the hooded figure was warning me against? Or had he just wanted to devour me like the other red-eyed creatures I saw in the shadows?

I followed the king's line of sight as he gazed over the people of Mara's Keep.

Everyone waited for the announcement, the official statement that'd claim me as King Drakkar's future wife, but all he said was, "let's feast."

That was it, *let's feast*.

I nearly snapped my neck as I raked my gaze over him. He forced his fingers into my clenched hand, spreading my fingers so he could slip his in between. When he lifted my hand as if to kiss my knuckles, he drew me into him with a quiet strength that held me in place.

Without turning his head or affording me the mere regard of looking at me, he spoke. "You're wondering why I didn't announce a marriage?" I huffed my agreement. "Because you never said yes."

"You never asked."

It still didn't make sense why he cared about my answer when I didn't have a choice. He said nothing else as he turned his attention to his people.

The crowd broke apart, spreading like stray dogs in Skaldir, searching for food and attention as they chose to dance or fill their plates with lamb and crusts of bread to coat with soft cheese or dip in buttered juices dripping from the steaming meat. Those who served in King Drakkar's castle moved with frantic ease, scurrying through the mix of guests and the hundred or so people who took residence with the king, advisors, friends, perhaps relatives.

While other servants carried plates and trays, distributing them to the people with practice, the woman who approached us held only a single bronze goblet. Her straight black bangs hung like a curtain above her eyebrows. The dangling earrings she wore set her apart from the other servants. Glittering jewels swung lower than the hair she kept cropped at her chin.

Presenting the goblet to King Drakkar, she met his gaze. They stared at one another for a long, tense moment, until she looked away. With her head angled to the side and her milky skin nearly translucent, I couldn't help but notice that her throat throbbed with an erratic pulse. Absent-mindedly, my fingers found their way to my throat where my own heart beat off rhythm.

What caused her spastic pulse? Sweat lined the curls of hair sticking to her forehead, and her jaw twitched with the subtle grinding of teeth. Was it fear, or the strain of work?

When my gaze slid back to King Drakkar, my breath snagged. He had yet to break his attention from her, as if this servant had enchanted him with the kind of magic my mother claimed she could once cast.

King Drakkar lifted the goblet from her pale fingers, and as he brought it to his lips, he stared at her, sipping without so much as a blink. Envy boiled in the pit of my belly, not for his attention, but for this strange power she wielded. What entranced him to her? Could such influence guide him? He was the head of this kingdom, but I could become the neck, the muscle that'd point his face to Skaldir and the other villages in need.

When King Drakkar broke his gaze, time seemed to speed up. The servant woman spun around and disappeared into the crowd. Bodies closed in around her, swallowing any trace of her, and the king downed the rest of his wine in a single gulp.

"What was that?" I asked as he turned, and pulled me with him.

He didn't so much as look over his shoulder as he dragged me to the throne. "That was my favorite drink."

"No, I mean the tension between you and the servant woman."

Finally he stopped and afforded me his full attention. He turned, facing away from the throne to meet my gaze, his blue eyes harsh and bright like sharp icicles. The thick sapphire cape he wore fastened at his throat seemed to darken the icy shade of his eyes as I took the whole of him in. He didn't wear a crown like I'd expected of a king in his castle.

He dressed rather plain for what I thought of a king. He wore no shining rings on his fingers, and no jewelry hung at his neck or on his wrists like I'd seen many Vyls choose to decorate themselves. King Drakkar had a simple style that suggested he was more of his people than of his throne, and yet, the warrior look made me feel small. As if he held power I couldn't recognize—from a hidden weapon or a skill with fighting that lavish belts and jewels would only restrict him from.

"Are you jealous of Thora, wife?"

"I am neither your wife nor capable of jealousy when it comes to a man I hardly know," I said, frowning to offset his curious smirk.

"Then why do you ask about her?"

"Because if you are to marry me, I won't have you distracted. And didn't you promise protection? In Skaldir, distraction leads to death."

He studied me, nearly as entranced, but without the unblinking stare. One of amusement. "Silver, I can't protect you until you say yes."

"You never asked." I set my jaw.

He turned and took a seat on his throne, his legs spread wide, one hand on his thigh, the other perched on the dull bronze of the throne's arm. "Sit," he said, all patience gone from his voice.

"Where?"

His eye flickered to the leg free of his hand and a faint twitch curved the edge of his lips as he looked back up at me standing helplessly before him. "You'll do what I say when you're in my castle, Silver. Sit."

"Is that what kind of wife I'll be forced to become?" I couldn't tamp down the fire raging within me. None of this is what I expected, and instead of succumbing to my nerves, I let anger flare. It felt safer to be outraged, as stupid as it was to argue with the king. But he said he valued truth, so I'd give him the truth—exactly what I thought.

"You won't be a wife at all until you sit down and say yes."

"To what proposal?" I snapped. Since he hadn't immediately called forth the executioners, I'd become too bold.

When I made no move to obey, he grabbed my wrist and pulled me down. He only afforded me a moment to adjust my skirts and maintain my dignity before his hand found my bare collarbone. He gently traced the bone with his fingers until his hand momentarily slipped over my neck, as if to grab me by the throat.

In reaction, I reached for the silver tree in my pocket. When his fingers found their way to my jaw, I loosened my grip on the necklace, leaving it still buried in the fabric of my skirts. He tipped my chin to face him.

"You'll be my wife, Silver?"

"Is that a question?" It sounded more like a statement.

"It is."

I rubbed the pointed end of the silver pendant, letting the sharpness dig into the soft flesh at the center of my thumb. I could accept him, or I could continue trying to protect myself. No other man could offer what a king could give me. Times of peace bred gentle men, men I was friends with and cared for, but not men with true power.

"I know what you need," he said, prompting me to give him the yes he longed for. "Remember, Silver, I *know* what you did." His eye fell to my hidden hand. To my pocket. To where I kept the weapon I'd used to kill two people from this very court.

My throat squeezed tighter than if he'd wrapped his fingers around it. Dread crawled over my skin as I remembered their boiling flesh. It seemed my own body bubbled and bloated until I was forced to push out an answer. I had a dozen reasons to say yes, protection from the shadows, an excused execution. The trial was the most important, but it wasn't until he pushed the reminder of what I'd done on me that I finally formed the word…

"Yes." I said, as if this betrothal—this sacrifice—would wipe it all away.

"Yes?" He wanted more.

I tried to swallow but my throat was too tight. "Yes, I'll be your wife."

He pressed a palm to my stomach, lifting me from his lap and to my feet as he stood with me. Instead of forcing his hand in mine, he offered his arm to me. All harshness had melted from his eyes and the wicked grin shifted to a peaceful smile, like an icy stalactite that'd melted in the warm sun. Like he was two different people.

The change was so odd, and yet I found it easier to take his arm, even with every muscle in my body fighting it.

He tugged me forward. His mere presence, having returned to standing now, quietly demanded the room's attention.

As dancing ceased and laughter silenced, King Drakkar lifted his chin, glancing at me before sealing my fate in front of hundreds of witnesses. "I'd like to officially introduce Mara's Keep to my betrothed. Silver Norn Quinn is to be my wife."

CHAPTER TWELVE

I woke to the roaring crackle of a fire. Rolling my head to the side, I found the source of the heat pulsing through an unrecognizable room. Flames licked high up into the flue above the fireplace, erasing my body's memory of winter in Skaldir. For once, my hands weren't painfully cold.

Too dizzy to move, I lifted my hands up to inspect my fingers. My skin glowed with a rare but healthy pink, even if I felt horrible.

Too much wine left me waking with throbbing at my temples. After the announcement, hundreds of villagers descended upon us, each clambering to grace us with their congratulations. Some I'd thought I even recognized.

Had one of them been Ragna? Impossible, she wouldn't congratulate this corrupt betrothal. But I'd seen her face in the crowd, I could swear it on Odin's eye. Shouldn't she and the other witches have been taken beyond Mara and to the wasteland?

I never had the right mind with which to ask King Drakkar. I didn't even have the opportunity to speak with my betrothed again after he'd officially introduced me, not with the swarm of faces asking to kiss their new queen's knuckles.

It was a title I never wanted and definitely didn't deserve. Hearing them address me as it over and over and over sent me into a downward spiral of thoughts as loud and as painful as the thumping in my head now.

Wine quieted it one sip at a time, until I'd lost track of myself.

And my father. I recalled seeing him speak with King Drakkar. I remembered my father saying goodbye, that he already planned to return to Skaldir.

After that, the last moment I remembered was a hand-maiden guiding me down a freezing cold hallway. Her name was Stella, or maybe Sara. My stupid drunken mind didn't let me recall the details, and now nerves rushed back with the force of a wave crashing over the fjords.

"I'm marrying King Drakkar," I said.

The room was vast and with a vaulted stone ceiling, but I didn't speak loud enough for the sound to catch an echo. My pulse thumped erratically. The wine was too much, I never drank it and avoided mead for the same reason, my heart felt like it'd burst from my ribcage whenever the haze of the drink sunk in. My body disliked it, but it had seemed my only escape last night.

This was another selfish choice, number one thousand and one. Likely twice as much, but I didn't actually keep count because tallying each mistake would make it too easy to slip into a cycle of dwelling. I already laid awake most nights replaying what I could have done differently.

I could have let Ragna make the choice she'd decided for herself.

I could have stopped my mother from sacrificing herself to the wasteland ten years ago.

I could have been an honest child instead of hiding in the hatch when the Grimward knocked on our door.

But those choices were in the past now and impossible to

change. Today, I could get out of this bed and track down the king.

I'd find where he practiced with that sword. Surely practice would occasionally draw blood. The blood the prophecy said I needed to follow in order to uncover truths about King Drakkar and pass Freya's trial.

My only other options were dependent on an external event; if he was attacked, or if a member of the Grimward tried to defect and the king cut them down, resulting in a scuffle.

Groaning, I rolled forward and dragged my pounding head up with me. I slipped my legs from beneath the blanket to hang over the edge of the huge bed. These bedchambers were nothing like the open space we shared in the longhouse. At home, we separated the two large rooms of the house with colorful tapestries and curtains strung up with glass beads.

Here, narrow halls stretched into an endless maze. I hadn't explored the other rooms, but if they were anything like this one, the tight hallways would open into oversized spaces with a large mantel over the fireplace, a deep oak cabinet, an ornate mirror placed precariously against a thick stand, a stone tub in the far corner, and a bed so large it could fit four of me. Like the castle itself, the bed was sturdy, heavy looking and gray with posts on each corner that reached up toward the ceiling in the imitation of spires.

I flattened my bare feet against the cold stone and stood. Like a fawn just born, my legs shook. Must have been from the combination of nerves I tried to lock away and hours of standing until late into the night.

The loose silver gown fell around my feet. Not a gown I ever remembered seeing before. Where my original dress had ended up, I had no clue. It damn well better have been the handmaiden who changed me and not King Drakkar, or one of the leering guards.

I brushed my palm over the sheer fabric as I shuffled

across the room. The gown was so light and airy, it clung to every dip and curve as I walked. I stood before the oversized mirror, feeling like a child's doll in the massive room.

The light weight of the dress felt wrong. A small gasp slipped out as I palmed the non-existent pockets.

My Y Tree.

I'd forgotten it was tucked away in the loose pocket of the clothing I wore from Skaldir. Now it was gone, along with the dress.

And my enchantment. I blinked at my black eyes. After waking, I always had to recast it to hide it, but not without first inspecting just exactly how many threads of darkness spread through the thin veins. I leaned closer, trying to spot any hint of white behind the inky black.

My mother's enchantment was almost entirely gone.

Which meant she was almost entirely gone. Claws seemed to squeeze my chest, like a giant had reached through my ribcage and picked me up by my heart.

I'd lost my pendant, my freedom, and almost, my mother.

Usually, I needed a bowl of water to speak incantations over for my concealing enchantment. Today, tears slipped from the edges of my eyes, rolling slowly down my cheeks as I whispered the familiar words.

I caught two teardrops in my palm and enchanted them to become a watery film that'd make my eyes look normal, at least for a day. Tilting my head back, I slipped each droplet back into my eye where the magic concealed the black.

The center of my eyes looked oddly pale and not fully round now, like a crescent moon clouded by a retreating storm, but I was used to it. And at least they weren't two black abysses.

The door to my bedchamber creaked as a small and pale servant, not unlike Thora, slipped inside the room. Gathering myself, I wiped the look of horror from my face and twisted to see a young woman so pale she nearly glowed luminescent in the dawn light.

She made quick work of laying a new dress across my bed and setting out several bracelets, a necklace, and earrings for me to wear. Her mouth hung open, breathing rapidly as her empty stare fixated on the dress for a moment.

She turned to me, her stare haunting as I returned it through the reflection in the mirror.

"Are you all right?" I asked, hopeful she would speak to me. The servants didn't exactly refuse to talk, but those I encountered last night didn't make conversation either. She'd only responded in single words, and when I'd asked for her name as she'd guided me to bed, she'd whispered it; *Embla*.

At least that much I could remember before the wine carried away most of the previous night.

"The king requests your presence at a celebration for your betrothal." It was all she said before she finally snapped her jaw shut.

"Another one? Didn't we celebrate last night?"

She hummed, but it didn't sound like a confirmation. "And now another day has passed with sleep. The time to be awake passed several hours ago. They'd like plenty of time to celebrate before dawn."

I rubbed my eyes. No way had I slept that much, but the exhaustion pulling at my eyes said otherwise. Perhaps I'd never become accustomed to the flipped schedule in Mara where the people prepared for the dark of the Polar Nocturne.

"You are to become our new queen," she continued. "I'm told there is a long process. Approval, appointing, and then application. But not to worry, it all takes place during the celebrations."

"Is this just an excuse for the people of Mara to drink more wine?" I asked.

She gave me the faintest shrug. I almost didn't catch it

before her frail shoulders fell and she pointed at my hair. "May I redo your braids?"

My gaze flicked from her to my reflection. I ran my hand over the heavy braid laying atop the rest of my hair. The side where smaller braids pulled tightly to my head had come loose with wild hairs after my night of drunken stupor. The heat of too many bodies had twisted the escaped hairs in weak coils.

Already, my hair had adapted to the humid southern weather. The curls changed so easily, so quickly, I almost didn't see Silver now when I looked in the mirror. This was King Drakkar's future wife, a woman I didn't know.

I sighed and nodded. "If you keep it in the style of Skaldir."

Women in the northernmost village wore two tight braids against their skull on either side, joined with a thicker braid in the center and then laid over free-flowing hair to imitate the fall of water over the cliff of Iskniv, the highest peak visible from our village.

Embla worked in silence, tugging lightly at my hair, quickly weaving and tightening each braid with her slight fingers. It didn't matter how many little questions I prodded her with, she only hummed in response. I didn't dare ask her where the king practiced wielding his sword, or if servants or courtiers ever tried to challenge his reign. Knowing where the king stored his weapons was likely not allowed, and I wouldn't get this poor girl in trouble.

Silence settled in my throat, but she continued to hum.

The soft pitch carried a tune. Steadily lifting until it matched the rhythm of a familiar song, one written by the ancient skalds. Village poets no longer wrote about the Gods, but this melody was old, as old as Sol herself. The pitch that climbed higher and higher represented the rising morning light as the God of the sun drove the chariot that carried it across the sky.

I closed my eyes, listening to the tune I hadn't heard since my mother sang it to help us sleep.

Embla no longer looked as stricken after I stopped inundating her with questions. Brushing and twisting my hair clearly brought her peace, and I was honored she kept to the Skaldir style without a fuss.

I didn't have time to sit with her for too long, but I enjoyed every minute of her presence. Though she was a young woman, maybe eighteen or twenty, her wide eyes and blond curls sparked thoughts of Alva.

How had Embla come to serve in Mara's Keep? I couldn't imagine this gentle girl causing bloodshed, and felt none of the crackle beneath my skin that I came with being in another witch's presence.

Perhaps she was another unknown. Villagers often explained away those who vanished by insisting that a wild animal had dragged them away. But those who were bolder, hinted that they were taken, either by monsters or other people, I didn't know. Nobody would ever clarify what they believed about it.

What if the same happened to Alva someday?

I gritted my teeth, suddenly set on getting to know Embla. If I could make her life even a little better here as the queen, it would be enough reason to take the title.

Once my hair was set, she helped me into the courtier's garb. The icy blue silk nearly matched the shape of the silver nightgown as it held tightly to my hips, my shoulders, my breasts. It dipped lower in the front than the dresses I wore in Skaldir.

The king wanted to parade me as his prize, or a well-dressed prisoner. I still didn't know where I stood with him.

Embla pointed to the mirror and then gestured for me to turn around. "Do you approve?"

"It looks just like my Skaldir braids." I gave her a gentle smile.

"Look again."

I furrowed my brow and turned, twisting to see as much of the back of my head as I could reflected in the mirror. A shimmer caught the glow of the room's candles from between my braids. I reached up to feel cold hard silver buried in my thick hair.

"My Y Tree," I whispered. She hadn't just returned it, she'd tucked it safely in the weave of my braids so that only a sliver of the top poked out. There were no pockets in this new dress with which to hide it, but Embla had found another way. I turned to cup her hand in mine, but she'd already slipped away to stand by the door. "Thank you."

Without another word, she opened the door and waved for me to exit.

In the hall, Embla trailed at my heels, silently pointing which turn to make next in this labyrinth of cold stone. I scanned every inch of the ground and walls in case there was a hint of blood, or anything that would clarify Freya's vision.

The Gods spoke cryptically, not because they wanted to play with the people of Midgard, but because riddles and challenges were the language of Asgard. It was all they knew, according to my mother.

I blew out a breath.

Mara's Keep gave me nothing. No hint of identifying markers on the doors, no peculiar sounds, and definitely no blood. The castle was so vast, I could spend a decade searching for the records and still not find them.

But I had King Drakkar to follow. He was the single clue in Freya's cryptic language.

With every turn, my heart beat a little faster. The next time I saw him, I'd be sober, wearing *this*. A blush bloomed over my chest where the skin was bared above my breasts. *Do you want someone inside of you?* I laid a hand over my red skin to tame the heat.

Why had he chosen to marry me? Could he somehow sense this sick and twisted attraction I had for him?

Now with a head clear from the shock of his proposal and the wine that flowed afterward, dozens of questions took my mind captive. I didn't have time to consider them in depth before Embla pushed through the double doors of the throne room.

Yawning ceilings stretched above us and ornate tapestries decorated the walls. For the first time, I was really seeing the details of the throne room. The room that housed the one and only true throne in all of Vylheim.

King Drakkar's throne.

I avoided looking in that direction until the warm flush of my skin was no longer visible. Taking slow breaths, I tried to will the heat away as I focused on the rest of the room's features.

Just like last night, the vast space was filled with courtiers and commoners alike. Tables full of soaked breads and hard cheeses, stuck pigs and berries of every color lined one side of the room. On the opposite end sat King Drakkar in his style-less throne, all gaudy bronze with wide armrests and pointed tips at the back twice as tall as the king.

Now that the heat had subsided, I marched directly toward him. I couldn't deny the flutter in my chest as his eyes fell on me. I was here because I wanted answers, not for him to look at me in this damn dress.

My heart skipped at the lie I told myself.

I seethed as the flushed heat slowly simmered again. Later, when I was alone in the bed that nearly swallowed me, I would relieve myself of this tension. Pleasuring myself would surely release this twisted craving and I'd be free of the depraved thoughts for a man I should have let Ragna kill.

King Drakkar turned at my approach, his mouth slicing into a crescent. With the eye patch removed now, his gaze roved over me, pausing too long at my bare collarbone.

His injured eye had entirely healed to its former glory, the color of ice reflecting a clear sky. Those in Mara who practiced salves and the work of healing must have been wildly skilled. He looked as if the witch had never attacked him at all.

When I was within reach, he snaked a thick forearm around my back and hooked me into him. "My wife."

"No." I didn't know why I still denied it. Even after hundreds of congratulations and commoners calling me their queen, this reality hadn't sunk in.

His brows peaked, not unlike when he came for me in Skaldir. Then, I'd run. I didn't feel the need now. If he wanted to kill me, he wouldn't be parading me around as his betrothed.

Hopefully.

"No?" he said.

"We're not married."

"In three days, we will be."

"Three? Approval, appointing, then application?"

He laughed, the sound of it sending ripples through me. "Something like that." With his free hand, he brought a goblet to his lips and tipped it back. The dark liquid stained his teeth red for a moment before his tongue swiped it away. I stared too long at his mouth, perhaps influenced by his behavior already. He really should get his staring problem under control. "It can do more than lick my teeth."

"What?" I blinked at him.

"My tongue, it can do a lot more."

The blush burned across my chest again. The last time I felt a tongue between my legs was more than a year ago. Bjorn was patient, skilled even, but my release had always required more, and more was what King Drakkar had promised.

I bit my lip hard enough to break through this depraved lust. Blinking again, I tipped my chin up. "What is this approval?" I'd start there with my questions. "Isn't it clear your people already see a future in our betrothal?"

Hand still gripping the goblet, he ran his knuckles along my jawline. "Eager to make this official, are we?"

I frowned. At least my face obeyed while my traitorous thoughts dipped into a darker realm. Once we were wed, he'd touch so much more than just my chin. My husband-to-be was just like the warriors in the sagas I craved, skilled with a sword, powerful, dangerous. The kind of man my mind always conjured when I slipped my fingers between my legs.

Strong in both will and form.

I wasn't short like my mother or slim like the women of his court, but he'd just as easily tossed me onto his horse as if I were the weight of the goblet in his hands. How quickly could he throw me on my back? How easily would he flip me so that he could sink his fingers into the softness of my waist as he did during our ride?

"We don't have to be married to do what you're thinking," he said.

I looked away, feigning sudden interest in the courtiers who eyed me. With this blushing distraction, I hadn't even noticed their harsh stares. Each icy glare served me well as it cooled the heat that'd flushed over my skin and built between my legs. Cooling now, the blush faded and King Drakkar would stop guessing at my thoughts.

"You have no idea what I'm thinking." I spoke through a frown.

"That the courtiers don't approve."

I snapped my eyes to him. He'd never taken his gaze off of me.

"You see beyond a person's surface." He said it as if he'd known me for years.

"And?" I challenged him. If he was so skilled at observation, what else had he learned about me? Did he know I wanted to find Ragna and free my mother? That I considered him the key to passing my trial from Freya?

"And that's what makes me fascinated with you."

"You know nothing about me."

He laughed and took another drink, emptying the goblet. When he stretched out his arm, a servant materialized from the dim shadows of the crowds, courtiers talking in muted tones, commoners dancing and eating recklessly.

The young woman did not fill his goblet from the bronze pitcher in her hand. Instead, she took the cup away and reappeared moments later with it full.

"Silver, I think you've forgotten we spent several days in deep conversation. That you slept beside me at the camp, your body curved into mine?"

"For warmth. That is what everybody does during winter travel." It was nothing more than survival.

"It isn't winter yet."

"The early snow begs to differ." I eyed his cup as he brought it to his lips. Not once did he offer it to me. The customs in Mara might be different than Skaldir, but from what I'd heard, it was normal everywhere in Vylheim to pass around drink and share food. "Tell me something I don't know about Mara." This was the most neutral question I could think to ease into my own version of an interrogation. I couldn't very well command him to lay bare secrets he and other kings had kept for a hundred years.

"If you come and sit with me." He slipped his hand into mine and pulled me toward the throne.

"Do you mean, on you?"

He glanced over his shoulder, his grin apparent by the lift at his cheekbone. He dropped my hand and turned, then gripping my waist with both hands, he sat and positioned me in his lap.

"Now look at the people, Silver. What do you notice about them that's different from Skaldir?"

"They're rude."

His laugh rumbled against my back. "That is obvious. I know you see more, dig deeper."

Even though I was a seer, this wasn't how a witch's magic worked. I didn't notice anything about others beyond a basic need for survival. If they weren't a threat, I stopped assessing them.

"The courtiers are cold and the servants act like they're in a trance. People from my village are sharp and full of life." I twisted to face him. Even if he said he valued truth, I wanted to see evidence of this on his face. "Where is Ragna?"

"Ragna?" His eyes were devoid of recognition.

I gritted my teeth. How could he forget her so easily? She'd risked her life to make a statement. Did he already wipe the other witch from his mind too? He hadn't even watched her execution.

"The woman you ripped from her home in Skaldir. She has a daughter named Alva and a newborn son and a husband, Rolf, and several other children along with a farm."

He shook his head and I scoffed. I shoved off of him but he hooked his arm around my middle and pulled me back down.

I nearly bit my tongue to keep from cursing at him. "The women you hunt down and drag away from their villages, have they already been shipped off to be forgotten in the wasteland until they die at sea for your exploration?"

"Ah." He smiled. "That Ragna. She is safe and taken care of. I can assure you, she is not exiled, nor part of this exploration."

"I don't believe you."

"I don't lie."

I chewed at my lip. Maybe I did believe him. He was so different from me, and I was the one who lied, often. Everyday, I lied about my true name.

What about King Drakkar made me believe him? Was it

that he mentioned the monsters? Or that he had no reason to lie? He was the king, untouchable, whether he created false truths or not.

He cleared his throat. "Also, that is not my exploration. It's the council's plan."

"To rebuild our population. Or do *they* lie?"

Another noise came from this throat. "Definitely. But that one is actually the truth and I can't deny they're right about this one thing. One." He laughed without joy.

In roughly five weeks, all the exiled witches would be sent to a watery grave, but my mother didn't even have that long.

"Where are the runestones?" I asked, emboldened by need.

"You have three nights until we're married, Silver. You must be patient. Then, and only then will you share in every truth that I have to offer."

I frowned. It was a bold question, stupid to throw out there so flippantly. Perhaps if I gave him more of myself, he'd open up. "Then I expect to see them. I like history."

"Because you're smart."

My lips parted, his compliment throwing a curve into my thoughts. I blinked and continued. "I know it's wrong to say, but I'm...intrigued by the ancient warriors."

His gaze sliced to me. The icy color of his eyes reflected brighter from the matching shade of my dress. "I should have guessed." His voice was lower now, heavy with heat. "That's why you look so thirsty when your eyes are on me."

It didn't matter how much I tried to hide, King Drakkar somehow always saw through me as if I was still wearing that stupid transparent nightgown. Talking around the truth was a waste of time with him, so I cut to the questions again. "Why do you carry a sword? Is it true that you cut down defected executioners yourself?"

"Yes."

"Are you skilled with it or do you only use it on such rare occasions?"

"A traitorous Grimward member isn't as uncommon as you think, and if you're looking for more to lust after, I'd be happy to show you my skill with a weapon." He winked and my heart skipped. This was the answer I needed. It was the only lawful and possible way I saw to get him to bleed. Then he'd be at his most vulnerable and I could pry the real answers out of him.

That was Freya's promise.

"Now?" I prodded.

"Another time. I only practice on an empty stomach and when I want to exhaust my body for sleep."

Shit. If my calculations were correct, my mother would only survive the wasteland for a couple more weeks. She likely required fresh water, and the substantial food that only a prosperous land could offer.

Two weeks to pass the trial.

Freya wanted me to understand her but I had to do her bidding to comprehend the way of a God. Only then would it be clear.

"You never lie, right?" I asked without waiting for a response. "So tell me, if the guard you practice with cuts you, is he held to the standard of the law of Vylheim?"

King Drakkar ran his teeth over his bottom lip. "I want to say they can never get past my sword, but I do value the truth."

He left it at that, but I didn't. This was enough proof that I had to watch one of those practice sessions, and witness the sight of his blood hitting the ground.

I wasn't going to wait for another time. It had to be now.

So when the celebration ended and the king retired, I followed him, because he hadn't eaten a damn thing all night.

CHAPTER THIRTEEN

A fter years of watching shadows trail me from a distance, I embodied their behavior. Or perhaps I already knew the skills of invisibility after a lifetime of hiding.

A shudder vibrated through me as I stepped into the chill of the drafty hall. All the warmth of the celebration faded away. Soon, my fingers would be as blue as Rolf's balls again.

A smirk lifted my lips for a moment before my heart sank. I had no idea where Ragna was now, or if she was okay.

I spotted King Drakkar's cape trailing behind him. Now that I saw it from a distance, the designs woven into it matched the shape of Vylheim. At least I think it was Vylheim. The fabric splayed out behind him as he marched around the corner.

I crept forward as he ducked beyond a nearby door. When the door clicked shut, I sidled up in front of it and pressed my ear to the wood. The clop of his boots stopped.

After several minutes, I dared to crack it open and peer around the room. Only silence greeted me.

I slipped inside to find a simple bedchamber, not the armory I expected. I suppose a room full of weapons only existed in the past, but it likely had a place in Mara's Keep. Where else did the Grimward, the appointed guards, and the king secure their swords and axes?

The room was a mirror of the one I'd been given though much smaller. The oversized bed at the center swallowed most of the space. A fireplace covered one wall and a cabinet crowded the opposite wall. The flicker of flames matched the sound I'd woken up to.

King Drakkar was nowhere to be seen, and there were no exits. That I could see.

Like the hidden hatch beneath my childhood bed, a crawl-space or hidden door might lead beyond the room. I checked the floor under the four poster first. Deeming it solid stone, I stood and marched to the cabinet. I swung the two doors open wide to find nothing more than a musty, empty space. After slamming them shut, I ran my hands along the walls to determine if they were as solid as the floor.

The stone rubbed rough against my palm. I circled the room and stopped at the large mantel. The fireplace was the only place I had not checked, but he would have to be a God to walk through the flames.

Unless I was missing something.

Crouching in front of the fire, I relished the heat, wanting to pause to warm my fingers over the flames. They'd turned blue again after King Drakkar let go of my hands.

From this angle, the back of the fireplace looked deeper. Rather than a shallow indent and then an upward tunnel for the smoke to travel, this fireplace stretched into chalky blackness. Like a tunnel.

Impossible.

Not even kings walked through fire without getting burned. Unless he lit it after passing through.

From the other side of the door, footsteps stomped. The rhythmic march grew closer and closer, and my heart matched the thumping.

I ducked from the fire and into a hiding place I knew too well. Slipping beneath the bed, I pressed close to the cold stone and watched the door swing open.

Heavy boots stormed past the bed. The gray leather marked him as one of the king's guards. The tip of the sword's sheath hung low at his leg.

This had to be the place I was looking for. Satisfaction curled at my lips. I'd been right about King Drakkar's plans before dawn; sparring.

When the guard stooped, I inched closer toward the wall. Holding my breath proved impossible with my hammering heart. I sucked in air in small intervals to keep from gasping desperately.

After a moment, water splashed over the flames, dousing the fire to mere embers. He stepped into the fireplace and his boots quickly disappeared into the darkness. When his footsteps faded to a distant thud, I dragged a gulp of air into my tight chest, and crawled out from beneath the bed.

I hurried to the fireplace, and, stepping inside, left the small bedchambers behind. Darkness stretched out before me so I was forced to follow by sound.

I quietly tracked the echo of his steps, carefully listening for every hint of change in the sound of his footfall.

Deeper inside the yawning tunnel, a faint flicker of candlelight beckoned me along. Only occasionally did I pass a candle left on the floor in a bronze holder, but each time it was a relief from the abyss of black.

Eventually, the tunnel broke off into several other hallways, but if I followed the sound of footsteps, I wouldn't get lost.

I committed each turn to memory. Right, right, right again. The floor sloped downward, inviting me lower and lower under the ground. I paused at a fork in the hall and listened carefully. Closing my eyes, I noted the clop of his feet coming from a slight left. My eyes popped open and I ducked to the left pathway.

The maze grew narrower and darker as I came to the top of a staircase.

Steps vanished down into more inky black where the path descended to the depths of Mara's Keep. If there was anywhere to hide weapons or the history the kings of the past didn't want us to know, it was down there.

When the echo of his footsteps faded completely, I had to force myself further into the darkness. I placed a hand on the wall to steady myself. The steps were thin and dropped rapidly, the walls narrow like a tomb encasing me.

In the sagas, only people who died dishonorably were buried in tombs. Those who lost their lives in battle, with a weapon still in their hand, were placed on a pyre and burned so their spirit was released where it could ascend to meet the Valkyries halfway to their descent. This gave them priority for Valhalla.

I recounted bits of history as I dropped deeper and deeper into the bowels of Mara's Keep to keep my mind from spiraling.

Suddenly I could hear the clash of metal on metal ringing up from below, and excitement prickled through me.

When the narrow stairs flattened out and the walls expanded wider, I smashed myself against one side of the stone.

The steps opened into a full armory with an open floor in the center. Racks of swords and axes lined the walls, their shine glinting faintly in the candlelight. Dozens of candles were propped on the shelves set between each rack. Scratches marred the edge of the axes, but most of the swords were smooth, pristine, maybe never used at all.

King Drakkar wielded a sword with a charcoal black hilt topped with a shimmering bronze pommel. A shape I wasn't close enough to identify was carved into the pommel.

When the guard lunged for King Drakkar, I held my breath. The tip of the guard's sword nearly slashed the king's arm, but he swung his arm away with blinding speed. He slammed the base of the blade against the same spot on his opponent's sword, and the hilts crossed.

King Drakkar shoved him back. The guard stumbled but quickly recovered, ducking to pierce the king low on his torso.

In the dry air, my breath came in shallow gulps as I pressed into the wall and kept to the shadow of the stairs.

The king easily side-stepped each angle of the guard's blade but it did not discourage his opponent. The guard was relentless, swinging, and then clashing. When their blades met, he used his weight to shove against King Drakkar, though it did not have the same effect it had when King Drakkar did it to him.

Each time the guard thrust, swung, or slashed, the king bested him.

I bit my lip, watching sweat gather across King Drakkar's forehead. Though this sparring was mere practice, he did not hold back. Slamming the blades together, he continued pushing the guard back, back, back toward the opposite wall.

King Drakkar was closer to a true warrior than any man I'd ever seen. I slid my eyes shut for a moment, committing the sight of him with the sword in his hand to memory. A slight ache burned low in my belly. The hours I'd spent dreaming of the men described in the sagas put me in trouble now.

Now I didn't have to imagine them.

Their dueling quickened with their breaths. They clashed again and again and again, and every time the guard came close to slicing the blade into the king's skin, I ceased breathing.

When the sparring suddenly stopped, the king marched toward the stairs. I flattened to the wall, my heart nearly slamming against the stone through my spine.

What would he do to me if he knew I'd followed him? What would he do to the guard who led me here? King Drakkar was discreet in his escape to the armory. As diligent as I was in following his every step, I wouldn't have found the armory if it wasn't for the guard.

"I'm starving." Came the king's voice. The guard grunted in response. "We'll resume this tomorrow before dawn."

The sparring had ended and the result yielded no blood. If only the guard's skills were sharper, this would have been worth it. Now, I was deep in a maze of tunnels beneath the castle with the king heading my direction.

I slipped up two steps as quietly as possible, but when King Drakkar's footsteps grew quieter, I paused and stuck my neck out just enough to see him swipe a linen cloth over the glinting blade.

His hands shook from muscle strain and lack of food. If he was careless, he might nick his finger.

But he didn't.

His gaze snapped up, and I swallowed a gasp. His eyes sliced to the guard who stepped in front of him and headed for the steps. To my relief, the guard had stopped walking to face his king.

"Be sure this week's vessel is ready for me," King Drakkar said. His icy eyes flashed red and my pulse skipped. When he spoke again, the tips of his teeth caught the glow of the candles. They stretched long, jutting out of his mouth as if they'd grown several inches in the blink of an eye. The ends were pointed, unlike his row of perfect teeth behind it. "I need fresh food."

I squinted, brows furrowed to narrow in on what I was seeing. Fangs were only for wolves, serpents, wild boars, and the undead. This couldn't be real.

Now I sounded like my father.

Draugr, or the undead people, tore the living apart, eating them like a wild animal would. At least that was what we suspected based on the poetic language of the only saga to mention such creatures. My mother believed they ate their prey's flesh, but Ragna had said she thought Draugr siphoned their existence simply from the joy of killing the living. A living being's breath was offensive to the undead. We believed the Undead, like all other monsters, once bled over from the other realms relative to Midgard.

I didn't have time to consider the reality of what I saw or the implications of my reaction. After the guard responded with a curt nod, he marched forward and straight toward me.

I spun and darted up the staircase as quickly and as quietly as possible. Following the directions in reverse, I went left three times, counting how many halls it broke off into to be sure I turned down the right one.

Ahead, I spied the light of the candles in the bedchamber. Tracking my way back was easier than I thought. Perhaps King Drakkar was right about my skill with observation, though this, too, was tied to my survival—or rather, my mother's.

Footsteps echoed in my wake. I was already breathless, but I shuffled faster, careful to keep my feet low and quiet against the stone.

The guard must have been in a hurry to end his night. Each heavy footfall gained on me. If he turned the corner, he'd see me. I broke into a desperate run for the mantle when a hand hooked around my arm.

Another hand slapped over my mouth before shock had me crying out. The shadow pulled me into the darkness of another, narrower hall just behind the fireplace.

My heart slammed thrashed against my ribcage as I squirmed to free myself, but my captor merely hushed me and tightened their hold. Their voice was low, belonging to a man, and barely audible at the edge of my ear as he tried to shush me.

The guard marched past, ducking through the fireplace.

I quietly squirmed against my captor, but his hold grew firmer and firmer with every muscle I flexed. Panic gripped my throat and I suddenly couldn't draw enough breath through my nose. His fingers dug into my cheeks until I couldn't so much as part my lips.

Had King Drakkar seen me? Did he take a quicker path to beat me to the exit?

Those fangs flashed in my mind.

Every story my mother told resurfaced. Draugr dragged their victims into the privacy of the shadows where they ripped off their flesh. Ragna's theories were worse. Images of the king tearing me to shreds just for the sheer entertainment of it clouded my mind. I refused to believe the latter, but my resolve did nothing to comfort me.

I'm starving.

A shiver rippled through me.

His eyes had turned red, just like the Draugr, like my shadows. I'd never heard of red eyes on the undead before, my mother claimed they didn't have eyes, just open sockets of sinew and hollow bone, but the sagas didn't confirm this. King Drakkar had both the fangs of the undead and the eyes of the figures who'd lurked at my heels.

They were one in the same—a king, my shadow, an undead monster—and he'd finally dragged me into the shadows to devour me.

Chapter Fourteen

Once the door to the bedchamber slammed shut behind the guard, my captor finally spoke.

"Don't scream." His whisper was a mere suggestion of voice, so low and quiet I would have thought him a ghost.

This wasn't how King Drakkar said his commands. His bold, unbothered nature never broke. Even his whispers were rough, and his beard scratched against my throat when he spoke into my ear.

The one who'd dragged me into the shadows carried none of this same energy.

Before he released me and spun me around, his hands forcing my shoulders toward him, I knew I'd been wrong. This wasn't the king.

I swept my gaze over him in the dim light, scouring for anything recognizable. Based on the green cloak, this was the same red-eyed man who'd tried to stop me from entering the throne room when I'd first arrived in Mara.

Curiosity mingled with fear, and rippled through me with the prickle of goosebumps.

The man's wheat hair was cropped short with the swoop

of a wave that hung down over one side of his forehead. Unlike the king, his facial hair was close to the skin, shadowy but without a true beard.

His eyes were nearly as dark as mine, two brown abysses beneath the sunny hair that didn't match the grave demeanor of his furrowed brow and the ragged scar that went from his eyebrow into his hair. The scarred skin cut through his cropped style like a sideways lightning bolt.

He was shockingly handsome for a man who crept through the shadows. If he hadn't dragged me into the darkness, my heart would be skipping for an entirely different reason.

"I won't hurt you," he breathed.

Astrid had said nearly those exact same words when she sank her fingernails into me and then threatened to taste my blood. Both she and Sten spoke about me like I was a tool or toy to be used, and then when I tried to run, they were faster. When I pulled away, they were stronger.

Icy fear melted into fervent anger. No stranger, no shadow, was ever going to grab me again.

I shoved my elbow into him, but the effort did nothing to move him. "Get away from me," I spat. "I am King Drakkar's."

My stomach roiled, resisting the words I'd forced out to deter this man.

"Not yet. He can't find out about this, Silver." His eyes flashed red in the dim light from the candles in the room beyond.

I opened my mouth to ask how he knew my name but the gold that followed the red in his eyes swept my breath away. He stared at me hungrily. A sudden echoing clank of metal and heavy footsteps triggered him.

With inhuman speed, his arms were a blur as he dragged me further into the black. This confirmed it, he had to be like one of my monsters. I hadn't imagined the rapid, impossible movements of Astrid and Sten, nor their strange eyes.

And if he dug his fingers into me like Astrid had, I'd have to fight my way free of him. Asking what he wanted from me was a waste of time. Both Astrid and Sten had refused to give me anything other than threats.

Whoever they had been, whoever he was, they all just wanted to use me.

"You have to come with me," he said.

I will taste your blood until you're nothing but a lifeless human husk. The memory of Astrid's words descended on me like icy ghosts coming to reclaim me. I'd buried their voices only for them to break free again, but with a new understanding.

Eating a human was something only a monster would say.

Astrid and Sten were not just courtiers. Full understanding finally dawned as the image of King Drakkar's fangs crowded my mind.

"You're all Draugr," I breathed.

My pulse raced with a sudden and guttural fear. I had to gulp each following breath as questions seized control of my mind. How many undead crawled through the court at Mara's Keep? How many craved to gut me? Was this why Embla returned my Y Tree?

And King Drakkar...I truly was engaged to marry a monster.

"Yes, that's why I need you—"

I scoffed. Fury stoked higher in my throat and I tried to yank away from him. His grip wasn't vicious like Astrid's, and I pulled free.

With my free hand, I reached for the top of the Y Tree tucked into my braid. It slid out, tugging tendrils loose from the weave of hair.

With him caught off guard, I managed to slash the tip of the Y across his arm as he threw his hand out to grab me again. He immediately dropped back, hissing.

The king's heavy footsteps echoed from below, and the man made no move to step from the shadows. I took the opportunity and threw myself from his reach, running for the fireplace before King Drakkar emerged. I prayed to Odin for the knowledge of what would keep me safe in Mara's Keep.

The bedchamber was as devoid of life as it'd been when I first slipped inside. I dashed to the door and shoved through. Bursting into the hall, I broke into another weak run. If the Draugr was trailing me, he'd catch up within a single heartbeat.

I glanced over my shoulder but nobody was there. My captor had been cowed by the mere presence of King Drakkar. This would comfort me if the king didn't have those same red eyes, and fangs like a wild beast.

For now, the king's unintentional protection served me well.

I slipped around the corner and forced myself faster. My muscles were already racing with my heart to be the first to threaten to give out. Erratic beats left me dizzy and unsteady on my feet. I needed to find my bedchambers before I collapsed.

I'm starving.

Come with me.

Did every corner at Mara's Keep present a threat? Was every courtier hungry for the taste of human flesh? For our blood?

The blood.

Freya's vision.

Suddenly, the gray hallway was swept away and a new vision enveloped me.

A woman stood before me, her golden hair tumbling over her shoulders in loose waves. Her pink lips parted. An ethereal voice came from all around us but it didn't seem to be hers and her lips didn't move.

I felt rather than heard the words, though I knew these

didn't come from Freya. The presence was a stark contrast from the feminine energy displayed by the woman before me. This was a man speaking.

"Cast off this colorless cage.

Let them think you're a coward, then rise stronger."

The woman reached out, something clunky and rough materialized in her hand. Like a small wooden sword, she held the tip pointed at me. Instinctively, I reached for it, only for her to snatch it away again.

A woman's voice breathed into my ear. *"It isn't Loki's time."*

The vision cut away with a sharp bolt of pain through my temples.

I came to my surroundings still in a world of stone. A woman had her arm crooked under both of mine as she helped me straighten. Bright hair framed her face. I squinted at her, trying to identify if she was the same woman from the vision, but it was already too foggy, like a distant dream after a rough night of sleep.

This woman guiding me around a corner was even more familiar than the person in Freya's vision.

She had that same golden hair in full waves like a mane, encompassing her slim body. Compared to many of the pale, entranced servants, her shapely lips and the round apples of her cheeks were a healthy pink.

If I believed in the angels of our ancestors' neighbors, I would have believed she was one of them.

CHAPTER FIFTEEN

I limped down the hall with the angelic woman's help. Staring at her, I tried to match her pace, but my body was having none of it.

Somewhere behind us, I was sure King Drakkar and the cloaked man were pursuing me. Though if they were, they'd already be upon us. Even with her hurrying and dragging me along, we wouldn't be fast enough to run from monsters.

"Walk quicker, my queen," she said. I slowed her down, and maybe made her one of their targets by proximity. Still, she walked with me, keeping me upright with a wiry strength not unlike Ragna's. "It isn't safe to roam the halls near dawn."

"Where's Embla? Are you my other handmaiden?"

Suddenly her pinched face and formal posturing vanished. Her brows furrowed and she let out a breath, slightly slumping forward. "Yes, clearly I'm your handmaiden. Why else would I be dragging you along like a sack of flour?"

"Because you're kind?" I muttered, still in a daze from the vision and the thought of her as an ethereal being.

She snorted. "Kind? Kind of a genius, actually."

I only blinked at her. My mind was too muddled from the vision, exhaustion, and the chaos of the last hour.

"And for your information," she said, all politeness now gone from her tone. "Embla is merely a Lady's Maid."

Before we turned another corner, I twisted to catch a glance of the hall behind us. My captor did not lurk our way, and neither was King Drakkar anywhere in sight.

Another servant passed across the end of the hall then vanished into a room.

Finally, we arrived in the same room I'd left so many hours ago. My original dress was clean and dry, hanging from a hook on the ornate cabinet. My handmaiden helped me climb into the high bed where I gently rolled and collapsed on my back.

Staring up at the ceiling, all I wanted was to slide my eyelids shut and sleep for days, but with every minute lost my mother was slipping away.

I turned my head to see my handmaiden pouring water from a pitcher. "Thank you," I said as she placed a full cup beside the bed on a narrow table with spindly legs. "Why did you say that, about the danger of being in the halls near dawn?"

Would she admit Mara's Keep was crawling with monsters? Did she know? I really needed to know if it was safe here in my room, or if it was as dangerous as the halls.. Not that I was going to venture out without resting, I would always listen to my body. If I pushed it to the edge, I would take care of it after.

"Because I can't let you get hurt," she said.

"Did King Drakkar assign you to protect me?"

Another snort. "Sure."

"And who protects the king?" I asked. Her brows scrunched. "I mean, if he were to slip up and get hurt, who helps him?"

"Are you referring to when his eye was wounded? Don't worry it has fully healed. You won't have a one-eyed husband." Judgment twisted her voice.

"I know it's healed, I've seen it. That's not—" I sighed.

She folded her arms and popped out her left foot. With a single brow arched, she eyed me. "Why are you asking?"

There was no easy way to form the slew of questions into words. If the mention of blood in the first vision was the king's blood, or the blood of one of his victims, it wasn't clear.

But I couldn't outwardly ask if the king and his courtiers were monsters. I'd out myself as a believer. And if the people turned on me, would the king?

My execution had been pardoned by him and only him. Now I'd found my way inside the castle that housed the rune-stones with the key to my mother's freedom. I couldn't throw it all away.

Blinking, my gaze slid from the dress hanging behind her back to her forest green eyes. "I need to know if he is safe, and if you think he is ever in any danger, would you tell me? Please?"

She clucked her tongue and dropped her arms. "King Drakkar is extremely powerful, but I've seen him argue with Ylva and Darius before."

Since she answered every question I'd thrown at her, I wanted to keep asking. "Have you heard of the lost history?"

She thought about this for a moment. "Maybe."

"Stories from our ancient ancestors to the wasteland war. My mother—" I stopped and swallowed my words. Nobody needed to know about her visions. "I've heard there are missing runestones hidden in Mara's Keep."

"There's a lot hidden in Mara's Keep. But if it's not in the kitchens, your bedchambers, the servants quarters, or visible from the windows, I can't help you. I'm sorry."

I nodded, sobering to the fact that even someone who'd lived in this castle for years didn't know how to find the runestones.

"Now," she continued, "you need to rest. The king says

you tire quickly and you get cold easily." She pointed to the fire. "I'll return in a few hours to keep it burning."

Without letting me speak, she swiftly marched to the door. I propped myself up on my elbows, though even that made me breathless.

"Am I safe here?"

She paused and turned at the door. The thick hem at the bottom of her skirts swished at her ankles. The pale green brought out the forest in her eyes. "You're the king's betrothed. Only someone stupid enough to sacrifice their life would dare harm you."

I swallowed through my dry throat. Would the man in the tunnels pay for what he'd done? Had King Drakkar spotted him in the darkness? They were both monsters. I had no idea how monsters treated one another, only that they'd left me as curious as I was unsettled.

Flashing red eyes would no doubt appear in my nightmares once I slipped into an uncomfortable unconsciousness.

"And what about the king, am I safe from him?"

Her pale lashes fluttered as she considered this. Finally, she shook her head. "Nobody is truly safe here. But escape is never entirely impossible. Even a bird with clipped wings can escape its cage."

Cast off this colorless cage.

My handmaiden didn't match the masculine energy that came with the vision, but her words struck me as oddly familiar.

With that she twisted the doorknob and swung it open.

"Wait," I nearly shouted before the heavy door fell shut. "It's shameful, but I was too drunk to remember your name."

Her arm shot out to stop the door, and her pink lips pursed in a playful smirk. "Shameful? No. Was it stupid not to drink water and eat plenty of food to soak up the wine? Absolutely. Next time you drink, I'm shoving bread down your throat. Then maybe you'll remember, I'm Stasia."

Stasia, nearly the same name as my mother's. Though her full name was Anastasia, she went by Anya to those who did not call her Mother.

When the door eased shut behind her, I lay back on the pillowy bed and pulled the blanket to my collarbone. Despite the all-consuming exhaustion weighing heavy on my eyes, I kept them peeled open so that I would not fall asleep.

The second vision told me to leave Mara's Keep. If the male voice belonged to Loki, I didn't know if I could trust it. He was the trickster God, the one who was always playing an angle that often got Odin and Freya, Thor and the others into trouble with the giants or the dwarves of the other realms.

I couldn't leave until I found the answers Freya promised me. I had a trial to pass before I could understand it all, and tonight led me a step closer to that understanding which meant Freya's guidance had proved perfect.

From tracking King Drakkar I learned it wasn't his blood that I would follow. Rarely would a king—or anyone in Vylheim—bleed unless they were involved in an accident. I didn't have to wait around for the king to slip up and the guard to slash him.

The blood he left behind was likely from his victims, whether he devoured their flesh and tasted their blood, or he simply ripped them to shreds and absorbed their life to continue his existence. Could this be when he was most vulnerable?

His claim rolled over in my head. He'd said he was starving. Even humans grow weak and touchy when they haven't eaten. For a monster, I could only imagine this was magnified, because the sagas hinted that the undead were never satiated. Never truly alive. Never fully dead.

I already knew the time to track him down. He fed just before dawn, confirmed by Stasia's warning.

Now I needed to know which shadows King Drakkar dragged his prey into to feed on them.

None of it completed a coherent picture. How would the king's appetite for human flesh give me the runestone that proved witches didn't deserve exile?

I could turn this question on every side. I could mull on it for hours and still come to no conclusion other than that I had to trust the vision.

Seers trusted their visions; they trusted themselves. But I'd been lying to myself for my entire life…

I shook that off and squeezed my eyes shut. That didn't matter right now. I only needed to focus on one thing; where the undead king killed his victims.

Chapter Sixteen

The stress of sneaking and running left me bed bound for too many hours. Laying awake, staring at the ceiling, wondering if King Drakkar, or my captor, or any number of Draugr would come to devour me.

Stasia's sack of flour reference was more than accurate. My legs swelled to puffy tree trunks and weighed about as much. Even rolling over left me breathless and my pulse racing.

I was used to my body shutting down, but not while surrounded by monsters.

If nothing else, the hours gave me enough time to think, and since I had plenty of information to mull over, I skirted on the edge of nerves, never sinking into a spiral of dwelling.

Astrid and Sten were undead which meant I couldn't have killed them, and yet, they'd collapsed with unblinking eyes. The only explanation I came to relied on the silver, though I never thought the Y Tree was truly silver since pure metals were unheard of across Vylheim. True silver and gold were said to be cursed, weapons against Draugr, but the only saga to mention the undead was also part of the history that'd been lost. We didn't have the details about what it meant to wield a weapon against a creature that was neither alive nor dead.

I decided that though they were undead, it was thanks to the purity of the Y Tree that I destroyed them. It was the only thing that made sense.

That left me with one impossible question. Why had King Drakkar allowed me to keep it?

This catapulted me into a hundred other thoughts that needed answers. I had no clue what an undead king would want with a human bride, or how these creatures came to be on the throne, courtiers, and members of the king's council. I'd sensed a threat in the cold stares of the courtiers, but I never expected soulless monsters.

At least one question was answered.

Now I knew why the shadows followed me. They wanted to tear me apart and use my life to fuel their existence, though that didn't explain why they'd only lurked at *my* heels. What about the thousands of other lives in Vylheim from which to draw life?

A shudder cut through me. I didn't wish this curse on anyone else. I didn't. Truly, I wasn't that selfish.

Evil.

Selfish.

Ugh!

The door creaked open and my heart caught in my throat. I rolled my head to the side—without getting dizzy. I didn't breathe until Stasia's cherub face appeared. Sliding my eyes shut for a moment, I exhaled as slowly as possible to stop my pulse from running away.

The thumping in my chest slowed to an off-rhythm ticking.

As Stasia bustled about the room, carrying a new deep magenta dress, and a cup of fresh water, I tested my recovery by lifting my heavy arm. When the effort didn't send my heart hammering again or sweep my breath away, I dragged my legs to the edge of the bed and sat up.

"Finally," I whispered.

"Seriously," she said, shaking her head. She set the cup down on the table beside my bed then spun and hung the dress over the cabinet next to my original clothing. "You've been drifting in and out of consciousness for hours, but I couldn't find a single bite on you. Also, my concoction of nettle, dandelion, and dark greens in broth barely helped, which really threw me. Usually that works. Trust me when I say I know my food."

I blinked at her. "A bite?" The Draugr had not sunk their teeth into me, yet. "From what?" I shook my head. "Wait, when did I eat?"

"Like I said, you were really out of it." She spoke as she smoothed out the bottom of the new dress. The lace beneath the overlay of silky fabric didn't want to lay flat. "I propped your head up and had you take sips whenever you were half awake."

Pieces of these memories resurfaced. I'd even tried to push Stasia away because I was too tired to take the broth, but I didn't have enough strength to do more than lay my hand on her arm.

The stress of getting caught, the capture, the running, it'd all stripped me down to nothing but heavy bones. My muscles were useless and my heart protested everything that wasn't the mere task of keeping me alive.

"Why did you mention looking for a bite on me?" I asked again.

Stasia spun around and motioned for me to stand. Her pursed lips gave no indication that she was shocked by this question.

I slid off the bed and eased up to my full height. Moving too quickly would bring back my dizziness and I didn't know if my shaking legs would steady me enough to walk, much less stand. But I stayed upright and my head remained stable.

"Stasia?" I prodded as I met her gaze, now level with her eyes.

She sighed. "We don't usually mention it directly, of course."

"The Draugr?" I dared. I didn't know Stasia. I couldn't even recall her name correctly before last night, but something about her kind face and the way she spoke so bluntly beckoned me to be straight with her.

Besides, time was cut shorter and shorter the longer I danced around the truth. I was sick of lying and hiding and if the king would have my head for mentioning monsters that weren't supposed to exist, he'd already have killed me.

She clucked her tongue. "Gutsy lady, I admire that. I'm more of a gut lady, myself. By that I mean, most of the time I'm thinking about what will go next into my gut. Tea, soaked bread. Ooh, or the thick crunchy crust when a round of sour bread is baked a little too long? I die for that. Honestly, I probably will be the first to die with this famine coming——"

"Stasia," I snapped. She was clearly avoiding the question, and the truth, but her presence set me at ease enough to push for answers. The answers seemed right there, on the edge of her tongue, even though she kept changing the subject back to food. Tired of dancing around the secrets in Mara's Keep, I pinned her with my gaze. "How can you ramble on about food when we *are* the food in Mara's Keep?"

Unfolding her arms, she laid her hands on my shoulders. I wanted to shrug away when the weight of her grip pulled me back into the moment my captor had grabbed me. Back into the shadows where the wheat-haired man had held me out in front of him.

"My queen, may I offer a suggestion that could help keep your sanity and save your life?" I opened my mouth but she didn't let me respond. Apparently, since I didn't immediately shut her down, she took it as an invitation to explain. "The best food in all of Vylheim is in this very castle. We have the best cooks, the best of every crop, and even we servants eat decently."

"What does that—"

"Shhh." She lazily pressed a finger to my lips and then spun toward the door. Marching toward it, she chattered on. Frustration built within me. My insistence for answers was not breaking through her useless rambling. We were having two different conversations and it was clear that was exactly what Stasia intended. "Listen, if you want to survive among the... non-living, you have to soak up every single tiny moment of satisfaction. And here? That's mostly just food. At least for me. Maybe for you, dancing could be added to that and, well." She stopped with one hand on the door as she pointed at the new dress. "You can delight in dress as well. But the rest of life in Mara's Keep is pain. Screaming. Have you heard the screaming yet? Probably not in this wing."

With that, she disappeared through the door, leaving me with the barest hint of a truth.

Screaming...

So the Draugr devoured their victims right here in the castle, like animals playing a human lifestyle?

To me, it always seemed the damp forest was the most dangerous, or the edge of a gushing fjord, or the thrashing seas. Not a stone palace with sky-pointed spires and throne rooms full of decadently dressed courtiers.

"Stasia?" I called out again. I took a shaky step forward, then decided it was safest to shuffle until the swelling in my legs subsided. Moving would help the blood flow.

I only made it three steps when Stasia shoved back through the door, awkwardly carrying a bucket of sloshing water. Steam drifted up into her face, twisting a few separate tendrils of loose waves into tighter curls. She dumped the water into the stone tub.

"Does everyone here know the king is a monster?" I asked.

She heaved a breath and held up one finger. Returning to the door, she hauled in two more buckets until the tub was full of heated water.

Then she pointed at it. "Let me get the last bucket. Then get in and I'll answer your questions. You're supposed to be at King Drakkar's side before the guests arrive."

"Guests?"

"Your engagement party, of course."

My brows lifted while my shoulders sank. "Another party?" How would I track him if I was with him every night? Waiting until the end of the celebrations proved tricky with how tired and nearly careless I became, and King Drakkar certainly didn't showcase any vulnerabilities while courtiers and council members, commoners and servants, all praised him for his upcoming wedding.

Of course, a king as arrogant and as powerful as Drakkar *never* bore any vulnerabilities. But I was promised that if I followed the blood he left behind, I'd see him at his weakest.

I'd receive answers.

And as close as I'd come to it last night, I hadn't passed Freya's trial. Only when I was granted sight of her beloved cats would I know it'd ended.

Stasia huffed as she poured more steaming water into the tub. I stared at the foaming bubbles at the base of the miniature waterfall, turning over the possibilities in my mind.

The king had been hungry which skirted vulnerability, but Draugr never truly tired. What else would pitch him into vulnerability? The blood trail... If my clues were what he left behind, was his weakest moment when he killed? Or when he fed? Weren't those one in the same?

With Stasia untying the ribbons at the back of the wrinkled dress I'd worn for nearly two days, I slipped free of it.

In the tub, the warm water enveloped me, easing every aching muscle with delicious, steamy comfort.

Stasia picked the weave of my braids apart and then soaked my hair beneath the water. Cupping my head in her hands, she allowed me to fully relax, where I could give my body to the water. As I melted into the warmth, sweat and oil washing away, my mind cleared.

Baths in Skaldir were rarely this soothing. Warm water didn't stay that way long enough to soak.

Fully immersed with my head under the surface, the world around me melted away. Something about the protective water stripped away my senses and swiped away every worry.

Until Stasia lifted my head. My sharp intake of breath after sitting up in the chilled air was too loud, too sudden after having suspended in the quiet beneath the surface.

I peeled my eyes open and sat up. Droplets streamed from my hair down into the rivulets of my ears. I shook my head and twisted to meet Stasia's eyes.

"So the Draugr?" I didn't even form a full sentence because with Stasia's casual way of speaking, our conversation felt as familiar as if I were joking with Ragna about Rolf's balls.

"Vampire," she said.

"What?"

"Draugr is a witch's term. Vampire is their chosen title."

I opened my mouth but didn't have a response among my scattered thoughts. Clearly, Stasia knew more about them than I did. My heart lifted and every bit of energy that'd been stolen from me slowly buzzed back into my veins.

I straightened and squeezed the water from my hair.

"Tell me, do these vampires eat human flesh to survive? Or do they just get life from the entertainment of brutality?"

She smirked. "Ah, the speculations are wilder and wilder every time I hear them. But I guess I wouldn't say they're wrong."

"So, they're true?"

She shrugged and tucked her hair behind her ear before helping me out of the tub. The smooth stone was as slippery when wet as it was relentlessly cold. "Most of the courtiers prefer a cleaner way of eating. They simply draw the blood from your veins until they've had their fill. But I won't say some don't get messy with their food."

"How can you talk so casually about it?"

Tapping her skull, she forced an odd smile. "Sanity, remember? Plus, I've served here for seven years, since I was fifteen. It's part of my everyday life. For now."

"How many of them are there?"

"In Mara's Keep? One hundred and nine vampires."

My chest sank and breath caught in my throat. I tried to swallow but my mouth was too dry. Speaking through it felt like my tongue had transformed into cotton. "So every courtier…"

"Is a vampire." She nodded. "Hey, look at you, New Queen is getting it all pieced together. You're observant. It takes some of the newer servants years. Though most of them are fed on and you forget things when you're missing so much blood, you know. Plus, vampires have a way of making their vessels confused so they don't talk about it. Nobody beyond Mara's Keep knows, unless they're vampires or part of the Grimward. Vessels eventually waste away, but before that they're too…" she paused and snapped her fingers. "What's the word for feeling lost but like you were just hit over the head with a wooden spoon?"

"Dazed?"

"That's it! Enchanted, dazed, in a trance."

I frowned. Was Embla a vessel? Her pale face and gaped mouth suggested the worst. Who fed on her? If it was King Drakkar, I could both save her and get access to the rune-stones when I found him in his moment of vulnerability. But he'd shown obvious interest in the servant who always filled his goblets.

"Does every vampire drink from... a specific vessel?" I asked. The word tasted bitter. Calling a human a vessel felt akin to Astrid's threat of making me a lifeless husk. The servant he'd claimed I was jealous of had a name. Thora was more than a vessel.

Tilting her head side-to-side, Stasia's spiral tendrils danced over her face. "More or less. Most vampires have their favorites, but if they get hungry enough they'll feed on almost anyone nearby. They have to let their vessels recover, or eventually they'll run out of options, and vampires like their options. Kind of like us, we don't want to eat the same food for every breakfast, midday, and supper."

"Have you been fed on?"

She nodded as she retrieved the new dress. The magenta silk puddled on the floor when she dipped it low enough for me to step into. Pulling the sleeves up, she draped them just below my shoulders.

The combination of silk and lace made for an odd but extravagant look. Black lace sleeves hung off my shoulders, baring all of my collarbone and an expanse of my chest. When Stasia slipped behind me to tighten the ribbons of the corset, my breasts lifted, but were still gratefully covered. The more skin I showed, the more it felt these vampires would want to bite into me.

I didn't know if I would get used to this style of clothing. Animal bones kept the corset's shape and the ribbons were pulled so tightly, I barely breathed. The people of Vylheim had no use for such inefficient and uncomfortable dressings, but the courtiers all wore it, so as a part of Mara's Keep now, I had no choice.

Stasia finished off the ribbons with a small bow at the top of the corset.

"So you've been fed on, but you're not in a daze, why?" I asked, hoping it wasn't too rude.

"I'm not a vessel anymore."

"At the risk of sounding like a child," I said. "Why?"

She laughed and shook her head. "It's complicated. Let's just say, if the fish you dined on could become a human if you enjoyed it a little too much, then you'd probably stop eating from it."

At that, words escaped me.

I let her chatter away about the food that'd be at the engagement celebration. Roast duck, milky eggs, dates wrapped in charred pig, cinnamon apples, cinnamon pears, and cinnamon almonds. She gushed over the selection of drinks as well, honeyed mead, ale, spiced wine, and mint tea, and as she claimed, it did lift my spirits to focus on the food.

"Do the servants eat as well as the guests?"

She snorted. "Yep. Vampires hardly eat at all, only for taste occasionally, and they want their vessels healthy. Ylva has even said humans have flavor based on what we eat the most. So I like to imagine I taste like bread soaked in melted butter and dusted with cinnamon. Obviously, the cinnamon-everything was my genius idea. Before you arrived, I was a cook, and when you're sleeping your life away, I go back to irritating the current cooks. I'm going to miss it." A little laugh escaped her.

Stasia's enjoyment spread like a contagion, and for the first time since coming to Mara's Keep, I smiled. Smelling of rosemary soap instead of sweat helped. I suddenly couldn't wait for the party, the food, and to track King Drakkar.

Now I knew exactly where the blood came from—his vessel.

All I had to do was find Thora. I'd follow him to wherever he fed on her, then I'd demand to know where he kept the lost history. Though they were all vampires, monsters, and would surely deny it, I still refused to be discouraged.

Freya said these trials would spare the witches, and that was all I needed to know.

That and exactly what she wanted me to do. Follow the damn blood. I'd repeated this to myself enough times that it should become a reality now. And it would, soon.

Once I received a visit from Freya's cats, the first trial would be over and I'd be closer to saving my mother. To sparing Ragna and the other exiled witches from death at sea.

Chapter Seventeen

Lively music and the warm scent of honeyed mead greeted me upon stepping into the throne room. Commoners danced, their ignorance a type of wild bliss.

North of Mara, winter already raged. Here, they still enjoyed flourishing crops late into autumn, but Mara couldn't sustain all of Vylheim. How long until starving villagers from Stormdal, Torsholt, Einnland, Daganfold, Myrr, and Skaldir flooded Mara? How long until their bliss ended in a desperate war over food and warmth?

The Dawn of the Exploration Age was supposed to solve this problem, but it'd only send thousands of people to their deaths when witches, like my mother, could yield successful crops if they weren't bound to hiding or exiled to the wasteland.

For some reason these vampires didn't like witches. They buried us and our beliefs, deeming our existence and the Gods fake, but to what end? To hide their true nature? Clearly, they didn't want the people of Vylheim to know they were vampires. Belief in monsters, based on the sagas, would have villagers suspicious—perhaps suspicious enough to cut them down.

What human wanted the undead to lurk among us?

Hiding witches must be motivated by self preservation.

But with the history, with the witches help, Freya would undo it all.

My gaze sliced from the dancers to the throne. King Drakkar sat with one ankle propped on his knee, his hands relaxed on the armrests. Two courtiers kept him engaged in conversation, but he still slid his eyes to me as if he sensed me watching him.

I didn't blink, instead, soaking in his gaze as it raked over every inch of me. Heat reddened where my chest was bared, and he instantly took notice. My lips parted. I sucked in slight breaths until I snapped my eyes away.

It was too easy to fall into his gaze, to want him to look longer. King Drakkar played the man of my dreams. Dressed like a warrior, powerful, dangerous.

I scanned the crowd of servants, of commoners, of vampires playing at being courtiers. Where was Thora? She'd been as pale as Embla, as quiet and discreet with her movements, but instead of Embla's long hair, Thora kept hers shorter than her earrings.

Had King Drakkar gifted her with jewelry? Bitter jealousy sloshed in my gut. With a thought like that it was almost as if *I* wanted to be his vessel. As if I wanted him to sink his fangs into me like there was dignified intimacy in being fed on.

But there was nothing dignified about it.

Vessels were innocent humans being used, and I was fucking insane to entertain the thought of becoming the king's. And yet, the weight of him watching me wrapped around me, like his hands encompassing mine when he saw my fingers were blue. Comforting. His behavior—and this feeling that came with it—didn't make sense.

Why had he claimed he was fascinated with me?

Worse, why did I still want him to be?

Vampires had no souls, no connection to the Gods, and they denied witches a free life. I should hate him as much as I hated myself for the warmth that pooled between my legs when I felt his gaze on me.

When we weren't together, he was just a distant king, but as soon as I became aware of his presence, my body and mind both betrayed me. Perhaps because he'd stopped my execution —the warrior who'd saved me. It was the dream of a foolish girl.

A selfish girl.

I dared glance at him again. He stood, eyes still on me, and my pulse flickered when he marched toward me, striding with purpose and a hurried eagerness I'd never seen from him. Heat built in my chest again. I swiped my hand over my breasts so my icy fingers would cool me.

He didn't miss a beat. His mouth sliced into a wicked grin.

When he reached me, he took both of my hands and examined my fingers as if he'd read my thoughts from across the room. His icy eyes ticked up and he gently cupped my hands in his. "You're cold again." I merely nodded, not trusting myself to speak. "Does your handmaiden not keep the fire burning in your bedchambers?"

"She does."

"The dress then," he said, "we'll have you wear a cloak over your shoulders." His eyes dipped to my bare skin.

"No," I said, too fast. I didn't need him to admire me. I was already bound to marry him, a vampire, a monster, the creature who exiled my mother. I didn't need him to stare at my bare skin, but I wanted it. Especially after watching that damn sparring. He'd become the warrior I fantasized about my entire life.

Everything was in Freya's hands now, if I didn't fuck this trial up with these depraved thoughts.

"Whatever you want, my wife." He dipped forward,

brushing his lips across my shoulder. A tendril of dark hair escaped the knot at the back of his head.

Desire unfurled low in my belly. When he tugged me toward the throne, my thighs rubbed together, slick with my body's betrayal. I couldn't want him—a king of monsters.

When a servant with cups passed by, he lifted one from the young man's hands and offered it to me. I stared at the liquid. This definitely wasn't the blood I suspected had been in the goblet he often drank from. I took a whiff of the sweet wine and I was suddenly thirsty for a sip.

Taking it from him, I tipped the cup to my lips. He waited for me to finish, before palming my lower back and guiding me to his heavy bronze chair.

At the throne, he hooked his hands over my hips and gave me a slight lift, propping me on the throne's wide armrest. Swiveling to take a seat, he smirked up at me, his bride.

I wanted to wipe that smirk off his face, with my mouth. *Shit.* I was in deep. Too many months passed since I enjoyed Bjorn, that was all this desire meant. Nothing less, nothing more. King Drakkar didn't need to be the one to release this pent up energy simmering between my legs.

He lifted his hand to toy with the ends of my heavy braid where it sat just at his shoulder. What would it do to my depraved thoughts if he pulled it? A man like the king, someone wielding his sword with the skill I witnessed the other night, was a man who wouldn't be afraid to yank on my braid.

Having his fingers in my hair was dangerous territory, like crossing the border from Skaldir into the forest alone at night. All it'd take was one little tug and I'd be begging for more. Bjorn had always been too cautious. If I told him to dig his fingers into my hips or nip at the sensitive buds of my breasts, he'd pretend he didn't hear me. He refused to hurt the Vyl's daughter. But I wanted a little pain with my pleasure, and that was just something Bjorn could never give me.

"One more day," King Drakkar said, carving through my thoughts with a husky voice.

I stared down at him, searching his icy eyes for any indication of why he wanted to marry me.

As a witch, I was the enemy. Or perhaps it was all about control, I had the gift of visions after all. Those visions gave me insight into the history he and his king had buried, but he didn't know.

"What is it, wife?" he asked after taking a sip of wine, the bronze ring on his finger clinking against the cup.

"I'm not your wife." I said it more to shut down my lust than as a reaction to his words.

He handed the empty goblet off to a servant with short black hair. She disappeared into the crowd.

Thora.

When she returned a moment later, the cup full of red liquid, my stomach turned. I pinned her with my gaze but she didn't seem to notice as she turned away and let the party swallow her.

I flicked my eyes to him, watching every time he took a sip. Watching for a spill. Watching any drop of what was surely blood inside the goblet.

He shifted in his throne to face me. "You can avoid the question, but your eyes are speaking for you."

I lifted my brows. "And what are they saying? That I want you?" It was what I expected from his arrogant lips, so I threw the suggestion out there before he could take control of the conversation.

The curve at his mouth spread wider. He gently picked up my wrist from where my hand rested. He pressed the soft pad of his thumb against the beat of my pulse, the blood pushing through thin veins at an erratic rate. "They say you're curious, excited, intrigued. Can I claim victory for inspiring such feelings, or is there something you haven't shared with me?"

I shifted my jaw, considering his offer to speak freely as I ground my teeth. I drew in a slow breath to calm my heart. It did no good because the thought was already committed to my mind. "Why did you mention monsters when you asked me to be your wife?"

Would he dare admit what he was? We would be married soon, I'd have to know.

The grin wiped from his mouth. He gripped my wrist and tugged me hard enough that I lost balance and fell into his lap.

Before I could get to my feet, he whispered in my ear. "Because they're everywhere, Silver."

I drew back far enough to examine his face, but his eyes flicked to the people celebrating. I followed his line of sight. The celebration was a revel, a blur of fine fabrics the color of wine and the colors of the fjords in the summer, rich blues and greens. Men and women holding tightly to one another glided together, some in scripted dances, others shifting slowly with hands all over their partners' bodies.

I turned back to King Drakkar who was observing me silently. "You believe in monsters?"

His throat bobbed with a hard swallow, and he dragged his gaze back to me where it landed heavy on my eyes until it slipped to my lips. "You see the truth already, my wife. Look a little longer. Look in a mirror. There is no need for belief when there is truth."

My heart skipped, shooting sharp pains across my chest. Were his words another reminder of what I'd done? Of the fact that he claimed to be like me? That we'd both spat on the sanctity of life and killed? "What are you suggesting?"

"Tomorrow," he said, cupping my jaw. His lips paused right over mine, brushing against me as he spoke. "When you *are* my wife, you'll share in every truth I can give you."

My pulse thumped faster and faster, yearning for all that

implied. Every truth. There was so much possibility wrapped in those two words, everything I'd wanted to expose the reality that my mother and the other witches weren't a threat. It could change the entire course of my life and the women I cared for

"Why did you say the plan to explore The Sea of Skalds wasn't your doing?"

"Tomorrow." It was all he said before he drew my face closer, pressing his lips to mine. Like the other kiss, he started gently, until I returned it. His aggressive hunger sunk into me with increasing firmness.

No. I refused to give in to this desire. Questions still plagued me, and Freya couldn't give me every answer I wanted.

Pulling away, I pressed him with questions. "Aren't you the king? How did the council plan something that is not sanctioned by the king himself? You're the one in control here, right?"

He sucked down the last of the blood from his cup and bared his teeth as he slammed to goblet down against the armrest. "Fuck, Silver!" he snapped. His teeth were stained with red until he swiped his tongue across them, and faced me with fury in his eyes.

There it was. The monster within.

He pushed me off of him and stood, raking his fingers through his hair. Nobody else noticed, servants too busy with their jobs and guests drunkenly dancing and laughing.

Turning his head to his shoulder, he kept his eyes on the ground. "Remember when I said you do what I want when you're in my throne room?" I didn't dignify his question with a response. He twisted, flicking his intense gaze to me. "Keep that pretty mouth shut about the damn council."

Finally, someone took notice of the king's outburst. A plump man I vaguely recognized fixed his eyes on us.

Darius approached the throne with a commoner at his side. A belt kept his buttoned pants from slipping off the hips that were buried by his oversized belly. Thoughts of a vampire overeating sent chills down my neck. How many vessels did Darius feed on in a given night?

"My king, the courtiers don't like that your betrothed sleeps late into the night," he said. What the fuck? That certainly wasn't what I expected to come from this man's mouth. He continued despite the fact that King Drakkar only grunted at Darius's first comment. "Rumors that she suffers from an illness do not appease them. Order and tradition say any celebrations hosted at Mara's Keep begin when the sun would set."

"There's no sun during the Polar Nocturne, so maybe we should give up these ridiculous and antiquated traditions."

"You know we can't do that." His meaty hands flexed into reddened fists as he shifted his gaze to me and then back to the king. King Drakkar only huffed and shook his head, not even looking at Darius.

The commoner cut in. "Illness or not, Silver is rude—"

Before he could finish, the king turned to him, fisted the front of the man's tunic, and yanked him closer. "Say that again."

Darius jumped to his friend's defense. "My king, you can't treat Vigg like this."

Vigg nodded. "I'm Ylva and Darius' guest, invited by the council—"

"Call my wife rude again," King Drakkar snarled.

Vigg grit his teeth. "The council will make you pay for this."

"Say. It."

Breath went stale at the back of my tongue. The music and blur of dancing kept most of the people oblivious to the scene, but several courtiers and a few commoners stopped to watch.

Vigg frowned at me. "She's rude."

The king shoved Vigg back, releasing the man before curling his fingers into a fist. The thick thwack of his knuckles across Vigg's face drew more onlookers. A yelp escaped me as I found myself sinking to perch at the edge of the throne. Vigg tumbled to the floor, smacking his ass against the black stone. He fell at the feet of the gawking dancers.

Blood poured from his broken nose, dripping down his chin and over his wrinkled cream tunic.

King Drakkar stepped over him, a spot of red dropping from his knuckles onto Vigg's forehead as he passed by.

Follow the blood he leaves behind.

Ylva materialized from somewhere beyond the crowd and shadows. Fury twisted her features and her mouth dropped open like a skeleton who'd wasted away to nothing but bone.

Looking from the king to Vigg, her eyes narrowed. "Have you lost your fucking mind?" she asked, between her teeth. "He's bleeding."

"And I'm the king."

"There are still laws."

Forgetting about Vigg, both Darius and Ylva flanked the king. His guards made no move to step in. King Drakkar twisted to meet my gaze, he shoved past them and put his hands on either side of me, leaning against the tall back of the throne. His entire body caged me there where I sat at the edge of the throne. I rolled my neck back to look up at him.

"I'll be back soon," he said. "Eat and enjoy some wine for me." Dropping his voice, he dipped his mouth to my ear. "If he calls you rude again, you have my blessing to gut him. I know you have it in you."

My lips parted and breath escaped me. When he pulled back, we locked eyes until he turned and stalked out of the throne room after Ylva and Darius and three other members of the council. My eyes trailed them until the heavy doors groaned and sealed shut in their wake.

I had it in me to attack, that much he knew, and maybe his fascination finally made sense.

The darkness in me called to the monster in him.

I should cut this thought out of me before I took pleasure in it, but he saw—he saw the real me.

For once, I wanted him to call me his wife again.

CHAPTER EIGHTEEN

After the guests realized King Drakkar would not, of course, pay too heavily for his crime of bloodshed, the celebration continued. The people of Mara danced, and stuffed themselves with figs and wine until they were laughing and sweaty.

I gave Vigg a wide berth, which was easy enough since he'd limped to a group of courtiers who eyed him hungrily. I didn't want to know if they were about to choose him as their next vessel.

Slipping from the throne room only minutes after the council had guided him out proved effortless. The door fell shut behind me.

Servants passed through the hall, but I was mostly alone with the draft sending goosebumps over my bare arms. I scanned both sides of the hallway until a spot of red caught my eye. Hurrying toward the drop, my heart thumped faster and faster.

Freya's trial was finally surging forward.

I crept down the hall and stopped where another corridor forked to the right.

Another drop of blood guided me to this new section that

branched off. Like all the others, this hall stretched into what felt like an endless abyss. With no end in sight, I kept walking, walking, walking until all sounds of the celebration faded completely.

There were no doors, no new corridors splitting left or right, just a straight forward stretch of deafening stone. If I'd gone the wrong direction, I would have lost half an hour already, but the last blood drop was in this hallway, so I stayed the course.

As I continued, time stretched on.

I followed the snaking hall with the only sound coming from my groaning stomach. I scolded myself for leaving the cinnamon pears behind. I hadn't touched the food, and by the time I made it to the end of this hallway, a door, anything, I would be another year old. I'd have wasted away but not from famine alone.

This doorless path felt more like a trick, an illusion to get curious villagers lost. Perhaps it led to the council so that lost stragglers could be taken for feeding once they came upon the council of vampires, because if they tried to run, there was nowhere to go but straight back toward the throne room.

Finally, the hall came to an intersection leading left and right. I stopped, carefully scanning for another speck of blood.

Nothing told me which direction to go, not Freya's vision, not a hint of where King Drakkar had gone. No blood.

If I failed now, in the heart of the trial, I would not have another chance. The Dawn of Exploration was set to begin in a few weeks and my mother was slipping away much sooner.

I closed my eyes before panic surged.

My chest tightened and air was harder to come by. The ground seemed to shift and sway beneath my feet and I knew if I dared peel my eyes open, black spots would prick my sight. Little by little my nerves frayed like the torn hem of an unraveled dress.

I crouched with my hand on the wall to steady me even in

this hunched position. The stone floor still rocked beneath my feet, threatening to topple me.

Tipping my legs forward, I dropped my head to my knees. I curled in on myself in the empty hall, praying to the Gods that no monster came upon me in my moment of panic.

With my head spinning, I forced slow breaths. One after another, after another. The single moment stretched and every minute that passed tugged the trial further and further from my reach.

I couldn't break down now. I didn't track the passage of time, but some of these attacks of the nerves lasted beyond an hour before I became stable enough to resume cutting the wheat, or following the other gatherers out of the forest, or facing my father after I embarrassed him by placing last in a footrace.

But I wasn't in Ragna's field with the faces of those who died last winter haunting me. I wasn't foraging wild berries in the forest outside Skaldir and spotting a shadow with flaming eyes.

I was finally following a full vision.

One that would eventually lead me to my mother.

Drawing a breath through my nose, I smelled nothing but the rosemary soap lingering from my own hair. I tasted a hint of sweet wine left on my tongue. Feeling the rough stone wall, I held my breath and listened for any sound.

Muted conversation came from behind me. *Finally.*

My eyes popped open and I straightened. Fully standing, I tested my steadiness with one step into the hall on the left. Panic still quickened my pulse, but I remained upright as I slowly shuffled toward the voices.

I'd finally reached a stretch of doors that peppered both sides of the hall.

It wasn't until I was outside the door where a wild voice full of venom drifted that I recognized Ylva's tone. I reached for the handle but thought better of it. Marching into a meeting in a room filled with vampires left my blood chilled.

Was this really his most vulnerable moment?

I didn't have time to think about it when the door handle dropped. I backed away but not fast enough. When King Drakkar emerged and spotted me in his path, the heavy door fell shut with a slam behind him, and I froze.

His chest heaved as we stood face-to-face. "Are you following me, wife?"

He certainly didn't look vulnerable. Instead, he was self-assured, powerful, dripping with the kind of strength I could only fantasize about from the warriors in my favorite sagas.

I said nothing, but a curl of satisfaction trickled through me. I'd found him, even if this wasn't the end of the trial. And when he called me by my future title, it left my veins buzzing.

"It's late," his voice was as rough as stone and his eyelids hung heavy and half-lidded. It was the same look I'd seen on so many friends and family, villagers who ran out of food in the dead of winter, pure and desperate hunger. Until branches of scarlet slowly stretched across the icy blue center of his eyes

My breath hitched.

I'd never seen a monster's eyes shift gradually, they'd always flashed red. When he blinked, the scarlet lines vanished, but only for a moment. Jagged branches grew longer and wider, gradually bathing the blue in blood red.

He dipped closer to me, his face only a breath away. "You shouldn't be here."

Was this the moment of vulnerability? After attacking a man for merely calling me rude? After being scolded by his own council?

My dry lips peeled apart as I straightened my spine. I had to press on. "Where is the lost history?"

Shaking his head, he pulled away and ran his palm over the back of his neck. "Not yet." He turned his back to me and placed one hand on the wall.

His head hung as he muttered something to himself, not in a rush to get away from the door in case Ylva or Darius came out to interrupt us. They must have been busy.

There was no use keeping my plan a secret now. I was waist-deep in Freya's trial. This was it. "The wasteland is killing my mother. If she survives that, she'll be shipped off to die at sea in only a few weeks because of your plan to explore—"

He spun around, and before I could blink, his hand wrapped around my throat. "Not me." His fingers tightened until any thread of air cut off from my lungs. "Do you hear me? It's not because of me. You witches are to do *my* bidding." Red entirely stained the center of his eye. Sharp-tipped teeth dripped from beneath his top lip, growing and stretching into long fangs.

Ylva's shrill voice grew louder and a hum of other voices responded to her. Muted footsteps approached the other side of the door King Drakkar had burst from.

Releasing me for a single breath, he pressed a palm to my stomach and swung open the door behind me. He grabbed my arm and pulled me inside, slamming me against the wall where the door fell shut beside us. Red eyes raked over every inch of me.

A shuffle of footsteps faded as the council disappeared down the hall. Once they were long gone, he sucked in a breath and dipped his mouth to my throat.

But he didn't brush his lips against my skin. I barely breathed, almost wanting it. No, definitely wanting it. What the fuck? *What the fuck?*

With the tip of his fangs grazing my throat, he spoke. His lips brushed my skin, sparking every nerve alight and tingling. "You will do what I want. Right, Silver?"

Yes, edged on the tip of lips. I gnawed at the inside of my mouth to keep from giving him a promise my body wanted—I wanted. The simmering heat flamed in my belly. I had to refute this depravity. My mother, the witches, the *Gods* were counting on me.

"I *am* a God," he breathed. "Well, nearly." My brow furrowed as I stared up at him. His fanged mouth tipped into a devious grin. Dropping his gaze to my lips he trailed it slowly back up to my eyes. "Yes, I can hear your thoughts."

A slight gasp escaped me. Arching my back against the wall, I pressed away from him as if the stone at my spine would block my mind from him.

He chuckled. "You can't get away from it." As he brought his mouth to the corner of my jaw and just below my ear, he brushed a faint kiss across my skin. "Not while you're aching for me."

"I'm not," I whispered.

"Liar."

Fuck.

"Yes, that's exactly what I want to do. And I know you do too. This heat you have for me is the only reason I can even hear what you're thinking right now. When you desire me, I know your every thought."

My entire body buzzed with his confession and my thighs were slick with wanting despite his blasphemous claim.

I am a God.

"Do you doubt that I can become one?" he asked.

I bit my lip and glared at him, tempering the desire coiling in my belly. Through the haze of it all, I managed a single clear thought. "Doesn't the king traditionally deny the Gods were ever real?"

Another hooked grin seemed to sink into me and reel me closer to him. I tipped my chin up as he spoke. "I became a vampire. I will become a God."

"Impossible."

The bright red in his eyes darkened to a pooling crimson. Hunger hollowed his gaze as it fell to my throat. He gripped my chin and tilted my head, stretching my neck to a curve. A sharp prick scratched across the pulse beating in my throat.

He was going to devour me, and I didn't even fight back. I wanted him to touch me.

The darkness within reared its ugly head, fighting every logical thought with baser, selfish desires.

He suddenly paused and breathed a string of curses. Shoving back, he left me panting as he stepped away. Before I could think, he yanked open the door and vanished into the hall.

CHAPTER NINETEEN

LOKI'S TRIAL

I had come too close to passing Freya's trial to let the king slip away now. I pushed off the wall to run after him.

Stepping into the hall, my foot caught on something small. I stumbled forward, catching myself with the heel of my palm on the opposite wall. Pain radiated through my hand and snaked up my arm, at the same time that a screech echoed through the hall with a chilling pitch. My blood went cold as I whipped around.

A dark blur darted into the long hall I'd first come down. Whatever it was left behind an oversized cat with thick gray fur. It twined around my legs lazily rubbing against the smooth fabric of my skirt.

Freya's cats.

"It's over?" I breathed. The first trial was over. Freya had confirmed it with this vision of the cats gifted to her.

"*Yes.*" A voice descended upon my mind, curling with eagerness.

I didn't know if it was safe to believe it yet. But it was real, Freya's trial ended and I'd...passed.

The dark gray cat came sauntering back around the corner, having forgiven me for tripping over him.

This couldn't be the end. I hadn't learned where the rune-stones were kept. King Drakkar gave me nothing. Would the next trial give me more?

Where was the lost history? How could I expose a vampire king and his council of monsters without it? King Drakkar was supposed to be vulnerable when I tracked him down.

And perhaps he was.

Hunger had left his eyes a haze of red, the anger made him reckless, and it almost seemed like he was running from me now. Running from a willing victim, like he didn't want to hurt me. If King Drakkar truly cared for me, maybe that was the real vulnerability.

Maybe that was my key to where the runestones were locked away.

It was that or trying to convince a council of undead crea-tures not to send the witches they hated to death at sea. Right.

I ducked back into the room he'd dragged me in. In a desperate hurry, I searched for anything hidden, any hatch, any false wall, but the room was a simple bedchamber, without a fireplace. I tried to the next door, then finally, the room the council members had disappeared into.

Disappointment fell heavy on my shoulders when I discov-ered it was nothing more than a meeting place. The rune-stones were probably hidden far more carefully than in a room near where the council might frequent.

I stood in the hall, my arms hanging limp and helplessly at my sides. Though I wasn't alone, the cats still slunk around my legs, I was empty of any ideas.

What was my next step?

The voice slithered into my thoughts again. No vision came with it, instead, this voice spoke as if part of me, though it came with that masculine energy again.

"Freya warned you? Told you he's a threat. A danger. A ruin wrapped in skin.

But tell me, since when did danger feel that good?

Curious little thing you are. And curiosity, well... it always follows, doesn't it?

Follow the cold.

Follow the screams.

Follow and find what I have to share, and there,

Fenrir, my son, the wolf, will appear."

Screams? This voice, it had to be Loki, he was Fenrir's father, after all. According to the vision, his trial came next, and only the God of chaos would encourage me to seek after danger. To seek pleasure from a monstrous king.

To go toward the screaming.

I wasn't flooded with the awe and admiration I felt whenever Freya's visions reached me. Loki was unpredictable and troublesome. But for now, he was all I had.

"I need a trail," I whispered. The larger cat's ears pricked.

I squeezed my eyes shut and listened. Surely enough a cry echoed from somewhere in the distance. I didn't breathe as I focused on the desperate plea. King Drakkar had been hungry, which must have meant this cry came from a victim he was feeding on.

The scream died away but not before I was able to pinpoint the direction; past the door where the council had met, further down the left side of the forked hallway. When I opened my eyes, both cats had vanished, leaving no trace of their bushy fur behind.

I set off, rubbing at my bruised palm and running when my breathing allowed.

Perhaps I was never supposed to be in this wing. Stasia warned me about screams even when my room was on the other side of the castle. Or so I suspected it was on the other side. The web of halls and matching stone always left me dazed and in awe of my handmaiden who so easily navigated this place.

A draft swept through the narrow space. Icy air curled around me, inviting me to come closer. Only a woman from Skaldir would run toward the cold.

I kept pushing forward as the temperature dropped lower and lower, because even if Loki scared me a little, he was a God, he was part of these trials, and he told me to follow the cold.

I tracked the chill because I refused to believe what I already knew was the whole of the information I'd learn from Mara's Keep. Freya had gifted me the visions that'd led me here, now Loki spoke to me.

And even if it was Loki, a thrill pulsed through my veins at the realization that a God talked directly to me. I'd passed Freya's trial which must have meant I was closer to the Gods, able to hear their influence more clearly.

Was this guidance his gift? It didn't make sense coming from the God of chaos.

The air in the dark hall dropped with every step I took. By the time I reached two large oak doors, my entire body convulsed in its natural attempt to stave off the cold and build heat. With my hand shaking, I struggled to grip the door handle.

Twisting it, I shoved the heavy door inward and froze at the threshold.

King Drakkar sat at the end of a four-poster bed with blood dripping from his hands. Red stained everything, the blankets, his clothes, pooling at his feet. In his arms lay the limp body of the man who'd approached the throne with Darius. Blood dripped from holes in his neck and his eyes were wide open, staring into an eternal void.

The king looked up at me with a single emotion coating his icy eyes. *Confidence.* Always cold hard confidence bordering on arrogance and pride.

An inexplicable gust of wind came from somewhere past him. My gaze flickered to a dark fireplace at the wall behind his bed before falling over the horrific scene in his arms again.

"He's…" I swallowed to soothe the ache in my dry throat. "You killed him."

King Drakkar stared at me in silence. After a moment, he lifted one hand to wipe at the corner of his mouth. A faint smile flickered over his lips. "He deserved it. Nobody calls my wife rude."

The pungent scent of sour iron and faint rot filled my nose. My stomach curled in on itself.

King Drakkar didn't just feed on vessels, letting them recover like Stasia suggested, he was a killer.

Now this poor soul's blood soaked the rug and the furs on the bed I was to share with the king. And the blood, the sick smell of death, it all looked far too familiar. The stain of red like a criminal's blood marking the earth after an executioner forced us all to watch the beheading.

I'd seen enough of death—too much.

I swallowed and whispered calming words my mother taught me when I needed to settle my panic.

All at once, I lost control of my body, but not to collapse. Instead, someone else seemed to be controlling me.

As if I were a child's doll controlled by an unknown force, my jaw expanded and words spilled out. These weren't the words running through my mind. They were foreign to me, thoughts that came onto me suddenly. A phrase I'd only heard my mother say came from deep within me. She always said the Norns weaved our fates.

"King Drakkar, bestow me the truth or suffer the Norn's twisted cords."

Did I just threaten him? An exhilarating thrill throbbed in my muscles followed by a swell of energy. Magic. This was the power of the Gods, Loki, Freya, and maybe even Odin flowing through me and igniting my tongue and mind with the courage to not only speak, but to demand.

But even though they gave me the power, what came out was *my* voice. My own words speaking a phrase I hadn't heard since I was a child, phrases from Loki's saga. And though I wanted to say it was Loki's invisible hands prying my jaws open, I knew the truth. The words came from me, perhaps simply laced with Loki's power.

Shock tightened my throat as my mouth hung open.

A whimper of relief and excitement escaped me. Visions were one thing, but *this*, the feel of pure power to fight back against the control of King Drakkar, and the royalty in this Keep, emboldened me.

After a moment of huffing, he responded. A dazed look clouded his chilling eyes, almost softening them to become the servant beneath my power—power I knew I'd just channeled from the Gods.

Damn it felt good.

"The truth?" He said, his voice faraway yet direct. I knew, without a shadow of a doubt, King Drakkar was compelled to confess exactly what I needed to know. This power would allow nothing else. This trance owned him, even if for a few moments. I already felt the vibration of exhaustion slithering through my muscles and veins. The Gods' power of this...this compulsion, would surely collapse me. "This is who I am. You already knew, Silver."

He stood, a shadowy silence over the stains, some fresh the color of cherry while other spots were the dark burgundy of dried blood. A twitch bolted across his face. He bared his teeth, his neck reddening.

He was fighting my compulsion and I felt every strain with pressure building in my head and throat and lungs, even pressing down on my tongue. I resisted, returning to what I was doing when I first felt this power.

Whispering calm phrases, I felt the strength within me rise

again. "I see him fighting the cage of magic on his tongue. I hear the echo of wind through a tunnel. I smell blood…"

His voice, still dulled with my compulsion, broke through. "I don't always kill everyone I taste, but everyone I kill I've tasted."

Sick.

More of this power tumbled out of my mouth with a demand for what I needed. "I compel you as I can with all of your kind. Give me what I want." *Give me the lost history.*

His icy blue eyes flashed to gold like an animal in the night before red replaced the gold. "You'll have to kill me first."

It was the truth. Somehow, an instinct carved in the marrow of my bones told me this was exactly what he'd been compelled to tell me, nothing more.

His broad chest heaved with the effort of fighting against my power. The compulsion slipped from my fingers, as if the power was water and I could not grasp it again until I had the energy to dive into it. I had to immerse myself in the sensations, in focus, something my tired brain could no longer keep hold of.

I licked my lips, claiming control of myself after the magic of the trance stripped me of my breath. "I'm not like you."

Anger built at the edges of his jaw. "What the fuck was that?"

"That was what it feels like to be controlled," I snapped. "Pushed around, like you and your damn executioners do to people every day."

"They're not—" He pushed out a hot breath and raked his fingers through his hair. His thick arm flexed from the effort until he dropped it at his side and pinned me with his gaze. "You know it's funny, you want the truth, but you sure like to lie, *Silver.* Want to share your real name?"

My blood chilled. It wasn't real. He couldn't have just said that.

Don't think about it.

Don't think about it.

Don't think about it.

I was just Silver, a simple witch from Skaldir.

He marched toward me. "I suspected the Gods had taken hold of you, but then whenever you were...wanting, I didn't hear a hint of them, so I thought you hadn't invited them in."

"I didn't—"

He huffed. "But I was wrong—damnit!" Slamming his fist against the wall behind my head, he didn't even wince as his knuckle smacked into stone. "I really hoped it wasn't true."

Chaos. I didn't know if this word came from Loki's voice or my own mind, but the king's flared temper was proof of promised chaos.

King Drakkar glared down at me until he hovered, bringing his face inches from mine. His wild eyes searched mine. "The only way to take back your mind is to sever your ties with the Gods. Bind yourself to the only thing out of Odin's reach. We have to move the wedding up, tonight, before the sun would normally rise."

I backed away, shuffling over the dress's crumpled fabric. "I won't marry a murderer."

He clucked his tongue and shook his head. "I'll either marry you, or I'll show you exactly how I kill."

I shouldn't have been surprised but claws clamped around my lungs and the blood-stenched air became scarce. "You'll kill me?"

"Not if you cast off the Gods."

Which meant casting off their gifts, the visions, this new... compulsion, everything that was meant to help my mother, Ragna, and the other exiled women. "Then you'll free the witches?"

"When did I say that?"

"The lost history says we aren't a threat and tradition says you must abide by the truth of history."

He laughed. "There is a lot of truth I want to share with

you once we're bound together. So what will it be? Marriage or death, my wife."

"You can't make me do this—"

"You have until first light to decide."

Every moment I thought he almost cared for me shriveled into distant memory. They were all lies. The monster standing before me had lost every bit of that desire for me. While he was once concerned for my bloodless hands, he now laughed at my sole purpose—the only thing I wanted.

My heart cracked.

"How can you be so cold?" I whispered. It was a foolish question because I shouldn't care.

"How can you let Odin ransack your mind?"

I shook my head. "He hasn't." Odin never spoke to me, and the day he did, I would fall to my knees, rejoicing for the connection to Odin himself.

"Whichever God is speaking to you doesn't matter," he seethed. "Odin is the Allfather, the fucking origin of them all. I'd hoped you would become mine, but you already belong to him." His mouth twitched, his fangs were no longer jutting out. "Unless you choose me. I will be your God."

Everything about this claim was wrong. Twisted. Blasphemous.

I frowned, defiance building with fervor in my chest and in the fury lacing my voice. "You're not a God. You're deluded. You're the king who ripped a mother from her children, twice." And so many more times I could not count. Hundreds of other families with witches suffered the same fate.

He said nothing, clearly uninterested in trying to defend himself. Though I'd put a few steps between us, his powerful presence still seemed to tower over me. His chest heaved as if desperate for a ragged breath and his eyes locked on me.

Cast off this colorless cage.

That was what this marriage would be, a cage built with stone walls and an iron grip. I had to run from this betrothal.

A betrothal that the thought of consummating shouldn't have weakened my knees and left my thighs slick.

But this clash of feelings was chaotic and exactly what Loki loved.

I backed into the hall. In my absence, the heavy door slammed shut and I abandoned this horrible scene in my wake.

Still vibrating with the swell of energy, I ran faster than I thought possible in these heavy skirts. I had to run, because even if he exposed my secret, at least I didn't bind myself to a lifetime beside a cruel king...a monster who murdered his own people.

CHAPTER TWENTY

I ran to the warmth. If nothing else, following the heat distanced me from King Drakkar. His words left me raw and coated in goosebumps.

I had until first light to decide if I wanted to give up everything I was, my connection to the Gods, my identity as a seer, hope for my mother and Ragna and bind myself to him—or die.

Heaving each breath left my throat tender. I couldn't collapse, so I stopped running and allowed my pulse to slow. Loki wanted me to leave this place, but was that the trial? I hadn't failed my mother if I could pass his and then Odin's in time.

The Gods would lead me.

I had to believe it because I was no closer to the lost history than when I'd stepped inside Mara's Keep for the first time.

"I'll lead you."

Loki's voice penetrated my thoughts again. King Drakkar was right, I'd invited the Gods into my mind and I'd never regret it. Focusing on Freya had helped keep the darker side of me locked away, but Loki...

"Let it out." His voice curled with satisfaction.

No! I'm not evil.

That was a lie.

He said nothing to confirm or deny this. Loki wouldn't care as long as I followed whatever cunning plan he had designed, and for now, I trusted him enough to follow this plan. How could I not? The power to put the king into a trance—a monster at my beck and call—must have come from Loki. He was the only one wild and chaotic enough to imbue me with such magic.

I could control a vampire, and for a moment, I wanted to relish in this, because what came next was Odin's trial. I had no doubt it would be the most challenging, more so even than Loki's chaos.

Loki was always a necessary evil in the history of the Gods, and perhaps that was why he was part of these trials. Perhaps they were designed specifically for me and the wickedness the Gods knew I carried within me.

Now it'd come to this, my wild escape to pass Loki's trial.

The shadows may find me again, but they'd find an honest woman, not a woman sitting beside a disturbed and cruel king. I just had to find a way out. Or find Stasia.

Even a bird with clipped wings can escape its cage. I hadn't forgotten her unusual words, as if she, too, considered escape.

The kitchens were my best bet, so I forged on, following the warmth. Surely, the hearths here would be the hottest part of the castle, not unlike the communal hearth back in Skaldir.

Shoving through a heavy door, I spotted her across the room and relief flooded me. Despite this, my face must have been the dazed agape expression of the vessels because she came to me at once.

"My queen," she breathed, green eyes as wide as a child's.

I shook my head. "Don't call me that."

Her brow arched. "You're terrified."

"It's that obvious?"

With a nod, she pursed her lips, pushing her pink cherub cheeks up. Her honey voice dropped to a whisper. "What is it?"

I stepped closer and kept my voice as low as possible. "You're planning to escape, aren't you?" Her strawberry lips parted. Sudden fear darkened her bright eyes. "Nobody told me," I said quickly. "I only know, or am guessing because I'm…"

"Observant," she said, relief lacing her voice. "I know, and honestly, it's about damn time, my queen." I narrowed my eyes and she cleared her throat. "Miss…Silver?"

"Just call me Silver." I winced.

She sucked in a breath and cupped my elbow. Guiding me out into the hall, I suddenly missed the warmth of the hearths.

"As I was saying." She clucked her tongue as she pulled me around a corner and we continued down a hall I actually recognized with the double doors to the throne room. "It's about time you want to leave. I mean, your betrothed is an undead monster."

My heart skipped. She was right, but in so many little ways King Drakkar didn't match that description. He'd cared for my cold hands, defended me for sleeping late when I needed rest, his mere words had made me wet with wanting.

But it was all a facade—and I would know.

A dull ache hooked into my heart and seemed to drag it to the depths. Of course a lying king would choose the woman whose entire life was a lie. We were the same.

Stasia continued talking quietly as she led me down a wide hallway. "Didn't you ever wonder why I left the kitchens when you came here?" I furrowed my brow and followed in her wake. She marched straight for two massive doors and shoved one open. "You have always been my ticket out. Since the moment I saw your expression when the king proposed to you, I knew you didn't want to stay here."

Air blasted into the hall, needling my face with icy

pinpricks. Stasia slipped outside and I stepped to the threshold. Stone steps lay before me, and beyond that, Mara. I'd been holed up in the castle so long, I forgot how high this fortress stood over the village. Flickers of distant candlelight dotted the landscape below, mirroring the glittering stars across the open sky.

Stasia grabbed my wrist and pulled me through. The door groaned as it fell shut behind me.

"Escape is simply walking out the front door?" I said, sliding my eyes to my handmaiden.

She tilted her head side-to-side. "*You* can simply walk out. You're nearly the queen, and as your handmaiden, I go where you go, even if it's just for a breath of fresh air. This is the tricky part. I can't leave the property, and I suspect King Drakkar wouldn't like you going far either. But from the windows, I've mapped a path that will keep us in the shadows."

My mouth popped open. I stared at her wordlessly for a moment, awe and appreciation stealing my breath away. And I'd known to seek her out, so a small slice of this admiration was reserved for myself, too.

It was as if Loki had sent Stasia to guide me through my escape from Mara's Keep. This trial was proving far easier than Freya's, which was definitely not what I expected from the God of chaos.

"Thank you. I–I don't know what else to say. This is perfect."

"Follow me," she said, trailing the shadow cast by the castle. The moon hung bright and shimmering behind the spires.

As easy as it'd been to walk out the front doors, escaping tonight, with heavy and tired limbs, would prove difficult. When and how would I rest once I was out of Mara's Keep? In there, I was surrounded by monsters, but out here, life was uncertain.

I'd take the uncertainty, even if my body argued with it. Thankfully, it wasn't long until the thrilling energy of escape bolted through my veins. This temporary boost would have to pull me through until we were able to stop and breathe.

Like the long halls, we followed the length of the structure for what felt like an hour before cutting to the right and slipping into a narrow space between overgrown plants. Spiked bushes clawed at my neck and arms as we ducked into the darkness provided by the bushes. Dim moonlight filtered through the thick branches, just enough for me to make out the shape of the delicate flowers. Roses.

Before my mother was sent away, she taught me about all plants. Plants to heal, plants to feed us, plants to protect us. She'd claimed blood red roses, thorned and often rare, were a gift from Freya, planted by Valkyries, to shield us from the monsters who slipped into our world from fractures across the Nine Realms.

Sliding along the narrow space between the stone castle and the crowded bushes, I allowed Stasia to guide me. So far, my shadow was nowhere to be seen and King Drakkar hadn't found us. Even if I didn't know Stasia well, I trusted she was capable. I'd seen her determination the moment she first came into my chambers. Truly, she was my only option and she knew Mara's Keep and this castle far better than I.

As I squeezed through the wild bushes, a thorny branch caught the soft flesh of my cheek. I swallowed a yelp and twisted away from it as the spike dragged across my face where it'd leave a mark to match my other scar. Frustrated, I shoved through the suffocating bushes with a curse at my lips.

We broke free at the back of the castle where Stasia grabbed my hand and pulled me beyond a grassy hill spotted with scattered headstones. Royals had been buried here for centuries, the hundreds of graves kept record of their high status even in death.

Descending the hill proved harder than I expected in the

heavy dress, but we made it to the bottom and ducked into a line of trees. Following a ragged path through the forest, I ached for Skaldir.

For a simpler time with the other gatherers.

For life before the winters grew dangerous.

For distant memories of foraging for berries with my mother. I trailed her into the forest with the other women and she taught me how to identify which plants were palatable and which were poisonous.

My heart ached. Would I ever see her again? She'd know how to translate Loki's clever way of speaking.

I'd escaped Mara's Keep as he said, so where was my vision of Fenrir? I shouldn't have trusted him, but I'd had no other options. And, of course, Loki was a trickster, he never gave straight answers. One could never see the end of his cunning plans.

What did his trial entail beyond escape?

My mother would know. She'd lift my hand as we prayed to Odin with the sacrifice of burning our most prosperous crop to strike down the men who harm us. Though we never spoke of it again, the shadow that stood outside her door at night was torn to pieces by a direwolf. His liver, his head, and his entrails were left scattered across her doorstep, as if the shadow's body was a gift, an answer from Odin and Freya. A reminder that they existed and heeded our calls even if it was outlawed to utter their names beyond the frame of stories.

I peered through the trees to catch sight of the gray stone spires reaching into the sky. I'd cast off the colorless cage, but Loki did not grant me victory yet.

His voice materialized across my mind like a wisp of smoke.

"He's coming, L."

L? A shiver trickled through me.

Forget it.

Forget it.

Forget it.

———

I didn't think it possible for the stretched night to get darker. The forest coated us with a strange silence. Here, the only sounds were the crunching of leaves beneath our feet and an owl's call. Moonlight no longer cracked through the dense branches as we stumbled along.

Finally, Stasia's footsteps stopped tromping and I paused behind her. Standing still now, I made out the shapes in the shadows and adjusted enough to find a soft patch of earth. We sank to the forest floor where Stasia produced provisions from a pack buried beneath her shift. Dried lamb and a small pouch of water that she shared plentifully.

"Do you always carry this?" I asked, pointing to the pack.

She patted the pack and winked. "Since the day I planned to leave Mara's Keep."

"Will you come with me to Skaldir?" I asked.

She stopped mid-chew and looked up at me, eyebrows raised as if I should already know the answer to this. "You don't expect me to keep playing at being your handmaiden do you?"

"No!"

With a laugh, she shrugged. "I was awful at it. I never braided as well as Embla."

"So, where will you go?"

Stasia hummed thoughtfully. "I don't know if I should say. You're going to think all that talk of my sanity was to cover up my lack of it." Swallowing, she smirked. "I mean, I'm not as wild as you—how long did it take you to want to escape an undead husband? Sometimes I think you're a little off, and it has nothing to do with your painted eyes."

"Painted?" I echoed. My hand shot to my eyelid. How

long had it been since my last enchantment? How far had the black spread from the center?

"It looks like the Gods spilled paint right in the middle of your eyes, and it's still spilling. Looking at you gives me the creeps, but then you say something amusing like 'will you come with me to Skaldir' and I remember you're my friend. But who would ever want to go to the coldest village with the least amount of food? Honestly, you did not do a great job staying sane in Mara's Keep."

I rolled my eyes but at the same time, the hint of a smile lifted my tired face. Stasia said exactly what she thought of me, and even if it was rude, I preferred that to whispers and secrets.

"You've never spoken of the Gods before," I said.

Another shrug. "I don't care for them, but I suspect you do. Anyone who is as well versed in Draugr, and believes in them before even seeing them, that's a person who still listens to the sagas."

"You're right."

"Clearly."

I eyed her as she chewed at the dried bit of meat. "You never said where you're going."

She didn't bother to swallow before she spoke around the lump in her cheek. "Once you're not totally helpless?" She lifted her brows and raked her gaze over me. Coming from her, I knew this was her way of showing she cared. She'd betrayed a damn vampire king to help me escape when she could have slipped away herself without the weight of my slow pace dragging her down. "I'm going to The Sea of Skalds."

"What?"

She laughed and nudged me with her elbow. "When you ask a question, Silver, listen to the answer."

I shook my head. "I heard you, but why would you go where it storms the most? Don't you know the only food at sea is fish, fish, and more fish?"

She smiled. "You're funny, and a little offensive. Teasing is my way of coping with this life, don't copy me. And clearly, I know that I'll only be eating fish, but even food isn't enough to keep me away."

"From?"

She spit out a particularly tough piece of meat and sighed. I didn't know if it was for the lost food or what she was about to say. Throwing her loose waves over her shoulder, she straightened and met my gaze. "From an executioner."

I merely blinked at her. Why would she chase after a member of the Grimward?

"Don't look at me like I've gone mad." She wagged her finger at me as if I were a child she was scolding. Lifting her chin, the moonlight bathed her face in a bluish glow. Her postural confidence drove me to sit up a little straighter. "I'm going to find him. Half of the Grimward has been sent to move the Exiles to the shore at The Sea of Skalds in preparation to set sail. First, I'm headed to the wasteland, but if I can't find him there, I'll wait at The Sea of Skalds. I suspect he's still at the wasteland because I haven't heard of the exiles being moved across Einnland and Mara yet."

"You're in love with an executioner?" I said, the words slipping out bluntly. I didn't even know if it was the truth, but the way Stasia's eyes lit up when she spoke of this mysterious man, I felt the love within her.

She eyed me, a smirk curling her lips again. I knew I was in for it and I couldn't help but return the smile, until a pang of sadness struck through my chest and tightened my throat. The playful teasing and Stasia's rough way of speaking was akin to my friendship with Ragna. They were both women I admired. I loved Ragna as if she were my sister, and apparently Stasia and I bickered like sisters, too.

My smile vanished.

Thoughts of sisters were not something my ragged emotions could handle right now.

"Maybe I am in love with an *executioner*," she said, her tone playfully mocking the way I'd said it. "And maybe you should shut your damn mouth and stop judging me. Don't you know that when you love someone, you don't care what they've done?"

Why King Drakkar flickered into my mind, I didn't want to know. I'd been too drawn to him. I'd killed, and so did he.

One in the same.

Two monsters giving in to our selfish needs.

There was no love between us, of course, but he'd seen me —the real me, and still wanted me. Even when he found out about Freya's visions and Loki's voice in my head. But in the end, he'd demanded I give those up.

The memory of his mouth dripping with blood turned my stomach and when Stasia offered me another cut of dried meat, I frowned and waved it away.

"You take the first watch," Stasia said, cutting through the bloody memory.

"What?"

She snapped her fingers and then clapped her hands together. "Wake up, girl. Are you already asleep? The king will be looking for us—especially you. Until we're out of Mara, we must be on guard." I was always on guard. After a lifetime of being followed, I could spot the movement of figures in the darkness and feel the prickle of eyes on my back. "And I need my rest," she continued. "Do you think this beauty comes without effort?" Though she was slim, not quite full with thick thighs and wide curves like the most beautiful women from Skaldir, she radiated a certain warmth that still made me want to call her an angel. I crooked a smile at her contagious confidence. "And don't worry, I know you need to rest. But I've become aware of the signs of your sickness."

She pointed at my fingers. They were pink since the high

and energy of our escape still flowed through me. It wouldn't be long until they tinted blue again, but we both needed rest, and Stasia was the one who'd mapped and guided our entire escape. I could manage a little longer while she slept and she knew it.

"Now shush," she said, "and don't talk to yourself. You won't hear our enemies over the sound of your own voice, however much you might delight in it."

After a few seconds of rustling, she released a long sigh and the shape of her torso melted into the earth.

I stared at her for a moment as she curled in on herself.

"What's his name?" I asked her.

Only silence responded. An owl broke the quiet until Stasia finally spoke. "Finan."

Once her breathing steadied, I stood, creeping quietly to a rock where I perched on the edge. Without our cheerful bickering filling the air, the silence tensed my every muscle. Escape had filled me with energy when we were still moving, still talking about our plans, but in the darkness of the Polar Nocturne, nearly alone, the grim possibilities spiraled through my mind.

I was a target, and I knew it wouldn't be long until we'd need to conjure a new plan to keep us safe.

Waiting for wild animals, or my shadows, or King Drakkar to come hunt me down, I fixated on the darkness.

Chapter Twenty-One

C reatures crawled along the forest floor and the flutter of bats occasionally startled me, but the time passed quietly. I sucked in a long breath that snagged at the sight of something large between the trees. I narrowed my eyes, my lungs frozen, as I scanned the treeline.

The shape of a man stood between two thick trunks, his entire body shadowed except the glint of his eyes, like an owl — like King Drakkar. My heart quickened as I recognized the shiny golden hue.

I shot to my feet, but didn't run. The man stepped closer, carefully, methodically, his hand lifted out in front of him as if he was approaching a frightened deer. Or perhaps he wanted to grab me, slap his hand over my mouth and drag me through the forest by my hair. I couldn't run and leave Stasia to fend for herself.

Blood rushed through my ears like a melted fjord crashing with deafening water. I'd run from my shadows as a young woman, and then I killed my shadows once they captured me.

But I'd faced the man who trapped me in betrothal. I'd compelled him. *Loki, can I do it again?*

I peeled my dry lips apart and my hot breath coiled into a humid mist. "You must leave."

He stepped closer.

Fuck. That was the opposite action of my demand.

The shape of his thick hair identified him as the wheat-haired man who'd pulled me into the shadows. His deep brown eyes drew my attention. In another realm, I would fall victim to those eyes, determined, sharp, handsome. Here and now, I refused to be any kind of victim. He would either kill me or drag me back to Mara's Keep, and I could not let that happen. "Silver, you have a duty—"

"To the king? To you?" I spat. No, I had to compose myself, to try again. But with the rush of blood vibrating in my veins, my heart thumping wildly, I couldn't think of anything sensible to say.

Speech abandoned me altogether and nerves over-whelmed my senses. If my mother were here, she'd instruct me to slow my thoughts and then manifest a sense of calm by giving voice to those thoughts.

When he stepped forward and closed the distance between us, all mindful control dissipated and I descended into muscle memory.

I reacted as if he were Ragna approaching me for practice in the shield hall. Throwing up my elbow and stepping back, I spread my feet in a wide stance. If only I had a shield and weapon, this would be a lot easier, but the hard bones at the crook of my arm would have to do.

"I'm not yours and I'm not going back to the king."

"No, but you are chosen."

My stomach convulsed, rejecting this with a dry retch. "I don't care what the king or his council wants, they're monsters."

Rustling leaves caught my attention and I glanced over my shoulder to where Stasia laid. The forest floor was empty, a soft dent in the shape of her body against the decaying leaves.

She'd taken her chance and left me. I sucked in a breath and turned back to see my shadow was upon me.

"I'm not here for the king," he said. "Listen to me, Silver. Your blood—"

"Fuck no!" Nobody was going to threaten to taste my blood again. I wouldn't give him the chance to flex that kind of power over me.

"Let me show you."

He seized my wrist, and every ounce of blood rushing through me pulsed with energy. I flipped my arm to twist his hold on me, but his grip remained steady. I threw out the heel of my other palm against his jaw, shoving his face away from me.

When his other hand found my free wrist, panic struck me.

Instead of falling victim to it, I listened to the panic, feeling the erratic nerves and noticing the changes in my body. My mother said self awareness was its own kind of magic, separate from the gods and witches. It was innate in every person, plain or powerful, as long as we listened.

I let the energy course through me, building to shove back against him. With all my might, I wrenched one hand free, but not for long. He was faster, far stronger, almost as if he was toying with me by releasing my arm. I kicked at his shin with the toe of my boot, which elicited a satisfying grunt from him.

Taking advantage of his reaction, I threw my shoulder against the center of his chest to knock him off balance so I could twist my other arm and be free of him. But he was as solid as a shield, unmoving.

If this were practice with Ragna, I'd locate her weak spot, below the block. I dropped low, my wrist still in his grasp and used my free hand to rip the tree pendant from my pocket. He yanked me to my feet again where he could snatch my other wrist, but I was prepared.

The soft spot of his palm found the sharp tip of the tree

pendant. His entire body reacted, throwing not only his arm back when the silver tree cut into his flesh, but all of him— and me.

With his hold still on me, he twisted and threw me to the ground.

His body dropped on top of mine, his hip pressed into my side, his leg pinning me to the earth. Because his movements were so quick, I didn't see his arm shoot up and pin my wrist into the slippery wet leaves.

He forced my arm above my head to keep the Y as far away from him as possible.

I wriggled and wanted to spit at him but my mouth was dry, my energy cut short. He'd overpowered me, his solid body pressing against mine.

His eyes flashed a blood red and my stomach dropped.

"You're the one who dragged me into the shadows," I said. It slipped out—an observation, something I'd already known.

His lip twitched and his mouth parted for desperate ragged breaths. Something formed from beneath his top lip, creating two bumps at the corners of his mouth. As if in a trance, I watched the solid shapes drop below his lip, gleaming with saliva but much shorter than King Drakkar's fangs and with blunt tips.

It was then I noticed only one of us pulsed with the rhythmic thump of a heartbeat.

"You're all Draugr," I said. "Vampires."

"Yes."

Purified silver. It is the most potent weapon against those cut off from the Gods. I'd once believed my mother was calling me a weapon, but it was the Y Tree itself. If only I could move my arm and embed it into his.

The vampire stared down at me, his eyes returning to a normal deep brown but rimmed with gold, full of hunger and desire. To take me? Heat simmered between us, the thrill of the fight, the pressure of our bodies imprinting on one another.

To kill me?

His eyes shifted from desperate to focused, and no longer staring at me. He wrenched his attention from me and sucked in a tight breath.

Why the unliving even breathed, I didn't know. I only knew what the poetic sagas said of them, spoken in flowering tongues and with the breath of a believer's whisper.

Breathing slower now and without any flecks of red in his eyes, he looked back at me. His throat bobbed with a swallow as he took me in.

"I prefer Kayn," he said. I searched his face, brow furrowed. He didn't hurt me, other than the pinching of his heavy hip pressed into mine. "You called me Draugr," he explained. "I prefer my name, Kayn."

"And I prefer not to be pinned to the ground by a stranger."

His eyes flashed and then trailed down my face and neck all the way to where our hips connected. "It wouldn't be necessary if you'd let me speak with you."

I opened my mouth but nothing came out because he was right. I couldn't argue that I'd only run from him, and then fought when I no longer could escape. He was just another shadow, threatening to claim me for unknown reasons. History told me I couldn't allow him to get within reach of me.

"I am not a threat," he said as if I would take his word so easily. I turned my head to break our gaze so he would know I didn't buy into him. He had to earn my trust after stalking me. "It seems you've already discovered this for yourself, but you cannot marry King Drakkar. At all costs, you must not."

Breath froze in my throat. I slid my gaze back to him. "On that, we agree."

"He wants what you can give him."

"And what is that?" I asked, irritation staining my voice

because as much as I wanted to hear the answer, I hated that he knew what I didn't.

"Your help."

I almost laughed as air escaped me in a huff.

His brows lifted in tenuous impatience. "He wants to use you since you are Volva." I snapped my attention back to him. "A witch."

"I know what Volva are." I considered trying to use the compulsion I wielded over the king, but he wasn't hurting me and I couldn't deny the curiosity welling within me. His interest in my betrothal was odd at best.

Besides that, I didn't need to show him just how much of a witch I was, in case he intended to get me exiled.

Even if he spoke of witches, it didn't mean he approved of magic.

I'd witnessed my mother communing with the Gods in an enchanted divination and then seen the aftermath at her doorstep. Magic—or witchcraft—had always been like a distant cousin whose name we refused to say aloud beyond the safety of our own walls. A living force that we were both proud to call a part of our family and yet a curse to be ashamed of since it was an old belief attributed to our simple-minded ancestors. The same ancestors who scarred the earth with the wasteland after centuries of battles incited by purposeless wars passed down from the conflict between Gods Odin and Freya against Loki.

"Then perhaps you know that you're the most potent of them all," he said.

"You say that as if I am a poison." My mind flickered to my mother's face. Perhaps she *had* intended to hint that I was a weapon. His eyes dipped to my throat again, his blunt fangs were still exposed between his parted lips. "Must I lay beneath you while you tell me what I already know?" Though he was the one with the fangs, I was the one with a bite in my voice. He'd pinned me easily and I hated that after years of running and practicing defense with Ragna, I was still over-powered.

His mouth curled in a faint smirk. "If you do not run, or stab me."

"I make no promises to anyone but myself."

"Then you'll never know the potential the Gods are trying to give you."

I frowned. "A Draugr speaks of the Gods?" The sagas said otherwise. Draugr were the only beings cut off from the Gods, since they were never living and could not die and go to Folk-vangr or Valhalla.

"I told you..." he held his small smile. "I prefer Kayn."

I forced a smile, mustering feigned respect for the man pinning me to the ground—or rather the shape of a man in Draugr's skin. Another monster who sent my stomach flutter-ing. What the fuck was wrong with me?

"Kayn, will you alleviate your hips from mine so that I may move and we can discuss why someone like you would even acknowledge Odin and Freya when neither created you?"

His smile flickered, too quickly. I wanted to see it again. "It is true, they did not have a hand in my creation. But your kind did. What if I said you can both make and unmake someone like me?"

I narrowed my eyes, and it was then he finally picked himself up, freeing me from the weight of his body. He held out a hand to pull me to my feet. One moment I was running from him, then fighting him, now we were in discussion. My mind could barely wrap around it.

Like the Polar Nocturne, each day, each moment, melted into one another like a blur of memories with no defining features to track the change in time. The sun wouldn't rise for several more days.

With the pendant still gripped in my fist, I stood in front of him. As long as he made no move to hurt me, in my fist it would stay. "Get to the truth, *Kayn*." I elongated his name to show I was listening. "Why are you following me if you already know I won't marry the king?"

"I want you to pass the trials so the Gods may reach you."

I had a hundred questions but only one came out. "Why?" Why would he want the Gods in contact with me?

"Because it is crucial for the survival of humanity."

A leaf crunched behind him and my gaze dropped from his eyes to the darkness beyond.

When another figure cut through the shadows, my shoulders went taut and my legs ached to run. If he'd brought more monsters, like Astrid brought her partner to drag me through the trees, any chance of escape was a distant dream.

But when the figure crept closer, they came with the confident gait of Stasia's swaying hips.

"Cavorting with the enemy, are we Silver?" she said. "I should have known someone named after riches was not to be trusted."

"Then why did you return?" I asked, refusing to mask the disappointment in my voice. She'd helped me escape Mara's Keep, but it hurt to see her spot empty when I'd stayed awake and on watch for us.

"To save your sorry ass," she said. Kayn twisted to see her, and she merely folded her arms, lifting her chin as if daring him to come at her. Stasia was truly a force to be reckoned with. Just like my mother. "Once I recognized who it was, I knew you were in for a good time."

"You two know each other?" I asked though it was likely a stupid question. If they both resided in Mara's Keep, sharing the castle with the other servants and royals, they'd have crossed paths many times. But Kayn didn't dress like the other royals. He prowled the celebration with the air of authority like the royals but clothed himself as a commoner.

"I know of him," she said. "He is the only royal to ever have been exiled. And here he is again."

A royal and a vampire. "King Drakkar did not throw you out, why?" I asked.

"He does not stoop to pay attention to me when there is a witch as powerful as you within his sights. When you arrived in Mara's Keep, I was able to walk in your path unnoticed."

Stasia lifted one arm and regarded her fingernails with mild disinterest. "So, Kayn can't bite us, and he won't drag us back to King Drakkar either, because he'll just out himself. The executioners always find the source of violence."

"Not when they're vampires," he said, snapping his attention to her.

"That's a lie," Stasia spat. "The executioners always find those who incite violence. They're bound to do it, or else they're…" her voice cracked.

When he turned to face her, he towered over her, his shadow blanketing her in darkness as one thin stream of moonlight broke through the canopy of leaves and branches. "What is with the two of you and your inability to listen? I said it once already. Not with vampires. Executioners don't even have the strength to cut us down, much less the knowledge to track us."

First came icy fear with the impact of what he'd said. Executioners, the masked men and women trained to cut us down and control us, couldn't even touch these vampires. If they couldn't, what hope did the rest of us have to survive?

Once the ice in my veins melted enough for my mind to work, a rush of thoughts crashed through my mind like packed snow tumbling down the mountainside. Vampires thought themselves untouchable, but they were not more powerful than the Gods.

If Odin could reach me, I could protect myself from the king and stop the exodus of witches to The Sea of Skalds.

It was what my mother would believe. The Gods answered our calls before, but they'd never called for us. Though why should they? The people had all but abandoned them, outlawed their names, forgotten that they kept the monsters of the Nine Realms from slipping into our world. If they were to call on anyone, it'd be the silent believers, those of us who hid our sacrifices in the dark of night.

Someone like me.

A liar who lived in secret.

I sucked in a breath and fixed my eyes on Kayn. His blond hair tumbled over the parts of his skull where it was cut close to the skin. "What do you know of my Gods?"

He released a sigh and I found myself wondering about the inner workings of Draugr, or vampires. Why did they have no beating heart but sucked air in their lungs? Were their insides decayed? Could something that's never been alive even decay?

"Not enough," he said, his jaw flexing. "There are three trials that they've extended to you. An offering not unlike the sacrifice of burning Henbane to destroy a shadow." I flicked my eyes to him, and my heart skipped. How could he know what my mother and I offered the Gods all those years ago?

Unblinking now, his deep gaze seemed to swallow me. Though his eyes were a simple brown, the darkness of them reminded me of my own. Black water in the poisoned pools of the wasteland, a sight I'd never seen but heard detailed sagas with poetic description.

"How do you know of these trials?" I asked.

"Anastasia," he said plainly. Instinctively, I glanced at Stasia.

She pointed to herself and then shook her head. "Don't look at me. I'm just a pretty face."

Mother? Without thinking, I reached out and laid my hand on his forearm. If he was near my mother recently, I wanted to be closer to him. It was only expected that I wanted to trust the creature who proved to have some connection with the person I cared for above anyone else. "You know my mother?"

"I can take you to her. She's not in the wasteland, she's been relocated to Mara."

In Mara? My mother was right here, close enough to reach within a day's travel. I didn't know if I could allow myself to believe it.

My heart thumped, lifting weightlessly with every beat. "Is this a trick?" Even as I asked it, I knew the truth. Because the only way he knew about what we'd done to protect her from the shadow outside her window was if he'd spoken with her. My mother would never have uttered it to another soul, not unless she believed there was a purpose.

"It is not. But I am not giving you an option either. I will pursue this until the Gods can reach you."

"So you threaten me," I said. I was growing tired of men and monsters wielding their power with words. I wouldn't bear another threat.

"I'm simply committed to helping you seal your connection to the Gods."

"As a vampire? Won't you lead us into the dark and drain our blood?"

When he opened his mouth, fangs, like King Drakkar's, descended from the pink above his row of teeth. Except his were shortened and without sharp tips. "I have not fed on humans in a very long time."

The sagas said Draugr drew strength from the life that flows within us. Otherwise, their strength came with age. Every Polar Nocturne that passed, their well of endurance and strength filled and filled faster if they spent a portion of the darkness in an unconscious state. I stared at his broken fangs for too long. I didn't trust him, but without sharp teeth, he was safer than King Drakkar. "Anastasia asked you to come for me?"

The muscles in his throat strained as he swallowed thickly. "Yes."

Stasia looked back and forth between us. "Don't tell me you trust him."

I lifted my chin. "She wants me to learn about these trials? Why?"

"You truly do not listen. Humans will not survive when Vylheim inevitably becomes overrun by monsters. Everyone here will either be a vessel or a vampire. Now with this Age of Exploration on the horizon, they're seeking food from beyond, there won't even be anywhere to run."

"What do you care for human survival?"

He licked his lips. "Maybe there's a human I care for. Once you pass the trials, you'll not only know the truth of monsters, you'll eradicate them."

Victory over these trials will spare your fellow Volva for years to come. Freya's words came back to me until Loki's voice cut through my thoughts.

"I told you he was coming, L.
Go on, ask him about the second trial.
About waking those who play dead."

A shiver stole through me. My gaze slid across Kayn's face. "If you know so much about me and my Gods, tell me, what do they expect me to do next?"

His dark eyes fell to my feet. "Loki wants you to give power back to the vampires who've been buried. We rest in graves, but once we're under the ground, we cannot rise up on our own. Only a vampire's connected vessel or a witch with compulsion can do that."

Breath stagnated in my throat. I was that witch with compulsion, straight from Loki. A vampire was who Loki sent to guide me to this trial? It was as chaotic as it was dangerous.

"And why would I help monsters climb out of their graves?"

"So you can kill them."

"Me?" I breathed.

He nodded. "Chosen by Odin."

Nerves ignited down the back of my neck and my throat tightened. Kill them? Was this really what the Gods wanted from me? I didn't yet know the details of Odin's trial, but Freya's showed me what these monsters were capable of, and Loki gave me the power to compel them. But Odin?

According to the single saga mentioning Draugr, the Allfather despised the sight of these monsters. They were an affront to the humans he'd given life to in Midgard. They were the only part of this world he did not have a hand in. The sagas said they sprang from the ground, suggesting they'd found a new way into our realm from wherever they came from that wasn't through deep water, like giants and the other monsters beyond Midgard.

I should have known he wanted them dead. But why at my hand?

I'm a killer.

I'm selfish.

Evil.

This is why they chose me.

Stasia huffed but when I met her gaze, she shrugged. "I guess I'm on board," she said. "Because if the council is dead, who would send the explorers to drown at sea? The exiles haven't left for shore yet, if someone's going to kill the council, it needs to be now, and I, for one, want to help make that happen." Hope pitched her voice higher. I couldn't argue with that logic, but I was a weak runner, a simple girl from Skaldir...and just wicked enough to kill. "It's wild that you're going to be the one killing them though."

I opened my mouth to defend myself. *I'm not evil.*

That wasn't true. Maybe Silver wasn't evil, but I wasn't Silver.

Stasia hummed thoughtfully, drawing me from my downward spiral. "I guess I should have expected this from someone who rolls around in the leaves with the enemy." She said it as an insult but the mischief in her jade eyes revealed that the wall around her fortress was cracked. She was considering this wild change of plans along with me. "Anyway, it's not like he can turn us in," she muttered, dropping her arms and marching past us. "So lead the way, Monster."

"Listen this time," he said, his voice ragged and as deep as when he was pinning me to the ground. He was speaking to her yet staring at me. "I prefer Kayn."

"Right then," I said, not moving. Truly, it was out of sheer exhaustion rather than stubbornness or the desire to flex my control over the situation. My heart was pumping too slowly, and my limbs were sluggish. Fighting often energized me, but that combined with running all night and the shock and fear that stripped me bare, I required plenty of sleep.

As much as Kayn claimed we didn't hear him, I listened well enough. My listening skills and focus were usually just reserved for when my body spoke. My failing heart demanded I keep a piece of my attention on myself at all times, for survival.

Was this how Freya expected me to spare my fellow witches for years to come? Kill the vampires?

I straightened my spine and fixed him with my stare. "Kayn, you may not need rest very often, but I do. We will sleep here and then when I wake, if you want me to do this, for whatever reason you refuse to explain, then you'll take us to her."

If nothing else, my mother and I could offer another sacrifice and cut my ties to King Drakkar.

CHAPTER TWENTY-TWO

Hours of walking left my legs wobbly. The two days my body demanded I rest had all of us impatient to move faster now.

Pure fear and determination had pushed us deeper into the forest than I had thought possible that night. Far enough that Stasia claimed the wasteland was only a few more steps beyond the trees and to the side of us.

And she was right.

Between the crowd of tree trunks, I spotted dead plants with branches poisoned in black and gray earth stretched over the ground. Red lines, like veins snaked through the dry-packed dirt, and the stagnant clouds that clung to the border of the wasteland, threatened to inch its way into Mara.

We'd hiked a path parallel to it as we made our way deeper into the southern side of the kingdom.

Curiosity had me glancing to the edge of the forest, hoping to glimpse the place that was only spoken of in sagas. Sagas that scared me as a young girl, leaving my imagination as scarred as the battles left the earth. It was a morbid curiosity, not unlike my interest in King Drakkar before I had proof of his brutal behavior.

"Once you cross into the wasteland, you lose all sense of direction," Stasia said from the path above. She'd turned to walk backward and explain this to me.

"Yet you plan to go there," I said, my voice careful.

"Eventually, I'd find my way to Finan." Her voice was simultaneously confident and tinged with sadness when she spoke of him. "And where else would I hide from the vampires while I look for him? Don't you think being lost is worth survival? Or are your delicate sensibilities as queen more attuned to self sacrifice for the glory of it all?"

She feigned being faint by draping the back of her hand against her forehead. In the time we weaved through the trees, she'd grown more comfortable teasing me.

Perhaps she picked on me because we were following my plan now, rather than hers. But Stasia didn't strike me as someone who needed to control others, more that she found humor in times of distress as a way to cope. Likely because of her many years spent serving that monster.

I found entertainment in her teasing as we trudged through the darkness.

"I do love glory," I said, fueling the pep in her step.

Besides, I relished speaking the truth out in the open air. I didn't know glory in my own life, nor care for it, but I adored the sagas of triumph, of the Gods and Valkyries selecting the honorable for Valhalla and the chosen for Folkvangr. It was outlawed to speak of it, but I kept my dream to myself, to someday be taken to Valhalla where I could hear the stories of the Nine Realms from Odin himself where he sat at the head of the table with his wife Frigg.

I hurried to keep pace with Kayn who was picking through the forest's overgrowth a step ahead of me. It wasn't long before Stasia fell behind us as she became distracted by the wasteland. Perhaps she hoped to catch sight of Finan, but we saw no life and no movement beyond the scarred border.

We emerged at a remote village, where the view of the

king's castle was only a scrap of gray against the rolling green hills. The scattered structures didn't form a village you would recognize. No signs indicated what was inside each structure or if they were actively used.

The hillside was bare, with little trees and shrubbery, different from the full rose bushes all across Mara's Keep and the surrounding forest of thick trees that reached into the sky. Here, stones were crumbling from the buildings, moss and vines cracked through the closest structure as if the earth's growth was slowly swallowing it.

The spiked roof that reached as tall as the trees was cracked at the tip of the spire so that the tip lay sideways, pointing south rather than to the sky. Stained glass windows were either shattered or splintered into cracks until the artist's rendering in the glass was no longer recognizable.

Stasia caught up with us as we paused, her breath heaving from the effort of climbing the steep hill. She could run like a hunted deer in the woods but climbing was not a skill she'd mastered yet with her thin body and minimal muscle. I was the opposite.

"Where are we?" I shot Kayn an impatient look. "You said my mother was in Mara."

Stasia made a strange sound and folded her arms as she eyed Kayn. "He's also a monster, I wouldn't put it past him to be a little deceitful. Vampires love to trick and lie to their vessels so the humans come back for more torture."

Kayn narrowed his deep brown eyes at her. "You instructed me to lead the way."

A defiant hum came from her as she turned away from him. "Just because you're an Exile who can't turn us in without getting caught doesn't mean I trust you. And it definitely doesn't mean I like you."

Ignoring her, he faced me again. "This is Mara. A forgotten side of Mara."

"This is hideous," Stasia said.

"Is it abandoned?" I asked.

"The Hall of the Gods?" He turned to me, his gaze sharp with the golden rim closing in, etching away at his dark eyes. "Yes, long ago."

Stasia gasped. "Oh damn, it's a temple! I've never seen one with my own eyes, all the temples near Mara's Keep were leveled long before I was born. Children climb and play on what's left but they're ruins, nothing so grand."

My body went cold. "My mother is in there, isn't she?" I stole a look at Kayn who nodded silently. "Did she escape the wasteland?"

"In a sense." He turned away from me to face the temple. "Mara's people call this The Forsaken Hall."

I didn't ask more about her escape, but I couldn't stop my mind from wandering. Perhaps someone gave her a pass, akin to when King Drakkar stopped my execution. Or perhaps she dared find a way to break free of the borders of the wasteland and hide in Mara.

My ear prickled with the sensation of his eyes on me. "Though she is alive, I should warn you, she isn't well. I had a nearby villager come to attend to her while I was gone, but I can't promise they followed through."

Though I already knew this, a pang struck across my chest with a skipped heartbeat. Heat crawled up my throat and my hand found its way to my collarbone where I clawed at my itchy skin. Worry manifested in a thousand prickles over my exposed flesh.

"She's sick." I said absentmindedly, preparing myself to see her weak.

If Valhalla came for her soon, I would only try harder to find a way there. Battles were a scar of the past, but divination could connect us to Odin. Surely, her life as a seerborn had already connected her to the glory of Valhalla. She would be a welcome addition with her knowledge of our history and the Nine Realms. Or rather, how she'd used that knowledge to protect witches before, the Gods' vessels, like the enchantment she created to conceal my eyes and hide my nature.

I had to catch up to this glory if I wanted to be with her in the afterlife.

"She is," he said, confirming the story my eyes already told. They were nearly all black now, and once the white was gone, she would be too. "This is only more reason for you to work faster toward killing vampires."

I shot him a look. His impatience set me on edge. I hadn't even had the chance to see or speak with my mother in ten years and he expected me to focus on killing right now? I didn't want to be that person now, or ever.

"Yes, I'm aware you have your own goal in this," I snapped. Though I didn't know what that goal was. After traveling with him for over two days, he still didn't share enough for me to get to know him beyond his name and what he was. "But my mother is my first priority."

"And then I trust you'll focus on the Gods' Calling."

"And become a killer?" I shivered at the word.

"Of vampires."

I frowned. "I need to see my mother before I agree to anything."

Stasia, two steps ahead of us now, twisted toward us. Her freckles mashed together in a stricken expression. "What we should be asking is if she's actually in there." Her green eyes sharpened and slid to Kayn. "Even vampires without fangs have to eat. You could cut open her wrist just as easily."

Kayn said nothing, only continued walking right past her. I didn't need them to get along, but Stasia and I were entwined now and if Kayn was leading me to my mother, I'd follow him.

I had to believe she was here, because the alternative was that Kayn was the monster I knew him to be and he'd learned what he knew about my mother before he killed her, just like

King Drakkar killed innocent humans so he could feed on them.

I forced a breath and stepped up beside Stasia. We walked together, climbing the loping hill where the Hall of the Gods perched at the peak. "What did they do at the temples? The sagas didn't speak of them, and in Skaldir we communed with the Gods in the secret of the forest or in our own homes."

My mother rarely spoke of official worship, because coming from her, it had sounded like she longed for it, perhaps even planned to gather other believers where they could all call upon the Gods. Though it was outlawed in the official capacity, the hunt for glory, to impress the Gods and die in battle to earn a place in Valhalla was what created the wasteland. We scarred our world to reach the next world. It was an act of stupidity.

"Sacrifice," Stasia said. "That's what Mara's history says."

"Silver." Kayn said, his voice dying away as he froze in front of the temple.

I stopped short to keep from colliding with him. His arms flew out behind him to feel for me. He pulled me closer, as if using his body to block me.

Before he moved me, I caught his line of sight straight to the temple's entrance. "Get behind me." But it was Stasia who moved. From the corner of my eyes, I saw her slip away from us, sprinting for the cover of nearby trees.

And then I saw why.

Between two stone pillars sat King Drakkar.

His elbows rested on his peaked knees, his back leaning against one of the pillars with his hands hanging limp out in front of him. Though he sat on the ground, his casual demeanor and wicked grin told me he knew he still held all the power here.

But Kayn was one of them. Draugr. Vampire. Would he stop King Drakkar if he laid his claim to me?

"No need to hide my wife from me, Exile. I'm the one who

let her leave, and I have to say, I'm disappointed with her choice." King Drakkar's grin spread wider as he met my gaze. I wanted to spit out that I wasn't his wife, but it was a waste of breath. He only said it to vex me and flex his authority over the woman he trapped into this arranged marriage. "I'll have her one way or another."

I shoved past Kayn. "Like Hel you will. I escaped you once and I will do it again. I don't care if you think you can drag me to the altar by my hair, I'll cut it off before I bind myself to you."

King Drakkar stood slowly, enjoying the audience as he raked his fingers through his loose hair. It wasn't tied back behind his head like it always was when he was inside the castle. Here he looked wilder, more intense. Less of the figurehead on the throne and more of the monster within.

But the cracks seeped through with the twitch of his mouth. The tension in his arms and shoulders.

He was on edge.

Was it because of Kayn? Or because I'd bested King Drakkar once already and he feared the trance I'd put him in?

"You will let me see my mother," I said, focused now on the movement inside the temple's open door. I could see her inside, laying on a bench, a blanket covering her thin frame.

There she was, my precious, amazing, sick mother. After ten years, I finally laid eyes on her again. Joy warmed every inch of my body, but in a single breath, it was replaced by prickly worry for her health. Still, she was *here*, right in front of me.

I suddenly felt like the little girl at her side again, staring up at her with wide eyes full of love and admiration. From the age I could recall memories, I had a well full of them of her enchanting witches with ways to conceal their magic, guiding them with portions of visions that told her where these witches could stay safe.

She was a hero, and I'd never loved anyone more.

And she was still alive.

Of course I knew this, or else my eyes would be nothing but inky blackness, but seeing her chest rise and fall with the breath of life was different. The buzz of hope was dangerously addictive, and it vibrated through my veins as I stared at her.

King Drakkar stepped to the side and beckoned with both arms. "After you, my queen."

I gritted my teeth and marched to the Hall of the Gods, brushing past him with every muscle in my body tensed.

Once I was through the door, I ran and dropped to her side. Her hollow cheeks sunk inward. Pale thin hands with crooked fingers rested on top of the blanket at her chest. Her eyes were closed until I laid my palm over her icy wrist. They split open in narrow slits, her eyes rolling beneath the lids.

"Mother," I breathed.

"Silver?" Her voice was like the sharp *shing* of an executioner sheathing his sword. Cutting, hollow, hopeless. But it was hers and I was hearing it for the first time in so long. Hot tears stung behind my eyes.

"What happened? How did you end up here? How can I help you?" The words tumbled out of me one after another. I didn't feel the tears streaming down my face until they dripped on the stone floor and over my folded legs, slowly soaking my skirts with salty dampness.

"Silver," King Drakkar said. I ignored him and tilted my ear to my mother's pale lips. Her mouth moved slowly but she breathed the words out with enough force for me to understand the shape of them.

"Henbane," she whispered.

The poisonous plant we'd cultivated so many years ago and then burned as a sacrifice had saved her once before—or rather, the Gods had as they accepted her offering and the risk of breathing the toxic smoke.

"Silver," King Drakkar cut through our conversation again.

I shot him a look full of vitriol. Kayn kept his distance from the temple, staying back several paces.

"Silver—"

"Shut up!" I screamed. I shot to my feet and willed everything within me to send him into another trance. "Tell me what you need from me and then leave."

The attempt at compulsion didn't work. I was too distracted by my mother.

He only shifted his jaw. "Invite me inside, and I'll carry her back with us."

"I'm not going anywhere with you."

"There are healers at the castle."

"Like I believe you'll treat us well after what I saw in your chambers. You're disturbed, disgusting."

"Monster or not, your words can still hurt me," he said.

"Perfect. I'll wield them like a sharp sword."

"Just say it." He stepped closer, filling the open doorway.

"Say what?"

"Come," a weak voice said from below. My blood went cold as I realized my mother had just beckoned the king inside.

In one smooth blurring movement, King Drakkar rushed into the temple. I half expected him to spark into flames since his state as a vampire was severed from the Gods. This place of worship was no longer active, but I still hoped it would destroy him, I hoped the Gods could reach out and strike him down.

He dropped to my mother's other side, opposite me, where he hovered over her. My jaw went slack and breath left my lungs as his mouth closed against her neck.

I tried to scream but I had no air. When I tried to move, my stomach retched. Instead of vomiting, I swallowed the bile back down and it was the dregs of energy I'd been clinging to after hiking here that seemed to spew out of me.

My legs shook beneath me.

Horror filled my every nerve with stinging, fiery pain. His fangs sunk into her papery skin and her eyes rolled back into her head.

Was this his plan? Kill the person I cared for the most to flex his power over me and drag me to the altar where he'd torture me for our entire marraige?

I would have taken life in the wasteland.

CHAPTER TWENTY-THREE

In a blur of images sweeping through my mind, I imagined King Drakkar at his knees with my harvesting scythe buried into his throat the same way his fangs were buried in my mother's neck.

The Gods knew I'd seen too many beheadings. It was too easy to picture the king's head severed from his body after he'd bitten my mother.

But I blinked the vicious thoughts away and suddenly shame coursed through me, hot and sickening where it pooled in the pit of my gut.

If I attacked the king, I'd be giving in to the darkest side of me again. I'd become what I'd locked away. Everyone would know the wickedness lurking deep within me.

But my mother wouldn't live to see the next minute if I didn't act, and that was enough to push me into action, even if I barely had the strength to take one step.

It took me entirely too long to move, to rip the pendant from my pocket and aim to plunge it into the king's arm so that he might suffer the horrific pain that he was inflicting on my mother. He was stooped over her, fangs deep in the soft flesh of her throat, kneeling in the middle of the Hall of the Gods where his kind was unwelcome.

Why had she called him to her?

The moment I forced my foot forward, time blurred. I threw myself at King Drakkar, ready to hurt him. To stop him from bleeding her dry in her most vulnerable state.

I lifted the Y tree gripped tightly in my fist and arced my entire arm down to land on his hand so that he'd let go and lose his grip. He held the edge of the bench where she lay so that he could hover over her, his other hand cupping beneath her head so that her neck angled open toward him.

Before the sharp tip sliced through his skin, his form flickered in a blur my eyes couldn't comprehend. In one breath, he dropped her back to the bench and shot to his feet with his fingers wrapped firmly around my wrist. With little effort, he held my arm steady, the pendant safely away from where it could touch his flesh.

"I need you to wait," he said, voice low, infuriatingly calm. "I only speak the truth, but I know you won't believe me. So wait." His icy gaze shifted to my mother and then back to me. "You'll get what you want, and then..." his wicked mouth curled in a sickening grin. He released a faint laugh, the force of the air puffing through his nose. "Then I'll get what I want."

When I glanced down at her limp, helpless body, thinking of the mere seconds we had together before he bit her, my eyes burned.

Tears stung at the edges until my vision swam and hatred laced my choking voice. "How am I getting what I want when you've killed the only person I care for?"

Fuck his claim to speak the truth, *she* was the only one with enough guts to say our history was tainted and incomplete. *She* was strong and brave and if only I could have been like her, I could have stopped him.

"Silver!" A harsh voice shouted from somewhere behind

me, the sound vague and clawing at the edges of my focus. "Call me to you."

King Drakkar's brow twitched as he used his hold on my wrist, pulling me closer where we stood over my mother's body. His face was a mere breath from mine and I resisted the urge to spit in it, not wanting to disrespect the most admirable person I'd ever known in case the spit dripped onto her. The red-stained gold in his eyes was receding, returning them to the color of water in the fjords.

He no longer smirked, but held his mouth in a steady, emotionless line. "She's not dead—"

"Turned into a monster then?" I cried, my voice squeaking and desperate like a young child who'd slipped through a crack in the ice. I sucked in a shuddering breath. "I know the sagas better than anyone else. She taught me every single one. Draugr can make more from the shell of our bodies."

Now he smiled, but for once, there was no arrogance, no amusement, just a hollow, lifeless lift of his blood-stained lips. Stained with her blood. My throat tightened, another well of sadness swelling within me. "Not every single one."

"What?"

"Silver!" I blinked, finally recognizing Kayn's heavy voice. "I can help."

I twisted my neck, if for nothing else than to angle my face away from the man I hated, to break our gaze before I screamed at him and descended into a pitiful, grief and rage-induced disaster. At the corner of my vision, I saw his dark frame in the doorway.

"Come," I whispered with as much effort as I could give to my splitting voice. It didn't help that aching exhaustion was tugging at my bones. I needed to listen to what my body was screaming at me, but another rush of tears blurred my eyes as I spoke the same word that was my mother's last word.

How could he claim she wasn't dead when I just witnessed

him drinking the life of another innocent person only two nights ago?

He'd done the same to her, sinking his spiked teeth into her neck until her blood coated his fangs.

Through the tears, I only made out vague shapes as King Drakkar's grip on me went slack. My arm fell limp at my side and I stumbled back, no longer held in place by his grasp.

Kayn was upon him before I knew what had happened. His eyes shining a brighter gold than I'd ever seen on the king. He ripped King Drakkar away from my mother, away from me, and slammed him against the wall between the benches. Somehow, Kayn was stronger than the king, able to pin him to the solid stone.

King Drakkar seethed, his eyes golden again, though not as striking as Kayn's eyes. "Think about this Exile. You cannot kill the king."

"I have nothing to lose."

"Don't you? Opportunity is a great stake." King Drakkar tilted his head, his mouth a wry smile even though Kayn still overpowered him and held him pinned like a criminal ready for the swing of an executioner's blade.

"You will leave," he said. "And I won't rip your head from your shoulders."

King Drakkar only laughed. "Try to kill me, Exile. You can't. We're perfectly matched in strength and speed, made by the same power. We'll destroy each other."

"Except I don't care if I die."

Another laugh slipped from the king. "Really? You're not hoping for a soul first?"

Kayn grunted, holding his gaze on the king. After a moment of thick air and little breathing, Kayn finally wrenched his hand away from the king's throat. His chest heaved with what I could only guess was a mixture of frustration and fight.

King Drakkar stared down at him for a moment before

shoving past him. He marched toward me but I thrust out the pendant as a silent reminder to keep his distance from me. He didn't bother to even glance at it, keeping his gaze on me. The iciness had softened. Was it that Kayn's threat had stripped the king of his arrogance? No, the arrogance remained at the corner of his mouth where his lips lifted in a perpetual curl.

"When you see what I've done, come to me," he said.

I recoiled. "Never."

"I'll either marry you or kill you, Silver, and I'd really hate to do the latter."

"Leave!" Kayn shouted.

King Drakkar didn't move, clearly unbothered by the vampire who could easily overpower him. He took no threats which only sent heat flaming up my chest and neck. Anger burning all the way to my tongue.

He'd threatened me, trapped me, used my past to claim me and now he'd done it again. I wanted Kayn's threat to bring him to his knees—no, *I* wanted to bring him to his knees.

What had made the trance successful? And how could I recreate it? If I could compel him to leave, he'd have no choice. Maybe I could even compel him to never return.

What had I done when I saw King Drakkar covered in blood? I'd nearly vomited.

But I didn't. Instead, I'd tried to calm myself. I whispered the incantations to keep my heart from exploding.

My lips parted, the phrases my mother used to say coming to my mind. "I am in control of my own fate." My mouth moved of its own accord as energy tingled through my veins. Freya's words in The Thorns of Betrayal, my mother's phrases, my incantations, memorized and repeated a hundred times to slow my pounding heart.

My pulse thumped twice and then paused, twice again then paused for too long as a pang struck across my chest and then the beating resumed slow, too slowly. "You're a blight upon this realm..." my voice faltered as my head spun. Black spots dotted my vision and a heaviness tugged at my limbs and face. My mouth felt as if it was melting off my chin, sealing shut as it slid down, down.

I slumped, my body suddenly thick and falling like gathered snow tumbling down the mountain. King Drakkar darted forward and I opened my mouth to scream but it felt like it was lost on the floor beneath me. I fell into the crook of his arm, as vulnerable as my mother, when darkness overcame me.

I'd pushed myself too hard and without enough rest. Yet Freya wasn't granting me a vision now. I was on my own, succumbing to the darkness that my foolish, relentless determination had driven me to.

I should have listened to my body.

When I peeled my eyes open, I was still in the king's hold, except now he was slumped too and I was laying across his lap. He leaned against my mother's bench, his head hanging. Something heavy draped over my mouth and I realized it was his arm. I jerked, throwing it off of me only to send blood splattering across my dress that was splayed out in front of me. It was then I tasted wine sweetening my tongue. I drew my hand to my mouth, my fingers coming away with the stain of the king's blood.

With my heart skipping, my gaze slid to where his heavy arm lay. A jagged wound cut up the flesh of his forearm with blood trickling out...and it'd been in my mouth.

Why did he feed me his blood? Why hadn't Kayn stopped him this time? Was this another way to turn a human into a monster? Or was this to poison me?

His words came back to me. *I'll marry you, or kill you.*

I scrambled away from him, frantically wiping the blood from my lips. Red seeped into the ridges of my fingers and stained beneath my fingernails. The worst part was that I wanted to taste it again, to fill myself with it like sweet wine warming me from within. I forced my legs beneath me so I could stand and back away from King Drakkar's reach.

Kayn stood over us, casting a long shadow from the flicker of torches on the temple walls. "You've done enough. Leave."

King Drakkar dragged his head up with a lazy smirk at Kayn. "I did what you could not." Weakly, he pulled himself into a straighter position, glaring at Kayn who stood over us.

When King Drakkar turned to me, his blue eyes heavy as they searched my face, he reached out and tipped my chin. I didn't recoil this time, something in his eyes pinned me in place. His touch was a mere brush against my skin, sending goosebumps along my jawline and down my neck where they spread over my collarbone and chest. "I didn't kill her."

"Liar," I said weakly.

He chuckled. "I'm not the liar here and you know that."

"I said leave!" Kayn shouted.

Again, the king ignored him. What was stopping Kayn from attacking him again?

King Drakkar dropped his arm. "When you're ready for the truth. Find me."

"I've already heard your plan."

I would never choose him. *Find me*, he'd said, as if I'd ever seek him out.

I could hardly believe this was my reality. Two unliving beings fighting over my mother's body in a forbidden and abandoned temple, when only weeks ago I was a hopeful, simple woman traveling into Mara's Keep in search of lost history.

"Here's a piece of truth for you, my wife." He pointed at my mother. "I pulled the poison from her. I took it, for now." My heart flipped. I snapped my gaze to her limp body. "This won't last, she'll grow weaker again, and I won't help her until you take my hand."

My eyes sliced back to the king. "How can I believe you

helped her when she was speaking before and she's helpless now?"

"I told you to wait. You'll see when she wakes."

King Drakkar thrust his hand out toward Kayn, silently demanding he keep his distance as he strode out of the temple, the cracking stone doorway looking as if it'd crumble around him. He stopped just outside and turned, his eyes first on Kayn then shifting to me, still soft but hardening to an in-between state like a melting icicle.

"I may be too weak to fight now, but I am still the king and you're in my kingdom." He held my gaze. "You will be my wife." I opened my mouth to reject this, but he continued with a steady voice, no malice, no passion, just a pure, icy calm that I could only achieve with incantations. "And if you choose otherwise, both you and your mother will die." He tilted his head, face devoid of emotion. "How tragic that will be."

"You're cruel," I said, my voice weak from my aching throat.

"Then I'll fit in perfectly with the other Gods," he said. "Remember what I said, Silver. You have until first light."

With that, he melted into the darkness beyond the glow of the temple's torches. The moonlight couldn't reach into the shadow cast by the towering structure, but it filtered in through the splinters in the stained glass windows.

The aura of his calm may have come from his weakened state, however that'd happened, but I couldn't help longing for it to remain when he left. How could the chaos and bloodshed caused by him end this way?

With him gone, perhaps I should have sought out Stasia, wherever she'd disappeared to. Or I could have thanked Kayn for his help. I did neither.

I simply dropped to my knees and draped my arms over my mother's body, my head resting on her chest. I twined my fingers into her hand and squeezed, but she remained limp.

Grief gutted me, scooping deep between my ribs and hollowing out my heart.

If King Drakkar truly helped her, there'd be evidence of healing.

I straightened and tilted my head over her chest. With my ear pressed against her, I heard it—a faint but rhythmic thump deep within her, growing stronger and stronger with every beat.

CHAPTER TWENTY-FOUR

After a night of forced rest, I woke to Stasia shoving a crust of bread into my hands. Where she got the food, I had no idea.

"If you're going to kill the council, you need to eat," she said.

I dragged myself to sitting up in the makeshift bed Kayn had created with gathered blankets. Stasia shuffled to where my mother lay and pressed her fingers to my mother's throat. After a moment without breath, Stasia nodded and I allowed myself to inhale. My mother's heart was still beating. She was still alive.

When Stasia turned around, I pinned her with my stare. "Where did you go when King Drakkar showed up?"

Folding her arms, she shot a glare right back at me. "Eat the damn bread, now. And I was in hiding, obviously. He can't know I'm still with you."

"What are you still with me?" I tilted the bread to my lips but did not yet take a bite. "What about Finan?"

She smiled. "I'll catch him when they move the witches to shore. They have to go through Mara. We are between the wasteland and the most southern tip at the Sea of Skalds.

There's no way they're going all the way up and around. Besides, you need your handmaiden if you're going to survive long enough to supposedly kill the council. I'm rooting for you, Silver."

Before I could thank her, she slipped through the door and outside. A blast of chilly air swept through the temple and a shudder rippled through me.

Though her offer to stick with me warmed me, goosebumps pricked my arms and I winced. A dull ache throbbed at the center of my chest. My heart had been working too hard with the effort of hiking to the Hall of the Gods, and then it nearly broke over the sight of my mother's limp body.

After filling my belly with the dense bread, I climbed to my feet and tiptoed to my mother's side. I listened to her heartbeat growing steadier when Stasia appeared again.

"There's a fire outside with a pot of stew. I'm going to rest. You're going to finish stirring it and then eat. Got it?"

"Okay, but where did you get food and supplies?"

"Again with the questions." She rolled her eyes for a dramatic effect. "The temple had cooking supplies and there are villages nearby selling food. I think you forget we're not isolated in the middle of miserable, frozen mountains like you Skaldir folk are used to."

I shook my head but did not argue with her.

"Anyway," she continued. "Kayn won't stop talking about these trials you have to do. He says you need to be strong, so he's been checking in on you even though I keep telling him that you need a lot of rest and even more food. In my book, strong means well-fed."

"Kayn said that?"

She hummed her confirmation. "My guess? He's worried you're not going to run off and kill all the vampires he said he wants you to kill unless your mother tells you about it herself."

His worry was spot on. I wasn't going to run off and kill anyone, again. I'd already done that, and it haunted me. I needed a better understanding of what the Gods wanted, or maybe I needed more time, something that wasn't just a cloaked vampire with broken fangs demanding I do what he wanted.

Stasia's voice cut through my thoughts. "I don't know what you're really planning to do, but for now go eat the stew so you can get strong enough to at least wipe that damn smirk off the king's face."

Despite my mother's condition, King Drakkar's threat, and everything else, Stasia managed to make me smile. I stood and nodded, slipping out into the night without another word and hoping to find Kayn on my way to the stew.

With my mother unable to speak, I had to rely on whatever Kayn knew about Loki's trial, which made my blood boil. Based on Stasia's comments, he was already growing impatient with me and we'd only just arrived at my mother's side. Not only was she sick, but she worsened, and I'd collapsed. What the fuck did he expect from me?

To wake vampires, apparently, and then kill them. I shook my head.

Waking vampires. It felt too dangerous, but I wouldn't expect anything less from Loki, and I expected everything from myself. Dangerous or not, it was my destiny.

I rounded the corner of the Hall of the Gods to find Kayn pacing the yard, tracking the graves in the darkness. I wrapped my cloak tighter around me as icy wind cut through the fabric and sent a swath of goosebumps over my arms.

The fire and pot of stew by the graves were a welcome sight. I was endlessly grateful for all the supplies Stasia had spent time digging out from the cabinets in the temple. I'd be lost without her, and freezing to death.

Orange flames flickered and tendrils of black smoke licked up into the air. I had no doubt Kayn had helped her build this fire since it was so close to the graves where he seemed drawn to hover. I was grateful for all the help he'd provided, feeding my mother and keeping watch over her here before we arrived.

He crouched beside the half-winged Valkyrie whose stone body lay grieving over the gravestone. His hand brushed over the dirt and weeds. In Skaldir, everything would still be coated in a thick layer of snow, unable to plant and cultivate. Everything there survived on stores during the Polar Nocturne.

Here, a dusting of snow melted away even in the persistent darkness.

When Kayn noticed my approach, he stood and weaved through the crumbling graves. Chunks of stone lay in his path, but he stepped over them and marched toward me. His cloak billowed in the wind behind him but he showed no signs of being chilled. I pulled my cloak even tighter to ward off the icy wind but it was no use, my body already convulsed in its natural attempt to keep warm.

I stiffened as I prepared to tell him, once again, that I didn't know if I could let myself kill someone again. Even if Loki's and Odin's trials would lead me to it.

"How is she?" he asked.

All tension melted as quickly as a snowflake in Mara. I released my fingers from where I'd buried them in the fabric of my skirts and reached for the fire. The blue tips wouldn't turn pink for upwards of an hour, if at all, but the heat of the flames soothed my soul as it promised even a little help.

"Not much better," I said as I sat on a rock by the fire. "There is nothing I can do for her other than attend to the wound King Drakkar left and keep her fever tempered. If the king hadn't fed on her, I believe she'd still be awake."

His jaw shifted. "We cannot wait for her to wake for you to trust me. You need to pass Loki's trial."

"Loki's yes, but I'm not a killer, Kayn."

"You can't kill what isn't alive."

I gritted my teeth, knowing he'd let me stew in the quiet. I wanted to wield the same weapon as him; silence. Every time he sealed his lips and refused to explain more, I was further and further from trusting him, from accepting his message. I needed to hear it from my mother's lips. Only then would I consider the task of wiping monsters from this world.

Kayn didn't even deign to tell me the details of why he wanted me to eradicate all of his kind—including him. He only mentioned caring for a human, but he seemed more alone than even me.

My skin prickled. Was this all a lie? He'd led me to my mother, he'd fought King Drakkar for me, but I knew nothing else about him.

"Alive or not, it still feels like killing," I said.

He sighed. "When a vampire is struck in the heart with a wooden stake, we turn to dust. It isn't like stabbing a human where there is suffering and blood. It isn't killing, it is destroying. A vampire can also be decapitated, though the body must be burned after or we may return our head to our shoulders and resume existence."

I pulled my hands back into my lap and him from over the steam. "And you think I, a simple girl from Skaldir, can cut off a monster's head?"

"I've heard you speaking with Stasia, I know you trained in secret with your friends back home, but beyond that, the Gods have—"

"Chosen me," I finished for him. "So you've said."

"You don't believe me?" His brow peaked as he took a seat on a rock on the other side of the fire. Hair fell into his face and he looked all the more my shadow as the flames cast dancing, erratic light over the darkness surrounding him.

"How can I believe what you barely say?"

I scooted to the edge of the rock and reached for the stone spoon. Swirling it around the soup, notes of warm honey and squash filled my nose. Stasia was a wonder with food. If I didn't know better, I'd think she was a witch and her particular power was cooking something from nothing.

My stomach growled with impatience. Ignoring it, I eyed Kayn.

Instead of biting back with a clever retort like King Drakkar, he remained silent.

The longer the silence stretched the more frustration swelled within me. I couldn't stay quiet another second.

"Why are you consumed with the thought of me killing your kind?" I asked. "It doesn't make sense and paints you as cruel as the king."

Though I supposed destroying bloodthirsty monsters for Odin and Freya wasn't akin to feeding on the blood of innocent humans. Still, I couldn't comprehend why a monster himself would pressure me to take up this call when it'd only end in his own destruction.

He scrubbed his hand over his chin, his brown eyes staring into the flames as he thought.

I tried to ignore the silence before I leaped over the flames and strangled a response out of him. That'd likely only further convince him that I was destined to become the chosen killer of his kind.

I fought the urge to roll my eyes. Perhaps I'd spent too many hours beside Stasia in the past few days.

I ripped my gaze from Kayn, and busied myself, dipping a spoon into the sweet soup and filling my mouth with the brew before I screamed at him. *You're my last connection to my mother, tell me why you sought her out. Tell me everything she told you. Mostly, tell me why the fuck she trusted you of all creatures.*

The soup warmed my throat and trickled down my chest. Sweetness lingered on my tongue, but not as satisfying as the cinnamon sweet buns, so I picked up the cloth of honey and let more drain into the pot.

After what felt like the entire Polar Nocturne, Kayn sucked in a breath and leaned forward, his elbows on his splayed legs. "I've been waiting for someone like you for a very long time." I hummed my acknowledgement, just enough to encourage him to keep talking but not so demanding that he shied away from me. "I'd almost lost hope when Ingrid vanished." I looked up at him now, unable to tamper my interest. "She was a witch too, chosen for this task of destroying us vampires. She'd connected with Odin and Freya, but it did not last, and I was left alone again to wander the graves."

"Wander the graves? Do you walk out here every night?"

Did he miss this woman? Or was she just another target of the Gods that he shadowed? Had he grown impatient with her and insisted she kill vampires too? Kayn never spoke of others but I couldn't help wondering if he'd cared for someone once, a mother, a friend, or perhaps a child, even a lover...

"I don't have a choice." He blinked away from me, his gaze lost on something vague in the shadows. "Have you ever made a mistake that consumes you even years later?"

Breath caught in my throat. Every muscle in my body stiffened as my lips dropped open and I drew a sharp gasp. Did he know? Astrid and her partner were dead, gone, thanks to the Gods' help, and the king had only known about their deaths because they'd never returned to resume life in the castle with the other royals.

Of course, I'd done worse than hurt Astrid and Sten.

I gave myself a little shake as if to rattle the creeping memory out of my mind. It was so long ago, and I'd only been a child.

I dragged my eyes back to Kayn. Focusing on him and whatever he was clearly wrestling with helped pull my mind out of an impending spiral.

He clenched and unclenched his right fist, seemingly unbothered by my reaction. Though I didn't find comfort in forming a fist, the movement was familiar; the repetitive action of calming oneself.

I, too, repeated the same phrases over and over in my mind to ward off thoughts of the horrible act I'd committed.

"What is it?" I prodded

"I persist," he continued. "Hating myself more with every Polar Nocturne that passes, and I've had many years, hundreds, for this to build upon itself. I turned too many innocent humans into monsters."

He'd made more vampires. No wonder guilt plagued him.

The twist of his mouth and sadness in his dark eyes sent my heart skipping and feeling every word he said as my own shame coursed through my veins. I hated what I'd done, but I'd only been haunted by it for twenty years. I couldn't imagine living as long as he had knowing this and while keeping the secret to myself.

I wanted to forget it, but I knew I never would.

I tried to catch his gaze, but his eyes were fixed at my feet. "Is that why you filed down your fangs? So that you wouldn't turn anyone else?"

He only offered me a grim smile. With a slow breath his dark eyes finally met mine. His throat rippled with a rough swallow. "After the only person I cared for died, I was entirely alone." He thumbed the pad of his finger against the flat surface of his broken fang. "It consumed me, drove me mad until I could no longer face loneliness. I found myself in a village of men and women and…" he swallowed again. "Children too. After I drained the first woman I found, I turned the rest. Every single one of them." Pain wracked every word he forced out. I stopped eating and sat forward, clutching the bowl in my fingers as I absorbed his story. "A child of the woman I drained followed me. He was a vampire then, too, of course. I'd turned him. I couldn't be rid of him. He thanked me because he said that as a human he was always starving and in pain. As this creature, he was only starving."

"You don't feel pain?" I couldn't help my curiosity. I cut through his story with the hot knife of my need for knowledge. I swallowed each piece easily, bites of truth I'd been dying to uncover.

"That's not entirely true," he said. "Vampires feel plenty

of pain, just as we do pleasure. But the boy was newly turned, he felt strong at the time compared to his weak human body. He soon learned vampires starve more often than humans."

Kayn dropped his head in his hands. After a moment, he sucked in a tight breath and looked at me. "Even after all that, I didn't snap my fangs off. Not until the boy had hunger pangs and the vessel I'd captured didn't have enough blood for us both. It's hard enough to resist human blood, so I took a stone and broke them off so that I'd have to rely on hunting and consuming animal blood so that he would have enough to drink from the humans we captured.."

"Where is he now? The boy?"

"With Hel," he said.

The underworld. Hel was the goddess of the place our souls descended if we were not granted passage into Valhalla or chosen by Freya for Folkvangr—both places of varying honor for life after death.

"He died dishonorably," I whispered my understanding. Kayn only frowned, not offering more details on the boy's passing. I wasn't about to ask. The twisted grimace revealed he was in enough agony already, but there was one question I couldn't tame back from my tongue. "Isn't it true that vampires no longer have souls? What part of him could Hel have claimed?"

He raked his teeth over his bottom lip. With a shuddering inhale, he forced the air out quickly. "Vampires age slower than humans, so by the time he stumbled upon Hel in Midgard, he was a young man."

"In Midgard?" I shook my head. Monsters dripped into our realm from the others, but Hel was a goddess, not even Odin and Freya came to Midgard. How could Hel? It was impossible.

"I don't know the details of her summoning, but she was here. I witnessed it with my own eyes. Once a human turns into a vampire, their soul is ash, but she didn't need to find the flakes of his soul, she took his body instead. I don't claim to understand why the gods, including Hel, do what they do."

"And you feel responsible for his death, too?" I guessed.

"Guilt ravages me for all of it." He nodded. His hand shook as he scraped his fingers through his hair. "The only relief I find is to act as though I am still the human that Freya and Odin draw sacrifices from. I know you're curious about why I'd want you to take up a Call that'd require you to eventually destroy me, but destruction will be my final relief from this guilt." He swallowed hard, the muscles in his throat tightening. I didn't know if Draugr could cry, but in the firelight, his brown eyes shimmered with an emotion I'd suppressed for too long; pure, all-consuming guilt.

I stood and walked over to him with the bowl still in my hands. Perching on the rock beside him, I offered him a sip of the soup. "I don't know if you enjoy human food."

He sat up and accepted the offer, taking the spoon and tipping the liquid into his mouth. "It's very sweet," he said, swallowing and squinting with displeasure.

I smiled. "You don't like sweetness?"

"I haven't tasted it in years."

"Not even sweet wine? King Drakkar nearly swam in it." When he wasn't downing his vessel's blood.

He shook his head. "No, but thank you for sharing. I've deprived myself of simple pleasures for so long. This guilt doesn't allow me to enjoy…anything."

I nodded, dropping my gaze to the wringing hands in my lap, because I knew he was describing my own fate. What he'd suffered all these years was coming for me next. I cleared my throat.

"I understand what it feels like to be unforgivable," I said. He dragged his gaze up from my hands and over my torso, searching every inch of my face as if he were looking into a mirror, understanding himself as much as he was getting to know me. "Thank you for stopping King Drakkar."

"You know if you accept Odin's trial too, you'll be free of him."

"I'll also have to cut down hundreds of people, and weren't we just talking of guilt and shame?" My teeth chattered as the wind shifted and carried the fire's warmth away from us.

He set the spoon on the rock and took my hand. He was surprisingly warm, like a living being, and I could almost trick myself into thinking he wasn't one of the undead creatures who crawled through the sagas. "There is no shame in destroying monsters for the safety of your own realm."

With his gentle hold, his thumb brushing over my fingers, I almost believed him.

My heart didn't skitter at his touch. When I first met him, I'd felt the flutters of blossoming attraction, but everything I was feeling for him now was akin to quiet comfort because we understood each other.

In that understanding, there was a strange sense of safety that made me want to sink into him.

Instead, I blew out a slow breath, tempering the nerves that crawled up my insides as my thoughts shifted. Staring at the flames beneath the pot, I could no longer think of anything but my mother. The witch who'd dedicated her life to looking into the future for the protection of others. If only I had half the skill of a seerborn that she did, I wouldn't have been chosen to kill.

When Kayn gave my hand a quick squeeze, I looked up at him. He released my hand and gazed at the fire. "You should start preparing for what Odin has asked of you. I can train you."

I cursed under my breath, but it was cut short as an idea came to me. Perhaps we could both get what we wanted.

"First, we heal my mother," I said. His brows lifted as I continued. Flames danced in his dark eyes as they sliced back to me. "I'll unbury a vampire and then compel them to pull the toxins from her blood." My gaze drifted to the graves. Light rain fell in scattered drops, dotting the headstones with dark gray spots.

A different shade of shame twisted my gut. Even if I wanted to become a killer, I didn't know how. I was chosen by the Gods, a seerborn, and yet I still didn't understand what they wanted from me. I'd misunderstood Freya's trial, and no doubt would Loki's be trickier.

Choosing me had to be a mistake.

Or maybe that was just the selfish side of me rearing like an angry horse again. I didn't want any of this. I was meant to be a seer like my mother, a protector of witches.

This was…different, darker. Dark enough to match the wickedness I'd locked away, the pieces of me that kept others at a distance from me. Not Silver—*me*. The person only my mother would acknowledge, and since she was taken from me ten years ago, I'd been alone in this.

"Okay," Kayn said. "Now you just need to learn how."

Learn how? How was I supposed to learn to wake a creature I'd only just discovered existed? I knew of vampires from the sagas, but I'd thought they were realms away, or relics of the past, not rulers of Vylheim. And now, I was being asked, by both Kayn and the Gods, to learn how to compel them, to wake them, and to destroy them.

My tongue became heavy in my dry mouth as I worked up to a confession. I shook my head and swallowed through the thickness. "I have no idea what I'm doing."

"That's why I'm here."

My heart skipped.

I'm here, my mother's last words before the Grimward dragged her away. She'd placed her hands over my eyes, reminding me her magic covered me and that my sight as a seer might give me a glimpse of her whenever I needed to see her again. It rarely worked, but I was grateful for the glimpses

I'd had, and the spreading blackness in my eyes to keep tabs on her life.

Kayn stood and offered me his hand. "I'll piece it together with you."

Though the rain extinguished the last of the fire, warmth coated me. I accepted his hand and he pulled me to my feet, before leading me through the steady rain to the graves.

Kayn was nothing like the other monsters. He'd stopped King Drakker. He'd admitted the horrible act he'd committed —something I wasn't even willing to do to myself.

He may have had his own goal at the end of my Calling, but something about his willingness to help me understand it and learn it with him comforted me. Nobody had been willing to slow down and hear me out since my mother. He not only heard the plea behind my confession, he offered to work through the lack of knowledge and training with me.

With my hand in his, I wasn't doing this alone.

Chapter Twenty-Five

Cold droplets beat down on my bare head as I followed in Kayn's wake. Water sloughed off his broad shoulders where the animal fur blocked it from soaking the fabric beneath.

When he twisted to see me behind him, I squinted through the sheets of rain to see he was pointing across the hill at the same stone Valkyrie. Nodding, I swept water away from my eyes and hurried to catch up with him.

His narrowed eyes and lifted chin made him look so determined. So confident in what we were about to do.

But I had no idea what that could be.

"Was Ingrid like me?" I asked, referring to the woman he'd mentioned earlier. "Or did she know how to pass the trials?"

"She did the best she could with the knowledge she had. She was a witch like you, but she was discovered and promptly punished for it, so she didn't have a lot of freedom to explore the Gods' guidance."

"Exile?"

I didn't ask if she was executed.

He tilted his head, seemingly understanding my confusion.

"Not everyone has the same punishment. Not when the king takes pity. King Roderic had taken Ingrid as one of his favored women before he knew she was a witch. When she was outed, he kept her close by deeming her punishment a lifetime as an executioner. I found her not long after, and she tried to become the huntress, but she could not handle the Gods' power. It drove her mad. But you…" he paused at the grave and turned to me. "You're aware of your limits."

"I have to be," I said, flexing my cold fingers.

His gaze rippled from my hands back to my face. A glimmer of pride, or hope, or perhaps admiration coated his soft eyes. "It makes you strong."

"I doubt strength will raise a vampire from deep sleep." I waved my hand at the grave.

"Awareness will. The answer will be unique to you."

I stared at him as if he'd suddenly provide an answer and deliver an explanation to me, but the only movement on his stoic face was the rain streaming down in little rivers. I trailed his line of sight back to the grave.

The Valkyrie with a broken wing lay with her body draped over the headstone, her face hidden in her arm. Her stony hair looked as smooth as if it were real waves and her wing was sculpted so carefully it could have been real feathers, which gave the whole sculpture an ethereal look among the pouring storm that could not soak her hair or send her feathers shuddering with the wind.

My eyes fell to the soil beneath her. Digging wasn't a smart option because vampires didn't wake simply by exposure to the air. I had Freya's visions, perhaps I could run and push myself to break to glimpse an idea. Except that this was Loki's trial, and he hadn't spoken to me.

I scraped my brain for an idea.

"Each huntress's Call is personal," Kayn shouted over the deafening rain.

I looked up at him while he kept his eyes on the grave.

"Huntress?" I'd heard it before but every time I said it, the word tasted sour. I didn't like the connotations that came with *huntress*.

"It is what you will become when you pass Odin's trial," he said. I swallowed a curse and turned back to the grave. "If you consider what behaviors make you who you are, it'd help narrow your unique abilities down."

I knelt over the grave, my hand brushing the stalks of grass that had grown over it. The grass squelched beneath my feet and it felt as though I was sinking into the earth one breath at a time. Was the storm more of Loki's chaos?

I closed my eyes for a moment, and the rush of the rain splattering the ground faded. When I opened my eyes, a spot of red drew my attention. A single red petal, like blood among all the green, quivered in the breeze as it caught between two blades of grass. I picked it up, examining the spidery veins as I rubbed the soft velvety texture between my thumb and forefinger. Looking up, I scanned the graveyard but couldn't spot where the petal had come from. No rose bushes grew anywhere near the abandoned ruins.

I pressed my hand against the soil, as if I could feel the shape of the sleeping vampire beneath. "What can I do?" I whispered.

The only person who'd know the answer was slipping away.

A sob caught at the center of my chest. My heart thumped painfully as I thought of existing in this world knowing my mother was gone. When she was in exile, I planned to go to her, someday, to see her again, to thank her for always teaching me the truth, and most of all, for believing me.

That was all different now that I'd found her here, but if I failed the trials where would she end up? She couldn't survive in The Forsaken Hall forever. Not now that King Drakkar knew where she was. Not with the council of monsters dragging witches and anyone they could grab to sea.

I could not fail.

A bang echoed from behind us and I startled. Kayn and I whipped around to see Stasia running toward us. "She's worse! Her heart's even slower now."

"Shit," I breathed.

Kayn crouched beside me, his voice steady. "Take it slow. What is a skill you know well?"

Working on Ragna's farm. Whispering the sagas with my mother. I could run but was never skilled at it, and my visions were sporadic and the result of beating my body into the ground. Did I have to do that for Loki's trial too?

Hope waned.

I dropped back down in front of the grave, scanning the Valkyrie, the headstone, the grass beneath. My hand splayed out on the earth as if searching for the pulse beating beneath our living realm.

Panic wrapped around my throat like the hand of Loki to choke the answer out of me. *This is your last chance.* My pulse doubled, tripled. Bile pushed up into my mouth, bitter and burning on the back of my tongue. With black dots spotting my vision, I knew I'd lose consciousness if I didn't calm down.

I closed my eyes and whispered, "I hear my voice. I smell the rain—" Before I could finish my routine, I lost control of the words, my mouth moving of its own accord until I gained command of my tongue again.

My mind flooded with what to say, like magic, like Loki speaking to me but without actually hearing his voice in my head. This compulsion was a pure kind of sorcery, wild and addictive in how easy it came to me. I simply knew what to say. Of course, the years of repeating sagas that spoke of Draugr and monster and Gods may have had something to do with it.

And I couldn't deny that it'd taken preparation. I could compel when I tapped into the sensations rippling through my body. Attuning myself to my own body and the world where it existed made me aware of everything. Aware enough to bend and control the will of the other person.

I knew this as if the Gods had simply placed this information in my brain. Perhaps this was what it meant to truly be connected to Odin and Freya, and by necessity, Loki too.

"Wake, Draugr," I said. My will and my senses seemed the source of how strongly it worked. The more I wanted it, the lighter the tension in my head became.

The earth pushed up from beneath me. Cold, dead fingers wrapped around my wrist with a painfully tight grip. A scream ripped from my throat as the hand yanked me toward the ground, the creature's strength overpowering the earth itself.

Kayn dropped beside me and reached for the hand, but I shouted for him to back off. I had to compel this vampire myself. I had to do this to pass the trial.

It was enough to know he was there if I needed him.

As if the soil was water and my arm weightless, the vampire pulled me into the soil all the way to my shoulder until I fought the voice in my head.

"Create chaos. Spite Odin. Destroy those who worship him."

No! I'm listening to you only for this trial.

I was doing enough. I woke the vampire. This had to be enough. I opened my mouth, ready for Loki to speak through me. "By breath and blood your will is mine."

All at once the monster's hold on me loosened. I scrambled away from it as both hands jutted from the grave and dragged the figure from its dark slumber. The earth seemed to shift beneath me as the vampire clawed out of the ground. Rain lightened to scattered droplets, as if the night greeted its monster with a calm welcome.

Her fangs were exposed already and her eyes blood red. She crawled toward me, lifting and dragging herself from the grave. I swallowed another scream and tried to form words around my fumbling tongue. This time, it was me speaking. "Your will is mine."

The vampire's eyes shifted from red to gold, and my courage bolstered. I pushed to my feet, and backed away from her with the dregs of energy simmering in my veins. "I am your path now. Come with me."

In a trance, she mirrored me by climbing to her feet. Soil tumbled off of her velvet dress, revealing the violet shade buried by moist dirt. The corset at her torso was covered with detailed embroidery. Not all royals were vampires, but perhaps all vampires had once been royals.

In my own kind of daze, I led her to the Hall of the Gods where I invited her across the threshold into the house of Freya and Odin.

Dizzy, I struggled to hold the compulsion, the invisible string pulled taut between me and my compelled victim. The vampire's fangs sank into my mother's neck. The last thing I remembered was compelling the vampire to drain only the toxins and then to stop drinking from her. And then, the clouds darkened.

The world faded at the edges of my vision first until I saw only one thing. A massive wolf towered over me, his eyes gleaming like two shimmering moons in the thick of his broad skull. His jaws split open and the echo of his howl resonated around me, all-consuming. But Fenrir, Loki's son and the most feared creature in all the Nine Realms, didn't attack me.

Because of this, I knew Loki's trial was complete, and I'd passed.

Chapter Twenty-Six

Odin's Trial

After two days of fluctuating between consciousness and sleep, I prayed it wouldn't take a trial of the Gods to fully wake me.

Divination felt closer now than ever before, as if I could call Loki to come down to this realm and ask him for help, face-to-face. Of course, Loki wasn't who I wanted help from, he had his own goals, fully separate from the people of our world, and I still couldn't grasp why he was part of these trials.

What did he want with me? Chaos, apparently.

I slipped away into another bout of restless sleep plagued by nightmares and it wasn't until a child screamed for me, calling me Anna, Lux, Silver, that I woke again with cold sweat coating my forehead and my chest heaving ragged breaths.

Out of habit, I allowed a hundred thoughts to descend upon me and whisk my mind away from the nightmare. I'd done it many times as a scared little girl after long, dark nights.

I knocked down the barriers in my mind that held the dwelling at bay and let the everyday fears consume my every thought until I could no longer remember the nightmare. Simple worries like if my father would scream at me again if I failed to properly conceal my black eyes when out in the village. He insisted I conceal them, yet denied that I used the magic I'd learned from my mother's enchantment to do it. Or if I'd accidentally wailed one of the Gods' names in my sleep like I had when the nightmares first crept in.

Light from the candles on the walls softly shimmered over the blanket draped across my chest. Stasia silently fluttered between the benches, stooping over my mother with a bowl in her hands.

If my mother reached for the bowl, I was only vaguely aware of it.

Perhaps it was a dream, or a chaotic vision granted by Loki himself. The swimming, blurred sight of everything suggested a dream that I didn't have the strength to wake from.

I opened my mouth to ask if she was doing better, but my voice came out weak and they were too far to hear me. Soft rain dripped into the windows, rhythmic and lulling me back into the darkness behind my eyelids.

Pressure coated me, like a body laying over mine. This feeling and the dream immediately transported me to when I'd first faced Kayn after our escape.

I expected to experience it again in this swimming illusion. To feel his breath on my neck, the crunch of leaves beneath my spine, but when I looked up, it was the king's eyes that met mine. His icy stare sent a shudder through my core and I found my gaze falling to his mouth as he whispered gently. *How long I've waited to call you my wife.*

I arched my back, the soft bed sinking beneath my spine as his lips brushed against my throat. He kissed along the curve of my neck, slowly working his way to my mouth.

His teeth hovered over my bottom lip, tugging with a careful bite as a moan escaped me. His finger traced my neck before he enclosed his entire hand around my throat. Though his grip tightened and I could barely draw in breath with another gasp, my stomach burned hot with desire and I shifted to spread my legs.

My entire body warmed with the heat between us coating the air, our wanting thick and desperate until he suddenly drew back and the fingers that'd been holding my throat were covered in blood as red as his eyes.

He smirked and told me he'd enjoyed killing and eating those whose blood he painted his hands with. *There's freedom in devouring those who follow you. Let's enjoy them together.*

This was no dream, this was a cursed nightmare. The Mare was the spirit of a woman who could shift into a horse and slip into the quiet consciousness of the sleeping. She preyed on us in our most vulnerable moment.

Not even sleep was always safe.

The nightmarish king's words echoed again. *Devour them…*

I woke to sickness souring my gut. I doubled forward, spewing the contents of the stew. My ears pulsed with blood and energy, muffling the sound of my retching until I could no longer hear it. Silence pressed in around me, the only sound a faint knocking—no, footsteps.

I didn't breathe so I could listen for the heavy rhythmic thumps again.

Though the thudding grew quieter, I managed to identify the weight and sound of the steps as clopping. Hoofbeats.

I bolted upright, my back aching and head pounding. The world filled in around me as the nightmare of King Drakkar's words slipped away. My mother often spoke of The Mare, blaming her for the nightmares I'd had often since the day the Grimward pounded on our door the first time, ten years before they returned for my mother.

This was the first time I'd heard evidence of The Mare's hooves.

The rain had stopped, but puddles still pooled in scattered

sections across the temple's stone floor. The stained-glass window in the wall above me shook as a gust of wind slammed against it. Flickering candles with flame as bright as Stasia's hair danced across the stone walls, and I tried to slow my choking breaths by counting every crack in the stone.

When a shadow cast over me, I drew my eyes up. Stasia hurried to me, cup in hand. "Take it in gulps," she said. "You look dreadful." I shot her a sharp look as I raised the cup to my lips and tipped. "What? It is your mother who says so."

I nearly choked on the honeyed stew. She'd made another batch, though it had far too much sweetness. Kayn would have retched.

"She's awake..." my voice trailed off as my gaze landed on the bench at the other end of the Hall of the Gods. It hadn't been a cruel trick of the mind.

My mother lay still for several long moments, until finally, she rolled her head to look at me. She lifted her frail hand for a weak but warm greeting.

"She is awake and stronger than ever. But it will not last, so I swore to go out in search of Henbane and Hawthorn root as soon as you were well enough for me to leave."

"The plants don't grow during the Polar Nocturne."

"Not in Skaldir maybe, but here, herbs last well into the darkness." Stasia pointed at the bowl and then folded her arms as if waiting for me to consume it all right now.

"What about the vampire? Why can't she draw out the toxins?" I asked, ignoring the too-sweet brew.

"After your compulsion faded, she vanished."

"Kayn didn't stop her?"

"She overpowered him."

"How? He's stronger, even, than King Drakkar."

Stasia sighed. "You just woke up from a fitful sleep sweating like a hog and yet you're full of questions."

With that, she snatched the bowl from my hands and spun around. I dragged my feet to the edge of the bench and, on wobbling legs, shuffled across the temple to sit beside my mother. Her chest rose and fell with soft but steady breaths. She'd fallen back asleep, her body still fighting whatever sickness had poisoned her blood. A rosy hue had returned to her skin and the hollow of her cheeks filled in. She'd been eating.

I smiled as I brushed a wisp of hair from her face. She was better, but not cured.

"You're okay," a deep voice said.

I looked up to see Kayn having appeared on the other side of my mother. Orange light of the candle's flames brightened his dark eyes. Though his features didn't match the hardened line of King Drakkar's mouth and his chin was cut clean of hair without a thick beard like the king's the golden rim in his eyes and persistent behavior reminded me of the king.

"So is she," I said, resting my hand on my mother's bony shoulder. "But Stasia says it's not for long. What happened to the vampire I raised?"

When he nodded, a strand of wheat hair fell into his face. "She's gone, yes. I couldn't stop her, even she had more recently fed on a human than I have. And she was newly turned, she doesn't—" He shook his head.

"Now what? I raise another monster to suck this sickness out of her? And then another?"

"Now you face Odin's trial."

Stiffening, I frowned and searched his face for any indication of what he was about to reveal. "I'm a seer, not a huntress. I protect, I don't hurt—"

"That isn't true" my mother said, her voice slight.

My stomach dropped.

Her eyes were still sealed shut, but her hand shifted, slowly moving across her chest to her shoulder where she found my hand. She held onto me, her grip firmer than I expected. But I wasn't surprised that my mother was the strongest person I'd ever known. Even in sickness and after two vampire bites, she grasped my fingers tightly enough to prove she was as tenacious as ever.

"What can I get you, Mother?" I asked, returning the squeeze of her hand.

She shook her head, eyes opened only to slits. "Nothing, Little Spider."

I swallowed, tears welling in my eyes at the name nobody had called me since she was exiled.

She groaned softly and released my hand. Her finger pressed into my palm. At first I thought she was tracing the lines across my hands until I recognized the vague shapes of runes. A mountainous spike, an upright line with two jagged protrusions, and two corners hovering one another. Chance, protection, survival.

With my brow furrowed, I stared at the flesh of my palm, trying to understand the runes with more clarity. "Loki, Freya, and Odin?"

"I had hoped you would not be chosen. The prophecy is very clear. Once you accept the Call and pass the final trial, you will be bound to this duty until it is complete, or else their power will destroy you."

"You knew?"

"I'd heard of these trials testing other witches in the past, yes."

I sucked in a breath. "Freya's made sense for a seer, but Loki's and Odin's…"

My mother squeezed my hand. "Perhaps you're not meant to be a seer, Little Spider." My heart hollowed and I didn't breathe until she spoke again. "You've always been a survivor."

Survivor. This was another word for fighter in the casual language of Skaldir villagers. Fighting wasn't allowed, but many of us still practiced defense in secret, and when winter came, those who fought off illness and hunger were survivors.

The words were one in the same, and my mother's way of reminding me what I'd done to *survive.*

A chill struck my spine and I dipped my head into my free hand.

"Don't spiral, Spider," her voice was as soft as it had been when I was a grieving child. "Commune with Freya and Odin. Offer a sacrifice and then you will know for sure. There will be no question, no more need for hesitation."

Kayn made a noise between a huff and a grunt. I snapped my gaze up to him as he paced the length of the bench and raked his hand through his hair. When he noticed my eyes on him, he stopped and fixed his jaw into a tight hold.

"Do you have something to share?" I prodded, though I already suspected the source of his thoughts.

He'd insisted I accept the Call of the Gods in its entirety since he stalked Stasia and I into the woods. He'd stayed by my side to ensure it. And as much as I wanted to fight him on it, I couldn't blame him.

My chest warmed with unexpected admiration for the man—the monster—before me. He'd dedicated himself to helping the Gods reach me, a human, when he was cut off from them, hated by them. And for what? To protect us? Passing Odin's trial would mean eventually killing him too. His presence here was a sacrifice that I couldn't help but respect.

Kayn released a breath and closed his eyes for a moment before meeting my gaze. Something akin to sadness, perhaps regret swam in his dark eyes. "You should be training to kill vampires, not offering sacrifices. You are the only one who can remove the blight on this realm."

My mother's voice fell to a whisper. "The power of the Gods will destroy you. If you don't kill every Draugr before Odin, Freya, and Loki overwhelm your mind. It has happened to every chosen witch before you. I've witnessed these visions, my Little Spider." I leaned closer and tilted my ear toward her lips so that I would not miss a single word. "It is a risk, but the Call is only for you to accept. I cannot tell you what to do any more than Kayn."

I hadn't considered where the Call would go if I didn't accept it. Once I passed on to Folkvangr or Valhalla, carried away by a Valkyrie not unlike the statue over the graves, another witch would face this same decision.

Unless, I spared her from it and saw it through…to whatever end.

My eyes slid back to Kayn who hovered over us. I straightened and cleared my throat of all emotion. "I will commune with the Gods. I will ask Odin and Freya." I spoke this decision aloud more for the sake of my own courage than to inform them.

"They require sacrifice," my mother said, her voice breathy but stronger, as if she forced the words out with the last dregs of her energy. "Freya always wants us to have wisdom, because there is freedom in knowledge."

"Like the lost history?"

"She would want us to have it. And Silver, my sleep was not all lost time." She tugged me closer to her. I leaned in, just as I had when I was a child and she'd whisper the sagas to me. "I asked her not to choose you, but her response was a single phrase in my mind. Silver is the queen."

My heart skipped. Did that mean King Drakkar would succeed in claiming me?

I pulled back and looked at her, my mouth hanging open like a child struck between awe and fear.

She smiled weakly. "I believe you will find the lost history and that it will restore the truths of our Gods. The Gods know what they're doing. The runestones could have been taken from this very temple and hidden in the castle. Seek the answers, Little Spider."

I nodded, numb from the suggestion behind her vision.

Standing, I lay my mother's hand back on her stomach and turned toward the back of the temple.

With one foot in front of the other, I approached the bloodstained altar. Runes carved into the dark Yew beneath the flat altar were once filled with the blood of sacrifices. I'd never seen a person give their life for the Gods, only an animal, but it was the way of our ancestors, to appease the Odin and Freya and receive answers.

If I wanted clarity, I had to offer a sacrifice.

Chapter Twenty-Seven

With every step toward the altar of sacrifice, my nerves frayed, leaving my skin sensitive with goosebumps and my heart thumping uncontrollably. I left my mother and the truth she spoke in my wake as I approached the center of the Hall of the Gods where our ancestors offered sacrifices.

"Silver," Kayn said, his voice rough. "What are you doing?"

I continued toward the altar before my courage waned. The Gods would want something from me, and based on the stained altar, and the runes below, they'd want what flowed through my veins.

"What is required for this sacrifice?" he asked, his footsteps pacing behind me.

I stepped up to the altar, the runes carved into the yew at my feet. Deep ridges created all twenty-four runes in the ground around the base. The altar was cut with lines like rivers snaking from the spike at the center.

He ran ahead and cut in front of me, blocking my fixation on the altar. "You've only just recovered from Loki's trial."

I rolled my eyes up to his face and lifted my chin. "What is my health to you? You've delivered your message, let me read it."

His jaw flexed. "Will this sacrifice hurt you?" I said nothing. It was obvious enough. "Let me heal you after."

"And risk turning into a vampire?"

"You're chosen. You will not turn."

"I will not drink your blood, Kayn." I placed my hand on his chest and pushed him back so that I might step around him and stand before the altar.

He let me push him away but grabbed my wrist and turned me toward him. "You don't have to." Breath caught in my throat at the sight of his blunt fangs jutting from above the row of teeth at the top of his mouth. "There is another way I can heal you."

"You can't bite me either," I said. When he shook his head, I furrowed my brow. If there were other options to heal a witch, why did we raise a vampire? Why did I deplete my energy compelling her? "I knew you were full of secrets, Kayn." I hoped the bite in my voice was as obvious as my frown. "Why didn't you do this when my mother needed it?"

He barely let me finish before his words tumbled over mine. "The recipient must first accept it, and any healing whether it's drinking my blood or not, requires a connection that I do not have with her."

I opened my mouth to argue, but found that nothing came out. Frozen, I stared at him helplessly. There was too much I didn't understand. Even after a childhood of careful teaching, warning of the monsters, and the pendant in my pocket, the sagas I'd memorized barely scratched the surface of the ice that coated the truth.

"How is it that a monster cares for my pain?" Nerves came through my voice with an edge.

I wasn't mad at him, but he was the one standing in front of me. I couldn't snap at the altar for requiring my blood and sacrifice. It was just a hunk of carved wood.

He was real, flesh and muscle, sending fire through my veins as I waited for his response. I didn't know why I wanted him to tell me he cared for me. It was childish.

But I wanted it anyway.

The gold in his eyes flared, nearly choking out the brown. "I wasn't always a monster."

"Fine, you may heal me after." I said it so he'd move. I was already fixated on communing with the Gods and he would not stop me, and he didn't give me the confession I wanted.

Maybe he didn't share the same interest that stirred within me.

As I'd hoped, he stepped aside and let go of my hand. With my hand free now, I thrust it into my pocket and pulled out the pendant.

Tipping the sharp edge against my palm, I stretched out my arms over the spike. I pressed harder and harder until the tip split my skin open. Sucking air through my teeth, I dragged the tip across the longest line of my left palm, the life-line. With every beat of my heart, I became more aware of the stinging. The persistent pain caused my arms to quiver, my hands shaking with every stretch of flesh I cut into. I pulled the weapon down, down until the line in my hand disappeared at my wrist.

Hot blood flowed freely over the spike in the altar. It dripped slowly at first and then filled the ridges quickly. Some dried up, the river of red stopping short, while two filled, the blood flowing to the edge of the flat altar and spilling over the side.

I swayed. My head suddenly felt too heavy for my shoulders and my legs did not want to support me. Rocking back on my heels, I expected to fall as darkness seeped in at the edges of my vision. Instead, a warm presence hovered behind me as Kayn made himself known. I tipped into his chest and was vaguely aware of his hands gently cupping my arms.

My knees gave away and I sank into him, but he did not

force me to stay upright. He dipped with me, carefully seating me between his legs as we slowly dropped to the floor, his strength the only thing keeping me from collapsing.

I blinked rapidly, desperately attempting to clear the dark spots from my eyes. As three runes beneath the altar filled with my blood, I craned my neck to see their shapes.

An upright line with one triangular protrusion and an open ending line at the bottom turned red as the shape filled the highest. *Raido*, meant to journey or travel the path ahead, often used in the sagas to refer to hunters traveling paths to their prey. Then a portion of the animals caught and killed would be sacrificed to Odin and feasted upon by his people. Next, the rune with an upright line and an open arm reaching to the sky, like a tree with a single branch, filled halfway. My path—my hunt—would be one of pain and transformation. *Kaun* symbolized suffering through change.

The majority of my blood pooled in a final, haunting shape.

An upright line with a peaked top, like an arrow pointing to the skies. *Tewaiz*, represented warriors.

It didn't matter how desperately I locked the darkness away, even the Gods knew I was meant to fight—to survive.

To become a huntress.

My hand stung and strength waned. My body threatened to buckle beneath me when the gift of an unexpected vision took hold of me.

Darkness enveloped me and before me a figure appeared.

Based on the descriptions I'd heard from the sagas, I knew Odin was standing before me.

His tall, gaunt body stretched above me. He was mostly concealed within the dark cloak wrapped around him, but I saw the long ragged beard hanging over his chest and stomach and the glint of his single eye, the other having been sacrificed long ago for wisdom. Two ravens perched on either side of him, their claws clinging to his bony shoulders.

Though this was like Freya's visions, I knew it wasn't. Not when the Hall of the Gods filled in around Odin.

He was visiting me—*me*. However briefly, he was here, standing before me, and I was both captivated and humbled at the same time.

All pain and exhaustion temporarily melted away as I focused every ounce of my attention on the Allfather.

"Kill the kings," he said. His haunting voice echoed all around me like a pulse of energy. "This is for you to do alone. Only trust yourself."

Another voice split through the haze of my awe, almost dissipating the entire scene of Odin standing before me.

"Do you have what you need?" Kayn whispered from behind me, his breath warm and soothing against my ear.

"Do you see him?" I breathed. "Do you see Odin?"

But before the words were all the way out of my mouth, Odin had vanished.

I let my head relax and I leaned into Kayn, finally humming confirmation to his question. I had what I needed, a visit from the most powerful God and a single command—a step forward. Though I didn't know why he spoke of more than one king. Perhaps that was my tired mind misunderstanding Odin's strange voice.

Kayn reached around to the other side of my jaw, cupping it gently in his hand as he twisted and carefully tipped my face toward him.

With my eyes half-lidded, I lazily scanned his tender expression for understanding. He bent closer to me, our lips almost touching. My breaths, which were already rapid, quickened as his dark eyes fell to my mouth.

He drew my face into him, his kiss soft, lingering, and with just the right amount of sweetness.

The pain in my palm faded with every breath that passed between us. I took his tongue into my mouth and deepened the kiss.

Whatever this healing magic was, I felt every inch of it knitting my flesh together again.

Breathless, I pulled back just enough to speak. "How?" I whispered.

"I can share my power to heal myself with those I..." he paused for a beat. "Those I desire."

Our lips collided again and I drank him in.

He'd admitted it. There was heat between us.

CHAPTER TWENTY-EIGHT

Three days later my hand had completely healed. No scar remained and the pain had ceased immediately. While Kayn's kiss had strengthened a connection between us, it was the vitality that channeled from him that ultimately healed me.

Now, I spent every waking minute training.

In nine days the Polar Nocturne would end, and King Drakkar would cut me down. Worse, the Grimward would be transporting every exile from the wasteland to The Sea of Skalds. Exploration would dawn, and Alva would never see her mother again. Two mothers and a daughter destroyed by King Drakkar and his council.

This haunted me until I wrapped my fingers around the solid cut of an ash tree.

With the weapon in my hand, the promise of destroying the king triggered a flash of hope. Sick and twisted hope, but hope for my mother's survival, for Ragna's, and selfishly, for my own.

Before training to fight, Kayn had insisted I practice every skill I could, even those that weren't powers granted from the

Gods. I expanded my knowledge of vampires by studying him. I ran to push my body to the brink to test Freya's visions, gaining glimpses of Mara's Keep, the graves, images I wasn't sure of but knew would be useful later.

For the compulsion, I practiced on him, building my resilience and strength so that the power would not strip all energy from me.

Starting with small commands, I compelled him to stop moving, then to look at me, then to come closer to me.

Each try drained me a little less, but my body was still in need of rest. My heart still hammered too fast with skipped beats and pain striking my chest.

No amount of training, no amount of power from the Gods, no amount of healing from Kayn changed this illness that plagued me, but I learned to train around it. To use the skill I'd learned from my mother to calm myself and observe. It forced me to slow down, to consider every angle and think before I acted.

This, Kayn said, would be my survival, and my greatest skill as a huntress.

And finally, he'd led me outside, his fingers twined through mine.

After enough careful training, it was time to learn to fight a vampire. If I could at all.

Moonlight coated the abandoned landscape surrounding The Hall of the Gods. Shadows from the headstones stretched like yawning arms over the dewy grass. Silhouettes from the trees beyond blanketed the weeping Valkyrie in gray.

We stood over the graves of the men and women of Mara who once dared to honor Odin and Freya, and the vampires who may or may not be buried with them. This is where I'd tease out Odin's gift and learn to cut down monsters.

Kayn enclosed his fingers over mine and around the branch. "A stake will work better than your silver pendant.

Because the tree of Yggdrasil is Midgard's connection to the Gods, any sharpened cut of a tree will destroy a vampire, not just hurt them."

As a witch, of course I was well versed in the understanding that Yggdrasil was the source of our magic since it was the gateway between Asgard and our realm. Odin had hung from the tree for nine days and nine nights for knowledge and to keep this connection between him and the people of Midgard.

But I hadn't known of the tree's power against monsters.

"Is this how you trained Ingrid? The last huntress?"

"Partially," he said. "She never destroyed a vampire so she never became a huntress."

I turned the branch over in my fist, then met his dark eyes. "And what happens when a vampire's destroyed?"

"We hollow out and then turn to dust. Without our souls, this decay is almost immediate."

I snapped my gaze away from him before my mind ran away with the image. According to my mother's visions, watching Kayn crumble to ash was part of my future as this huntress. If I didn't destroy every single vampire, I'd eventually lose my mind to madness. Every other witch before me had suffered this same fate.

Kayn angled the tip of the stake to the right of his ribcage. "Our hearts don't beat the same as humans' do, but you have to cut through it all the same." I frowned and tugged the stake to pull it away from his chest. He held it steady, reminding me, once again, I could never overpower a vampire.

"It will take effort to push it through," he continued. "But with the right angle, you don't have to be strong, just precise."

I sucked in a breath and nodded. With Loki's power of compulsion, I didn't need exceptional strength or speed to bring a vampire down, but their bones and muscles still maintained a tough barrier to break through. This would be so much easier if Odin granted me a powerful body. Until I uncovered whatever the Allfather would give me for this task, I had to rely on Freya, Loki, and Kayn.

Thanks to Freya's visions, I would be able to track the undead and catch them in their most vulnerable states.

Like a true huntress.

A tremble snaked down my spine. My mother encouraged this. Odin wanted this. The Gods wanted this. They wanted me to kill, and yet I couldn't shed the part of me that clung to becoming a seer. If I grew into a witch who helped and protected others, I'd strip away every selfish choice I'd made and replace them with decades of service to my fellow witches.

That was the Silver I knew, not the huntress with her hands wrapped around a stake.

Kayn tipped the stake up. "Aim to the side of the hard bone at the center." His free hand tapped the middle of his chest and then shifted to his left. "Point up and into the soft spot between the ribs. Try it."

I shook my head. "Not on you."

"I'll stop you."

"Can you? I'm the huntress. What if this draws Odin's power out of me?"

"I can't die except to a stake made from the tree of Yggdrasil."

I tilted my head, my lips parting. "But you're—"

"Different. I told you." Something akin to regret shimmered in his abyssal eyes as if reflecting the darkness in my own. "This isn't Yggdrasil, but it is an ash tree. A stake sharpened from any ash tree will sink through undead flesh without much effort if angled correctly."

My eyes flickered to the line of trees behind him. No wonder The Hall of the Gods was built so close to a forest of ash. "Then why hasn't the council burned all the ash trees?"

"Because it's not a threat. Nobody is fast enough to even think of getting a stake at the right angle. Remember, we are not human. We are predators, created to be pure power."

"And they've never suspected a huntress like me might be a threat?"

His hair fell into his face as he shook his head. "Like Anastasia said, history proves that the chosen witches lose themselves to madness long before they ever become a threat. Right now, the council has one main concern; their food source dwindling from the harsher winters." Glancing over his shoulder, his eyes scanned the line of trees. "Winter also doesn't make it easy to burn the forest. The perpetual dampness keeps the trees from being their target. For now."

"So they won't expect a huntress at all?"

He turned back to me, the warmth in his eyes, like charred wood and just as dark. Concern pressed his brows together. "I didn't say that. You can't hope to catch them unaware. If you get too complacent, or reliant on Odin and Freya, you'll be ripped apart." Grimacing, I tried to keep Ragna's belief in a Draugr's feeding habits out of my mind's eye. "I can't let that happen, so we'll keep training."

"Nine days," I breathed.

Matching my frown, he trailed his gaze over my face. "Nine days," he echoed. He brushed the soft pad of his thumb over my knuckles and then pulled his hand away. Tipping his chin down toward the stake, he prodded me. "Try it."

My hands quivered. I peeled each finger off the wood and then tightened my grip. With both hands and the entire weight of my body, I shifted the tip of the stake upward. Blowing out a hard breath, I shoved every bit of energy I had into him. The stake was pinched between his ribs but did not melt through him the way he said it would for other vampires.

A wince flickered across his face and he drew a sharp breath.

I yanked the stake away. "I hurt you."

He scrubbed his palm over his clean-shaven chin and huffed. "Only for a moment. You need practice to get the aim correct. Try again."

"No."

"Silver." A line deepened between his brows. He reached out and placed his hand over mine again but didn't adjust my grip or tell me to tighten my hold. He simply held onto me until I met his gaze. "You need to train. Over and over. Vampires are blindingly fast and incredibly strong."

"And I can compel them." I wouldn't cause him any more pain than his guilt already did. Hating oneself was enough punishment, and he didn't deserve it. Even if he'd made a mistake as a monster, he was doing everything to rectify it now. Somehow, he'd overcome his soulless self and found empathy for the people he'd turned.

"Compulsion exhausts you, so you have to strike in the right spot the first time."

I chewed on my lip and shook my head. "It's all set up for my victory. The Gods made sure of it."

Except we still didn't know what Odin had granted me. When would the power he'd give me surface? Or did he not deem me worthy of one? *That* I could believe.

I wasn't worthy of anything more than the shame that clawed through my gut.

"Again," he said.

I narrowed my eyes and glared at him while running my thumb over the rough wood. "I don't like hurting you."

His gaze dropped to the stake in my hand, and then to the grass beneath my feet. After a moment of only an owl hooting, he shook his head. "It may have been a mistake to seal this connection between us."

My arms went limp at my sides, the stake at the edge of my grip. "You mean it was a mistake to kiss me? Just because I don't want to watch you in pain?"

"Yes!" He snapped. Dropping his voice, he stared at me from beneath his brows. "Because I'm a soulless creature, Silver, not a human man. My desire should be secondary to protecting you, and I gave in to it."

I recoiled. "So what's this connection between us? Does it mean I'm soulless too?" I would believe it. I had believed something similar for most of my life.

"It means we understand each other." He held my gaze as if a thin thread connected us, pulled taut with increasing tension. "It means I'm here for you. I'm your support. That I —" His eyes sliced to The Hall of the Gods behind me. A flutter of wings beat as two black birds burst from the trees and took flight above us. He cleared his throat and faced me. "I care about what happens to you."

"Because I'm helping you destroy the monsters you made."

"Because I've sought solitude since I turned an entire village, and then I met you." He grabbed the stake and lifted it with my arm. "Let's do this again. Tip it up."

I did as he said. Without prompting, I dug the sharp end into him. It was tougher this time, until I dropped the thicker side lower and shoved it into the soft spot between bones. He gasped and I yanked it back.

"It's done," I said. "Now, tell me what meeting me means. I can imagine you've met hundreds of people in your existence."

"And I haven't admired any of them the way I do you."

I tipped the stake up again, as if it was a threat. "I'm not someone to admire." The truth slipped out. I pursed my lips and scolded myself with a dozen silent curses. He didn't need to hear about my past as much as I shouldn't dare unlock it. Except with Kayn, I wanted to. He understood the shame that ate away at my heart.

"We'll have to decide to disagree on that."

I frowned. "You don't know what I've done."

"And you know exactly what I did, yet you still trust me to be here for you and teach you."

I lowered the stake and shook my head. "That's because of my mother's visions. I trust her powers as a seer. She saw you training me, so I'm taking your training." Again, the silly need for him to admit he cared for me cropped up. It was as childish as it was foolish.

This man was a monster that I was destined to destroy. I looked away from him, observing instead the hills around us.

Icy wind swept through the abandoned valley, tugging tendrils of hair loose from my braids. Stasia was right, she didn't have the talent that Embla had for styling braids. Shivers made my grip on the stake unsteady.

Kayn stepped to the side to block the wind from me. "That's exactly what I mean. Your love for your mother, your trust in her, it's admirable. I forgot what it looked like to care for anyone except myself."

I knew that.

Damn I really knew what that was like.

As much as I cared for my mother, Ragna, Alva, and now Stasia, I'd put myself first too many times. Kayn and I were more similar than I ever would have expected. Maybe it was time I agreed with him. We truly did understand each other, so maybe when he said he admired me, that was true too. A truth I couldn't simply deny because I believed it wasn't the right thing for him to do. He was free to believe what he wanted.

"I never wanted to get to know the other vampires, and I definitely didn't want to watch humans become vessels, so I preferred solitude. But you feel familiar."

I scoffed. "Because we're both living in regret."

"And now working through the mistakes that led us here."

When King Drakkar had said we were the same, I denied

it. I refused to believe it. I didn't delight in death like a cruel king. But with Kayn…it felt right to say.

"We're the same."

His mouth lifted into an unusual smile. Unlike King Drakkar, he didn't walk around with a wicked grin cutting across his face. He was unlike King Drakkar in so many ways. For one, he admitted his mistakes, his weakness. He also wanted to give me this power of becoming a huntress, of training, rather than trying to claim me like a prize to sit beside him on a throne.

And of course, Kayn never threatened to kill me.

Anger simmered with determination and I held tighter to the stake. If the king wanted to try to cut me down, he'd have to fight me first.

I lifted the stake. "Again."

Kayn nodded, holding his smile steady, the softness of it inviting me to relish in this desire I felt for him. As hours slipped away and my arms ached, I tallied hundreds of different strategies. None of it unearthed whatever power Odin may have granted me but repeated practice lifted my spirits and my confidence.

Despite the moments of pain, Kayn praised me for my effort, complimenting me every time I struck with accuracy.

I began to crave the praise, pushing myself to keep going, keep training, until my breath was ragged and my blue fingers could no longer grasp the stake.

On the edge of collapse, Kayn drew the weapon from my hands and tossed it aside. He wrapped his arms around me, letting me collapse against his chest. Catching my breath while sinking into him, I soaked in the moment of rest, of trust, of every word he'd said.

He was here for me.

He was my support.

With Kayn, I could do this.

Once my breathing slowed, he gently released me. He

threaded his fingers through my hair. Cupping the back of my neck, he pulled me closer. His eyes dipped from my gaze to my lips. The taut thread between us snapped and our mouths crashed together, urgent only for a moment until it melted into gentle embers.

It was never desperate, or hungry, or possessive like the king's kisses. With Kayn, this intimacy lingered, slow and careful.

We broke away only when a shrill voice sent goosebumps over my arms. Stasia shrieked from somewhere behind us. Kayn snapped his attention to her as I spun around.

In the dim light, a flash of beige dashed toward us. Stasia's usually light voice was twisted with distress. Exhausted as I was, we both ran to meet her halfway. She'd returned from the village to purchase cooking supplies for food and medicine for my mother with the little money Kayn carried around.

Breathless and with shaking hands, Stasia swung her arms wildly as she tried to speak. "I saw them," she said, between breaths. "I saw them in the village. They're passing through Mara. On their way to Einnland."

My gut lurched. The exodus. "Stasia, slow down. Are the Grimward moving the exiles?"

She nodded and slapped her palms to her knees. Though Stasia was wiry like Ragna, she didn't have the muscle and endurance. Her breaths still came quick and choppy. "Hundreds of witches and the executioners—" A sob cut her off.

I bent to scoop my arms beneath hers and gather her into a hug. "I'm sorry."

She fell into me and I stumbled. Kayn pressed a steady hand to my back to keep me from falling.

Her voice was a whisper now. "I saw him. I didn't get to see his face but it was his mask. The Wolf."

"Finan?" I asked, though I already knew it was only him she cared for. Still, I knew so little, Stasia kept her heart close, speaking only of her passion for cooking and teasing me.

She drew back and wiped at her eyes. For a second, she wasn't the confident handmaiden who'd helped me escape Mara's Keep. In the silence and with a tear-streaked face, I saw Alva in her. A child wanting nothing but to be in the arms of the person she longed for.

She swallowed and closed her eyes. "I spoke to him, Silver. I told him to run with me before he dies at sea." Pausing, she gathered herself. "He said he didn't know me and that if I didn't step out of the way, he wouldn't hesitate to hurt me. But it was a lie. I know he recognized me. I know he did."

The pressure of Kayn's hand slid higher up my back. He stepped to the side, casting a shadow over Stasia. "This exploration, it's so they can find more vessels. More sources of food before the population in Vylheim dwindles. There's too many vampires."

My mouth went dry, but I peeled my lips open and looked up at Kayn as I spoke. "I have to kill the council before they force everyone to leave. I won't let them send Ragna and the other witches to die." I glanced at Stasia. "And Finan."

How many witches had Finan sent into exile? How many people did he execute based on claims of violence? This wasn't for me to ruminate on, not with Stasia staring at me like that. I didn't know him, but I wanted to make her tears stop. Tears on Stasia's perfect cherub face looked unnatural. She was born to be full of joy and food and hope.

"You need more training," Kayn said. "I won't let you march to your death, Silver."

Stasia heaved a shaky breath, drawing our attention. "Ylva and Darius and several other council members were overseeing the exodus, but King Drakkar wasn't there. The castle might be empty for a few more days."

"I have to go now—"

"Once you can both compel me and strike me at the same time." His tone was insistent, but not demanding like the king's commands.

I chewed on this, thinking carefully about my response.

From the moment Kayn tried to stop me from walking into Mara's Keep, he'd intended to save me from the king and his vampire courtiers. I should have gone with him then. I should have listened to him the first time.

"One more day of training."

He nodded. "One day."

CHAPTER TWENTY-NINE

I stood before the grave with the Valkyrie after another full day of training with the stake, with compulsion, and hoping to tease out Odin's gift. I turned my hand over and a beam of moonlight cast over my pale palm, giving enough light for me to see that the lifeline from my hand to my wrist wasn't even red anymore.

All evidence of my sacrifice had been erased now. Not even a scar was left. Thanks to Kayn, and our connection.

"Isn't it ironic?" I said to Stasia who was inspecting the open grave. "That the pain of a sacrifice required by the Gods was healed by the creature they condemn?"

"Not all of them. Loki seems to like the monsters in the saga of the *Children of Ragnarok*," she said. "Also, the sacrifice gave you an answer. It's not like Odin came down here himself and forced your hand over the altar. Just like when he chose to hang from the tree of Yggdrasil, you chose to sacrifice yourself. And it was only a little cut."

Stasia was no stranger to giving voice to what needed to be said, though neither of us was entirely right. We weren't wrong either.

I stared at the grave where Kayn had just buried himself.

This was my last act of training, raising Kayn from sleep with compulsion. Since I'd only tried that once, and it'd been a process of trial and error riddled in shock and fear, I hadn't noticed any subtle powers from Odin that may have mingled with Loki's compulsion.

After a few minutes to allow him to slip into sleep, I'd drop to my hands and knees and wake him. This time, focusing on any extra abilities, strength or speed, though none of those would make sense with raising a vampire from his grave. Still, this was the task remaining and I'd only practiced it once. And Kayn wasn't about to let me leave without attempting everything that might draw our knowledge of what Odin had gifted me.

I needed all the help I could get against the king.

I blinked up at the Valkyrie. Her hidden face piqued my interest. Why keep her a mystery? I wanted to see the eyes of the warrior woman who served Odin. Why did the Gods keep their answers a mystery? Freya could have given my mother a vision.

But I supposed the Gods were not here to serve me, and as Stasia reminded me, the *Hávamál* taught the history of Odin, which gave the example that not even a God himself was above sacrifice. The Poetic Edda said he hung from the tree for nine days and nine nights with a spear in his side in order to access the runes they used to communicate with us today.

Stasia snapped her fingers in front of my face. "I release you from your trance." Coming from Stasia, I knew it was a joke, though how she spoke so lightly of witchcraft, I didn't understand. "Look, I'm in awe of her beauty too." She nodded toward the statue. "And I've definitely wondered what it'd be like to kiss a Valkyrie. But I'm willing to bet your lips are reserved for the Exile, so what are you doing staring at my woman?"

I smiled to mirror her smirk. Heat burned my neck and I curled my bottom lip under, remembering the connection between me and Kayn, the pulsing energy that enclosed us in a moment of his pure compassion and my eager willingness.

Our connection was quiet, similar, like an unspoken prayer. He knew and accepted that I needed protection when he first guarded me from King Drakkar, and later, he knew and accepted that I needed someone to catch me, to heal me. Finding him through my mother was no mistake, no coincidence. She'd once been the only one with an arm around me, willing to accept me as I truly was, and willing to heal me despite the risk to her.

"Huh," Stasia's voice cut through my thoughts. She was grinning even wider now. "Now I assume you're lost in thought about kissing *both* the Exile and the Valkyrie together. And while I definitely don't blame you, I hate to have to tell you that this Valkyrie is just a statue. Her lips would be as cold as Kayn's."

I raised my brows. "Contrary to what goes on in your mind, I wasn't fantasizing about kissing. And Kayn's lips aren't cold."

She shook her head. "I still don't understand how a creature who is neither living nor dead can heal a human."

"A witch," I corrected. Though I was technically both, there was still a distinct difference. "And I don't get it either. But my mother says she once received a response from Odin that said the answers to everything are lost in our history. That's one of the reasons she insists on not letting the true history of our ancestors die. What she can remember, anyway."

"Speaking of an answer from the Gods." She shifted her eyes to the grave. "Does Kayn think you're ready?"

"Yes. He hasn't said it, but I can tell." *In the way that he praises me.*

"So your plan is to sneak in and kill the king first?" Her green eyes were brightened by the surrounding grass. Snowflakes caught in between the blades of grass and along her eyelashes, but they melted quickly. The last stretch of the Polar Nocturne was always the coldest.

"I can only compel one vampire at a time, so yes. Him first, then I'll track down each member of the council."

I palmed my hand to my stomach, willing for the contents of it to stay within me. Sour bile sloshed and pushed up my throat but I swallowed it back down and finally dipped to my knees. The soft earth bent beneath my legs as I prepared to raise Kayn from his sleep. Ever the loyal friend and hand-maiden, Stasia kneeled beside me.

"You look worried," She said with a frown. "Need food?" Using the Valkyrie's broken wing to pull herself up. I glanced up at her, shaking my head. She stood over me now, casting a thin shadow from the light of the moon. "I don't believe that. Worried looks require food. I'll skin those rabbits Kayn caught for us and make a stew before you leave." She stooped over me and slapped me on the back. "I promise, once you have stew in your stomach, that frown will turn over." When she straightened she patted her stomach and turned around, hiking in long strides to the front of the temple.

She wasn't gone long when a scream split through the night. The silence of the Polar Nocturne carried the chilling sound across the cloudy sky and it seemed a drop of water slipped down my back, trailing over my spine. My blood went cold. Had I lost myself in a dream—a nightmare—again? Was it in my head or real? I pushed out a slow breath but cut it short when I recognized the tone of Stasia's voice. This was real and happening right now.

I shot to my feet and gathered my skirts in my fists. Running across the graveyard proved difficult when I had to weave through headstones and my every step sank into the soft grass. Snowflakes caught on my eyelashes and, when I blinked them away, the moisture left my vision blurred.

The scream fell away as I cut around the edge of the Hall of the Gods. Stasia stood several feet back from the temple doors, her chest heaving and breath ragged. Before her lay a body with blood pooling on the stone around it.

I drew a sharp breath and slapped my hand to my throat where overwhelm squeezed me tighter and tighter. Dragging my feet forward, I made my way to my friend, my hand half heartedly lifting to land on her bent arm and comfort her.

"Forget food," she said, spitting the words out. "I'm never eating again." She hinged forward with her hands on her knees as she cupped her hand over her mouth.

I ripped my eyes from her and finally took in the dead person lying across the temple's steps, like a sacrifice, as her blood seeped into the cracks along the stones.

Holding my breath, I dipped to a crouch and carefully shifted the scraggly hair from her face. Stasia screamed again, the pitch piercing in my ear. The shrill sound cut off abruptly when she spun around and spewed everything in her stomach over the snow-flecked grass. I scanned the dead woman's face, the sharp point of her nose, the pale skin, a slackened mouth with splits in her dry lips.

"Embla," I said, releasing my breath with her name. The young servant woman in the castle. No wonder Stasia had screamed, they'd likely known one another. Perhaps they were even friends.

Two distinct holes were pierced into the curve of Embla's neck where a vein bulged.

She'd died by vampire bite, and it was messy.

CHAPTER THIRTY

W aking Kayn wasn't like raising the vampire who'd been buried for so long. Instead of being dizzy and afraid, I simply waited for him to rise up. Was it due to our connection or had this strange magic become easier?

He climbed out of the grave with plenty of strength and none of the bloodlust and snapping jaws of the woman who'd wanted to consume me.

A strange combination of relief and exhaustion had me rubbing my hands over my face. He stood over me, hand out to help me to my feet. Perhaps the moonlight illuminated the distress on my face because he wrapped his arms around me and held me in silence. I let my head dip into his chest as he encompassed all of me and held my drained body upright.

The dwelling and overthinking always left me hollow, like my mind had cycled every thought possible and then they'd spilled out of my body where they crawled away to take effect into the world. The only part left was the erratic thump of my heart, striking pain across my chest with every beat.

After an indeterminate amount of time relishing his embrace, I gathered the strength to speak. "King Drakkar left me a message. He killed one of my handmaidens and dropped her outside The Hall of the Gods."

Kayn released me just enough to look down at me. I turned my face up to him. The sight of his mouth and the smell of him, fresh soil and a crisp wine, struck me with sudden clarity.

Kayn lifted his hands, cupping my arms in his grip as he leveled with me. "King Drakkar is strong, but you're ready."

Am I? I wanted to believe him. Those were the same words my mother had said to me when she sent me outside of the tent to keep watch for patrolling executioners. They killed us for any act of violence, but they punished us for any hint of a belief in the old ways.

More than once, I'd run screaming inside the tent when fear rattled me—when my nerves frayed and the thoughts became too much. I'd picture the executioners stripping the skin from my body, setting fire to my hair, whatever other horrors my father said they did to those who dared whisper the Gods' names.

More than once, I'd failed.

Tears pricked my eyes, stinging hot and heavy where they gathered in a pool at my eyelids. I squeezed my eyes shut and let them fall. I cried not for what lay ahead, but for causing my mother's exile. Surely, if she'd been in Skaldir, she'd never have been struck with the sickness that poisoned her veins. If only I'd not succumbed to dwelling. If only I hadn't screamed at the images in my mind and shouted Freya's name into the busy village, calling attention to my beliefs and the woman who'd taught them to me.

Kayn brushed a tear away with his thumb and then gave my arms a gentle squeeze. "Freya will grant you a clear path. You know where King Drakkar is so tracking him will be easy. Killing him may reveal Odin's trial." He glanced at my empty hands hanging limp at my sides. "You need to take the stake with you. You are almost the huntress."

My tongue soured. "I hate that name."

"It isn't a name. It is a title, and who you are."

It was who I'd become. I couldn't yet claim to be the huntress who destroyed the creatures of the night. I wasn't half of Sunna, the God who shined light on Midgard with the sun. I didn't drive away the cursed Draugr with a burning shield. Instead, I'd wield a single cut of wood that I'd have to use to kill one monster at a time.

I wasn't a God. I was just a girl afraid of her own thoughts. Thoughts that forced me to look at a situation from every angle.

"I can do this," I repeated. I could track King Drakkar right back to his bedchambers and strike him in the center of his chest as he fed on the blood of another innocent. I could stop him from tormenting humans and taunting me with our betrothal.

Though I'd rendered control of my mind, my body didn't follow. My chest heaved in gasping breaths as the chill of the Polar Nocturne sliced through the fabric of my dress. Kayn slipped out of his coat and draped it over my shoulders. Before I could thank him, he was gone, disappearing into the shadows.

I opened my mouth to call out for him but he'd returned just as quickly, a snapped branch in his hand. With his free hand, he gripped my arm and lifted it, pushing the branch into my palm. "You're ready," he repeated.

He tapped the center of his chest where my head had just taken rest. I wanted to lean into him again, and he must have sensed it, because he stepped closer.

I struggled to swallow through the thick emotion gathered in my throat. "If I start this, don't I have to end it?" My eyes scanned every curve and scar across his face.

"Yes, you will have to destroy me too. I will not let you descend into madness."

A sob caught in my throat and I swallowed again. I opened my mouth but said nothing.

What could I say to that? We'd only just become close. He trusted me to wake him, and I trusted him to hold me.

He's a monster, Silver. He's a monster. He's a monster.

Despite the words cycling through my mind, I tilted my head back, my fingers grasping the stake tighter at my side. He raised his hand and cupped my chin, gently, nothing like the way King Drakkar had grabbed my throat and forced me closer to him. I followed the slight tug of Kayn's hand and angled my mouth toward his.

Our lips met in a language more intimate than words.

I couldn't deny that the Call of the Gods demanded I kill him, too, but I could show him I didn't want to. I never wanted this Call, and though I needed to wipe the plague of monsters from this realm, he wasn't like the others.

Need I destroy him when he didn't even feed on humans?

I'd receive that answer when I came to it. I'd commune with all of the Gods next time, cutting my hand over the altar where I could watch the blood fill multiple runes.

When we parted, breathless, he wrapped his hand over mine. Tightening his hold on my hand that held the stake, he showed his support of my fate—of who I was—even if it meant I had to kill him.

"You're not like King Drakkar and Ylva and Darius... I can't kill you."

"But I *am* a monster, Silver, and you are my huntress."

CHAPTER THIRTY-ONE

I touched my lips, recalling the ghost of Kayn's kiss from last night. We'd trained together, discussed this plan together, lived together for the past few days that felt like months with the long hours and intense training. But now I was completely alone on the trek back to Mara's Keep.

After pushing myself last night for a vision about how to approach the king, Freya made it clear Kayn could not accompany me. It was too dangerous. If I relied on the vampire who trained me to step in when I needed it, it would be that hesitation that killed me.

The vision showed only me entering through a tunnel on the left side of the castle as I tracked the trail of roses growing along the outside. I approached the king's throne from behind with the stake in my hand. Then King Drakkar at my feet, begging for my blood before cursing Freya's tears.

I trailed the path Stasia and I had taken to escape. This tracked a wide berth around the central village and led me behind Mara's Keep.

Every step back to the castle was fraught with pain. Each time my foot struck the path, the throbbing in my head pulsed and spread to my temples. I rubbed at my skull with the heel of my palm but it was no use, my head was at war with my heart and I suspected it was Loki's doing.

Of course he didn't want me to track and kill one of the creatures—the most powerful of them—that caused chaos for Odin's people. Perhaps he'd hoped I would wake more vampires before Freya reached me. Loki likely wanted our realm overrun with monsters so he could strike trauma in the heart of Odin as he watched his people suffer. But as it occurred in the sagas, Loki's plan often went astray. Freya and Odin and the other Gods saw through his tricks.

"I am the huntress," I said, trying to distract myself from my throbbing temples. The sound of my own voice holding steady soothed me. "I am the huntress who will protect Odin's people."

The more I said it, the more I'd accept it, believe it, become it.

This late in the Polar Nocturne, the sky above Skaldir would glow the blue of the fjords in the spring, lavender, and the orange-red of a sunset. This contrast of color in the all-black night was the Gods' gift to those of us who lived in the northern villages. The northern lights lifted the spirits of the hungry and those who'd lost loved ones during the long winter.

Darkness coated Mara, deep and impenetrable. The only light to guide my path were the candles glowing in the windows along the village.

A restless silence had settled over Mara. The people were no longer celebrating in the streets because King Drakkar's betrothal was postponed. Without this change, their lives would continue as always, with people going missing, a monster for a king, and royals who could behave as they pleased while the villagers were under the executioners' thumbs.

I positioned my thumb and forefinger at the opposite sides of my head and squeezed. The pressure didn't ease the throbbing, and with another step, the striking pain radiated across my forehead.

"I am the huntress, Loki. Whether you like it or not."

My heart skipped as if in an argument with my thoughts. *Damnit.*

This Calling went against everything I'd known. Even my mother taught that the wars between us caused the wasteland. Though that shouldn't have cut us off from the Gods, because if the Gods wanted to grant us tenable soil and prosperity, they'd find our sacrifices worthy.

But they did not always spare us.

I sucked in a painful breath, my throat raw from breathing so heavily. I paused at the bottom of the hill by the graves of kings. Like the villagers, the royals did not creep out into the darkest part of the Polar Nocturne.

Torches were alight across the castle's outer walls, their flames flickering in the wind that swept over the hill. Before approaching, I plucked the pendant off of its silver chain and wrapped the chain around my leg. The pendant fell heavy in my pocket again. With the chain against my thigh, I pushed the stake between my leg and the silver. I seethed as the rough wood scratched red marks into my skin, but the stake held in place.

As I walked I got more comfortable with it again after having practiced concealing it this way during Kayn's training sessions. The stake matched the length of my thigh and moved with me as if it was meant to be a part of me.

I skirted to the right where the king claimed the entire section of the castle. The light of the moon cast a gray glow over the side of the castle. Here, no torches warmed the cool hue across the stones. I quickly returned to the front and snagged a torch from its holder before hurrying back into the cover of branches.

The bushes lining the side wall still bloomed bright with roses. The petals furled outward, full and deep wine or blood-hued in color. Without the light of Sunna's shield, I didn't know how they survived, or how the petals had found their way to the graves outside the Hall of the Gods.

Carefully squeezing past them, I followed the roses just as the vision promised.

Halfway to the back of the castle, the stone was cut away in the shape of a small cave, buried by overgrown bushes. It was nearly hidden, and without careful inspection, appeared to be nothing more than a natural indent in the shapes of the large stones that made up the castle walls.

Each stone was unique, with curving, smooth shapes, and fit into the structure, and with the cover of plants, every stretch of the castle walls was a new sight. But this indent was deeper and the roses themselves caught my interest.

Full of deep blackness, I hesitated to step closer but the rose bushes stretched into the tunnel, the flowers themselves fuller and fuller the closer they grew to the cutout.

"Freya?" I whispered. Only the child of a woman like Anastasia, a witch, a seller of herbs and plants with runes scratched in the surface of their leaves, would care to notice the subtle differences in the roses here compared to the front of the castle.

I forced one foot in front of the other and thrust the torch forward, trying to brighten the cave of stone and roses. It was just wide enough for me to fit through without catching the bushes on fire. I lifted the torch high enough to keep away from the branches that stretched across the base of the bushes. Orange light glimmered over the low-hanging ceiling. Shapes were carved into the stone, smooth and intricate. At first glance, I expected runes, but every carving took the form of the flowers blooming beneath it, and instead of lines cut into the stone, the shallow indents were gentle dips as if the artist carefully scooped out the stone piece by piece.

I lifted the torch higher, examining the artistry with breathless awe. Not even the Valkyrie draped over the grave was as detailed and stunning as these roses. I'd never heard of a God leaving art for the people of this realm, but I couldn't deny that the level of craft looked divine. Was there truth here about the Gods?

"What is this?" I whispered. The wind caught my voice and carried it down through the tunnel. A shiver trickled over the base of my neck. Tendrils escaped the tight braids that followed the curve of my ear and were fastened at the top and back of my head along with the rest of my hair. The loose hair whipped in front of my face as I stared into the darkness.

I pushed deeper and deeper into the tunnel, finally reaching the pale light at the end. An opening by my feet glowed with dim light from the room beyond. It was large enough to crawl through, not unlike the tunnel that led from the fireplace to the room of weapons where I'd witnessed the king practice sword fighting.

I ducked and crawled through the opening, emerging through another fireplace.

My pulse thudded but not in painful skips. This was King Drakkar's room.

Dark, nearly black, marks stained the fur-skinned rug at the base of his four poster bed. Bile burned the back of my tongue but I swallowed and stepped into the room. The chill left my arms prickling with bumps.

If I thought about King Drakkar covered in blood, about Embla's death, about his cruelty for too long, overwhelm would strip me of all logic and I'd be lost in my mind and a slave to my nerves. The delicate balance came with grounding.

I can see gray, nothing but gray stone. I dared to close my eyes.

I smell the honey on my breath.

I hear…nothing. I didn't know what I expected.

I exhaled and experienced each sensation as focused as if my vision had just gone black and I was about to collapse.

I taste the lingering honey.

I feel... The goosebumps on my arms had melted away. If I stood absolutely still, I wasn't as cold. Was it just that the door had closed and I couldn't feel the draft from the tunnel?

I feel warmth? That was nothing new. It was colder nearest King Drakkar's bedchambers, but it was never *warm* in this wing without the fire that'd blazed in my room. But I'd just come through the fireplace and no flame burned in the tunnel.

Another fireplace was being used, and it was nearby. How odd and yet, an invisible tug drew me to seek out answers.

My eyes flew open and I scanned the room.

The draft from outside swept over my skin, dancing with the icy chill of the Polar Nocturne's last days.

But right here, by the base of the bed, where I'd hurried away from the stain of blood, the freezing air wasn't as biting. I shifted my gaze down to the rug beneath my feet. Stomping with the heel of my boot, a hollowness echoed in response.

I dropped to the rug and ripped it out of the way, refusing to acknowledge the reminders of the innocent man's death.

The draft sucked my breath away. Beneath the fur-skin, beneath the blood, was a hatch door, not unlike the one in my childhood room. I frowned and dropped my ear to the wood.

"Battle and blood," a woman's voice said on the other side.

"Ragna?" I whispered. The king had insisted she wasn't exiled, which meant she could be hidden somewhere in Mara's Keep. But why?

"Blood and tears, tears and sacrifice," the woman's voice pitched higher, more strained, and louder with each word, building and building as my heart sped up with it. "Sacrifice and pain, pain, carve the pain! Carve it out!"

I knocked against the hatch. The woman fell silent. "Ragna?" I said again. "It's Silver."

"Silver," she echoed. "Silver and gold. Gold and curses. Cursed for sacrifice."

I tried to pull on the hatch's handle but it wouldn't budge.

Trying again, I determined it was locked on the inside which made little sense. Why would the king put a prisoner in a room that only locked on the inside?

"Can you open the door?" I asked, causing the woman to pause again.

"Silver?"

Her nonsense wasn't unlike my overwhelming thoughts when they became repetitive, and after weeks trapped beneath a vampire king, listening to him kill and drain other humans… I held my breath to stave off the sickness that was rising from my belly. "I can help you climb out, if you can open the door. The king is gone. He won't hurt you."

Something shifted on the other side of the hatch and the door suddenly fell inward with me on top of it. In a flash of skirts and tangled braids, I smashed against the stone floor with the torch knocked from my hand and clattering beside me. I gasped for the breath the impact stole from me. Coughing and dragging raspy breaths into my lungs, I blinked and focused on my surroundings.

Candles flickered from a table beside a bed, casting a weak glow over the room. A single bed was pushed against the far wall. Heaps of blankets were piled on top. A harp with horse-hair strings was laid across a tapestry on the floor at the end of the bed. Two bedside tables flanked the charcoal bed frame. A mirror sat above a dressing table to the left and behind me was a wardrobe.

The vast space was exactly what I could have hoped for Ragna's living quarters, but the woman hovering over me with salted streaks of white across her dirty blond hair wasn't my friend.

Age gently wrinkled the backs of the hands she held covering her mouth. When she slowly dropped her arms, lines pulled at her lips where years of frowning dragged her face down. She wasn't much older than my mother, based on the brightness still blooming in her hair, but it seemed time had not been kind to this woman.

I stared up at her like a child with my mouth hanging open.

"Silver and gold?" she asked.

"I—" I cleared my throat and found my voice. "I don't have any. I thought you were—" I shook my head. "Who are you?"

"Mother," she said, placing her splayed hand over her chest.

"Mother?"

She held her flattened hand halfway up her legs. "Little Drak."

I slapped my hand to my mouth, mumbling, "Drak? You're the—the king's mother?" He had his own mother trapped beneath his room? Narrowing my eyes, I noted the subtle features that matched the king. A strong brow, thick hair, the curve of prominent cheekbones, and an icy, blood-chilling stare the color of rushing water beneath a melted fjord.

As I examined her, she did the same. Her blue eyes squinted and the crease between her furrowed brows grew deeper and deeper as her lips parted. She nearly leaned into me, eyes darting back and forth as if trying to look at both of my eyes at once.

With a sharp gasp she threw herself away from me. Shaking her head, she backed up further and further until her back bumped into the wooden leg of her four poster bed. She slapped her palms to her heaving chest.

"They're in you. They're there. They're inside." Her voice was frantic and her eyes flung wide as though she could see the darkness within me.

"What's wrong?" I asked, carefully climbing to my feet. My ass throbbed, radiating with an ache that started at the hump just above my tailbone. I winced, and straightened as best I could.

"Evil. Inside."

Evil? I stilled, my heart stalling with me. I coughed to jumpstart it and it beat too quickly, sending black spots in my vision. Steadying myself with a single breath, I found my voice again. "Me?"

"Inside." She hit her chest. "They're clawing out. Torture. Battle and tears, tears and sacrifice—"

"They?"

"They called, they called, they called and..." Her voice faded, she raised her index finger to me. I finally took a good look at her beyond King Drakkar's resemblance. Cuts and bruises covered her arms. Long scars were dragged down her neck like stripes. One of her ears was mangled, as if smashed. "You must not answer."

"What?"

Her eyes darkened as her chin dropped to her throat. Staring at me with unblinking eyes, she gulped rasping breaths. "Gods are evil. You will be too, their chosen, their vessel. They hurt and hurt and hurt and we all hurt." Her words built to a sob and she suddenly spluttered, tears dripping over her eyes as she sank to the floor with them, her back following the length of the bed frame.

I closed my gaping mouth and steeled my face. This poor woman didn't know what she was saying. How long had she been held captive here, fed this filth about the Gods from her son? She was human, which meant she may have witnessed him turn into the monster he was today. Now that he was severed from the Gods, he must have wanted her to hate them. But why the...the hurt? She said it as if the Gods themselves had come down and caused the scratches across her arms.

Who else had access to her but the king? Her own son had trapped and tortured his mother.

Acid churned in the depths of my gut, but it was the rage between my breasts that burned. If he could do this to his own mother, what had he done to Ragna?

Determination set my jaw. My entire being quivered with an all-consuming need to cut the king down.

I peeled my dry lips apart and spoke in the most gentle pitch I could muster even with the fire blazing in my chest. "Do you know of any others here besides you?"

With a shaking hand, she wiped at her cheeks to sweep the tears away. "My boy before he was like a terrible ghost. My boy and the others. The others follow him. They follow him above. So sick and cruel and bloody. They feed, always at the coldest hour." She shook to emphasize this. "Now. Servants bleed and it drips here." She pointed to the ground where dark spots mottled the floor. I glared down my nose at them. "Drip. Drip."

"I'll be back for you—"

"No!" She suddenly flung forward, closing the distance between us with her hands thrown out. She shoved me back "Not with that evil. Never come back."

I ducked away from the woman.

She followed me to the wall beneath the hatch where the stones were curved. Repeating her demand, she yelled louder and louder until I was out of the hidden room and into the king's bedchambers. She scaled the wall twice as fast as I had and slammed the hatch closed, nearly catching my fingers between the door and the floor.

After a moment of shock, I scooted back. Now I understood exactly how easy it was for King Drakkar to rip mothers away from their children. He trapped and tormented his own mother, likely no longer caring for their relationship since he'd become a vampire.

King Drakkar deserved the scars and bruises that riddled his mother's body, but when I destroyed him, there'd be nothing left.

Climbing to my feet, I was more resolved than ever to hunt him down.

Chapter Thirty-Two

I tracked the vision, slipping into the throne room through the king's entrance so that I'd come from behind the throne. Though none of this made sense. Why would King Drakkar be sitting alone in an empty throne room?

It was not for me to question Freya's visions. She'd led me this far. The Gods had given me an escape from this marriage and a way to save my mother and all witches.

The stake had become loose during my fall into his mother's room, but it didn't matter because I pulled it out from beneath the chain and wrapped my fingers around the end. With the weapon in my hand now, I was emboldened.

I moved as silently as possible, my eyes scanning every inch of the room.

Bronze candelabras suspended above me with low candles flickering. Wax dripped to the smooth floor, spotting the polished black stone with dots of beige. The mess was a sure sign the council had taken their vessels—many of the servants, with them to the shore at The Sea of Skalds.

While his council forced exiles and half the Grimward to set sail, the king sat on his throne, being fed blood in a goblet.

I gritted my teeth, gripping the stake in my fist harder. I

was ready to sink it into his chest, to end his reign the way I should have let Ragna end it weeks ago. Without the king, chaos will unfold, just as Loki would want it. In the interim, I would be ready to hunt each member of the council and then the courtiers until Mara's Keep was stripped of vampires and the people of Vylheim took back their safety.

This was the duty of the huntress.

Kill.

Kill.

Kill.

I twitched and sucked in a sharp breath as I drew closer to the throne. The massive chair sat only a few steps from the servant's entrance that came directly from the hall across the kitchens. From here, a whiff of charred sour bread stung my nose.

Silently, I crept forward, the vast space threatening to catch and carry every scuff of my boots. The dim room looked entirely new and yet almost comforting in its familiarity. It felt like years ago when I'd flooded into the throne room with my father flanking me and half of the people of Mara's Keep scrambling to get a glimpse of the king and his council.

Like that first day, the faint whiff of sweet wine filled my nose along with a sickening tang.

Blood? I'd never smelled the thick liquid in King Drakkar's goblet before, but now it surrounded me and curdled my stomach more and more with every breath.

A bang radiated throughout the room and sent shocks through my skeleton. I froze and didn't dare breathe until I identified the source of the sound. The king had slammed his goblet down on the throne's armchair, sending the clang echoing against the tall ceiling. He released an exaggerated sigh with a quiet string of curses.

I drew careful breaths and tried another step forward. If I rounded the throne, I wouldn't be able to reach him fast enough. I wanted to get in front of him in order to compel him. The only compulsion I'd done without looking into the vampire's eyes was waking them, which was so much more exhausting and difficult than simply speaking right at them.

I had to see him first.

And thankfully, he wanted to see me.

I'd approach as his betrothed, not his huntress. Lying came easy for me. Way too easy. And as long as I didn't *desire* him, my thoughts would stay hidden.

Pausing halfway to the throne, I lifted my skirts and tucked the stake between my leg and the chain again. I brushed my braid and the remaining loose hair over my shoulder. Straightening, I swallowed the bitterness staining the back of my tongue.

I had to lie.

This was a good lie. If that were possible.

My father said the lie I'd been telling my whole life was a good lie. But my father wasn't a good man.

I had to either lie to get in front of the king, or risk him attacking me. If I didn't manage to compel him first, I didn't stand a chance.

It was always lie or die.

My pulse thudded faster and faster. *Fuck.* This wasn't the time to spiral. I squeezed my eyes shut and felt every aching beat.

Don't think about it.

Except I couldn't stop. King Drakkar already knew the truth. *You sure like to lie, Silver. Want to share your real name?*

I was Silver. This Call from Freya and Odin proved it. Gold and silver, pure metals were weapons against the undead. I was a weapon.

I am Silver.

I am his betrothed.

I want to marry King Drakkar.

The lies stacked in my mind like cuts of wood ready to be incinerated in a fireplace. King Drakkar sighed again. The goblet clinked against the bronze throne as he picked it up again. From my angle, I saw only his hand as it swiped the cup.

This was for Ragna, for my mother, for the witches and all Exiles. I straightened and forced myself to round the throne.

He sat low in the chair with his legs spread wide. His eyes sliced to me and he said nothing as I took light steps to stand before him. The flat line of his mouth ticked up ever so slightly.

Since I wasn't running and hiding away from him, he likely assumed I was here to accept his hand.

I dropped into a faint curtsy, not low enough to dislodge the stake from my thigh. Dipping my head, I offered feigned respect.

"Silver." His voice pulsed around me. "I knew you'd come back. Can I finally call you my wife without you biting back at me?"

The lying started now. My blood turned to ice.

I straightened and met his eyes, as cold as my chilled veins. Swallowing, I lifted my chin. "Yes."

For a second, he didn't move, didn't blink. He didn't meet my acceptance with an arrogant smile as expected.

In another breath, he bolted forward. I gasped when he was already upon me, his hand at my throat, cutting off the air I grasped for.

I scrambled to reach for the stake beneath my skirts but King Drakkar was faster. He snatched my wrist in his hand and tugged my arm behind my back. The hem of my dress fell to the stone floor at our feet as I struggled to free myself from him. Still, he was faster, grabbing my hand and pinching it into his other hand behind my back.

Dark corners cut his face into a mask. His mouth curved like the smooth edge of one of the rose carvings. "That's a lie and you know it."

I was a damn good liar, and I knew he couldn't read my

thoughts when I wasn't heated for him. This was bait. I had to keep playing along.

I tried to twist my head into a slight shake. "No," I breathed. I only had to get him to release my throat. Then I could whisper each sensation and take control of myself and the vampire in front of me.

His smirk spread into a wicked grin. "Oh *Silver,* I know you better than that by now. The woman I proposed to would immediately correct me." His grasp on my wrists tightened as he pulled my arms lower where his knuckles pressed into the swell of my behind. The hold forced me to arch my back, driving my torso up and closer to his body. "Because even if you were accepting my hand, we wouldn't be married yet and I have no doubt that little side of you that has to be perfect all the time would tell me that you're not my wife yet."

With his hand still on my mouth, his thumb stretched, brushing soft sweeping gestures across my cheek. "This is how this is going to go, when I let go of you, you're going to tell me the truth. Because we both appreciate the truth. Don't we, Lux?"

Goosebumps spread over every inch of my skin. My nerves went raw with the sound of that name on his tongue.

This couldn't be real.

Lux?

Lux.

Fuck.

I wouldn't think about it. I wouldn't let the thoughts clawing at the edges of my mind take control of me.

It didn't matter who Silver or Lux were. I was the huntress.

As soon as he released my throat, I gulped for air.

He tilted his head, his icy eyes intense as they raked over me, perhaps trying to understand why I'd returned. "So, what are you really doing here?"

I squirmed against his hand gripping my wrists but he only

tightened his hold, pushing his body flush against mine, squeezing my wrists raw, his fingers pressing harder over my lips. He dipped so close the only thing separating our mouths was his hand. His eyes narrowed as he took me in.

The truth. My heart thumped harder and harder. At one time, I'd do anything for answers, for another piece of the sagas, for remnants of our ancestors, our history. Now, I had to trust that I'd receive enough of that from my mother. King Drakkar couldn't tempt me.

I couldn't speak yet, so he filled the silence.

"Your body is so warm, and yet, this room is so cold. How is it that you're burning up?"

Because I was enraged, ready to fight and kill him. Because I'd climbed the hill that led to this wretched castle. Because my heart betrayed me as each beat skittered too quickly from one to another.

What could I do trapped in his hold? *I can't do this.* I was just that little girl again, screaming Freya's name, getting distracted and failing the task entrusted to me.

I couldn't fail. The Gods had chosen me. I had the power to raise monsters from the ground, then to compel them.

I barely put a voice behind my whispers. "I see ice in his eyes. Feel his hands on me…"

He chuckled, the sound low and taunting as it seemed to stretch down the tunnel with the sweeping wind. My eyes flew open. "I feel you, Silver." His gaze glazed, but he fought it, blinking rapidly. "I feel you trying to take hold of me."

A crease formed between his brow as he resisted the power slipping into his mind, my gift from Loki. My gut sloshed with a sudden heaving sickness. It cracked my concentration as I swallowed the stinging bile back down my throat.

I hadn't felt it before, but I hadn't experienced a vampire trying to fight the compulsion either. Something about the flicker of wetness in his eyes, the pain that lanced across his face with each twitch of his brow struck me. Why should I care if it hurt him?

I wanted to be a witch who helped others, not hurt them. Still, I pressed, letting Loki's chaotic power mingle with my words.

"How could you kill Embla?" I said between my teeth. I couldn't help myself. If he spelled out his cruelty for me, turning him to dust wouldn't be so painful.

This shouldn't hurt, but seeing him now, hearing him say...my name.

Lux.

Lux.

Lux.

King Drakkar knew who I really was, which meant he likely knew what I'd done. When he said he knew me better than to buy my lie, curiosity simmered in my chest, along with something else. Something sinister—like appreciation for a cruel king, for a monster who *saw* me. Really saw me.

Now I was scanning him, holding him with this power.

A glaze layered over his blue gaze, the compulsion taking control.

King Drakkar shook his head, wisps of the hair knotted at the back of his head escaped. "Embla?" His voice was emotionless from the forced answers. "She is missing."

"You killed her, you fucking monster! What purpose did it serve?"

"I didn't kill her. When someone goes missing, I have to look the other way. I can only suspect the purpose was the pleasure of gluttony."

"You're sick."

"It wasn't me." He flinched.

This was pure truth. The compulsion didn't allow him to lie. But if he hadn't killed her, why did one of his servants end up on the temple's step? The vampire I woke wouldn't have traveled to the castle just to pluck a random girl and drag her all the way back to the feet of the witch who compelled her.

"Who then?"

"There are many vampires. I cannot say who may have drank from her.."

Except she wasn't drained, she was bleeding out on the stone. This was murder, plain and simple. Black spots dotted my vision and I knew that if I didn't stop, I'd go limp in his arms.

I opened my mouth to compel him to release my wrists but I couldn't find the words. If I were free to grab the stake, I'd act on instinct. After so many hours of training, I knew exactly how to grip the stake and where to angle it. I could lean into muscle memory and let this Call of the Gods commence.

But if he let go, I'd also have to kill him. I'd turn him to dust and he hadn't even been the one to hurt Embla.

"You didn't kill her," I said.

He shook his head. "No."

"Stop the Age of Exploration."

He huffed. "I can't do that. I don't agree with the council on many things, but humans and vampires will both starve if we don't go forward."

"Then release the exiles!"

"They need seers to guide the way, to make it through the storms."

"Let Ragna go then."

He cursed and squeezed me harder. "They took all the witches."

Frustration rippled through me.

Why couldn't I kill him?

My tongue turned sour, and all at once, I dropped the compulsion. My chest heaved with the effort of the magic. I should have demanded he release me, but I'd been too consumed with a twisted sense of justice, as if getting him to confess that he'd killed Embla would help her now. And now I didn't have the energy to compel him again.

"Why can't they simply work with the witches instead of holding them prisoner?"

He frowned. "Witches have been proven dangerous and the vampires don't trust them, this is part of why they are exiled and then forced to do the vampire's bidding."

Something familiar flickered in his eyes, almost mirroring me. Frustration? He had my arms in his hand, my life in his palm, yet his breathing was as shallow as mine. His jaw bulged as he gritted his teeth.

"You hate this," I said. My gaze rapidly switched between his eyes, examining every flicker of emotion.

He said nothing.

I tilted my head, eyes narrowing. "It's the council. They control you?"

"Remember when I said to shut that pretty mouth?"

"But this is something more than that. You were mad about the council then. Now, you're...seething."

"Ragna was one of *my* witches."

A foreign feeling hollowed out my gut. My lips parted but breath stagnated in my throat.

He tilted his head, his icy eyes intense as they raked over me, perhaps trying to understand why I'd returned. "Are you...jealous?" he asked.

"Absolutely not." I quickly flipped the conversation back to the witches. "What are you doing with them? Killing them?"

He laughed. "You forget so much. I told you I'd share my truths with you when you marry me."

"Then I'll compel you again."

"You're tired." He spoke plainly. This was a fact and we both knew it. I couldn't lie to him. I'd lied my entire life, to everyone, even Ragna, but King Drakkar already knew the truth and he already knew me. "You're leaning against me, and I won't let you fall. So I have a better idea than compulsion."

I scoffed. He raised his eyebrows and continued. "Because you're so inclined to deny your attraction to me, I'll make it easier for you to explore safely. For every kiss you give me, I'll reward you with an answer. I want you to know everything."

Everything? Would he share the lost sagas? Our history? My heart thumped.

He released my wrists and I let my hands fall limp at my sides. Staring at him, a hundred questions competed to be the first from my mouth.

"We can start with whatever you'd like," he said. "How many vampires live within these walls? What plans I had for Ragna. What I thought when I first saw you." His voice turned ragged as he brought his lips to my ears. "What I'm thinking of doing to you now..." He kissed where my pulse beat just below my ear then pulled back, sucking a breath in.

This was for Ragna. I'd tell myself that over and over. It was only half of a lie.

Finally, I tilted my head back until my mouth found his.

He kissed me back with such hunger, I'd forgotten how it made my heart stutter. Nothing about his touch was soft or intimate like when Kayn held me. King Drakkar wanted to claim me, to consume me, and nothing about his obsession with me was quiet. He was open and honest and raw with every moment of his wanting and I couldn't help appreciate that he didn't hide his thoughts and desires even when they weren't quite...right.

His free hand cupped my jaw as his fingers pressed into the soft spot of my cheeks. Pulling me harder into him, I spread my lips and allowed his tongue to explore me. Even when he let go of my face and we parted, I couldn't breathe.

"Are you going to hurt Ragna?"

"No."

"What will you use your witches for?"

When he said nothing, I reached up, feeling for his jaw. His beard was rough against my palm as I drew him into me. He nearly devoured me, kissing with such fervor that it left me shaking, whether from desire or fear, I didn't know.

When he pulled apart, it was he who was breathless this time. "For a ritual."

"What ritual?"

Again, I kissed him until he drew back and answered me. "Summoning Odin."

"What? You want me—"

"Not you. The other witches. I already have plans for you." He smirked. "To be my wife, of course."

"Then why threaten to kill me?"

I leaned into him, enjoying this kiss too much. Maybe it was that he mentioned Odin and it was so rare to hear those words aloud, like I was in the room with another believer. Maybe it was simply that King Drakkar answered every single one of my questions without hesitancy. He always did.

"Because if you don't marry me, the alternative is your insanity."

That was it, that was all he said to explain this threat that loomed over me.

"And death is better?"

"No, but I'm selfish. I will not watch the Gods play with you like a toy. You deserve to die honorably, to fight and ascend to Valhalla. And Silver, I know you'll fight back when I come for you. I know you won't let me try to kill you without throwing everything you have at me, and that effort will give you a chance to honor them."

I searched his eyes. None of this made sense. "Why would you help me go to Valhalla when you hate Odin?"

He inhaled, deeply, purposefully, and teased out my bottom lip with his thumb. As if he'd trained me, I tilted my face up, kissing him hard. When he pulled away, I sucked in a breath and grazed my teeth over my lip. A low hum vibrated in his chest as he watched my mouth, and then forced his eyes to meet mine.

"It's what you want," he said. "Anyone who loves the sagas and history as much as you would. And Odin won't be there for long. It may be his palace, but palaces can be taken, just like I took Mara's Keep."

"You should be worried about your own sanity."

He only laughed.

"Why would you care if madness takes me?"

"I didn't, at first—" he cut off. A moment of silence followed until I felt his chest rumbling against me. He chuckled and then clucked his tongue. "You almost tricked me again. Now I'll take what I'm owed." Before I could respond, his warm hand dipped beneath the coat draped over my shoulder and his palm pressed against my bare chest just below my collarbone. He shoved me to the side and behind the throne.

Against the cold bronze back of the king's chair, he pinned me.

He kissed me with his whole body. Every inch of him pressed against me until he pulled away just as quickly as the kiss had begun. I gasped, almost reaching for him.

"I told you before, Lux. You fascinate me. I once only admired your ability to reject control. Then I noticed the way your lips inevitably part when your heart has lost its rhythm. You spent time here with me in the castle and I learned more about you. And now..." I knew he pressed in closer to me based on the heat of his body. His hand found my hip and his thumb hooked around the bone at my hip, his fingers were hot on my skin even through the fabric of my skirts. "Now I admire all of you. How could I watch you succumb to insanity?"

"How do you know about..." I couldn't say the name—my name. *Don't think about it. Ignore it. Ignore it.* I coughed and cleared the word away. "What can you tell me about the lost history?"

His only response was a sigh. Perhaps he was disappointed I'd forgotten to kiss him again before presenting him with the question. Silence followed.

Instead of taking the kiss that he was owed, he let go of my hip and found my hand.

"Come," he said, lacing his fingers through mine, as if we were the husband and wife he claimed he so desperately wanted us to be.

My heart skipped, but I didn't know if it was for the answers I so desperately wanted. The answers I came to Mara's Keep seeking in the first place.

Or because his hand fit mine like it was designed to mold together. All at once, he felt familiar, like I'd known him for an entire lifetime.

CHAPTER THIRTY-THREE

Anticipation buzzed in my veins, not unlike the moments before the send off at a footrace. I craved the skip to the next moment, to know everything about our history all at once.

When we emerged from the throne room, the hall was empty, devoid of life, and yet, I still felt eyes on us. I twisted to scan the dark stretch of stone behind us but only saw what appeared to be an open door. Nobody stood in the hallway.

King Drakkar squeezed my hand tighter and tugged me closer to him. With his lips at my ear, he whispered. "Stay close."

As we wound through the maze of halls, the stake rubbed the skin on my leg raw. I was supposed to be killing the king, not letting him lead me through the castle like a pet on a leash. I'd sworn that the promise of the lost history wouldn't tempt me, yet here I was tracking his every step with my hand tightly in his.

Glancing over his shoulder, he yanked me closer and then pulled me into a nearby room.

"What—" I started.

He pressed his finger to my lips with a low shush. Falling silent, he waited by the door. We'd arrived in another bedchamber, this one plain but with another fireplace that looked suspicious, though this fireplace did have a back to it. The ashy stone was covered in gray where it wasn't charred black. The bed appeared unused.

King Drakkar chewed at his bottom lip with his regular, human-looking teeth, his fangs weren't descended, and yet the crease between his brow hinted at worry. What did a vampire king have to be afraid of? I slid my gaze to him.

After a tense moment, he turned and, with a smirk, nodded toward the bed. "Are you ready for this?"

I followed his line of sight and then scoffed. "Let me guess, for the lost history you want more than a kiss?" I frowned, and when I tried to tug my hand away, he held tighter.

He stepped into my space, his face inches from mine as he looked down at me. His mouth curled into a smirk. "Clever. I'll keep that in mind."

Gripping my hand like a vise, he pulled me with him as he made his way to the fireplace. He finally released me and dropped to a crouch. The movement of his cloak sent a few ashes puffing out of the pile at the bottom of the fireplace. He craned his neck, twisting to look up into the darkness above where the fire vented up and out of the castle.

"What does a pile of ashes have to do with the lost history?" I asked, impatience curdling in the pit of my gut. The more I thought of Freya's favor of wisdom, the more I wanted him to give me the damn answers.

King Drakkar's gaze fluttered to me and he held his half smile steady. "Don't touch the ashes," he said as he straightened, looking down at me now. He lifted a finger to my chin and tipped it up. "And I should warn you, this is far more than an answer to a single question, so I'll require more than a kiss." When I narrowed my eyes, he let go of my chin and raised both hands in mock surrender. "It was your idea, my pretty little wife."

My hand itched with the desire to rip the stake from my thigh and plunge it into his chest. But I didn't. I didn't so much as push his hand off my chin. I *needed* the lost history, and for some insane reason that I couldn't comprehend, the vampire king was willing to give it to me. Perhaps if he hadn't spoken the truth before, always willing to bring up the Gods and monsters even when Father said Vyls, as well as kings, had been beheaded for less.

And if I was as honest with myself as King Drakkar was with me, I'd acknowledge the sickness sloshing in my stomach at the very thought of destroying someone—even a monster who'd bled an innocent man dry. Perhaps it was because this violence was against everything I'd been taught, or perhaps I couldn't bring myself to kill the one person who'd respected me enough to answer my questions.

Without another word, King Drakkar reached up into the flue. His foot balanced on a jutting stone at the back of the fireplace and his arm flexed as he pulled himself up and into the darkness. After a moment, his feet reached to the inside wall and he disappeared inside the flue where the smoke of a fireplace was meant to vent out of the room.

"Is every fireplace in this damned place fake?" I muttered, mildly annoyed that even I hadn't noticed this little trick.

"Not fake." His voice echoed from up inside the flue. "A fire was burning here just this morning. Now come."

I hesitated. Willingly placing myself into another dark and tight space with the king didn't sit right. Freya favored wisdom, and nothing about this was wise—except that I was meant to track a vampire, and here the vampire was, giving away all his secrets, even beckoning me to follow him right to the source of our history.

His hand appeared in the opening of the fireplace. "Need a little help?"

I scanned the room, my eyes falling on the empty bed. My blood simmered hot enough that I lifted cold hands to my face to cool myself off. *Don't think about his kisses. You didn't like them.* He was a true monster, and the man I was going to kill, despite how deeply I'd felt his kiss.

"Oh, and bring the torch," he said.

After a forceful breath, I snatched a lit torch from the wall, took his hand, and kicked my foot out to the jutting stone. My skirts swished over the pile of ashes, gathering gray dust at the hem. He brought my hand to a curved stone on the other side where I gripped the edge. His other hand lifted me as I pushed off with my foot and hefted myself up into the flue, climbing the inside wall like a rocky ladder. Soot coated my fingers until the tips turned black.

It wasn't until he pulled me onto a dark stony ledge inside the flue that my mind even registered where he'd been balancing. Behind him and high above where we sat was a square wooden hatch, charred black from years of smoke. He stood, offering a hand to help me up beside him. I swayed on the curve of the rock. Twisting, I stared down into the fireplace, hoping nobody would come with fresh firewood and strike a flame below us.

The king pulled a chain that was buried beneath his clothing. At the bottom of the bronze links hung a key the same dull shade of brown. He thrust it into the keyhole at the corner of the hatch, twisted, then pushed the hatch inward.

I never expected such a vast room hidden behind the squat hatch. King Drakkar stepped inside and then turned, holding out his hand to help me step over the edge of the hatch. Mindlessly, I took his hand and allowed him to guide me inside where I froze, my mouth agape, my heart slowing, as I tried to look at everything all at once.

Shelves nearly as tall as I'd imagined Yggdrasil were carved into the stone. Flat stones were stacked one on top of the other across each shelf. Scrolls rolled and bound with string balanced on each other in great piles from the bottom of the shelf to the top. Records of every kind from across Vylheim were kept safe here in this hidden library, each type indicative of the age from which it came. A fur-skinned rug spanned the stretch of ground. The stone slightly sloped with a lift in the center of the room.

I floated over to the closest shelf, hardly aware that I tripped on the rug and King Drakkar had to catch me by the elbow. Vaguely, I noticed him slotting the torch in a holder on the wall and then returning to my side.

I dragged my fingers across the edge of a runestone, a flat stone on which our ancestors had carved pieces of our oral sagas.

Breathing in shallows gulps, I plucked a book—one of the more recent forms of historical records taken up by scribes—and eased it off the shelf. We had a few books in the long-house in Skaldir that had helped me learn to read, but they were dull, records of the death of recent Vyls, village council meetings, what food had lasted through our previous Polar Nocturne and what we might need to do to prepare for the next length of darkness to avoid losing more villagers to sickness, frost, or starvation.

I ran my fingers over the spine of a book. A small tree with dozens of branches swirling like snakes at the top was etched into the side. "The Tree of Yggdrasil," I breathed.

Heat encompassed my back. I twisted my neck, eyeing the king from the corner of my eye.

"You really should see it," he said.

I said nothing. That was bait to get me to ask a question.

"It's breathtaking," he continued. "But nearly impossible to find. The only reason I've been there was because I went to burn it so nobody could carve a stake from it and kill me. I thought I'd be untouchable. Turns out, I'm not *that* king, and anyway, I might want to die someday, feast in Valhalla and all that."

I didn't know what any of that meant. He couldn't go to Valhalla or Folkvangr or anywhere, because, like the rest of the monsters, he didn't have a soul. Once he was destroyed, he'd be nothing more than the dust that coated these stone shelves.

He reached over my shoulder, letting his body press against mine, nearly pinching me between his chest and the shelf. "You'll find this one particularly interesting," he said as he slid a runestone from the shelf. I shifted so that he could use both hands to lift the heavy stone, but he didn't need it. Effortlessly, he brought the runestone down from above my head with one hand and angled it toward me.

I recognized most of the runes immediately, but I'd never heard of any saga with this title before. With a gentle touch, I glided my fingers over the ridges in the stone. "What is this first word?" I whispered.

"Vampírkarl," he said, his breath on the back of my neck as he propped the runestone on the shelf in front of me.

"*Vampírkarl: The Undying Witch.*" I traced the runes that followed, my eyes flitting from one piece of the text to the next, trying to absorb the entire saga at once. It spoke of a seer who prophesied the fall of her loved one in a combat called "Battle at Folkvangr's Gate." Though I struggled with the next few runes, I understood the basics. This witch trained as a warrior, perhaps a shieldmaiden, and then followed him into every battle, hoping that if she died in combat with him, they'd both be chosen to feast together in Valhalla.

"Lux," King Drakkar said softly. He brushed a finger down the back of my arm.

When the witch saw her own afterlife was chosen by Freya for Folkvangr, she fought harder, trying to change this fate, hoping to be cut down by their enemies with a weapon still in her hand so that the Valkyries may deem her worthy to sit at Odin's table. As her lover died, she witnessed a Valkyrie, becoming the only person to have ever seen one of the warrior women. She touched the bottom of the Valkyrie's wings as the Valkyrie carried her lover to Valhalla.

"Lux." His finger traced back up the line he'd drawn down my arm and his hand rubbed down my back. Slowly, he dragged his hand down my side until his fingers hooked around the bone at my hip. His grip grew firmer as he leaned his whole body into me.

My lips parted and my breath quickened as I deciphered the runes as fast as my mind could keep up. The witch vowed she would not succumb to death until she figured out how to thwart their eternal separation, and having touched the Valkyrie, she gained the power to take a soul. She could turn the near-dead into a state between living and death. Existing. Undead. Goosebumps prickled over my shoulders and down my chest.

She created the first vampire to siphon immortality from —as long as they fed on humans.

She chose a friend who'd fallen in battle, a man bleeding out from an abdominal wound. A man named Kayn.

A gasp escaped me and my hand flew to my mouth. The saga ended with a line about the first vampire set apart from the rest. This vampire created all the rest, robbing warriors, shieldmaidens, innocent humans of the afterlife they'd fought for.

The next rune called Kayn the "king of monsters."

It explained that he could only be unmade by a stake from the tree of Yggdrasil, the tree that this runestone said was branded into his skin—the mark of the first witch. A mark that said he was created by her power, according to the history.

With my eyes fluttering, the runes blurred in front of me. This was the source of the guilt he spoke of. And now he wanted me to do what he couldn't. He wanted me to wake, track, and eradicate all the monsters he'd created. I already knew this, but not the addition that sank my heart.

My eyes flew over the runestone, absorbing the last lines explaining that when the first witch made Kayn undead, he'd lost his soul—a soul he could never get back.

But it said that he *could* take someone else's soul as his own, if they unmade every monster he'd created.

Like he'd asked of me.

Like the Gods had asked of me, but Kayn had a vested interest. This wasn't just about protection for the people of Midgard.

He didn't care about humans. He didn't care about me, only what he could get from me. If I followed through with this, he could take my damn soul.

Anger burned hot in the base of my belly.

Kayn was gambling with my entire existence, my afterlife.

"Lux," King Drakkar demanded my attention as he grasped my arm and forced me to spin and face him. Shoving me back against the only smooth wall in the library, he seemed to enjoy pinning me against cold stone.

My back slammed against the stone and I couldn't stop what came out of my mouth. "That hurts. Fuck!"

He tilted his head, a wild and hungry look glazing his icy eyes. "That's exactly what I want to do." I looked away, not giving him the satisfaction of my focus. "You seem to have forgotten our deal. You asked a question, and I answered."

"No, I—" I snapped my mouth shut. I'd asked about the rune I did not know. Annoyed at the interruption, I quickly stretched my neck and pressed my lips against his.

When I cut the kiss short, his mouth twitched. "Oh no, my curious little killer got everything she could have asked for, now it is my turn. This room is full with as many answers as I can possibly give you. I did tell you, I'd give you every answer I can."

"For a price."

"If you want to look at it that way. Really, you're the one benefitting."

"Am I?"

He smiled wickedly. "You'll see. I have a taste for you now."

I should have retched, should have spit in his face, should have fought the monster pinning me to the wall. These were nearly the words Sten had threatened me with. Except King Drakkar's words weren't a threat, and for some reason, I wanted to know what he'd say next. Perhaps because he always said exactly what he wanted.

His grin held steady as his eyes searched my face. "You've been teasing me with these kisses."

"You asked for them—"

He slammed his mouth against mine, silencing me with his lips. When he pulled back, it was just enough that when he moved his mouth, his lips nearly brushed mine. His forehead gently pressed against my brow. "I asked for *you*. Because I really don't want to have to kill you."

My breath stalled. He lifted his free hand and dragged his thumb over my bottom lip, parting my lips so that he could kiss me openly again.

He finally allowed me to breathe when he spoke again, his voice ragged, full of craving, and drenched in desperation. "How else am I to convince you to marry me?"

I drew in a breath, gathering courage with the fresh air in my lungs. "You're so arrogant that you think your mouth will make me forget that you murder innocent people?"

He only chuckled and his hand fell to my hip again. He dragged it down, down the back of my thigh. "I suppose you're right, this is a weak excuse to have you." When he tilted his head again, his eyes narrowed. "And Lux, I *will* have you. But I know you admire honesty, so allow me to confess that I do hope that this helps change your mind."

"I've already kissed you."

"And now I must have more."

I stooped to reach for the stake at my thigh, but something

stupid crawled at the edges of my mind and stopped me half-way. He looked down at my hand and smirked.

Why did I want him to touch me again? Only a day ago I'd been in Kayn's arms, only giving my lips to him and by choice, but now I couldn't even think of Kayn without gritting my teeth.

The king of monsters didn't deserve me, not after he'd kept the real reason he wanted my help from me. A sudden ache flared in my chest. I thought I could trust him, but he'd only wanted to use me. To wipe away thoughts of Kayn and ease the ache, I parted my lips and tilted them to the king's mouth.

"There's more," I said when I broke the kiss. He only laughed and shook his head, a wicked smile bent across his face.

Slowly, he gathered my skirts in his fist, pulling it up higher and higher until my thigh was exposed. His hand slipped under the fabric and closed over the stake bound to my leg. Another chuckle rumbled in his chest as he gripped the stake. "Clever girl." His arm flexed as he pulled at the stake, yanking the silver chain that'd held it in place. "I will take what I am owed, and that was in the way."

For one horrible second the chain link dug so deeply in the soft flesh at the back of my thigh that I had to swallow a scream. Finally, the chain snapped and he threw the stake on the ground behind him. It rolled across the rug and clattered on the stone by the far wall. The back of my thigh stung where the chain had ripped along my skin.

He seemed to sense this because his cool hand quickly found its way to my thigh again. He cupped the raw flesh, his fingers a relief against the burn. I sucked in a few quick breaths as shame wriggled in my gut for relishing his touch after he was the one who'd caused the pain.

Tilting his face to me, he closed his mouth over mine as if quieting my rapid breaths. He gripped the side of my thigh and squeezed so hard a yelp escaped me. "Good," he whispered. "I wanted you to forget the feel of the weapon and instead remember my hand on you. Remember who you belong to, my wife."

I jutted out my chin. "Funny, I don't remember our wedding."

"So you're not a seer, but perhaps you can sense what's coming next." His hand brushed over the top of my thigh to the inside of my leg. He turned it over and dragged two fingers along my core, eliciting another gasp from me.

Before I knew what was happening, he dropped to his knees in front of me and shoved my skirts up. Breath caught in my throat and my entire body stiffened as his tongue followed the same path his fingers had just trailed. He licked along the sensitive center between my thighs. I breathed faster and faster, my heart pounding, my entire body flush with goosebumps.

Desperate to hold onto anything, my fingers plunged into his hair, pulling it loose from its knot. His tongue swirled over me from a new angle each time and it left me feeling intoxicated as the sensitivity built and built. I gripped the bundle of his hair tighter and tighter in my fist until my fingers ached.

His two fingers found my core again where they split me and dipped inside. I sucked in a breath and threw my head back, forgetting the stone wall behind me. I hardly registered knocking the back of my skull against stone, too entranced by the feeling building within me. Tension climbed up inside me, begging to be released. I whimpered, involuntarily giving voice to this begging.

His fingers slipped out and he pulled back for what I thought was a breath. Instead, he stood and he lifted his fingers that'd been inside me only moments ago. They glistened wet against the flickering light of the torch. He dipped them inside his mouth while he watched for my reaction.

My chest heaved as I imagined his fingers not between his

lips, but deep inside me again. He slowly pulled his fingers out and his mouth curved into a grin.

His eyes lingered on my heaving chest until he tilted his head and whispered into my ear. "Don't look so surprised, Lux. A kiss is a kiss." He pulled back, his eyes consuming me. "And now you know what it feels like to be teased."

CHAPTER THIRTY-FOUR

I'd traded myself for a glimpse of the lost history, but shame didn't crawl its icy fingers up my neck as I'd expected. Instead, desire for more left me breathless and slick.

As King Drakkar stepped back, allowing me to fully breathe again, I lifted my chin.

"Have I changed your mind?" he asked, his icy eyes glimmering. "You marry me and all this is yours, Lux. And a lifetime of this." He brushed thumb over my core, eliciting a gasp from me as every nerve ignited.

Despite the need burning between my thighs, I frowned and chewed at my bottom lip.

Giving in to the intoxication King Drakkar offered patched the hole left by Kayn, at least temporarily, but marrying a murderer wasn't an option.

Even if the lost history was right in front of me. The history I'd dreamed of. Everything my mother spent years offering sacrifices to the Gods to recover bits and pieces of. These were the stories of our ancestors, the stories that created the world we live in. I could lie and perhaps he'd allow me to see more of the library, but even the thought of lying left my tongue bitter.

"You'd lie to me?" he asked. The crease between his brow made him look as if he was actually hurt by this.

My heart jolted. I hadn't said it aloud, had I?

"No," he said. "I heard your thoughts."

With my back snapping straight, I bore into him with a fevered glare. "I was really hoping that was a nightmare? You really can read my mind, can't you?"

With a chuckle he shook his head. "I can catch glimpses after I've…connected with a human. And then when they're heated. When you want me. Part of it is simply observing how your body reacts to your thoughts."

Rage built within me. "You tricked me into this twisted little kissing game so you could invade the privacy of my mind, didn't you?"

He brushed his thumb over his lip and suppressed another chuckle. "Again, no. The human has to…*want* me, both in spirit and sex, in order for the connection to form. It goes both ways, and I didn't know if you felt more than just the heat—"

"No."

"Hmm."

I cursed. There was no way I could want anything beyond base attraction.

"So," he began, his wicked smirk taunting me. "Shall I ask again? Is this library a wedding gift worthy of your hand?"

I shook my head and absently toyed with the tip of my braid. Two smaller braids from the sides of my heads were intertwined with the larger one that I draped over my shoulder. "There is so much we don't know and I want all of it." I was that same girl my mother tasked to watch for the executioners—the blade at which the truth stopped. She always knew they were hiding our history, but not for what purpose

This hidden library proved her right.

"Why? What can lost history do for you now?"

I opened my mouth but stopped short, unsure if I could explain the will to live to an undead creature.

He grinned. "Speechless? I know another way to leave you without words."

I mirrored him now, folding my arms. "You wouldn't understand the answer."

"Try me."

"Survival."

He opened his arms and looked around. "What is mere survival when you can have all of this and live in the castle in the wealthiest village in our realm?"

Our realm. The way he spoke almost drew me to him, like an invisible thread pulled taut between us. Or perhaps my body was still tense, still wound up from the frustration of his teasing. "I want freedom. And for someone like me, black eyes and with a pulse that beats to the rhythm of the Poetic Edda, it is only a matter of time until the executioners come for me. But you, my…" I stopped. His lips parted, but he said nothing. "What?"

"You don't know what to call me."

"I'm not declaring you *my king* and certainly not calling you my husband because that's simply not true."

"How about Drak?"

"How about Killer?"

He stepped up to me, brushing the back of his finger along my cheek. "Only if I can call you that too." I gritted my teeth.

"See? You wouldn't understand. You killed for pleasure. I killed for protection. That is what survival means." A weight lifted off of me though the shame still lingered with a chill trickling down my spine. This is what the Gods needed from me; survival for me and my mother, for Stasia, and the people of Skaldir.

He cracked a half smile, but it wasn't full of amusement as it often was.

"If my eyes speak for me, then it is the shape of your mouth that speaks for you, even when it is closed," I said.

"My mouth is very talented." Though he spoke suggestively, his half smile faded.

I pursed my lips. "I haven't offended the king, have I?"

"There is something more precious than survival, Lux." I ticked my brows, prodding him to continue, as if a monster could even understand the need to protect oneself. "Revenge." I huffed. "And," he said, cutting me off before I could argue. "Freedom."

My heart skipped. "Those are the titles of Loki and Freya's sagas…"

"And I'm a monster cut off from the Gods," he said. "Yes, I'm aware."

"Are the full accounts here?" I pushed past him and trailed my finger against the stone shelf. Would Freya's full saga hint at these trials? Perhaps I could confirm if the answer I'd received after the blood sacrifice was correct. Could a huntress also be seer? Reading the entire saga dedicated to her would give a deeper insight into the God I was never allowed to speak of.

He caught my elbow and yanked me away from the shelf. I stumbled into him and shot him a venomous look. "That's enough."

"You have to release this history," I said between breaths. My heart beat faster, anticipating what could be if only he'd listen to me. "When it's exposed, the council will have to let the witches out of exile. The people of Vylheim will recognize the truth."

"I can't do that. There is already unrest in Mara because of the Age of Exploration. This will tilt humans into full on war."

If I wasn't helping the witches, then what was the point of any of this? My mother was still dying. Ragna was still locked away somewhere, and I'd still be forced to marry the king or die.

He turned his back to me, giving me a second, one single second to act.

Desperation melted with the simmering fury and I lunged for the stake.

He spun around, his eyes flicking to the weapon before his smirk spread into a sinister grin. "You won't kill me."

"Like you won't kill me?" I challenged, speaking through my teeth. Despite my earlier hesitance, I refused to give up my power again.

His smile wavered. "I told you, I don't want to, but if you refuse me——"

"You would have killed me already if you had the balls to do it."

He laughed. "I've killed more people than you've met, my wife."

I frowned and gripped the stake tighter. "But not me. What is it? Because I'm a witch? I've communed with the divine. Is the king afraid of the Gods?" Squeezing my throat harder, he finally frowned, which meant I'd hit a painful truth. It was my turn to smirk. "They're more powerful than you'll ever be, my *king*."

"I thought I told you to call me Drak?"

"I thought I told you not to call me your wife?"

He laughed, though the sound didn't have a lick of joy in it. "If you'd just trust me, you'd know that is a compliment and for your benefit."

"If you'd just tell me why——"

With a huff, he ripped his hand from my throat and stepped back, shaking his head. "This world is a game, Lux——"

"Silver."

"Lux."

"Fuck you!"

He laughed again and lifted his arm to tug at the strings of
my dress that now hung loose. My chest was nearly bare with
the ribbons having come undone. His narrowed eyes raked
over the swell of my breasts before he met my gaze again.
"I'm playing to win with you on my team. Unfortunately, the
other team has more players."

"Consider me on the other side."

"You have no idea what you're saying."

"Then. Tell. Me."

He drew his tongue over his top teeth before flexing his
jaw. Dropping his hand from the ribbons at my breast, he
smiled without amusement and sighed. "I can't risk it."

"Risk what?" I demanded.

"Losing you."

My lips parted. This was the last response I expected. He
didn't know me, he didn't care for me, he *used* me and fucked
with me, but that was where our connection ended. Or where
it should have ended. My damn body still wanted him. The
line between anger and this dizzying need to release the
tension he'd built thinned. I forced the depraved thoughts to
quiet.

"I'm nothing but a piece of the game to you," I said.

"You're the only one strong enough to believe in the Gods
despite the executioners and you've yet to succumb to the
Gods' affairs."

"Does this have to do with your revenge and freedom?"

"My revenge, yes, but everyone's freedom."

I brought the tip of the stake to the center of his chest.
Even if he knew I wouldn't kill him yet, I liked the position of
power. "How?"

"When we're married, I'll tell you everything." I closed my
eyes, frustrated with his useless response, then, surprised to
hear his voice again, I peeled them back open. "I'm not only
speaking to you right now. I can't trust that they aren't
listening."

"They?" I breathed. Though I posed it as a question, I already knew. How did he know the Gods warred within me?

"Because you're one of the few people brave enough to still believe in them despite the executioners, and you're the only one to fight back, so of course they'd choose you."

I released a string of curses under my breath. "You read my mind again. *That's* how you know about the Gods."

"No, in your mind or not, a vampire could never hear the Gods. I hear *you*, and only when you—" his lips bent into a wicked grin, the suggestion heating me from the inside out. The darkness within me beckoned for him, curling and twisting to reach for him. It wasn't just my body that wanted him to touch me again, but my spirit, poisoned black with a corruption that found comfort in the familiar corruption within him.

I straightened, finally lowering the stake to my side. I refused to let go of it, but I no longer wielded it against him.

"I'll marry you," I whispered.

His sharp gaze pinned me. "What did you say?"

"Release the witches, risk this war you claim will happen, and give Vylheim the true history of their people. Let everyone remember the Gods, and I'll marry you." With Drak still as their king, he could release the truth and temper this war. We could not risk another wasteland, not with the winters growing harsher. As much as I just wanted freedom, I had to be smart about this.

I could be the queen at his side, giving the real history to the people of Vylheim.

Shaking his head, he let out a cruel laugh. "That's not how this works. You will marry me because I told you to."

"I thought I had to accept it?"

He breathed a curse. He hated not being in control. Maybe I knew him as well as he claimed to know me. "I will not release Ragna or any of my witches until they've summoned Odin."

"What is your obsession with this summoning?"

"Is that understood?" He hardly let me finish speaking before barreling over my words with his own question.

I narrowed my eyes, keeping my chin lifted. I would not back down now, I'd already failed Odin. I'd already decided not to follow through with the single command he'd given me. Valhalla and Folkvangr were the dreams of a foolish girl. They were afterlives meant for someone better.

Could the Gods really fault me for wanting to save her? They knew who they'd chosen—a sick and twisted witch. Their choice was a gamble from the beginning and I had no doubt they were aware of it. Odin was aware of most things, especially when it came to witches.

Now it was either pass the trial given to me by the Allfather, or take what I wanted, and I was exactly selfish enough to take what I wanted.

"After we've tried summoning him then," I said. "And it can't take longer than a year from when we're married."

His fists flexed and released, flexed and released. He was fighting every instinct to demand control. I would not win him over by stripping him of it.

Maybe I could give him the illusion of control. Maybe that'd tip him over the edge. Maybe he'd agree to risk everything.

He'd asked for kisses in exchange for the answers he gave me, but it was obvious he was desperate for more.

"You will agree to this and for tonight, I'll do whatever you want." Even saying it stirred something low in my belly. The pleasure he'd given me only left me aching for more.

His eyes darkened and the tips of his lips tilted. "If I agree to this, you'll be my wife soon. I've no need to convince you."

"But you want to."

"And what do you want?"

Isn't it obvious? If he didn't hear my thoughts, the wetness between my legs would expose the truth if he ran his hands up my thighs again.

His gaze roved over me, hungry, consuming, as needy as he'd left me since bringing me to the brink of full pleasure. "By the flush over your chest and that look in your eyes? Yes, it's obvious, my wife."

I didn't fight it. At least he didn't call me Lux.

"So?" I prodded, impatient both because I wanted answers and because I needed more from him.

He tilted his head. "I have a very specific idea that I've been thinking about since you sat on my lap in front of everyone."

"You made me do that."

"And now I'm going to make you come, on my throne, and on me."

I barely breathed. I shouldn't be so distracted with this, but the offer had worked. "Then you will agree to my terms?"

"I will do everything in my power to release them on your timeline. I swear to you."

It would have to be enough. A king so desperate to control everything wasn't going to give me another inch.

I nodded and, finally giving in to the need building within me, I slipped my hand in his and kept my grip on the stake with the other. He was malleable now, intrigued by my wants, and I couldn't lie, I was more than intrigued whenever we touched.

Depraved thoughts slipped into my mind. Thoughts of his hands all over me, as I led him down the secret passageway and towards the throne room.

Chapter Thirty-Five

The candelabras burned so low now that several had extinguished. Wax dripped to the floor like a circle of runes surrounding the throne. Every nerve in my body buzzed with anticipation as I pulled Drak into the throne room. If he was to become my husband, perhaps this craving wasn't so depraved, monster or not. It was selfish, yes, but not as disturbed as some of my past choices.

And if I chose to be honest with myself, every drop of pleasure from Drak shifted my thoughts away from Kayn.

Dim light flickered over the shining bronze throne. I stepped up to it and spun around to face him, dropping the stake at our feet. The hollow clatter echoed through the empty room.

"So, you have me here, what is it you've been imagining?"

My heart sped as he draped his hands on either side of my waist and inched me back step by step until the back of my legs stopped at the cold bronze. I reached out and linked my arms around his neck.

He dropped his mouth beneath my chin, brushing his lips over where my pulse thudded in my throat. Lifting his lips to the shell of my ear he whispered, "You on the throne as my queen."

"That's it?"

The spread of his smile stretched against the soft skin at my neck. "Both of us on the throne. Now is the only time we'll be alone in this room. Soon it will be filled with the council and our wedding guests."

Nipping at my ear, his palm followed the curve of my torso, snaking to the ribbons at my back. He tugged, slowly, unraveling the tie and then pulling the ribbon looser and looser from each notch. My hands cupped the back of his neck, fingernails digging in more than I intended as every slow release of the ribbon tested my patience.

I'd denied this attraction to him since he framed my body on the back of that damn horse. Every nerve in my body begged for me to succumb to selfishness once again.

This desire was weak and stupid, but it was mine. The only thing that was mine, for right now. The Gods wanted me to dedicate my life to being a huntress. My father wanted the connection my marriage to the king would give him. Kayn wanted my soul.

I wanted a monster.

I wanted him to tear me apart and carve out the key I'd hidden inside me, unlocking every memory I'd buried. I wanted him to wipe my mind clear of the prickling nerves that tormented me with shame. Nerves that brought me to my knees, shaking and dizzy and spiraling with thoughts that I'd lost control of.

He was just disturbed and violent enough to do it—if it were possible. But he *could* make me forget. For now. And despite every threat and the murder I'd witnessed in his bedchambers, he was safe.

Drak had never lied to me.

With the ribbons undone, he slid the sleeves off of my shoulders. The soft fabric slipped down my arms and off of my hips, rippling to the black floor in a puddle of red. Naked now, a shiver brushed over my bare skin.

Candlelight flickered muted yellow over the curves and dips across my body, creating shadows.

Spinning me around, he pressed his palm against my stomach and anchored me against him until I could feel every muscle and bend of his body, his cock harder than stone against my ass. His hand ran up my middle and found my throat, his fingers closing around it. When he dipped to sit down on the throne, he guided me with him, positioning me on his lap.

Kissing along the curve of my neck, he coaxed a groan from me. The sharp graze of his fang only heightened the sensation.

With my legs on the outside of his thighs, he spread mine wider. If anyone stepped into the throne room, I'd be on full display, the future queen spread out for King Drakkar's pleasure. His fingers squeezed tighter at my throat.

"It's for your pleasure too, Lux," he said. I sucked in a gasp, remembering he could read my mind in the heat of the moment. His other hand slid down my body and cupped the inside of my thigh. He swiped a finger across my core, and the hum of his chuckling only made me want to melt into him. "My curious little killer, my wife, you're dripping wet. Is it for me? Or just for release?"

I opened my mouth but my throat was full of the tension that hung between what I wanted to say and the truth. I couldn't lie to him.

"For you," I whispered. *Fuck.* This was sick and wrong.

I don't deserve any pleasure.

I'm evil.

I—

"Focus on me," Drak's voice ripped through the spiral circling my mind. His grip tightened until I could no longer breathe. Even though I'd made my decision, I couldn't help the thought clawing at the corners of my mind. What would the Gods think of me giving myself over to him?

Drak pinned me with his half-lidded gaze. "I am the only one you worship, Lux. I am your only thought right now."

But I'm fucked up.

He released my throat only to grip my chin and force my head to the side. For a moment, I thought he'd sink his fangs into the flesh stretched over my throat, but he only held my face in front of his. Searching my eyes, his icy gaze drove shivers through me. "Only me. Right now I am your God, your only obsession, and I better not catch you thinking anything like that about yourself again. Is that understood?"

I expected a hundred thoughts to twist and writhe in my mind, but he slipped his fingers over my core again, adding pressure so that the tips dipped into me, and my mind went blank. He slammed his mouth against mine. Releasing my face, he ran his palm over my neck. His finger tipped my chin back until I let my head fall to his shoulder.

Splitting his fingers, he formed a V around my core and teased, guiding his hand up and down so that only the base of his fingers at his palm brushed over my most sensitive nerves. I groaned, my body squirming and begging for more without me having to utter a single word.

I rubbed my ass against his cock until his fingers dipped into me again, fully this time. After pumping twice, his fingers slid out with slick wetness that he spread over my center. Rubbing intoxicating circles, he cultivated the tension and teased out a sob building inside of me.

I drew sharp breaths, just enough air to sustain me. Every touch made my head swim with pleasure. Every second tipped me closer and closer to the edge.

Drak whispered in my ear, guiding me to give him—give myself—the ecstasy.

"When you're in my castle, what do you do, Lux?"

I whimpered as he circled the outside.

"What do you do?" he repeated. I worked my tongue in my mouth but my voice would not obey. "Come on, my wet little wife." His fingers split me open again, slipping out drenched in the evidence of my need for him. He released my throat only to pinch at my hard nipple.

I writhed against his cock again, licking my lips. What would it be like to bring the king to this same bliss?

He chuckled again and lifted his wet fingers to my lips. "I know you want to use that pretty mouth to taste me, but for right now you'll just have to enjoy what's left of you on my fingers."

I opened my mouth and sucked off the slickness.

"What did I tell you the first time you sat on my lap? Say it, Lux. What do you do in my throne room? "

"I do what you say," I breathed.

"Good girl."

Rewarding me, he finally circled my core again. With this pleasure climbing closer, closer to the edge, it only took one more circle before I unraveled. Ecstasy rippled through me, my nerves not frayed but on fire. I gasped and arched my back, pressing my ass harder into him.

"That's it," he said. "I've been wanting to watch you come on my throne since you first walked in here. But I had to share it with you so I could feel you against me. Tomorrow, after we're married, I'll sit you on my cock right here and make you come again and again."

My eyes peeled open and I straightened, twisting to look at him. "Ask me again." He tilted his head. "To marry you. You never asked according to my standards."

A grin split his mouth and his eyes dropped to my lips. "What are your standards?"

I stood, glaring down at him. I took a moment to enjoy this temporary power before I gave everything over to him. Even if I was naked, baring all before him. I didn't care.

"Get on your knees," I said.

He slid to the edge of the throne and, eyes locked on me, he dropped to his knees. "Marry me. Tomorrow."

"Beg for it." It may have been because of my selfish side, the darkness within me, but I wanted to relish this. I wanted to pretend the man who was insisting I marry him actually wanted me more than anything in the world. It was a childish wish, something a village girl in Skaldir may have had in a different life. But I was born a witch and a believer in the Gods and a cruel person stained with a hollow heart full of Freya's tears. I didn't deserve this moment for myself, but I took it anyway. I took it because I needed him to convince me to forget everything and give myself over to him. "Beg for me, Drak."

"As soon as I heard about you fighting off two vampires, I had to meet you. As soon as I met you, I had to get to know you. As soon as I tasted you, I had to have you. As soon as I got to know you, I..." The muscles in his throat rippled with a hard swallow. "When I said you fascinate me, it was mere interest, but after seeing the fire inside of you." *You mean the darkness?* "I became obsessed. So, please, I beg you with every ounce of my immortal life, marry me."

He took my hands in his, rubbing his thumbs to bring life and blood to my blue fingers. My heart pinched. He saw what plagued me, he recognized my struggle, never dismissing the silent and nearly invisible illness that I'd been taught to hide.

He knew to warm my hands without a word, so when I gave myself over to him, it wasn't a lie.

"I'm yours."

CHAPTER THIRTY-SIX

The come down after our enjoyment on the throne left my head swimming. I slipped back into my dress, my legs trembling. I wasn't going to bother with the ribbons when Drak came up behind me. The fabric clung to me as he softly pulled the ribbons tighter and secured them at the middle of my back.

If this was how he'd behave during our marriage, it'd be so easy to forget the blood all over him, that he killed and tasted others. Killing was the way of Draugr. The undead sought to extend their existence, they had no souls.

Kayn had no soul, and now he wouldn't have mine either.

I flexed my fists and Drak cupped his hand over mine. "Cold?"

I shook my head as I turned to him. "I need to know who killed Embla. Do you have any idea who would have bitten her but not drained her? And why would they leave her for me to find?"

He brushed his thumb over my hand. "Someone who wanted you here."

"Who else but you?"

When his eyes darkened, he blinked and let go of my

hand. Raking his fingers through his loose hair, he cursed. "Fuck. The council returns today."

"What does that mean?"

"That means they wanted you here when they came back."

"For what?"

He opened his mouth then promptly snapped it shut. His eyes flicked to the massive door. Without moving, without breathing, he stared as if in a trance. Finally, his gaze sliced to me and the frown that twisted his face warned me what was coming next. "I don't know, to stop our marriage? To make you their vessel. To kill you."

I sucked in a breath that cut off with the slam of a door.

A figure dripped out of the darkness as they stepped inside. A man I vaguely recognized as one of the council members strode into the throne room. His cloak was embroidered with intricate vines, leaves like Creeping Thyme in thread the color of the hills in summer across Skaldir. Fangs jutted from his pale, sickly-looking lips and his waxy taupe eyes fell hard on me.

Cold shivers skittered over my skin and I slipped my hand in my pocket, feeling for the silver pendant.

He flicked his attention away from me and to the king. "King Drakkar." His voice fell flat, and he tipped into a faint bow that looked more like habit than a gesture of respect. "The council has spoken."

The king clenched his hands into fists, but was otherwise still. My eyes darted between them. I knew the king had a council, and that likely the royals took a part in the decisions for Mara, but this newcomer said it as if the king wasn't part of that same council. In Skaldir and the nearby villages, the meetinghouses were open for all to discuss life and law with the Vyls. Though the last meeting before we left was split on the decision for my father to seek help from Mara. And my father did it anyway.

"She must go."

King Drakkar sucked air through his teeth and slowly shook his head. "The last I checked, I'm the king, Dante. Not you. Not the council."

"And who put that crown on your head?"

"Me," King Drakkar growled, his voice rough with finality. "Why are you really here, Dante? You're always at odds with the council. You and Astrid and Sten like to play at being in control but you can never sway Ylva and Darius and Sitric."

Astrid and Sten. They weren't just courtiers, I'd destroyed two council members with the silver pendant. A shiver cut down my arms.

Dante's grimace deepened. "They're not here. So maybe we're no longer playing. Not now that we've bargained with Silver."

All at once, my heart stopped.

I'd made no such bargain. But I also wasn't Silver—not the real Silver.

She's gone. The Grimward killed her. Forget her before I have to beat the memory out of you. Echoes of my father's voice filled in my mind. It was as cunning as Loki's but far crueler. Father always said the same thing until he hardly spoke to me at all.

You are Silver now. There is no Lux.

My gaze sliced from Dante to King Drakkar. The king went rigid. Fury flamed in his eyes and his jaw flexed. "You didn't release her."

For the first time, Dante smiled. "You went too far with this God complex. We will not have a God as our king."

"I will not be directed like a child." He marched over to Dante. "That's your cue to leave."

Dante only scoffed, refusing to back down. "I'm not here for you, my king."

King Drakkar's arm shot out behind him as if reaching for me. "Lux. Compel him."

Dante smiled, and before I registered the king's demand,

the other vampire was upon me. He gripped my neck and wrenched my head to the side. My empty hands fruitlessly reached for the stake I'd left on the ground by the throne, but it was too far and my desperation was useless.

My heart wove a frayed rhythm. In a single breath, King Drakkar grabbed him and threw him against the black stone floor.

It only took one blink before Dante shot to his feet and past the king to lay his hands on me again. He gripped my shoulders and sank his fangs into my throat, the pain hot and slicing. I couldn't help the shrieking gasp that escaped me.

Finding my voice now, I opened my mouth and spewed the power granted by the Gods in rasping breaths.

Dante released my throat and I gulped air thick with the rich smell of blood. I pawed at my neck where his fingernails had sliced into the soft flesh, just as my captors had.

Once free, I saw why the king hadn't come for me. Another vampire had barreled into him. Drak was stronger, but not as fast as the wiry man. Familiar gold eyes flashed. The cut of his high cheekbones evident when the king slammed him to the ground and the man gritted his teeth.

Drak's attacker had been in my nightmares, in my shame. *Sten.*

Impossible, I'd destroyed him with the pendant, with the power of the Gods. I saw his flesh melt and his body go limp.

Of course, killing the undead was tricky. I'd thought Odin had been able to intervene to help me bring the vampires down for the simple purpose of saving my life.

But I'd never killed my captor.

Evidence of this lay in front of me as Sten kicked the stake across the room and launched towards the king again. The stake rolled toward the back door, hopelessly far from me now.

Drak shoved Sten as my strength waned. Dante gathered himself again just when I could no longer hold the compulsion. I dropped the compulsion, my chest heaving. Sweat beaded on my brow as I scanned for the sensations again, drawing my awareness. It was all I could do to try.

I peeled my lips open but before I could compel Dante, Drak grabbed him by the back of the neck and threw him at the ground face first. He tried to block his fall, managing to only stumble forward.

Turning, he seethed and spat at Drak. "Either you kill her, or we will."

"Boys!" A sharp voice cut from beyond the doors.

Lithe legs slipped out of the darkness as a vampire with chestnut hair piled on her head like a messy crown stepped forward. She tugged another figure along with her.

My heart dropped to my stomach. I did not blink.

Astrid, too, had survived the stabbing from my silver pendant, but it wasn't her and the scarred flesh at her neck that captivated me.

The woman in her grasp met my eyes. As if looking into a mirror, I saw the same umber and auburn hair, the same striking wide eyes full of fear, though they were dark brown, not spilled black like the cursed ink in mine. Her hands were bound behind her back like a criminal.

She looked the same when the Grimward dragged her out of our room twenty years ago.

"Silver," I breathed.

Red thread stretched from between her chin and her mouth to her upper lip, sealing her mouth shut. White scars dotted each spot where they'd sewn into her lips. My sister's nostrils flared because she could not gasp or breathe deeply since she couldn't open her mouth.

My soul hollowed. How long had my sister's mouth been sewn shut? What had they done to her?

Astrid marched toward us, yanking Silver alongside her just as she had with me back in the forest outside Skaldir. Except her fingernails didn't dig into my sister's skin. Silver didn't exactly move with her, but she didn't fight back either.

The twisted lines of Astrid's perpetual frown stained my memory. Her cold steel eyes drilled into me. The closer she drew to me, the clearer it became. Who else would have killed Embla in cold blood? She must have known I would blame it on Drak and come here after him. Astrid and Sten had wanted to capture me from the beginning and this lured me right to them.

Sten scrambled to his feet as if ready to salute Astrid, but Dante paid her no attention as he slammed into the king again.

This time, the king was ready for him. He reacted faster, and, sliding a small dagger from beneath his cloak, he ripped it through Dante's neck. In one smooth move, Dante's head slid from his shoulders and his body dropped to the floor. Blood spilled from where his throat was severed, pooling over the black stone and triggering a rush of bile forcing its way up into my mouth.

I snapped my eyes away from the headless body and locked onto Silver. She was staring at me, her nostrils still flaring.

I took in her clear dark eyes, the dotted scars only I would notice after she'd caught a fever and a pockmarked rash riddled her neck. She'd scratched at the rash so hard it left permanent marks. Her hair had grown darker with age, but she still kept it short just like when we were children. She wore it pinned back around her face with dozens of shiny bronze pins.

With her bulging eyes and simple dress, her pink cheeks and a string of beads hanging from her fist, she reflected the child she'd once been. I knew that toy. It was the same beaded doll she had carried with her everywhere as a young girl, even when the Grimward grabbed her, she didn't let go of it.

That moment was etched into my memory forever. Her little fist holding the doll. The executioner lifting her off the ground by her hair.

The blade at her throat.

They hadn't killed her, but my father insisted she was dead. That they'd beheaded her when they dragged her away. I didn't know what to believe, but I chose to forget her. It was supposed to be the safest choice.

Twenty years ago, the executioners came for me, but they took her. King Roderic had called for the capture and execution of a young witch with dark eyes, more powerful than the others.

I was weak, selfish, *evil*, and I sentenced her to a lifetime of *this*.

Sourness bubbled in my throat. Black dots spotted my vision but I blinked and refused to succumb to the swaying in my head. I would not let my knees buckle. I would not be weak again.

Astrid clucked her tongue as she stared down at Dante. "What a waste of time," she said. "If you boys had just listened to me, he wouldn't have to spend the next few months healing."

"If I don't burn him," King Drakkar growled.

Astrid only rolled her eyes. "Whatever. A waste is a waste."

"Astrid," Sten said. "We had to act before the rest of the council returned."

She shook her head, her look deadpan. "I love you Sten, but you're a fucking idiot. I told you both to wait for me to retrieve her first."

"You were taking too long," he spoke through his teeth.

"I arrived precisely on time." She tipped her head to the side, shifting her gaze to Drak. "Isn't that right, *my king*?"

"I know what you're doing Astrid," Drak said. His fists flexed and released, flexed and released. It was taking every ounce of his control not to attack. And why didn't he? Because they were part of the council and she was not coming after him like Dante had?

Astrid's messy hair stayed in place as she dropped her

head back and laughed. Silver winced and tried to pull away from her but Astrid tugged her back and then shoved her forward. Stumbling into Drak, Silver could not catch herself with her hands roped behind her back.

I lunged for her but Drak was faster. With his eyes still locked on Astrid, he stooped to catch Silver in his arms. She fell into his chest and he righted her easily.

I stood at his side, unsure if I wanted to reach out to give Silver a reassuring touch. Everything seemed to cause her to flinch. The poor child.

No, she was twenty-six, the same age as me. We were no longer children, but she was just as terrified and I was…just as selfish. I'd successfully pushed her from my mind. For twenty years, I willfully forgot the real Silver.

When they stole her away, I stole her name, her identity, her life.

My father said it would keep us all safe, that the Grimward wouldn't come back looking for the black-eyed witch if they believed they'd already executed her.

So I forgot Lux. I became Silver.

I hid behind her name just as I hid behind the hatch door under our shared bed.

Everything within me wanted to brush my fingers over her face, to twine my hand with hers. We used to fall asleep holding hands, snuggling for warmth and for the love we'd shared since birth. Even if she wasn't a witch, she honored the Gods just as much and our mother raised us the same, secretly, with the truth of our ancestors and the Allfather who created us all. I'd follow in my mother's footsteps as a seerborn, and Silver was supposed to be right there with me, gathering supplies for sacrifice, watching for the eyes in the darkness that lurked after me and our mother.

She'd always helped protect me, but I didn't do the same for her when the time came.

"So," Astrid said, folding her arms now that her hands

were free of Silver. "I trust that you don't need your little seer wife to tell you what will come next?" Her smooth plump lips cracked into a crescent smile. Her eyes slid to me.

Drak stiffened. "You let Silver out to fuck with me?"

I flicked my attention up at the king. His gaze slid between Astrid and Sten.

Astrid's laugh radiated like the clang of metal on metal. "Did I even need to let her out for that? Your betrothed would find out eventually." Turning her gold eyes on me, they flashed red. "What *is* your name anyway?" I opened my mouth, unsure if I would actually tell her when she cut me off. "Actually, I don't care as long as your little betrothed kills you. Which I have no doubt she'll do now that she's seen what you've done to her sister."

"You have no idea what you're doing," he breathed. "Lux isn't just a witch."

Astrid's brows peaked. "You think I don't know? She's the huntress. Those hideous eyes prove it. The black ink of Odin's runes is written into her very soul."

I drew a jagged breath. Even Astrid knew more than I did about my Calling. The courtiers and council members knew the real history. They knew of the Gods. It was never about believing Odin and Freya didn't exist, it was about hiding the truth. Like King Drakkar, I suspected they all wanted to be Gods—in control. The witch hunts, exiling anyone who dared breathe Odin's name was evidence of this. Evidence I should have seen a long time ago.

But as much as I wanted to be, I was never truly a seer. Not like my mother. I was never selfless enough to see into the past, into the future, for the good of the people of Vylheim and all of Midgard.

Silver shuffled away from King Drakkar, but his hand shot out and wrapped around her arm. His hold was so tight her skin turned white.

I seethed. "Drak, what's going on?"

Astrid swept her eyes over me. "Don't you see, girl? Your king has kept your sweet twin sister imprisoned and tortured. He could have released her when he took King Roderic's throne, but he didn't. In fact, he ordered for her lips to be sewn shut."

Pain lanced through my chest. My heart ached with every erratic beat as my gaze sliced from her to the king.

"Is this true?" I whispered, unable to find the energy behind my voice.

His jaw flexed and it was enough for me to understand. Even still, he confirmed it, and King Drakkar never lied. "Yes. Your sister is unstable—"

"No." I shook my head and stepped back. Silver's eyes darted from me to him. The poor girl. My sister never deserved this. "What the fuck is wrong with you? She's been here all this time and you let me believe you actually cared about me? All while you kept my sister trapped."

His voice dropped low and curled with menace. "She's unstable."

I scoffed. "Like your mother? Do you torture that poor woman too?" Like Silver, I'd shoved Drak's mother out of my mind. I'd locked away the pieces of this world I wanted to forget, and I'd done it successfully.

This was my greatest skill and the only way I survived—selfishly ignoring the people who suffered the most. I was so good at it that I didn't even think of her when I kissed her son. When I let myself enjoy it, and almost enjoy him.

I was even more fucked up than I wanted to admit.

"I don't torture anyone," he said.

"Right, you just kill them and then taste their blood." I nodded, mouth twisted into a grimace.

King Drakkar turned to me, towering over me. Like Astrid's, his eyes shifted from icy blue to gold, then red in a blink. "Silver wants my throne."

A strange laugh escaped me. "What?"

"She's threatened to take it many times—"

"Is that why you sewed her mouth shut? So you wouldn't have to hear it?" I wanted to reach for her and rip her from his arms, but she was already so frightened, like a small rabbit, cowering in the claws of a wolf. And even if I could take her, what would Sten and Astrid do? What would King Drakkar do? My stake was discarded by the servant's door and my pendant couldn't take all three of them down. Not without the element of surprise that my burning blood had given me in the woods against Astrid and Sten.

"She can compel vampires too."

"You're fucking sick," I spat.

"It's my throne, Lux." He spoke clearly, unafraid of upsetting me now. He didn't care for me, he never had. All he cared about was his fucking throne and claiming a wife to sit on it with him.

My stomach knotted at the thought of what he did to me on that throne. What I wanted him to do.

"Let her go," I said.

He shoved past me, pushing Silver forward with him. "I can't do that."

Astrid's laugh boiled in my blood. I gritted my teeth and glared at her as she waved her hand toward King Drakkar as if to present him to me. Sten had shuffled to his partner's side.

King Drakkar hissed at her as he passed by. "I'll deal with you two when I return."

"Good luck," Astrid said. "The rest of the council has returned. We'll be tied up with the Blood Council for hours after you beheaded Dante."

He cursed under his breath as he marched toward the door, my sister still in his grasp. I ran after him, stopping in front of the doors to block his exit. "No way in hell are you going to lock her back up."

Astrid's laugh echoed again.

"You can't stop me," he said.

"I won't marry you."

He cursed again, shouting so loud this time it made my sister jump. "It's too late, Lux. You'll be my wife tomorrow. I told you, at first light you will either marry me or I'll kill you. The council is returning before the sun, and they're expecting the end of the huntress just like I am, whether that's through binding yourself to me or your death."

"I came here to destroy you." The words slipped out before I could stop them. I couldn't help it. Seeing my sister flinching away, his fingers holding her with such force her pale arm was already bruising.

"You're buying right into what Astrid wants. She wants us to kill each other so she can take over."

"Because everyone wants your throne?"

"Yes."

I stood my ground. "Then add my sister to the deal. I'll give up the Gods and on becoming the huntress if you let her go too."

He released a string of curses this time. "You're fucking impossible. That's not happening, Lux. We already agreed on the deal and Silver is not part of it. Unless you want to add her to my deal? Marry me or you both die."

My heart lurched. Cold fear curled around it and slowly crystalized in my veins. Everything hurt. I could have accepted my own death, but her's? After a lifetime of suffering? I couldn't allow that.

King Drakkar tilted his head, throwing his chin out to direct me to the side with a mere flick of his head. "Now get out of my way or I'll be forced to imprison you too."

I could not move. Even if the smart decision would be to stab him with the pendant and run for the stake, I could not do it.

My eyes fixed on my sister and I only thought of her. I would not risk scaring her more. What would King Drakkar do to her if I attacked him? I opened my mouth to compel him but I could not even do that. Exhaustion stripped me down more naked than I had been bared before the king. Then, I was only without clothes. Now at the vampire king's whims, I was vulnerable, broken down to my bones.

Exhausted or not, I remained upright. Here in front of the king, at the threshold of his throne room, I stood my ground.

I only moved when he grabbed my arm and forced me to move.

When he dragged me to my bedchambers.

And then when I crawled to the door after he tossed me to the ground inside the room. A lock slid shut on the outside.

CHAPTER THIRTY-SEVEN

Everything that led me to being locked in Mara's Keep and in a marriage with a monster was my own decision. The last night of the Polar Nocturne could have stretched endlessly. Each second tormented me as time crawled to first light, to the moment I'd take King Drakkar's hand and marry the man who tortured my sister.

I came here for answers and I'd gotten them, but it changed nothing.

I came here to destroy him. That I would still try.

Sitting on the cold stone, I leaned my back against the side of the four-poster and released a coil of misty air. Nobody came to light the wood in my fireplace so I sat in the chill with my icy fingers tucked beneath my arms. Only a single candle beside the bed flickered with a warm orange glow.

I hadn't gathered the strength to climb onto the bed and curl within the blankets.

Besides, Silver likely didn't have the comfort of blankets, or a bed, or even the ability to take a full breath through her mouth. All of it was King Drakkar's doing. Why the former king hadn't executed Silver like we were led to believe, I didn't know.

But I knew what King Drakkar wanted from her. His chosen witches, like Ragna, were set to summon Odin, though he'd never given me the full reason behind it. If she could compel vampires, she must have had a piece of the same powers I did and perhaps he believed her a stronger witch for it.

The hard wood of the bed's bottom panel dug into the back of my head. I didn't care to adjust for comfort.

Soon, the Polar Nocturne would end. The sun would rise, damning all the vampires to stay within the castle. This was my only hope.

I toyed with the chain of another necklace that'd been left in my bedchambers with fresh clothes. After locking me away, the king at least had the sense to send a servant to help me bathe. He didn't have the sense to keep the jewelry from me.

I planned to wear the chain with my own pendant at the end, tucked into my wedding dress. I would stab King Drakkar with the pendant, and then run behind the throne through the servants' door. After that, all I had to do was get out into the sun where vampires would weaken. All I had to do was get to an ash tree and fashion another stake.

Then, I'd return with a new weapon and all the determination in Midgard to become the huntress and cut down every single vampire for my sister's sake.

I would never question Odin and Freya again. I was twisted enough to become their chosen killer, and now it was all I wanted.

Freeing her was all that mattered. First, I had to turn every one of her captor's to dust, starting with the king.

Maybe I should have felt relieved when I saw Astrid and Sten alive. Or when I witnessed my sister alive, too, because that meant I'd never actually ended anyone's life. But it gave me no comfort because I would have killed them, and Silver's survival had nothing to do with me.

Until now.

I rubbed the soft pad of my thumb over the cold silver. The pendant shimmered against the glow of the single candle that burned on the bedside table. Tracing the shape of the Y, I swore to find the tree of Yggdrasil someday.

Someday, when all the undead were hollowed out and left in piles of ash, I'd take Silver with me and we'd find the tree Odin hung from for nine days. We'd gaze upon it and thank the Gods for the powers they shared with those of us who had a connection with them.

Without these powers, I had no chance of finding or destroying a vampire. I wouldn't even know they existed. I'd be a simple girl in Skaldir with a desire to run but no purpose for it.

My head dipped forward. This exhaustion demanded rest. My body demanded penance for pushing it so hard. I'd need the energy tomorrow when I would stab King Drakkar in the throat with the pendant.

Even if it wouldn't kill him, it'd hurt, it'd scar, it'd send a message. And if I was lucky, he'd be in enough pain that I could run.

It was a pathetic plan, but I had nothing else. I was locked in my bedchambers in a castle teeming with monsters. Maybe stabbing their king would show them that I would not give up. That I would do anything to get answers that could help free my sister.

Dozing tugged me into a dazed state. I slipped through the layers of consciousness and darkness until I nodded awake one last time and then finally fell into full sleep.

Tangled nightmares of Silver's sewn mouth and the murder in King Drakkar's bedchambers left me fitful and restless until the crunch of rough metal sliding over metal jarred me.

I woke to the groan of the door easing open.

A figure stepped inside, all wiry muscle. Blinking sleep

away, it took several seconds for me to place the clean-shaven face, the swoop at the top of his cropped hair.

"Kayn?" I whispered. He dashed to me, stooping to lift me off the floor. "What are you doing here? How?"

"We're connected, Silver. I feel when you need me."

Of course he could, because he'd connected us so that he could steal my soul.

My skin prickled. When he set me on the bed, I recoiled from his touch. "Get away from me."

"Silver?"

"No." I shook my head and scooted further onto the soft bed and away from him.

"I know what you want from me."

Recognition shined in his eyes. He frowned and scrubbed a palm over his mouth. For too long he stood like that, absorbing what I said, acting helpless at the end of my bed.

"You found the lost history," he said, his voice flat except for a quiver of worry. Staring at the edge of the bed, he didn't meet my eyes.

"Some of it," I said. "Enough of it."

"I don't want your soul."

I said nothing. He didn't deserve a response. I had no doubt he was here to convince me to kill the king. At least in that, we agreed.

Finally, he dared look at me. "I did. I'm still tempted at times, that's the truth. You deserve that truth as much as it kills me to say it. I never intended to care for you. All I'd wanted was a soul before. When I told you that you're my huntress, I meant it. You will destroy me too."

I sat up and narrowed my eyes, keeping my glare steady on him. "And how does that work? When I stake you in the heart, my soul transfers to you?"

He shook his head. "No, Silver. I watched you sacrifice your blood at the altar. I watched you stand up to King Drakkar for your mother's sake. You reminded me what it means to be truly honorable. Because of you, I see now that even if I took your soul, or anyone's soul, it wouldn't be the right way to go to Valhalla. I wouldn't have earned it. You would have killed all the monsters, not me."

Again, I said nothing, though I was tempted to ask what changed.

His thick hair clung to his forehead like he was a human exerting enough energy to sweat. Though I supposed monsters grew tired too.

All the rage I felt in the library returned tenfold. Instinctively, I slid out the pendant from my pocket and kept it tightly in my fist.

I didn't believe him. I couldn't, not after this betrayal.

The tears I shed for Silver dried sticky and tight on my cheeks. I sniffed and forced the emotion in my throat down, trying to keep my voice steady. "You lied to me. I can't trust that you're not still planning to take my soul. The runestones are the source of truth, our history, so I will trust when it calls you the king of monsters."

His throat rippled in a slow swallow. "I did not lie."

"You omitted the truth."

"I said I'd made a mistake and that it consumes me—"

"And now you want me to rectify it." I stepped closer while raising the weapon to his throat, not pushing too deep into him but not relieving him either. "How much time have we spent discussing these trials, Kayn, and you failed to confess you pursued me for this purpose? This isn't about human survival, like you said."

"It is."

"You've known me long enough now to know that I wanted the truth from the beginning. That you weren't doing this for me and my people, but to rid yourself of your own guilt and climb your way to Valhalla, damning me to Hel's underworld."

Carefully, he nodded "You're right." His voice was wound

tight. "I need your help to unmake me and release me from the guilt. The first witch made me. I was dying and she used her magic to suspend me between life and death so that she may siphon this immortality from me. There was no one else like me, and when she started to lose control of her magic, I knew I'd end up alone." He cast his eyes down for a moment before dragging them up to meet my gaze again. "So I made them. I cursed hundreds of dying men and women to this existence so that I would not be alone. So that she could use them and turn me back. When she didn't make me human again, I became enraged and turned more of those fallen in battle from human to vampire. I am their maker. I need you to unmake them before I persist for yet another generation, after these hundred years, ravaged with guilt." A quiver placed his voice somewhere between desperation and grief.

My hands shook with the skipping of my heart. It pulsed once, then three times, pausing, then beating twice as fast again as if my heart was reacting to the single last word he'd said. The Gods knew my lingering illness worsened when my mind dwelled on guilt.

Kayn had created monsters, but he didn't choose to become one. I had. Through each choice I made, starting twenty years ago, I slowly accepted the darkness within me.

And now with Kayn here, I actually had a chance to take down the king, to save my sister. Though it would never make up for what I did to her, it was the only thing that mattered now.

I would do whatever it took to free her, even though it'd never relieve me from the shame that twisted and stretched this soul I supposedly had.

But Kayn? He had no soul to twist, only hundreds of years of shame.

Of course he wanted to unmake the mistakes he'd turned into monsters. Of course he wanted a soul. It only meant he still honored the Gods, and that he still longed to spend the afterlife in Odin's palace, preparing for Ragnarok with the other warriors.

I couldn't blame him for craving the same ending to this life that I did.

My pulse grew more erratic. It wasn't until the swimming tears in my eyes spilled over my cheeks that the cycling thoughts silenced.

Without a word, Kayn sank to the bed and pulled me into him, his arms encompassing me. I let my whole self collapse into him. He steadied me against his chest and placed one hand on the back of my head as if consoling me.

"I cannot imagine," I said between breaths. With the hand cupping my head, he slowly brushed it down over my braid. "I cannot imagine living with this guilt and shame for so long."

"Vampires are not alive. You have done nothing wrong, Silver."

"I'm not Silver." He stopped caressing my hair and sucked in a breath. I twisted to look up at him, gathering every bit of courage within me. "My name is Lux." Keeping the flat line of his mouth steady, he merely listened.

"You feel guilty for lying about your identity?"

I shook my head and pulled away from him, wiping at my cheeks like the child I was twenty years ago. "For sentencing my sister to death." His dark eyes flashed, but he stayed silent, even reaching out to brush a tear away from my cheek. "You didn't have a choice in becoming a monster. But I did."

The rage melted away and cool relief washed through me. The truth was a balm to my soul. A truth so long buried and even more precious to me than the lost history.

I opened my mouth, but a sob caught in my throat. I huddled into his soothing touch. A touch that wasn't a trade. He'd answered my question and had demanded nothing from me. He didn't even expect me to explain how I'd damned Silver to certain death.

But speaking of her felt so good. Addictive even, to

someone who didn't immediately tell me to shut up and never mention her again. And unlike the king, Kayn wouldn't demand more of me right now.

So before the dwelling returned, I opened my mouth to release the persistent and aggressive thoughts that repeated in my mind.

"She was my twin," I said. "My sister, and I allowed her to be taken by the executioners." He tightened his arms around me as if to affirm that he did not cast me out for this confession. "When villagers discovered I exhibited signs of commanding witchcraft, they sent for the executioners to come for me."

I shivered at the memory of our door slamming open, their thundering footsteps, the sharp *shing!* of their blades, my mother's screaming and begging.

My voice became smaller and smaller as I spoke. "I was so afraid. Silver was braver than me while I ran away. There was a hatch on the floor under our bed that led to a crawl space. I hid and listened to them grab her and drag her away. They called her Lux and I didn't stop them. I didn't correct them, and I didn't tell them the truth."

Thick tears rolled down my face one-by-one.

"It's my fault she has been missing for twenty years. My father erased her and forbade me to speak her name. Even my mother started calling me Silver and I became so wholly her that I…I forgot about her. I almost forgot my real name. Everyone else believed her dead, but I refused—" A sob choked me, and I allowed the emotion to overcome me.

Forgetting Silver hurt my mother, but it broke me. And then, ten years later, when the Grimward took my mother too, my mind simply cracked. Even at sixteen when I could have fought for people to call me by my own name, I had to continue to be Silver because it was the last name my mother had ever called me.

"You were only a child. Survival is an instinct." His gentle voice was as much a blanket as his arms around me.

"I'm a killer as an adult too. When my shadows caught up with me only a few months ago, I killed them. Or I thought I did, until I realized they were vampires." I cleared my throat. "But the point remains, I gave in to the darkness within me and sentenced more people to death."

"For survival."

I sat up and faced him. "It's selfish. What is the survival of a single sick and disturbed woman? I'm not worth it. I've never been worth it."

He brushed an escaped tendril of hair from my face and then let his hand brush over my cheek, catching a tear as it slipped down my face. "I'm grateful for your survival."

"Soul or not, you still need me to kill the vampires."

"And I've also grown to care for you."

"What if I can't do this? Be the huntress? I don't want to give in to the darkness and kill again. I can't, and that's all you want from me."

He took my hand, and then flicked his gaze to my face. "Lux, no matter what you choose to do, I will care for you." The truth softened his dark gaze as he gave my hand a reassuring squeeze.

Though this wasn't a trade of kisses for honesty, I wanted nothing more than to taste his mouth. We both bared our truths about the mistakes our weaker selves had given in to as another weaker part of me wanted to give myself to him. To share a deeper truth beyond where words could reach.

Never had anyone listened with such attention, much less spared me their judgment.

I searched his eyes to be sure. There was nothing but softness in his gaze as it ticked down to my mouth. The softness grew harder as he brushed his fingers under my chin, beckoning me into him. I unfolded my legs and propped them on either side of him, slowly climbing into his lap to straddle his legs while keeping my eyes on him.

His hands snaked around to my back as he gently pushed me closer and tipped his lips to mine.

All at once, he consumed me, first my mouth then all of me as his hands slid down to my lower back and his lips parted to invite my tongue inside.

He only pulled back to carefully bite at my bottom lip and then trail hot kisses along my jaw and down the sensitive curve of my neck. His blunt fangs, having protruded, were hard against my skin. I arched into him, slowly rocking my hips forward and then backward to feel the hard length in his pants against me too.

When he released a groan, my pulse quickened and I repeated the motion to elicit another response from him. It wasn't until his hands slipped beneath my skirts that I recognized the sound of myself moaning as I pressed my core against his solid length.

His palm ran over my bare thigh and then over my waist until it was stopped by the tight corset laced around my torso. Desire pricked the tips of my breasts until they were unbearably sensitive against the tight fabric. I made quick work of unlacing the ribbon that kept it caged to my ribs.

"Lux," he breathed. I paused to look up at him. "Are you sure you want this? You've been through a lot. I will not take advantage of that."

His words warmed me from the inside out. Even in the dim room with nothing but silence and the icy air, I didn't shiver, didn't shy away from the desire to unlace the ribbons at the back of my dress so that I might feel his hand on my stomach. My breathing slowed and suddenly the tight ribbons didn't feel so restrictive without my chest heaving.

But the truth of what I'd done with the king on his throne cracked through the pleasure, twisting my gut. I suddenly had to put distance between us before the shame pricked my skin. I quickly unfolded my legs and slipped off of the bed.

Standing, I faced him with tears stinging my eyes. "We shouldn't do this. I just gave King Drakkar parts of me."

Kayn only tilted his head, listening intently. No judgment or anger flared in his eyes. They remained a rich brown not flashing with the crimson of vampire fury.

"I traded touching and kissing and..." I swallowed. "More. But I wanted it too. He was supposed to be my husband and, I don't know, I just wanted pleasure to help me forget everything."

And I'd wanted him. But I never should have. The darkness in me needed to stay locked away, not broken open to find solace in his darkness.

He stood and reached for my hand, brushing his thumb once over the back of it. "You owe me no explanation."

"I feel like I should tell you that I'm sorry."

He caught a tendril of loose hair that'd escaped my braids and tucked it back. "There is no need."

"Tomorrow I'm going to walk into this wedding and try to destroy the king. And then I intend to run to find a weapon."

"I will bring you one."

I nodded. "But all of the council will be there. The courtiers too. I don't know if I'll survive. I have to do this, at least try to do this, for my sister."

"Let's leave, tonight."

"Not without Silver. If I don't show up to the wedding, King Drakkar will kill her. He's threatened to end both our lives by first light if I'm not there."

"Then you have to go to the wedding," he said, understanding what I needed.

I nodded. "I have to go." I met his gaze, holding it without blinking. His eyes flickered to my mouth.

The tension of our argument and from the life or death

discussion shifted. We were together again, possibly for the last time.

Together. That one word had stuck in my brain since he offered to help me. We didn't have to do everything alone. We bared our secrets, our shame to one another, and we shared the weight of it. I couldn't hold his shame, but I could hold him.

"But I don't have to leave yet." The words slipped out and the tension thickened as understanding flashed over his face.

His eyelids dipped and lips parted. "We have tonight."

The wanting in his eyes stalled my breath.

"This could be our last moment together," I whispered my thoughts aloud because it was suddenly all I could think of.

I could die tomorrow at dawn. So what did tonight matter? King Drakkar couldn't be the last person I connected with before my death.

Somehow, Kayn understood more of what I needed again without me saying a word.

Time and space ceased to exist when he dipped his lips to mine. Our connection imbued me with fiery energy, as another more sensitive spot ignited with hot desire.

Deepening the kiss, I welcomed his tongue inside me, tasting him, all of him as the connection built and the vitality knitted my skin together and strengthened my muscles. As addictive as this feeling could become, I wanted the feel of his hand on my bare hip more. I wanted to straddle him and invite his hardening length between my legs where my desire left my thighs slick with wetness. The abrupt ending to our previous kissing left me more frustrated than I'd realized.

"I need you," he breathed the same phrase he'd said when begging me to take up the Call of the Gods.

"I know, it's okay. I'll help you—"

"No, Lux, I need *you.*"

A candle flickered just over my head, casting orange and red hues between the dark shadows across his face. My heart stuttered as his eyes raked over me before we collided again, my hands gripped at the fabric of his tunic. His hands roved all over my body as if he'd never get enough of me. I tilted my head back only for a moment of air when he nipped at my bottom lip and then kissed along my jaw, working his way back to my mouth.

He groaned and walked me back to the wall, consuming me with every step. Unlike when King Drakkar slammed me into the stone, he placed a hand between my lower spine and the wall. Whether it was an excuse to feel my ass, or for my comfort, I didn't care.

The fingers of his free hand plucked at the ribbon tied neatly to the front of my corset. As he unlaced it, his tugging grew faster and more desperate so the corset slowly expanded. I clutched to the back of his arm like my life depended on it, drinking every kiss in as if I'd been parched for as long as Kayn had been plagued with the shame of his mistake.

I wanted more of him and suddenly my skirts and corset, his tunic and pants were frustrating obstacles separating us. Understanding me, he paused to yank the tunic over his head with one hand. Runes in crude black ink covered every inch of his chest, including a mark of the tree of Yggdrasil.

Heat flushed over my neck and down between my breasts. As soon as the ribbon was fully loosened, the boning inside the corset peeled away from my skin and he ripped it off of me, dropping it behind him as his kisses followed a trail from my mouth down the curve of my neck where my pulse thudded heavily. He paused, his blunt fangs grazing the vein along my throat, and then continued over my collarbone and down to the swell of my breast where the tip tightened with anticipation. He gently sucked the bud between his lips, eliciting a long groan from me while he unbuttoned his pants. In the same breath, he bunched the fabric of my skirts at my waist.

When he dipped and his hand at my back slipped beneath my ass, I leaped and allowed him to lift me. Though my spine was flush against the wall, I only felt his hands, his tongue, his mouth.

"More," I said between breaths. "Give me more. Give me you."

With my legs wrapped around his hips and his hands splayed on the wall behind me, he thrust just enough to enter me with the tip of his length. I gasped and dug my hand into the base of his neck to encourage him closer and closer to me until he finally thrust halfway.

"More," I begged.

He squeezed his eyes. "I'll come undone, you've bewitched me, Lux."

I kissed him harder, my fingers exploring his hair until I whimpered, begging for him to thrust again. "Deeper."

Finally, he rewarded me with the whole of him and I released a gasp that echoed throughout my bedchambers.

He sucked in a sharp breath. "You're going to unmake me here and now, like this."

If only it were that easy. But unmaking Kayn as I carried out the Gods' Call would be *my* undoing. I couldn't destroy him…

Perhaps he'd spare me, and destroy me first.

The tension built and built between my legs until I lost all awareness of the world around me. My legs shook and my breathing stalled. A curse escaped him as he arched his neck back. We consumed one another, coming undone together, his thrusting sending ripples of addictive pleasure through me.

And for the first time, I felt the full scope of his healing— not because of our connection and his vitality as an immortal being, nor because of the peaking pleasure.

Because he knew me, knew of my darkness, knew my destiny to kill—even him—and still, he cared for me.

CHAPTER THIRTY-EIGHT

Before dawn, Kayn retrieved a new stake for me cut from an ash tree, then left me with a promise that he'd be there for me. He'd slip into the wedding and be ready to help me attack the king.

Together, we had a higher chance of success—of survival. Together.

As the night crept toward first light, I wanted less and less to let him go. But if Drak found him here, he might consider it a compromise to our marriage. I wouldn't risk my sister's life. Even if watching him leave left me hollow.

I was alone, again. Alone until I could see him at the wedding. If I survived my attack on King Drakkar.

Goosebumps spiked across the back of my neck.

Close to dawn, the door opened again and I held my breath.

Three servant girls, wiry and with wide eyes not unlike Embla, came into my bedchambers carrying my wedding dress. I kept my attention on the dress, trying to wipe thoughts of Embla and every dead human I'd seen since learning about vampires. Was the truth worth it? Or had life been better when they were mere shadows?

One of the servant girls beckoned for me to step into the dress while the others held each side, careful to not let it wrinkle. Obediently, I stepped forward, and allowed them to pull it up and over me. The smooth fabric seemed to mold to my body as silky as water, tight but with enough give for me to move and breathe freely unlike a tethered corset.

The girl pointed for me to face the mirror while the other two made quick work of brushing through my wet hair. The warm bath had been a welcome reprieve for my body, but the quiet had left me dwelling. My mind had circled the same thought over and over.

I can't marry the man who sewed Silver's mouth shut.

I can't marry King Drakkar.

How can I bear to marry a monster?

For my sister. Staring at myself in the floor-length mirror, I pulled myself into the present moment and raked my gaze over the image of me as a bride.

Like the royals' decadent embroidery, the wedding gown was a shimmering gray, almost silver. When the light caught it, the fabric nearly shone white, but in the shadows, it was as dark as my inky eyes. Embroidered blood red roses lined the hem, swirling vines and trailed each edge with jagged, dark green thorns. The sleeves grew wider and wider the closer it came to my wrist and more roses encircled the long, swooping sleeves. The back plunged so low it nearly exposed my entire spine to the cold drafty air that swept through Mara's Keep.

A miserable frown tugged at my mouth and shadows darkened the hollow of my eyes. I was an unbecoming bride, not meant for this moment or this wedding, yet I supposed it was always my destiny. No matter what the Gods had intended, it was the Norns who truly determined each person's life by weaving their individual's threads in the way they saw fit. My mother had predicted I'd end up queen of Vylheim, and now I was only minutes away from fulfilling that vision.

Except it'd never come to fruition.

A strange twinge contorted my chest. My mother was a true seerborn, her visions were never wrong.

Before I could dwell on it, one of the servant girls yanked my hair. I yelped and she quietly apologized as she tugged my loose hair into braids. All life and personality and hope had been stripped of these girls. How long had they been serving in Mara's Keep? How long had they been at the whim of the vampires' appetites? Though they were likely nineteen, perhaps even twenty years old like Embla, they reminded me of scared children. Of myself. Of Silver...

When I became the huntress, I would end this. Then, even the executioners would no longer be needed, because all the vampires would be vanquished, gone, and we'd be free of this life as their blood source.

They twisted my hair and pinned the intricate braid like a crown at the back of my head while two braids hung down to frame my face. The first girl secured a real, glittering crown just above my hairline. Without a word, they vanished from the room, leaving me to glare at the bride in my reflection.

She was empty, the hollow lifeless husk that Astrid had foretold I'd become, though it wasn't at her hands that I'd been drained of all life and hope. I'd fought so hard, only to find myself in the same place I was several weeks ago, bound to an arranged marriage, desperate for Silver's safety, even if I wasn't Silver anymore.

Though the wedding dress didn't have a pocket, I couldn't give up my pendant. In a daze, I sat on the bed and dragged the skirt up to my waist. Securing the chain around my thigh, I let the pendant hang against my bare skin, cold and sharp against my soft flesh.

Staring at the stake beside my pillow, I leaned over and grabbed it. I forced it between the chain and the muscle along my thigh until it was securely pressed against my leg.

A knock echoed throughout my bedchambers and I let the skirt fall over my feet. When I stood, the dress' long train flowed around me like shimmering water. I floated to the door, but it swung open before I reached it and two vampires stepped inside. Even if Darius's guest had offended King Drakkar, neither Ylva and Darius were as cruel and cold-hearted as Dante or Astrid. They hadn't murdered Embla or tried to kill us. They were just bloodthirsty monsters bent on keeping their food source safe.

Ylva and Darius gave me instructions I only half heard.

"Follow me."

"You'll approach the throne veiled."

"Do not…"

I trailed at their heels, my heart beating slower than I could have ever expected at this moment. Instead of dizzy and overwhelmed with nerves, everything within me numbed. The hallways closed in, the stone walls taller and narrower than I'd recalled.

Think of Silver.

For the second time in twenty years, I was about to see my sister's face. That, at least, was something to keep my feet moving forward. And perhaps once I laid eyes on her, I'd have the strength to lay the truth bare before Mara. The people needed to know what monsters lurked in Vylheim.

Ylva yanked the veil that'd been tucked beneath my crown and draped it over my face. The doors to the throne room groaned as Darius pushed them open. I stood at the threshold, scanning the vast room through the transparent gray fabric.

Hundreds of pairs of eyes, human and vampire both, royal and even some commoners, stared at me. King Drakkar sat on his throne, his crown like mine but larger and with darker jewels. My gaze fell across every face, my eyes darting for any sight of a face like mine.

Where was Silver?

Ylva prodded me forward with her sharp fingernails poked into my spine. I blinked suddenly and shot her a grave look. A spark ignited through the damp ashes of my numb heart.

I stepped forward, but not because Ylva forced me to. Instead of locking eyes with my betrothed, I refused to look at the king. With every step past the hundreds of people standing on either side of the room, I searched for her.

I twisted to look behind me, trying to see each face in the crowd. The dress dragged in a massive sweep like silvery liquid behind me. A familiar face sent my heart skipping.

Instead of my sister, I caught sight of blond hair jagged with the line of a scar, a clean-shaven jaw fixed with determination. My gaze flickered to the king whose eyes only seemed to see me. Kayn must have slipped in undetected. I remembered his explanation for how he snuck around so successfully. *The king does not stoop to pay attention to me when there is a witch as powerful as you within his sights.*

When our eyes met, he gave me a slight nod and I averted my gaze to avoid bringing attention to him.

Like the first time I spotted Kayn in the throne room, he slipped through the crowd, matching my path to the throne but under a different kind of veil. The hundreds of bodies pressed into the room so tightly meant nobody cared to notice a single exile shifting through the crowd. Vampires were likely too arrogant to believe anyone would dare interrupt this ceremony, and the humans' faces were agape with a mixture of fear, respect, and awe for their king. They knew just enough to be afraid but not enough to change the way of this world.

That was dependent on me.

The chain of the pendant dug into my skin and the rough cut of the ash tree rubbed my thigh raw with each step. I dragged my gaze to the king who still watched me with an all-consuming stare.

He was getting what he'd wanted all along. What had led my father to believe King Drakkar would even listen to him? How long had the king been planning this?

My hand flexed and I itched to grab at the stake as I stopped before the throne. It seemed the entire crowd didn't breathe until I dipped into the expected curtsy. My stomach churned, acid and anger mixing. I curtsied to the man who'd tormented my sister, who'd threatened to kill me. Even my body knew this was wrong. The twisted sickness of it sunk into my bones, seeping through my raw skin and aching muscles.

If I dared think of stabbing him too early, I'd lose everything I'd bargained for. I had to wait until he was close enough, until I could angle the stake right between his ribs and drive it up and up into her heart.

Think of Silver. Where was she?

Still kneeling, I craned my neck to search the faces at my sides, young and old, vampire and human, so many strangers. I spotted another familiar face. This one, stoking the fire that had ignited within me.

Astrid and Sten stood near the front. If I had truly killed them all those months ago, perhaps King Drakkar would have left me alone.

Perhaps I'd already be the huntress Odin wanted me to be.

I frowned. Sten toyed with his hideous bronze ring, the ruby at the center looking like a drop of blood on his thin fingers. Astrid looked as cruel as ever with the hard line of her mouth peaked into a sneer. She must have believed we would end up killing each other once I saw my sister, me as the huntress and him the most powerful vampire, and since that hadn't happened yet, she was fuming that her plan did not work to eliminate us both.

After the appropriate amount of time, I rose up to my full height again. Lifting my head, I saw King Drakkar had stood and stretched his hand out to beckon me to him, but I didn't move.

Bind yourself to a monster.

I frowned and marched to the throne. Laying my hand in King Drakkar's, it seemed I'd taken a dose of poison because my tongue tasted bitter and the sickness at the pit of my gut roiled.

I locked eyes with him and searched for answers, but they were flat, unreadable. They'd never been as expressive as his mouth, but his lips revealed nothing either.

"She better be safe," I breathed.

He stayed silent but his mouth still gave me a response. A grim smile, hollow and cold curved at the corners of his lips.

A figure stepped out from behind the tall throne.

"Silver," I whispered.

She was alive and safe. The needle piercings around her mouth were dozens of empty holes now. The thread binding her mouth shut was gone and her arms were free of ropes. Hope lifted my heavy bones.

She wasn't even near any other vampires, other than King Drakkar. He may have stood between us, but he didn't know I had the stake with me, and Kayn close by.

Could she control him? Together, we might have a chance to get out alive even with me exposing the Blood Council. Before I could conjure another thought, he tugged me closer to him and, just like the first time we stood before his throne together, he whispered into my ear.

This time, he didn't tell me to kiss him.

"Lux, you have to run." His voice was low, rough, as if he could barely speak. My pulse rushed through my ears and I barely heard him repeat the warning. "Run. I cannot stop her."

Movement caught my eye and I snapped my gaze to my sister. The room was flooded with candles and torches along the walls and in the candle holders hanging above our heads. The flames caught the shine of something in Silver's hand as she raised it.

"Lux, please." Desperation laced his words. This had to be a trick. All he'd wanted was to marry me, and now he told me to leave?

"Silver?" I said.

Her lips spread into a grin and her knuckles went white

around the blade in her hand. She kept it low and her body in King Drakkar's shadow.

Perhaps this was all a trick that I couldn't wrap my mind around. I'd learned so much truth, the vampires, pieces of the lost history, that the Gods I'd always believed in were real and active, and yet I was still left in the dark. Seeking truth and understanding was an endless quest.

Silver angled the blade with the tip up. It wouldn't kill King Drakkar so why…?

"Lux!" Drak begged. "I can't move, but you can."

My mind caught up with his words and my heart, skipping and dancing, pushed cold blood through my veins. As Silver stepped forward, I knew based on the bloodthirsty look flashing in her eyes that she wasn't focusing on Drak, she had her gaze fixed on me.

Silver wanted to kill me.

I didn't stop to dwell on the reason, or how we'd come to this moment. Before she could thrust the blade into my gut, I dropped back and fell into a crouch. I yanked the fabric of my skirts out of the way and, breaking the chain, pulled the stake free. In one fist, I held the pendant, and wrapped my other hand around the stake.

In the moments that followed, chaos erupted. The vampires must have seen the blade and understood my sister's intentions because Astrid was upon us and shouts rang out.

Silver bent forward and brought the dagger down in an arc. I swung the stake to intercept her arm as it dropped toward me. The force of the impact knocked the dagger from her hold and she shrieked.

Someone grabbed my veil and yanked me back, having gathered it and pulled it tightly against my throat. I fell back on my tailbone and Astrid pinned me to the floor, her knees on my shoulders.

"Do it!" Astrid screamed.

My sister scrambled for the blade but Ylva and Darius and

a blur of a dozen other faces filled in the space around the throne. The distraction must have broken her control over the king because he swung a fist at Darius who barreled into him.

Ylva kicked the blade from my sister's reach as Silver shouted. "I have to kill her!" The first words I'd heard my sister utter in twenty years were about my death. "I am queen."

"That wasn't the bargain we made with you, witch," Ylva said as she gripped my sister's throat. I didn't know why she didn't control her, or if she even could right now, but Silver only continued screaming about being queen.

"I will lead the vampires to victory! Astrid, tell them—" Her voice cut off. Ylva must have squeezed harder.

Astrid was too distracted with ripping the stake from my fingers and launching it away from me. It slammed into the throne and clattered to the ground where Silver had stood. Astrid's fangs were exposed and her eyes red as she grabbed my now empty hand and brought my wrist to her mouth. The sharp ends sliced through the thin skin over the veins in my arm. With the pendant still in my fist, I twisted the tip to face out and smashed it against her cheek.

Suddenly, her weight lifted off of me and I scrambled to my feet. King Drakkar, having knocked Darius unconscious, threw Astrid away from me as easily as she'd thrown the stake. She fell face down against the stone floor. None of the other vampires dared approach the king now that he wasn't under Silver's compulsion.

Free now, I dashed to the stake and swept it off the ground. It was a weak reassurance in my aching grip.

"You can't kill Lux," Ylva hissed as she released Silver. The vampire woman went rigid, having been rendered immovable the same way my sister had controlled the king. "If you kill her, the first witch will use her body to resurrect. Even you can't match the power of the first witch. Silver!"

Silver didn't listen and she slunk toward me, her shoulder

smashing into Ylva as she passed her. Her gleaming eyes fixed on me and she didn't so much as blink when Ylva shrieked at her.

"Stop her!"

"You'll thank me later," Silver retorted.

Astrid lunged at the king again, and with his attention fixed on me, she caught him off guard. He stumbled, shouting for me as he righted himself and turned to face her.

"Lux, run!" King Drakkar's voice was muffled from the pulse thudding in my ears and the haze of fixation I had on my sister. She wanted to kill me, and could I blame her after what I'd done to her?

Saving her was never going to free me from the darkness.

I adjusted my grasp around the stake, my fingers suddenly tingling. I gripped it tighter, keeping it angled out in case any vampires approached me. I'd been ready to destroy King Drakkar once I knew my sister was alive, but it wasn't until now, when I recognized the truth within me that Odin granted me this gift; strength.

A shriek jolted me from the stupor and I snapped my attention to it. Astrid attacked the king but he tossed her away, and I saw my opening. The crowd was slowly parting as if to create another aisle for the bride to walk down. From the chaos where some of the guests stood and gaped while others ran, Kayn emerged.

But not the Kayn, I knew. Not Kayn with his hood up, sneaking through the shadows.

He wasn't wearing his cape at all.

Instead, his tunic was untied, open and baring his chest. Though he wasn't as broad or built like a warrior like the king, his lean muscles were shaped from his survival of hunting animals, and before that, hunting humans. At the center, glowed the same shape etched in ink across King Drakkar's chest, the tree of Yggdrasil, the mark of our connection to the Gods, a witch's symbol, on the body of a vampire.

For some reason, the other vampires backed away from him.

Kayn walked through them like he was parting water. Every monster's eyes nearly glowed with whatever power ebbed and flowed beneath that mark. The same way the king's tattoo brightened as if moving beneath his skin.

Every vampire froze, except for King Drakkar, who glared at him with eyes so full of vitriol, I thought he might charge him. Almost as if he knew what had happened between Kayn and I the night before.

And perhaps he did, we weren't exactly quiet.

Even so, King Drakkar made no move to attack Kayn. Likely because it'd be a stalemate.

Kayn couldn't kill the king back at the Hall of the Gods and the king couldn't kill Kayn. At least as I understood it and it had to have something to do with this single matching mark —the only piece of these two that connected them.

Suddenly, their equally matched strength made sense to me.

This mark…it had to be the one from the first witch mentioned in the runestones, which meant she would have made them both. I'd forgotten about it, my mind having been crowded with thoughts of my soul, of the trials, of the king's touches and demands.

But how could King Drakkar have the same mark? He wasn't alive all those years ago when Kayn was made.

I didn't have time to dwell on it now.

Kayn stepped forward, his mouth forming around my name when Astrid flung herself at him again.

I ran to Kayn, my pendant and the stake still in my grasp while my sister's shrieks rang in my ears.

"I will kill her!"

CHAPTER THIRTY-NINE

With the rest of the vampires giving Kayn a wide berth, and the king and Astrid locked in a wild and relentless fight, we were free to run. At least in the seconds that Silver's control still focused on Ylva.

Human guests were frozen with shock, their mouths hanging open as they witnessed the bloodshed unfold. Their minds likely couldn't catch up with the scene of monsters, and I didn't blame them. Vampires had kept their secrets close.

The door groaned as Kayn shoved it open and pulled me out of the throne room along with him. The hem of my wedding dress collected dirt, darkening the edges until I looked less and less like the bride King Drakkar demanded.

Guards shouted at us to stop from where they were posted at the front of the keep. I pivoted. Switching now, I led Kayn away from the castle's main entrance. We could escape through the tunnel in King Drakkar's room.

My sister wouldn't be aware of it, and for now, she was the greatest threat, even if my mind wanted to reject every part of this. I'd come to save her. She'd come to kill me. And of course she did, because my attempt to rescue her was too little, and far too late.

The labyrinthine halls swallowed us in a maze of stone. I navigated the path with Kayn at my heels. Footsteps echoed behind us. I didn't know who I expected to see pursuing us. My sister? Or the vampires.

We ducked into a room, Kayn pulling me into the shadows behind the door and between the wall and a massive wardrobe. Falling silent, we barely breathed as the footsteps stopped at the door. Kayn positioned himself in front of me, ready to take down whatever vampire dared to face him now. When the footsteps faded, we emerged from the room and I led the way this time, guiding Kayn to the king's wing where we could escape through the tunnel. If one of the vampires followed us, I prayed they didn't know of it. And if my sister did, we'd surely lose her.

In the king's bedchambers, I paused over the rug.

"What are you doing?" He asked, looking at me and then back to the fireplace. "We have to keep moving until Odin grants you his gift."

I pointed between my feet. "The king's mother is trapped here."

Kayn's eyes shot to my feet. "Ingrid?"

My stomach dropped. The king's mother was the last chosen witch before me? But...

Before I could respond, the door flung open and the king stormed into the room. Instead of coming for me, he crossed the space in a single blink and slammed Kayn against the wall beside the fireplace, his hand at Kayn's throat. In his other hand, he gripped the dagger he'd used to roughly hack Dante's head from his shoulders.

Sickness sloshed in my gut as clarity hit. He intended to decapitate Kayn and without having recently fed on a human, Kayn didn't stand a chance. They were both created by the first witch's power and should have been equally matched, if Kayn wasn't honorable. If he'd never cut off his fangs and existed on a diet like mine, he could fight off the king—now he relied on me.

"All you have to do is answer the Call. One more step, Lux."

The last step to come into my full power. The last step to become the huntress chosen by Loki, Freya, and Odin. The last step to end life as I knew it.

I traced my forefinger down the rough ash, the wood splintered where Kayn had ripped the branch in half. All I had to do was drive the stake through the king's back, straight into his heart and it'd all be over. I'd be free and Kayn saved. So why the hell wasn't I burying it between his ribs?

A guttural groan escaped from Kayn as his resistance waned. The king pressed the blade into his throat and the pure white gold singed Kayn's skin. With every second the cursed metal pressed into him, the weaker he grew.

"It was you who made her a monster," King Drakkar breathed over him. "Wasn't it? The Exile who needed her help. I should have known the moment I saw you with her at the Forsaken Hall. Ever the dutiful servant to Odin. It's a shame I didn't pay closer attention until I saw the other vampires giving you space the way they do me. You're their true king."

King Drakkar leaned in closer, his fangs bared at Kayn, his eyes fiery red and boring into him. In a desperate attempt, Kayn shoved him away, but the king was just as strong. "But you're in *my* kingdom and when I told my wife to run, I never intended it to be with you. And since you were the first vampire, made by the same power Silver has now, do you know what that means?"

Kayn grunted.

The king didn't let up on Kayn's throat long enough for him to respond. He kept him pinned, and answered his own question. "It means I don't need that damn tree's stake to destroy you. Unlike everyone else, I can kill you with my bare hands."

Kayn could die.

He was going to die if I didn't do something. Anything.

I raised my arm, gripping the stake tighter and tighter until my fingers ached, all thought of the life I was accepting forgotten at the sight of pain twisting Kayn's mouth. I charged forward and brought my arm down just the way he'd taught me, with the same arc I'd done a thousand times in the shadowy hours practicing with Kayn among the graves.

Stake to heart.

King Drakkar dropped the dagger and whipped around before I brought it down. Behind him, Kayn sank to the floor, his hand at his throat where the curse scarred him. The king's hand wrapped around my wrist and yanked me closer to him, the stake still tipped to the center of his chest. All I had to do was push. One push and I'd destroy the man I was supposed to marry today. I had the strength to overpower him, thanks to Odin. Kayn groaned from beneath us, free of the threat but still weak from where the gold drained him.

The king's icy eyes glittered with an unknown emotion. Hatred? Fear? No, the flex of his jaw and curve of his mouth said otherwise. He was the same cruel vampire who wanted to claim me as his wife. Facing the end of his existence did nothing to change the cold hard confidence that shaped every firm angle of his face.

"Don't give in to the Gods, Lux."

A laugh escaped me at this blatant lie.

"Listen to me!" His rough voice cut me like a jagged blade. I didn't want to listen anymore. All I'd wanted was the truth, the lost history, to say the Gods' names aloud without fear of executioners, but I was done with it all, ready to become what they intended the moment they sent my mother the vision of the Call. "Why don't you find out for yourself? Compel me, Lux. This truth I'll be forced to give you. But I'm already telling you, the council is at odds. Astrid and Sten and Dante went astray from Ylva and Darius. They let Silver out and now everything hinges on you marrying me."

Another empty laugh burst out of me. He closed the distance between us.

Not touching me, he beared down on me with only his presence, his eyes intense and his face inches from mine. "Fuck if the Gods are listening, Lux, the vampires are preparing for war. I'm sure of it now, and neither side will win, because if the vampires are the victors, truth will only be restricted more."

"And if the humans win?"

"The Gods will have free reign to use you in their games."

Of course he didn't trust the Gods, he was a creature cut off from them. It was impossible for him to understand humanity's connection to Odin because he wasn't created by him. The vampires were created by the first witch, and then the king of monsters. This much I knew of the lost history now.

But none of that brought Silver back to me, and it made my stomach revolt and anger burn at the pit. I shook my head as I gave him a hollow smile. "You threatened to kill me and my sister. Why shouldn't I destroy you right now?"

"Because I'm the only thing standing between the Blood Council and the humans. Everything they do is to protect our source of sustenance."

Like the executioners. I'd always felt how wrong it was that we couldn't even defend ourselves without the executioners being sent to cut us down.

"I don't need you. I'll kill them too——-"

"Because you're chosen. I know. But killing the vampires won't free you." He pressed a finger to my brow. "The Gods already have you, and when the vampires are gone, they'll have everyone. It's all about control."

"No, the Gods don't control me, they grant me power. *You* control me, your executioners control everyone, and why?"

"For the blood source."

I huffed and swallowed back a swell of bile.

Even pinned, he showed no fear of me. Only a strange sadness swam in his eyes.

"What about my sister?" I asked. "How is she part of all this?" As much as I needed to run, or to stake him, or to give in to this ache inside me and crumple to the floor, I still begged for answers. I still wanted the truth.

And after all this time, I was more lost than ever.

"They want to kill her but they can't yet. They fear her body can be used as a vessel by the first witch to reincarnate and control all vampires. Just like yours. But this is a risk they'll be willing to take to kill both of you and me, because they know that together we're a threat to their way of life and they'll go to war to keep their control. If the lost history is accurate, none of the chosen have come this close since the war that left us with the wasteland. Lux, this means you've terrified them."

The wasteland. The war. Each of these words frayed my nerves a little more each time I thought of them, but it was the mention of Silver's death that struck dread in my heart.

I adjusted my grip on the stake, my arm growing tired. Blinking away the black spots in my vision and resisting the dizzy spell thrust upon me by my erratic nerves, I tried to process everything he'd said, stopping at one odd point. "Wait, *us*, as in you and me?"

"Silver made me a vampire." That wasn't possible, but instead of arguing, I soaked in his words. "And when we discovered you were chosen by the Gods and granted the same powers of the first witch—powers Silver already innately had—we knew you were tied by more than sisterhood. If she dies, they cut off your powers and I become...human again. I've no doubt they'll kill me."

This was why he'd begged for marriage. Not because he cared, not because he was *fascinated* by me or whatever bullshit he'd fed me. Because he didn't want to become a vulnerable, mortal human again.

And my sister was never a witch. How she'd come by these powers now, I didn't know.

"I wanted to blame you for this life my sister led," I spoke just above a whisper. "But I was the one who sent her here."

"I know the story. My mother was one of the executioners who was instructed to find you and take you to King Roderic." My heart skipped. "Silver and I grew up together."

When he spoke her name, his voice cracked, as if she were a childhood friend he'd lost long ago, not someone who he'd had her mouth sewn shut.

"No."

"Yes. And it wasn't all terrible, but I can't tell you any of it was good. For either of us."

"It's my fault."

"You were scared, Lux. Not evil."

That coming from the man who'd threatened to kill both Silver and I just last night. It was laughable, but I had no energy left. He'd carved me out, left me raw with the truth.

The night the Grimward came for me, I was scared. So fucking scared.

I hid, and I didn't come out when they thought Silver was the one they were searching for.

"I was the witch the executioners came for, not her."

"Yes, but when the first witch tried to be reborn, her powers were split. I suspect you became a seer while Silver carried the power the first witch learned regarding the undead she created. Powers that you now have because the Gods can't stand that they don't have total control."

So it was possible. My sister had powers similar to mine, similar, but entirely different. She could make the vampires, I was destined to unmake them. Was this all the magic of the first witch? We'd always been the opposite—I, the scared girl who would run and hide, while she dared spit on the executioners' boots as they walked by.

Had our mother's pregnancy destroyed the first witch's attempt to be reborn? There were two of us, and according to the king's understanding, it split her powers. I rolled this over, trying to process it.

Though it made sense, I wasn't ready to absorb it all just yet.

King Drakkar continued, unaware of the questions taking my mind captive. "But if we cut those powers off, we free you, and Ylva and Darius will leave us be. They'll have no reason to risk killing your sister and bringing forth the first witch."

"And you get to stay a vampire—" I cut myself off. Who cared what he was if it saved my sister's life? It was time I stop making the selfish choice. I never wanted to take this Call and now I had a reason to reject the darkness within.

"You have to choose to bind yourself to me."

I barely breathed. It all sounded too unbelievable, but also, so intricate that he couldn't have conjured it from an amalgamation of lies. King Drakkar never lied, and I knew he wouldn't start now with my stake at his heart. Why lie about his own vulnerability? The man who liked to grab my throat just to flex his power because he was so desperately afraid of any sliver of control he had slipping away.

"Marry. Me." He tugged me even closer, the tip of the stake pinching into the fabric of his shirt now.

I recoiled. "Is that all you think of? Binding and controlling me? Do you have someone lined up to take your place as my husband? Some sort of sick legacy of power?"

"Never." His voice was low, grating, as his eyes searched mine. "I could never see you with someone else."

Again, I was faced with destroying him and I could not do it. "Let us leave now or I'll kill you." My gaze dropped to his hand around my wrist. He wasn't hurting me, but he held on tightly enough to pull me into him once more, the stake the only barrier between us.

"Do you really want to kill me, Lux?"

I couldn't speak because I didn't want to lie. No, I didn't want to, and I suspected he knew that. But this was my destiny. This was exactly what Odin had asked of me, so why the fuck was I hesitating?

"Eyes up, Lux." Drak's voice was softer than I'd ever heard it.

I dragged my attention from the weapon to my betrothed —my first kill, if I could bring myself to do it.

He licked his lips and gave me a slight nod as if to praise me for listening to him. "Good girl, now push. I know you have it within you." My mouth parted. He wanted me to stake him? "You should determine your own future and if this is what you really want, I'm here for it. "

None of it made sense. I sucked in a breath. "Why would you want me to kill you?"

"Because this is what you want. Isn't it? I'm fucking sick of watching the Blood Council get their way. I'm fucking sick of watching the Gods control us all, especially you. But if this is what you want, not the Gods, *you*, then at least I can give somebody a decision. Nobody else gets to make their own choices Lux. Life is all a game but the pieces are moved by the Gods or the Blood Council or men like your father. Now the only person I care for wants the same things I do, revenge and freedom. I get to give you this decision, so take it."

"Why me? You swore to kill me if I didn't marry you."

"It was either marry you or we would both die. Lux, once upon a time, I just wanted to take you from Odin, but now I want to take you. All of you." His eyes dipped to my mouth. Feral hunger flickered in his gaze. He drew a sharp breath and tore his focus away from my lips. "And since you won't have me, I refuse to watch you become his puppet. I'd rather be dust than lose you to the Gods." He tipped his chin back and leaned in, the stake now digging into his flesh. "So kill me."

Accept the call. Kayn's voice echoed in my head. Or maybe he'd said it aloud, I was aware of nothing outside the bubble enclosing me and King Drakkar. It could have even been Odin screaming at me from Valhalla.

I had the strength. The Calling was within reach, all that would allow me to unearth the truths and stop the injustice thrust upon all of Vylheim from the Blood Council. I met the king's icy gaze and a shiver rippled through me. *Why can't I do it?* He was the only one who'd ever told me the truth and for some reason, despite every life he'd taken, that was enough to keep me from thrusting the stake into the hollow of his chest.

Footsteps echoed in the hall, drifting in from where the door was left open.

"You will let us leave." I released the pressure on the stake and helped Kayn to his feet.

"For now," King Drakkar said. I shot him a glare before we stepped into the tunnel. "A war is coming, Lux, and I want the huntress on my side."

"No way in hell."

"You already know I'm not very good at asking."

CHAPTER FORTY

Though the Polar Nocturne came to its end and we had the reprieve of daylight against the vampires, we did not stay at the Hall of the Gods. Staying in any one place for too long would only make us a target. I wouldn't risk my mother and Stasia too. Now that Kayn and I had escaped and reunited with them, we moved as one, slipping through the villages under the cover of the chaos that had erupted in Vylheim since the wedding.

Not only did the Blood Council want to strip me of my powers and stop me from accepting the Calling, my own sister was out for my blood. I was no longer just running from the king's demand that I marry him, I was also tracking Astrid.

A small village, west of Mara, named Ravensund, was where we heard the news.

Astrid had escaped the wedding unscathed and a woman named Silver had been seen in an encampment on the border of Mara and the wasteland. The vampire and the human woman fled to the edge of the wasteland with hundreds of men and women with red eyes. The Dawn of Exploration was stalled when the king demanded the exiled witches return to the castle. Then he released them, not all, but several, and Ragna among them.

He'd been so adamant that Ragna was his witch, as if she belonged to him like an item of clothing, but he'd chosen to give her her freedom. I didn't dwell on it for too long because if I did, creeping interest for Drak, longing even, would seep into my heart, and that wasn't an attraction I should have ever acknowledged. I'd been so helpless to the temptation before, and I knew I would again be if I saw him.

We only dared travel to Skaldir for a single night, for me to catch a glimpse of Ragna in the field at her farm with Alva by her side. I had to see it with my own eyes to believe that he'd actually let her go.

This only comforted me for a few hours. Thoughts of the dozens of witches still under King Drakkar's whims sent me spiraling.

Loki had won the chaos he wanted.

Vylheim wasn't the same. The people were emboldened to fight the control we'd been buried beneath for so long. Instances of attacks on members of the Grimward spread throughout the villages. Some commoners even tried following the executioners back to the king's castle where they tried fighting courtiers and council members.

I couldn't fathom the bloodshed staining the streets of Mara. A war was brewing.

The unrest stirred as more gathered the courage to speak of what they'd witnessed in Mara's Keep with the stake and a pendant in the shape of a tree at the center of the stories. Even if I hadn't exposed the full truth of the Blood Council, the weapons I'd brought to my wedding were enough to spark questions, and for once, the rumors and whispers cycling through the villages were all true, and they inspired witches to come out of hiding and dare to speak of the Gods. Because if the royals fought against themselves, who would command the executioners to cut down the believers?

Villagers knew the truth told through pieces of events from that night. Monsters with fangs fought one another at the king's wedding. His betrothed left with one of them and hadn't been seen since. Perhaps the people assumed I was dead, but the vampires would know I wasn't.

And so the shadows returned.

Weeks after the wedding, I glimpsed the one vampire who dared come after me knowing I was with the true king of vampires.

Kayn, my mother, and I sat around an open fire while Stasia slept peacefully beneath Kayn's fur coat. We couldn't keep running like this. My mother was well again thanks to the medicinal concoctions and food Stasia seemed to produce out of sheer magic, but she was still worn from the stress and demand of constant movement.

"We can't survive in the wasteland," she argued.

"I don't see any other option," I said.

"Lux is right." Kayn nodded. Something flickered behind him. I blinked and narrowed my eyes, trying to make out the shape among the trees.

Sadness tugged at the corners of my mother's eyes. "I still don't believe Silver would hurt you if we could just talk to her."

"That's not an option either," I said, focusing my thoughts on the army she'd gathered to distract from the pain striking my heart. Since my sister wanted me dead, she'd claimed a small victory over me, because something inside me did die when I saw her. Or perhaps it was King Drakkar's words that scarred me. Had my father known of vampires and planned to give me over to one all this time?

"That's a shame." My mother's vacant voice was distant to my ears.

We couldn't waltz into an encampment with that many

vampires when I wasn't even the huntress yet. I couldn't accept Kayn's help, not after what Odin insisted. And I'd never defy the Gods' Calling again.

So I'd have to find a way to do this alone—or as alone as I ever could be. Loki would sear through my temples with the resistance to my Calling while Freya and Odin beared down on me to kill. This continuous battle within me left my head aching. Only the calming incantations and grounding practices cleared their voices from me for long enough to drift into a few hours of restless sleep.

How long would it be until they drove me as mad as Ingrid had become?

"Once you complete Odin's trial, I trust you'll have the strength to enter the encampment." Kayn added as a reminder of why we were so close to Mara again.

Visions of Astrid hiding out in Mara's lower villages nearly led us back to the heart of King Drakkar's kingdom.

"I'm trying. But this is tricky, and—" I shook my head, cutting myself off. It wasn't a vision from Freya or a rumor I'd heard. My fear was simply an inkling. Astrid was leading us straight to Silver's encampment where they could ambush us.

Without the huntress, they could wage war on humans far easier. But I didn't want to speak this aloud, because my only other option would be to accept Odin's trial by killing the one vampire I had within my reach. Kayn was the only one I wasn't itching to destroy.

My heart skipped at a flicker among the leaves in the darkness. A shadow darted between the trees. Had a vampire dared to come to me? I stooped to pick up the stake at my feet and found myself drifting into the woods.

"Lux?" Kayn's voice trailed me.

"Odin says I have to do it alone," I repeated the phrase I'd reminded him of a dozen other times he'd wanted to be at my side since we'd been on the run. Each time I hoped to catch a vampire in the dead of night, and each time it'd only been another creature lurking through the woods, a wolf searching for prey, a vulture feeding on a deer carcass.

Tonight, I sensed a difference. Though I didn't get a vision, I knew Freya walked beside me, tracking the vampire who'd dare come near me.

A twig snapped beneath my boots. My skirts rustled over the dead leaves that coated the forest floor. The dense woodland kept Mara separate from Torstad but neither village claimed the land as their own since executioners cut down every single man who dared to fight for control of the game-filled forest. Torstad suffered from the lack of meat while Mara's farmlands flourished and produced enough food for half of Vylheim. But suffering never mattered to the Blood Council. As long as the people were alive with blood in their veins, they didn't care. It all came down to one twisted truth, we were just never allowed to waste a drop of blood.

Drops of blood were what I trailed now. Dark spots among the leaves, a streak of red across a tree trunk. Someone was hurt, and despite this, they darted through the trees with the speed of a vampire. My skin prickled as the figure stooped in the shadows. They were waiting for me to come to them.

This was a trick, but when I crept closer and caught a ray of moonlight filtering through the branches above, I didn't care. Her cold eyes reflected the silvery glow of night and the cut of her cheekbone was indistinguishable.

My captor had come for me again. Though instead of ambushing me with Sten, she was alone. Since he was destroyed and gone, she lured me to her where she must have thought she'd overpower me. Perhaps Sten was the wiser one of the pair and without him, she wasn't thinking clearly. Why draw me out here when she was already hurt? What had hurt her? Or was the blood part of the trick?

My heart skipped and I had my answer. Each drop of blood was supposed to bolster me to run toward her believing this would be an easy fight.

I knew better. I had Freya's wisdom, Odin's strength. I was almost the huntress.

The screech of a raven echoed from above and I gripped the stake tighter, ready to pass Odin's trial once and for all. If his messengers, Huginn and Muninn flew overhead and tracked me from tree-to-tree, they could return to the Allfather and tell him I'd cut down my first vampire. Eradication of the Draugr was about to begin.

I took another step, pausing to wait for her impatience to overwhelm her. If I remembered correctly, Astrid would rise to the occasion. Her temper easily pushed her over the edge with only Sten's shouting to snap her out of her and make her realize...my blood had made her burn. She couldn't drink from me. None of them could.

Wind rushed through the trees like an applause for my final trial. I barely breathed as I froze in the shadow of an ash tree's trunk—a tree just like the one Odin hung from to gain knowledge. He'd sacrificed himself and it was time I did the same.

Don't give in. The memory of a deep voice echoed in my head, sending a shudder down between my ribs. Was it Loki's will warring within me, or had King Drakkar's words sunk into my skull and made a home where they didn't belong? It didn't sound like Loki, and more of the king's words filled in my memory.

I'd rather be dust than lose you to the Gods.

No! This isn't losing. Not for the humans who'd been under the lies of monsters for too many years. This was our victory. I shook my head, resisting the urge to squeeze my eyes shut. I kept them peeled for any sign of movement from Astrid while the king still lurked in my mind.

Kill me. He'd said it. He'd told me to destroy him.

I seethed. I should have done it.

My fingers ached around the base of the stake. When was she going to give in and attack me? Rage boiled from my gut, leaving my throat raw and fire spreading through my limbs. Itching to lunge, I stepped from the darkness. I'd become the one lurking in the darkness. *I* was the one who'd inspire fear now, the shadow come to destroy her.

I'd exposed myself to the light and triggered her attack. Astrid lunged from beneath the cover of brush and slammed into me. A flash of her gleaming white fangs reflected the moonlight. My ear smacked against a rock and though it immediately went hot with a heavy ache, I ignored the pain. I smashed my elbow against her throat, throwing her to the side. In the span of a single breath she returned to her place on top of me. The heel of her palm bore down on my cheek as she pressed my head against the jagged rock.

Just like the first time I'd met her, she had no weapon, only the sharp teeth jutting from her mouth. But she couldn't touch my blood, much less consume it. Bolstered, I twisted my neck and swung the base of the stake toward her head. It cracked against her skull and she hissed as she stumbled off of me once again.

I flipped to my knees and raised the stake. The crows screeched again as if screaming for me to begin—begin my destiny as the huntress and end this vampire's immortal life.

Another sound, echoing, evil, radiated from her. I blinked down at the monster beneath me to see her chin tilted up, her eyes wide. She was laughing. Each huff of breath that came from her sent shivers through me. I wanted nothing more than to silence the disturbing sound but when I struck with the stake, her hand shot out and blocked me.

She wrenched my arm toward her, dragging the stake closer and closer to her though the tip was now angled out. With her long fangs exposed, she drew my wrist to her mouth.

Shock trapped me in place. Only my lips were able to move as I stared at her, willingly ushering in her own painful death. "You can't drink from me," I said weakly.

"When the tree burns, you'll be nothing," she said. "You'll

be the lifeless human husk I swore you'd become. I can die knowing I won."

I broke through the shock, and yanked my arm from her hold. I raised the stake, but before I brought it down, she spoke again, baring her fangs and fixing her hungry eyes on my skin.

"Long live Silver," she said, her tongue flicking out from between her fangs. Moments before sinking her teeth into my fragile flesh, she made sure I met her gaze. "Love live the queen."

When her fangs dipped into my skin like a hot blade through wax, I screamed and the ravens took flight, the beat of their wings matching the rush of blood pulsing through my ears. This wasn't bait for her to attack me alone in the woods. This was a sacrifice.

For my sister's sake.

I yanked my arm from her mouth and grabbed the stake with both hands. I lifted my body and threw my entire will combined with Odin's strength into the strike. Arcing from overhead, I swung the tip of the stake down and buried it between her ribcage where her heart should have been. Astrid grunted but managed a sickly-looking smile as blood pooled at her lips and spilled from her mouth.

She wasn't human but she bled just like one—until she didn't. Where her own blood touched the surface of her skin, the flesh turned gray then crumbled like ash.

I pulled the stake back and stood, my eyes transfixed one the horrifying beauty of a vampire's death. Red bubbled from the center of her chest where the open wound spread, slowly stretching across her body where she was already turning to ash from the inside out. Her skeleton held the shape of her body as every piece of her, flesh, organs, turned to ash. Finally, her bones followed and a gust of wind swept pieces of her away with dead leaves that skipped along the forest floor.

Like my blood, hers had destroyed every piece of her soul-less body.

My chest heaved, but not from the effort. A hundred thoughts bore down on me, the pressure greater than when she'd pinned my temple against a rock.

Astrid had known she was going to die, for Silver, which meant...had my sister wanted me to become the huntress? It didn't make sense. I was stronger now, able to pick off her army one-by-one, unafraid of the monsters she gathered to place her on the throne.

Or was it a message? For me to give in, to finally expose the darkness within me that'd damned her to a life with the undead?

Revenge and *freedom*, perhaps we all wanted it. Perhaps we all wanted to expose the truth in different ways. Perhaps she wanted me to admit I was a monster.

A scream rang out, slicing through the silence that had fallen with the end of our combat and Astrid's final moments. The high-pitched shriek echoed from where I'd left Kayn and my mother by the fire, but it sounded like Stasia's voice.

I bolted through the trees, racing the crows that screeched above me with every step. Bursting through the trees, I found the fire was doused. Not even a single ember still glowed in the ashes.

Stasia no longer lay among the leaves. No evidence of Kayn or my mother remained. They were gone, all of them, disappeared.

"Kayn?" I breathed as I stepped up to the fire. At the center of the soaking ashes was an odd shape. I blinked, adjusting my eyes to this dimmer, denser part of the forest.

A limp doll, her eyes black as the sky at the beginning of the Polar Nocturne lay in the middle of where the fire had burned. She was unscathed. In a trance, I dipped my fingers into the ashes and scooped the little doll into my hands.

"It was a message." My voice was foreign to my ears. The

wound at one of my ears throbbed but I didn't feel the pain of it, only the erratic thumping with every beat of my heart.

Silver had taken the only people left who meant anything to me. Whether she'd already killed them, I didn't know. But I wouldn't stop until I took them back.

She wanted me to be a monster? Easy.

But she couldn't kill Kayn, not without a stake cut from the tree of Yggdrasil.

The echo of Astrid's last words ignited a flame of understanding. *When the tree burns, you'll be nothing.*

"No..." A puff of white breath swirled in front of me. A clear thought sliced through the noise in my mind. The tree was our connection to the Gods, the barrier between the Nine Realms, without it humans had no hope of winning a war against immortal creatures. Without the few witches having divine access to the Gods and my Calling, it would be an uphill battle—worse, we'd lose hope when we'd only just felt the effect of the Gods again.

The vampires never wanted Freya and Odin to reach us, if Silver led them there...I'd become this monster, only for my powers to strip away when they cut Yggdrasil down.

One of the crows swooped down and landed at my feet. His head tucked sideways and his beady black eye flicked up and down. The other's wings beat above my head as he descended upon me and his clawed feet landed on my shoulder. His talons sank into the thick fur of my cloak as his beak nibbled at my bloody, smashed ear.

I stood with the doll still in one hand and the fingers of my other hand wrapped around the stake. I was no longer the God's chosen witch tracking a single vampire, I was their huntress in pursuit of an entire army of undead, and I vowed to cut down every single vampire until they were ash at my feet.

CHAPTER FORTY-ONE

Everyone deserved the truth. *I* deserved the truth.

Even if that meant hiking the half day's journey back to the place where I'd been imprisoned as King Drakkar's betrothed. I'd set the course the moment I understood my sister's plan to burn the tree of Yggdrasil, but I'd wanted to return even before that.

I'd wanted the other truths the king could give me.

I dragged my feet through the dirt. Blood from the villagers' attempted attacks stained the earth nearly every step of the way to Mara's Keep. The castle cast a yawning shadow across the kingdom now that the Polar Nocturne ended. Never had a sunrise seen so much blood. And the war hadn't even begun.

While humans sharpened their weapons, vampires bared their fangs. If only it were as clear as that. Humans on one side, vampires on the other. This battle would be so much easier. But our enemies took both. Both vampire and human. Kayn, Stasia, and my mother.

Led by my sister, they intended to use and destroy both and I was the only person who could stop them. It didn't matter how much I'd learned, or how much truth the last few weeks had shed upon the people of Mara's Keep and Skaldir.

The slice of daylight was quickly clouded with a heavy gray. Rain slowly soaked the ground, dredging the stained blood from the dirt and washing it away in little red rivers like veins. I pulled my head up, ripping my eyes away from the blood, trying with everything within me to forget how I'd once wanted him to feed on me. How I'd dared even think of becoming his vessel.

I hated everything about him. I hated that he'd insisted on marrying me, swore to torture me. I hated that I was exactly like him.

Rainwater dripped down my face, soaking through my cloak and sticking my curls to my neck and face. I took the steps to the castle two at a time, but then paused on the landing in front of the towering double doors.

I skirted to the side, to find the side door that I knew led to Drak's sanctuary, the dark room. There, I could bypass the servants and find him directly—if there were any servants left as battle preparations began. Would the people abandon their king? I had. I'd run from him. I spent weeks running from the monster I was bound to marry.

And yet here I was, throwing all that effort away, putting aside every ounce of vitriol I carried for this man.

Here I was, outside his door. Wet, defeated, alone. That was the thing about Drak, as cruel as he was, as many people as he'd drained and killed, as many threats as he spewed at me, he'd never once lied. He was the only person in my life who could claim that.

I raised my fist and pounded against the wood until it groaned from the pressure and then swung open.

Drak's normally sleek hair was disheveled. He held a bronze goblet in one hand and leaned on the frame of the door with the heel of his free hand. A smirk curved his mouth as his icy eyes raked over me, taking in the sight of my return.

I was the huntress, the creature designed to destroy his kind, but I'd choked down every bit of pride and even more hatred to stand here and drag my eyes up to meet his gaze.

"Well, if it isn't my wife."

I chewed on my lip, trying to bite back the instinctual response I wanted to spit at him. "We never married."

"Not yet." He downed the rest of the blood in the goblet and dropped it at his feet. With his hand free now, he stepped closer and tipped my chin back. "But you're here now, aren't you?"

I didn't recoil at his touch. "I had nowhere else to go."

I didn't just let his thumb brush my mouth, I parted my lips for him, inviting him closer to me. Was it the need for comfort? I couldn't explain it. How could I let the man who swore to torture me touch me—spread my lips, snake his other arm around my waist and pull me into the dark room I'd fled from.

I huffed and straightened, shaking this need off of me. "They've taken Kayn and Stasia and my mother. I have to find the tree of Yggdrasil before they do. You know where it is." Fuck. No matter how plainly I spoke, it didn't convince my body not to lean into him. Every time we came close, it seemed the Norns tied us together, weaving our fate into one thread that I didn't have the blade to cut. But he was a vampire. He had no connection to the gods or the Norns or anything else in the Nine Realms...

"Except for you," he said, reading my mind. Another part of him I hated. "You're the only part of this world I'm connected to, Lux."

He pulled the door shut behind me and darkness shrouded us. The only light came from a weak flickering candle by the four-poster bed. The extravagant resting place he never used for rest.

"Because we're both monsters," I said, far more breathlessly than I'd intended.

His smirk stretched into a wicked grin and he dipped his face to mine, our breathing intertwining as closely as our fates. "Because we need each other."

He was right. But I didn't just need him and that only sickened me more. A piece of me still wanted Drak. I buried it, suppressing the heat that burned low in my belly. It was so wrong, but now that we were alone together, I couldn't help but think of why I hadn't just staked him in the empty space where his heart belonged.

"Remember who you belong to, my wife."

I ripped my eyes away from him, letting them land at his feet. "You want me because we're both corrupt."

"Honestly? Fuck whatever you think is wrong with you, Lux. I want all of you."

All of me. He accepted my darkness.

And when I killed Astrid, I did too. I wasn't a protector like the seerborn I swore the Norns had weaved into my fate.

I was a huntress, a predator, shaped by the need for survival.

My gaze flickered to the bronze ring on his middle finger. I'd seen that same blood-red ruby somewhere before. "Is that... Sten's ring?" I snapped my attention back to his face. He only smirked, so I said what he wasn't giving voice to. "You killed him, didn't you? That's another reason for Astrid to have aligned with my sister, to try to unmake you so she could kill you."

He raised his brow. "Ever the curious little killer you are. Yes, I killed him. I didn't like that he suggested he'd had his way with you when he and Astrid captured you, so I cut off his head, burned his body, and took his ring as a reminder to everyone else about my promise to protect you, even if it's just from rumors."

"But I'm not married to you. You have no obligation to any promise."

"I can feel the difference in you, Lux. You're the huntress

now, which means you killed someone, just as I killed Sten. I'm guessing Astrid was your victim? She was always relentless."

I drew in a breath, expecting to argue about my role as the Gods' weapon against the plague on this realm, but he said nothing. What had made me think he'd help me? He hated the Gods, but perhaps he hated the Blood Council more. It was my only shred of hope. "You were right about the war." He stayed silent. "So whose side are you on? Human or vampire?"

"It's not that simple and you know it. There are humans who want the power vampires can give to them and there are vampires like the Exile who only want to exist with human vessels that choose to offer their blood. Besides, there are more than two sides. I still have many subjects that are faithful only to me."

"Whose side?" I demanded, because he could just as easily cut down the tree and sever our access to the Gods, but he hadn't, and I didn't want to give him the idea by having him lead me there.

"The side that frees you from the Gods." His mouth cut into a hellish grin. "And enacts revenge. Remember? It was always for revenge and freedom after Odin took my mother's sanity. Now they've taken you, and I'll do whatever it takes to reclaim you."

"What about your obsession with summoning Odin?"

"I'm working toward it." He leaned against the door frame with his arm bent. The fingers of his other hand brushed over my lips. Why did I want him to grab my chin and drag me to him? For him to consume me? Because we never finished what we started. Something inexplicable drew me to him, but I resisted the traitorous urge, praying he couldn't sense my thoughts. "Do you still want my help?"

"Will you help me find Yggdrasil?"

"If you say it."

He wanted me to beg? "Fuck you!"

A dark laugh came from deep within his chest. "Not that, my wife."

"Stop calling me that. I'm already the huntress, you can't stop that by binding me to you now."

"If you tell me the truth, I'll help. Say you need me."

I sucked air through my clenched teeth and glared at him from beneath my brows. It did nothing to deter him.

"Say. It."

I grabbed his arm and yanked his hand away from my mouth, but he was just as fast. Gripping my wrist, he pulled me flush against his body where I felt every inch of him, firm and feverish.

I swallowed the saliva I nearly spit in his face. I was the one who came here. I'd climbed the castle steps and knocked on *his* door. Even more, he'd told me the truth every single time I'd ever asked. He never failed to respond to me, and I wasn't going to be the first to lie or conceal what should be said. Especially not when he was asking for it—no, demanding it.

I tilted my face up to him. "I need you."

———

Thank you for reading.

To keep reading about the king and the huntress, dive into book 2 of *The Boodrune Saga: Wrath of the Ruined.*

Please consider leaving a review at your favorite place to purchase books! Also, a share with your friends who love badass FMCs and their possessive MMCs would be greatly appreciated.

For a bonus chapter 35 from King Drakkar's perspective: Join the Frostborn Baddies Facebook Group or join my newsletter at Elsa Frey Romantasy Books.

To stay up to date on new releases and connect with me, join the Frostborn Baddies Facebook Group or follow me on social media under Elsa Frey Romantasy. I love to hear from readers, so please slide into my DMs and chat about books! If you'd like to learn about my cozy fantasy books and follow me there, look for Author Emily Fluke on Tiktok, Instagram, Threads, and more.

A NOTE FROM THE AUTHOR ON NORSE MYTHOLOGY AND ANXIETY

On Mythology:

I've always been fascinated by Norse mythology and the world the Vikings lived in. Weaving that into a fantasy story was both a challenge and a joy. I dove deep into researching Viking history and myth to ground *The Bloodrune Saga* in as much authenticity as possible. My goal was to portray Vikings realistically, while also remaining faithful to the spirit of Norse myths.

That said, I also took a lot of creative liberties to craft a fully immersive fantasy world. For example, while *draugr* are rooted in Viking lore, they weren't quite the vampires you'll meet in *Vow of the Undead*. If you're interested in exploring the real history and mythology, there are many fantastic resources out there. I hope *Vow of the Undead* inspires you to learn more about the Viking's true culture and what they believed, not only how they're portrayed in popular media.

On Anxiety:

Everyone experiences anxiety differently. For some, it's a passing moment of unease; for others, it's debilitating. It can leave you shaky, faint, or completely unable to go about your daily life. Many aspects of Lux's anxiety, and her heart failure, are drawn directly from my own experience with multiple congenital heart defects and the anxiety that accompanies them.

Even so, what's portrayed in *Vow of the Undead* is only a glimpse of what people with anxiety or chronic illness go through each day. I've done my best to represent these struggles in a way that feels honest and relatable. Lux's journey in Book 1 and beyond is, in many ways, a love letter to my own.

Like Drak is for Lux, I wish for everyone living with chronic illness—mental or physical, visible or invisible—to have someone who sees you, understands your needs, and stands beside you.

About the Author

Anemic and sarcastic, much like her favorite female protagonists in vampire novels, Elsa writes about what she's obsessed with—possessive paranormal guys and badass FMCs. As much as she loves reading and writing about them, she'd never survive as a vampire in sunny California. After all, with the personality of a golden retriever, she craves her daily walks in the sunshine.

Join the Frostborn Baddies Facebook Group or follow me on social media under Elsa Frey Romantasy. If you'd like to learn about my cozy fantasy books and follow me there, look for Author Emily Fluke on TikTok, Instagram, Threads, and more.

www.ingramcontent.com/pod-product-compliance
Lightning Source LLC
Chambersburg PA
CBHW060216030726
47499CB00004B/1072